I0663578

Printed in the United
States of America

First Printing 2016

ISBN 978-0-9975100-0-3

RainEpicEra Publication
https://www.facebook.com/Rainepicera1/

The Power of Sex

Dedication

Rodney Ray "Rat boy" Campbell, I Love You. I never got the honor to tell you that I appreciated all that you taught me. You told me not to settle for anything other than greatness. It's been what, eleven years? Well, it still feels like it was yesterday when you were putting up with my whining ass. After all, they don't call me "Rain" for nothing, but you were my umbrella on cloudy days and long nights. Me and T.T. love you lots. Damn, why did they take you away? You'll always live forever in our hearts. "One monkey don't stop no show."

Rest in peace, bro

This is for you, by the way. Kiss mom for me. My best friend Nikki Farris passed away while releasing this book so I felt it necessary to add her to my dedication page because she was truly like a sprinkle of sunshine in my life. She taught me how to be a lady and never steered me wrong. I love you Skittles.

Acknowledgements

Of course, it would only be right to embrace the man upstairs—my wisdom, strength and conqueror. This is my second novel, and I am humbled to be in this position. To my offspring Deyjuan, Tyrone, Tyreshaun, Breauna and Tony, I love you. Thank you to my father Jerald Butler. I love you pops. A special thanks to my aunt, Katherine Dixon. To my sisters, Mohangany Knox, Demetrius Knox, Tesha Rough, Kendall Ledbetter, Jasmina Ledbetter and my only brother Stefon Ledbetter. To a very special man in my life, Phionex LittleJohn. My mentor and advisor, Jay Jackson. Thank you for teaching me new things every day. A special thank you to Michelle Powers, my editor. Your ideas and suggestions brought my book to life, and I can never thank you enough. I meant it when I said that you are the greatest. To my typist, Patricia Beck. A special extended thank you to the Butler and Knox family.

Let me not forget about the ones who kept me laughing, gave me ideas and gave their strong opinions, which were brilliant—Shamika Wilson, Tyrone Hamilton, Ashley Anduze, Jennifer Wheat, Charlette Cohee . Nikki "Skittles" Farris, we were roommates. We took turns going through the storm, but we managed to make it through it. You'll always be like my sister.

Now enough with the mushy shit. Anya "Ki"

Wimberly, Courtney Ives, Stefani Swantek, never a memory but a reminder that only the strong survive. Shout out to my haters; it was you who made this possible. Gotta give it to you. Find your niche and stay off my cl... (laughs) Joke is on you. Love is truth!

Let's get to the good shit....

Prologue

Smack! *Smack*! *Smack*!

Flesh against flesh. Hot, steamy sex and mounds of increasing pleasure were the sounds coming from room 216. Chauncey slipped two long fingers in D'mico's mouth to muffle her pleading.

"Ohh. Mmm...Oh, please don't stop!" she purred, gripping Chauncey's body so that he wouldn't get away. One lick, two licks, three licks...four.

Chauncey feasted on the next best thing for a black man other than fried chicken—black pussy. D'mico's body squirmed, twitched and jerked under his tongue. His chocolate lips had her throbbing clit in a choke hold that she couldn't run from. Chauncey made a point to swallow all the juices it produced. Round and round his thick tongue roamed across her pearl like a mini vibrator, sending D'mico into shock.

She didn't know whether to scream, cry or burst as she welcomed his suction. Her panting guaranteed that she'd soon be creaming all over his handsome face.

In D'mico's eyes, Chauncey was far from a pro in the bedroom. The nigga was a guerilla beast; he ate and served her pussy full throttle every chance they got. Standing at 6'4", Chauncey had an athletic build and was equipped with all the right tools, if you know what I mean. The first time D'mico got a glimpse of his lumber, I swear her pussy took off out the door. To top that off, Chauncey told her that he was a masochist. In other words, Chauncey loved to give and receive physical abuse while having sex. Ignoring the burning sensation traveling down his spine from D'mico's fingernails, Chauncey concentrated on making D'mico cum. His dark chocolate complexion loomed over her in the dimly lit room, showing off the multiple tattoos that covered his entire backside and forearms.

After giving D'mico two peaks, Chauncey moved to a more likeable position. D'mico parted her legs open to reveal her tenderness. The temptation to taste her pussy again had Chauncey drooling like a bloodhound. Instead of his tongue making a grand entrance, he filled her lava with dick. Once he was inside, he showed D'mico no mercy as he thrust his body forward, pumping in and out of her warmth fiercely, causing her knees to buckle and shake.

Damn, how can something so good be so bad? he thought, rubbing the rim of her asshole with his index finger. I know you're wondering what he meant by that.

Well, outside the bedroom, hotel room or wherever they decided to meet up, D'mico was damaged goods. Actually, Chauncey couldn't stand D'mico. Yep, that's right. He hated her fuckin' guts and especially the nigga she represented. But inside the bedroom, the bitch was like "Whoa." She was as good as gold. Nah, fuck that. She was platinum. Whenever Chauncey got in her treasure box, he literally had to pry his dick away from her.

Most niggas say that all pussy feels the same. Shidd, Chauncey had to disagree. D'mico had that argumentative pussy. Any nigga would break his neck to get a piece of her bubble yum. She had that shit that would give you a permanent lisp. Word! Not only did she have that rock-a-bye-baby snapple, but there was something alluring and sexy about the way she moved her hips to the thunder of his dick when she was on top. Her pussy was a magnetic force pulling his dick in, and he loved the response. Although the pussy was fire, D'mico wasn't a beginning chapter in his life. If anything, she was the root of all the problems in his life, little did she know.

Chauncey bit down on his lip while he watched his shiny dick go in and disappear inside of D'mico's volcano. Chasing his nut, he quickly flipped her over into a doggy-style position, giving her ass two loud smacks.

Whack! *Whack*!

"Do you want to keep this dick?" he asked, driving a strong hand against the back of her neck. He lunged her forward so her ass was in the air and her nose to the floor. "Has he been in my pussy?" He pressed down harder on her to force an answer, speeding up his pace.

"No-No...No, this is yours, daddy."

Chauncey hid behind his amusement with a look of malice. He grabbed a handful of D'mico's hair and yanked her head in the direction of the mirror. He traced his fingers in a circle around her nipples before squeezing her breast with a firm but gentle touch.

"You sure about that, 'cause you slackin' like a muthafucka. What, you tired?" he added, hitting D'mico with long strokes. Chauncey knew what to say to get D'mico going. Although she was a little flustered, she turned around with a light push of her hand. She eased Chauncey on his back. Her hazel eyes swept over Chauncey's six pack and then his dreamy eyes, making him weak. Already her exotic eyes had him gone. She slid down on his thickness until she matched his rhythm. She flexed her round ass against his thighs as her pelvis moved counterclockwise to the tune of his rod. Chauncey threw his head back, enjoying the feel of D'mico's pussy muscles as they clinched his dick. He could feel the side of his jaw tightening as his mouth prepared for a toe-curling, incoherent utterance. Two minutes on top and already she had him about to eject a considerable amount of semen. He squeezed his eyes shut and fought the urge. Taking control, he lifted D'mico off of him.

"What's wrong? What did I do? Did I do something that you didn't like? Whatever it is just tell me and I'll fix it," D'mico whined.

Yeah, that's right. Beg. Chauncey had D'mico right

where he wanted her, right in the palm of his hand. She didn't do anything wrong. If anything, she did it just right, but he was running the show, and getting pussy-whipped wasn't part of the plan. Just like the saying goes, "there's power in pussy," there's power, authority and big benefits in a strong dick, capable tongue and a mouth piece that flows like the Pacific Ocean. He left women "dick sick." Daily they would line up in anticipation for the antidote he had access to. Continuing what he started, he filled her up again. This time he maintained control the whole ride to cloud nine. Thirty minutes later, their session of rough sex came to an end.

"So, now that we're on the same page, you know what you gotta do, right?" Chauncey asked D'mico, blowing a cool trail down her sweaty back. D'mico stared off into the distance paralyzed. The guilt of betraying her man rushed back to her heart, but the power of sex made everything feel right for the moment…only for the moment.

"Mmm-hmmm. I know." she confirmed, easing her eyes shut.

Not only was D'mico's boyfriend, Tyreke, one of the filthiest lynch bosses out there, but the man D'mico was secretly in love with was one of Tyreke's henchmen. The line that D'mico was crossing could lead to severe consequences and repercussions. Too bad she didn't know that Chauncey had a plan to end her life.

Let The Story Begin…

Chapter 1

D'mico pulled up to her cozy, three-story home a little past nine. After punching in the code to the alarm system, she waited a couple of seconds for the light to turn green which would allow her to pass through one gate to be stopped by another. Any other time, the gate would be wide open, but since the gate was now closed, she knew that Tyreke was out doing what he knew best—working the streets—which was okay with D'mico because the less he came around, the better she would feel whenever she hooked up with Chauncey.

D'mico checked for signs of infidelity that would blow her cover before getting out her Audi. Once she covered her tracks, she made her way to the door, humming an oldie while clutching a string of shopping bags used to back up her lies if need be.

Inside it was dark. The only light that gave D'mico passage through the spacious house came from the kitchen. The smell of fresh linen and Febreze permeated the air causing D'mico to smile. *Home sweet home!* she thought, hitting the light switch to the living room. As D'mico removed her stilettos and looked up, she nearly jumped out of her skin.

"Aah—" she screamed partially, wrapping her hands around her mouth. Tyreke was sitting on the couch with his arms spread out eagle style with a half-empty bottle of Hennessy dangling from his hand. His eyes were bloodshot, and from the looks of it, he'd been waiting on D'mico for quite some time. In a sudden burst, he jumped to his feet, waving the bottle around violently.

"Where the fuck have you been? Bitch, I got you a cell phone and a pager for a fuckin' reason, so where the fuck you been?" D'mico looked towards the bags that she placed on the marble countertop, and then she faced Tyreke.

"Ty, you don't have to call me a bitch. Why is we together if you don't trust me? You know damn well where I been. I went shopping, and then I went over to Leslie's. I didn't know I needed permission to be gone," D'mico stated matter-of-factly. She rolled her eyes and headed up the stairs, dismissing their argument.

Tyreke watched D'mico ascend the steps in bewilderment. He took a good look at the woman in front of him who appeared to have grown a pair of nuts within six hours. Tyreke followed after her. D'mico was trying to manipulate the situation, and he wasn't going for it. D'mico looked over her shoulder and smacked her lips when she saw that Tyreke was following her to the room. She mumbled a few words about him being drunk and turned around, entering the room with an attitude.

Drunk? I'll show her ass drunk! Tyreke thought, putting down his Hennessy bottle. Without warning, Tyreke grabbed D'mico by the waist, lifted her in the air and slammed her down on the bed hard. "Bitch, don't ever think you gonna walk up in my shit without telling me where you been then step into my muthafuckin' face with some reverse phycology bullshit. I'll fuck yo ass up!" Tyreke responded with rage. D'mico shrunk under Tyreke's hands. He purposely wanted D'mico to feel exposed. All he needed was an ounce of an indication that D'mico was fuckin' around on him to end her life and the life of the chump she was creepin' with. With force, he ripped off her pink capris and stuck his face in between her legs. His nose traveled down the depths of her bayou while he inhaled the scent of her nectar. Frowning at the sight of her hairless mound, he came up.

"Didn't I tell you not to leave this house without any panties on?"

D'mico lay motionless on her back with eyes full of tears. This was the first time Tyreke had done this, and she didn't know what to make of this sudden outburst. She was scared shitless. "Tyreke, why are you doin' this? I would never try to play you." D'mico sobbed, saying the first thing that came to mind.

"Yeah, we'll see," he said, taking in another big whiff. After violating D'mico's space, Tyreke came back to the surface.

SMACK!

Tyreke slapped D'mico across the face, causing her head to shift to the right. "That's to let you know how serious I am." SMACK! SMACK! "And to show you that I'm not to be played with. If you ever raise your voice or try to play me close like you just did, it won't be my hands teaching you a lesson. Fair warning is fair game; consider yo'self warned," he threatened, getting up. He walked to the dresser, picked up her cell phone and pager and threw them at her chest. "Next time, don't forget 'em. That's your lifeline. Get up and get dressed. The car will be here in one hour. Be ready!" Tyreke finished, walking out of the room. When he left, D'mico exhaled her fear. She looked down at her cell phone and pager that she intentionally left home in the hopes that it would give Tyreke a good enough reason for why he couldn't reach her. I guess her plan failed.

* * * *

Tyreke cooled off in the backseat of the limousine as he waited impatiently for D'mico to drag her ass out the house. He could've sworn that he'd told her to be ready in one hour. D'mico passed the hour mark twenty minutes ago. *No wonder some black men wander off to fuck with the opposite race—sistas just wasn't obedient enough,* Tyreke thought to himself. However, there was something about black women that he couldn't get enough of. Nevertheless, he had an important meeting to tend to, and here he was counting away lost dollars.

Tyreke checked the time on his Rolex a second time. Five more minutes had passed. Infuriated by the delay, he picked up the car phone and dialed his seven-digit home number. On the first ring, D'mico stepped out the house wearing a flashy, champagne-colored Versace evening gown designed for top notches only. Tyreke slammed the phone down in irritation. He poured himself a glass of Surrenne Tonneau and relaxed in the comfort of the leather seats. He watched D'mico intently as she took her sweet time getting to the limo. Laughing to himself, he lifted his drink to his lips and took a sip. Although the sight of D'mico extended his dick to a full erection, he knew that she was trying to get under his skin by wearing an outfit that left little for the imagination.

When she got inside the limousine, immediately the sweet smell of *woman* circulated throughout the spacious car. Instead of snuggling under Tyreke, D'mico cut her eyes at him. She refrained from being lovey-dovey with the man responsible for her pounding headache and swollen cheek bones.

From his seat, Tyreke basked in D'mico's presence. Her caramel skin was without defect. Her lips shimmered with pearl peach lip gloss, giving her face a down-to-earth look. Three-inch earrings dangled from her ears matching the gold pendant holding up her hair, which was wrapped in an intricate bun. She had a curvaceous body that most females only dreamed of. Her flat stomach; big, silky legs; and her voluptuous booty were nothing compared to her lust-filled, hazel-green eyes and killer-ass smile. Dime piece? Nah...D'mico was a silver dollar from long... long... ago.

The thought of another man filling his shoes made Tyreke's dick limp. Instantly, he was reminded of the skimpy gown. "You hardheaded as fuck, you know that?" he said, tapping the window to let the driver know they were ready to roll.

D'mico rolled her eyes to the ceiling, "And, nigga, you're drunk." She folded her arms over her breasts. Tyreke ignored her accusations. He put down his glass and camouflaged his breath with a piece of Winterfresh gum.

"You over there actin' like a school girl, yet you're dressed like a woman looking for customers. Why you buy dat dress after I told you not to? And didn't I say one hour? I don't understand what took so long...shit, you ain't wearin' nothin'. You won't have enough until a nigga start going upside yo damn head," Tyreke stressed. D'mico sighed in aggravation. Tyreke was really full of himself, and he was beginning to get on her everlasting nerves. She crossed her thick legs and leaned further back.

"Whateva, Ty. I'm not tryin' to argue. When we get back home, I'll throw the gown away, alright?" she responded nonchalantly.

Tyreke hated the fact that he had to talk to D'mico like she was nothing. If only she knew that she meant so much more to him than the words that spilled out of his mouth suggested. I guess you could say his male ego got in the way or that he loved her so much that he couldn't possibly think of losing her to somebody else. No matter what they were going through, he had no right to put his hands on her. He could easily blame it on the liquor in his system, but he was man enough to admit that he'd fucked up. All he could do was hope and pray that D'mico would forgive him.

"D'mico...look at me, ma," Tyreke spoke up. D'mico turned away from the window and pierced Tyreke with a hateful look. "I'm not one of dem cats who have to confirm what their woman can and can't wear. I just don't wantchu to be one of dem birds my partners be talkin' 'bout. Nobody got love for a hoe or a female who don't respect herself, feel me? You was there, babe, when I was down to my nuts, and you stuck with me through that. Every day I thank God for you. You're my spine. You put up wit' my issues, and I thank you for that. I trust you wit' my life, D'mico. I can't expect for you to hang on when I'm putting my hands on you. I want to apologize for that," Tyreke said sincerely. Tears flowed like raindrops from D'mico's eyes. She wanted to believe Tyreke, but the painful memory—the reason why she was sleeping with Chauncey in the first place—played in her mind.

* * * *

On a typical, cold Friday afternoon, D'mico received an unusual call from Tyreke. He asked her to do a pick up.

"Yo, if you can't do it, then I can try and send someone else. I really don't like to get you involved in my business, but I'm kinda tied up, babe," he expressed on the other end of the phone. Since D'mico was only a few blocks away from where Tyreke wanted her to go, she agreed with no questions asked.

"Sure, daddy. I gotcha," she said in anticipation, ending the call. She loved it when Tyreke leaned on her to do things. It made her feel productive and needed.

D'mico reached the townhouse in less than ten minutes. The smell of fresh potpourri and cinnamon welcomed her when Chauncey opened the door, giving her a warm feeling all over. She smiled and stepped inside. Chauncey's crib was laced. The living room had a country style to it like one of those fancy houses in the magazines. Kind of feminine but overall it was nice.

"Lemme go get those," Chauncey said, walking towards the back. "Eh, make yo'self comfortable," he called out over his shoulder. Snooping around a bit, D'mico picked up a picture frame surrounded by two flower-filled vases sitting on top of a mahogany end table. Chauncey and an older lady sat side by side.

"Here you go," Chauncey said, startling D'mico.

D'mico held up the picture. "She's pretty. Is she your grandmother?"

Chauncey frowned. He took the picture and put it back in its place. "Nah, that's my mother. She had cancer. Died a few years ago."

"Oh, I'm sorry I—"

"It's all good. You didn't know. It happens to the best of us." The awkward silence was broken by the sound of D'mico's phone.

"Do you mind if I get this?"

Chauncey grinned. "Go ahead."

A big smile appeared on D'mico's face when she saw that she had a text message from Tyreke. He probably was texting her to see if she was okay. He was sweet like that. Once she skimmed the message, her smile turned into a cup of bitterness. The message wasn't for her; it was for another woman.

Coco, ya boy running late.
Gotta grab some XLs Ty.

D'mico was flabbergasted. *How could he do this to me?* she thought, fighting back her tears.

Who the fuck was Coco? The nerve of him to send her on one of his runs while he fucked around with another bitch. The nigga mentioned XL condoms, funny. Where was the extra sagging latex going? XL? Yeah right. Tyreke wasn't a little man downstairs, but he wasn't large neither. His lumber jack was a satisfying seven and a half inches. The same seven and a half he obviously was sharing with another woman. D'mico felt lightheaded. A piece of her heart ached, and the other piece shattered inside her chest. She snatched the duffel bags away from Chauncey and made her way to the door. Immediately Chauncey blocked her path.

"Whoa...slow ya roll. What's wrong?" Chauncey asked, showing concern. Unable to hold back tears, D'mico choked on her words.

"I-I'm fine."

"Yeah well, I would have believed you a minute ago. I don't know what information you just got, but you ain't leaving this crib mad like that. What if something happens to you? Tyreke wouldn't forgive me, and I wouldn't forgive myself." The mention of Tyreke's name caused D'mico to cry even more. Although Chauncey was playing the concerned, comforting male on the outside, inside the nigga was a snake in the grass. He knew exactly what it was that bothered D'mico. Hell, he was the one who sent the text message to her phone.

Last week, Tyreke stopped by to pick up his weekly dividends. While he was there, he misplaced one of his phones. Later on that night, Chauncey stumbled across it. The text message meant for another chick was perfect. Chauncey was dying to get close to D'mico, and this was his chance. Going in for the kill, Chauncey planted a warm kiss on D'mico's lips. The taste of her raspberry lip gloss settled on the tip of his tongue. Breaking contact, D'mico's face lit up with shock. She wiped her lips with the back of her hand. Chauncey was an attractive man and all, but he also worked for Tyreke. Tyreke would murder their asses.

"Nigga, you must be out of your mind. Do you know what Tyreke would do to you if—"

"If what? Matter of fact, let's talk about Tyreke and why he would send you over here to handle a job that he normally takes care of himself. Better yet, let's talk about why you're cryin'." Chauncey preyed on D'mico's vulnerability. He knew that a woman's weakest moments occurred when she felt hurt and betrayed. He could tell by the devastating look on her face that she could easily be manipulated.

With a firm hold on D'mico's insecurities, Chauncey wrapped his muscular arms around her waist and looked into her soft hazel eyes.

"Let me make you smile. I won't ever hurt you," he

lied. D'mico's gullible eyes met his gaze for reassurance. She completely let her guard down and opened up to Chauncey. One minute they were talking, and the next minute Chauncey was taking the bags out of her hand. He pulled her pants down to the floor and buried his face deep inside her hidden valley. All of her sorrow and confusion were replaced with sexual gratification. His powerful tongue took all of her worries away. For now.

* * * *

Tyreke and Chauncey stood side by side looking like night and day. Tyreke was a twenty-seven-year-old redbone, mixed with black and Native American. Standing at 5' 10", his lean build; slanted, almond-shaped eyes; thick, curly hair; and trimmed goatee gave him an overpowering and confident quality, and you could tell he knew it by the way he carried himself. His skin tone was the color of umber, smooth to the touch and flawless to the eye. Although his baby face gave him the look of a humble man, his heart and mind were that of a cold-blooded killer. No doubt. He maintained a low profile on a daily. Tyreke was smart about not attracting extra attention because he knew that it called for extra problems, which he didn't need.

Chauncey, on the other hand, created problems. He was a lengthy 6'4" in height. He had a Hershey-chocolate complexion, a commercial smile and muscles for days. He wasn't the type of dude you could afford to sleep on. Blink once and you were liable to miss everything. The majority of his time was devoted to seeking revenge. Like I said, night and day.

D'mico watched from the second floor as both men, who shared an equal amount of space in her heart, engaged in what appeared to be a serious conversation with the Chief of Police and several advocates working in the Senate office.

The way Tyreke worked the crowd was amazing. Everyone was of one accord when it came down to business. Piece by piece, they took in his instructions without further details. His milk-white teeth sparkled every time he opened his mouth or displayed a smile. Tyreke was exceptionally handsome. Once upon a time, he was all hers. What happened?

D'mico slouched against the railing wondering how her relationship with Tyreke went from a natural high to a terrible disaster. She did her best at holding his attention in the bedroom. Well, at least she thought she did. She couldn't understand what she was missing. She sexed him good and sucked his dick with honors. She kept up with her appearance, cooked, cleaned and did laundry. She tried to be his superwoman, and what did Tyreke do? He cheated. Consequently, D'mico's self-esteem went from colossal to shit. All the love and affection Tyreke had for her was gone. Sometimes she felt like a low, down-and-dirty slut for sleeping with Chauncey, but the sexual attention he gave her outweighed the bad. He gave her purpose when Tyreke failed, and he was there when it counted the most. How can you go wrong with that?

D'mico shot a hurtful look in Tyreke's direction. Not once did he look up to make eye contact with her. Instead, he smiled and threw his head back in laughter, enjoying himself as if he didn't have any worries.

With a motion of his hand, he waved over a waiter. Once everyone grabbed a glass off the tray, Tyreke lifted his champagne in the air for a toast. On the sly, he reached inside his pocket, pulled out a thick envelope and released it into the chief's hand. The chief smiled in acceptance and threw an arm over Tyreke's shoulder.

D'mico turned around in disgust. She hated cops. Daydreaming, she stared off into space towards the tall chandelier hanging from the ceiling. Slowly, she drifted off into her past.

* * * *

At the age of sixteen, Trish was a young, free-for-all addict who would try and do anything at least once. Threesomes, bestiality and robbing Johns were only a few of the things she'd done to supply her crack habit. One night, Trish had sex with five different men and ended up pregnant. Nine months later, she gave birth to a healthy baby girl that she named D'mico. Out of all the random men Trish had had sex with that night, she didn't have the slightest clue as to who fathered her child.

Growing up in the toughest projects in the 9-1-8 without a father and a crack-addict mother was tough on D'mico. The frequent drug dealings in their apartments only exacerbated Trish's drug habit. Sadly, the only time D'mico got a hot meal was at school or from local churches. Scandalously, the $255 monthly check Trish collected from the government went straight into the hands of her pusher who then invested the money into his household. However, D'mico wasn't the only one who was S.O.L (shit out of luck), so was the unborn child Trish had in her stomach. Being five months pregnant didn't stop Trish's ongoing habit. If anything, more drugs were shoved into the hands of the helpless woman.

D'mico sat on top of two twin-size mattresses with no bedspring. Underneath her buttocks were two frozen T-bones she hid from her mother. She didn't know the first thing about how to cook the steaks, but she knew one thing; she was hungry as I don't know what. Shoot, if the damn things weren't frozen, she'd eat 'em raw like a thirsty vampire. Wishing she was invisible, D'mico sat on her bed hoping that her mother wouldn't burst through the door. Already, she could hear her shaky voice vibrate her bedroom walls.

"Damnit, D'mico. Da-mee-co! I know damn well you hear me, little girl. Where the hell is those steaks I put in the freezer earlier?"

With her entire upper body in the freezer, Trish moved several empty ice trays out of the way before screaming for D'mico again. "D'mico! Girl, if I have to come in there, I'ma spank yo little behind," Trish threatened, rubbing her belly up against the ice box. The steaks were gone and so was any other kind of meat for that matter. As a matter of fact, the only contents in the freezer were the empty ice trays. Nothing new. In frustration, Trish slammed the freezer shut. She looked in various places that she'd already checked three times, as if the fourth time would present anything different.

Trish stormed to D'mico's room. It was obvious that D'mico was trying to ruin her plans for the night. Although the father of Trish's baby—excuse me, soon-to-be father—worked for the police department, the man was no saint. For years he received sexual favors from Trish in exchange for cash. The pussy became so convenient that June—that's the name of that piece of scum—grew attached to Trish. Even though he told Trish that he would never leave his wife for her, he promised to take care of the seed growing inside her belly.

Unfortunately, being a "smoka" and a prostitute didn't go on June's chart of likes. That left Trish with the role of being his bottom bitch. Today, Trish wanted to show June that she could offer so much more if he just gave her a chance. She had their evening already mapped out in her mind. His wife would leave around five, and when she did, Trish always got to come over. She would cook June the best steaks ever, give him some ass and then tell him about her decision to live a drug-free life. One way or the other, he was going to be with her or else she would tell his wife everything. Although Trish had plans to get help, she had to get high one last time, so she did. Once an addict, always an addict. No, that's not true. Trish called her addiction a "sickness." Hell, the woman was sick alright. What kind of woman would starve her child to go and feed a well-established, capable, grown-ass man? A sick muthafucka, that's who. As Trish moved through the house, she began to get the shakes. She hated the feeling of her high coming down. It made her feel like she had bugs living inside of her body, not to mention it made her very nauseous, causing her baby to do multiple flips inside her stomach. D'mico stared at her off-white, chipped door in silence. The ice from the steaks was beginning to melt, and the cold water was seeping through her underwear. It was a Friday afternoon, exactly two days before Christmas, and all she wanted was for her mother to show her love. Since she couldn't get that, she wouldn't mind having something to eat that would soothe her hunger pains and the feeling of her ribs touching her back.

D'mico no longer looked forward to Christmas. While some eager kids dreamed of the expensive gifts they would receive on Christmas day, D'mico prayed for time and a little bit of effort from her mother. Every year D'mico made a wish list to the big, fat man in red everyone called Santa Claus. Love was the first thing on her list followed by family. D'mico even went as far as putting the list in the mailbox, addressing it to the North Pole so Santa could get it. But she was only left disappointed. D'mico never got her wish. Take, take, take is all Trish knew. She took her love, kept her hugs and never released the three magical words that would later destroy D'mico completely.

Trish entered the room with the look of discipline on her face. "D'mico, did you hear me calling you?"

D'mico swallowed hard and shook her head no.

Trish sucked her teeth. "Don't sit there and lie to me. Now where is the meat I put in the freezer?"

When D'mico didn't answer, Trish started to snatch D'mico off the bed to shake some answers out of her, but the sound of a horn blowing outside the apartment caused her to change her approach.

"D'mico, that's June out there. Give yo mama the steaks."

"But I don't have them," D'mico pleaded as she

started to cry.

"Baby, please don't do your mama like this. When I come back, I'ma cook you somethin' to eat," Trish lied. D'mico looked up into the hazel-green eyes that matched her own, but the glow she saw when she looked in the mirror was far gone in her mother's ghostly appearance. For the hundredth time, she wanted to believe her mother.

The horn echoed inside the apartment once again. Although her dilated pupils spoke the truth that Trish didn't give a damn about her daughter, D'mico wanted to believe otherwise, so she got up and handed over the only possible meal she had to look forward to. Wasting no time, Trish snatched the steaks and took off out the door.

"Mama, please don't forget this time," D'mico said, trying to keep up with her mother's pace. "I'm really hun—"

Slam!

Before D'mico got the words out, Trish was already out the front door. D'mico's shoulders slumped forward and tears poured from her eyes as she peeled the curtains back. Trish jumped in June's car, kissed him on the cheek and off they went.

* * * *

Two hours had gone by and still Trish hadn't returned. D'mico flushed the toilet, attempted to wash her hands and face with a tiny piece of soap and went into her room to find some shoes to wear. Many times her mother would get canned goods and other nonperishable items from churches, so D'mico decided to save her mother the trouble by going out for help herself. Maybe that way her mother wouldn't have to do all of those disgusting things she witnessed her do with other men. The best thing D'mico could come up with was a pair of Skechers that were given to her by a local church two years ago. Although they were a size too small, D'mico managed to get her feet inside with the exclusion of socks.

For hours D'mico traveled in the bitter cold in search of a church that was open. However, every church nearby was closed, leading D'mico deeper and deeper into the urban area. Flustered, she stopped and examined her cold hands which were a shade of blue and red, nearly numb. Tired of walking, she wanted to drag her butt back to the house but thought against it when she realized that she had traveled too far to turn back. Besides, the long walk back with an empty stomach would definitely cripple her. D'mico scanned the area up ahead. A big, white church with several parked cars in the parking lot gave D'mico hope. In front of the big church on the side, next to the steps, stood a white sign that read, "OPEN TO ALL OF GOD'S CHILDREN."

A crescent smile appeared on her face. Her feet were already on the move again. Warm and cozy are the words that came to mind when D'mico walked inside the lovely church. The temperature instantly felt like the heat coming from a kindled fire upon her cold face. Looking around, D'mico admired the large display of the Last Supper covering the walls around her. Plaques and pictures of the church's congregation were placed neatly on the wall for visitors to view. Against the wall on the left side was a wooden box with a drop-off slit on the top.

It had a sign that read, "Prayer Request." D'mico tore her eyes away from the box and fixed her eyes on the array of lilies lining the broad hallway. Matching its white nobility lay white carpet with a pinch of maroon speckles. Careful to not destroy the bell-shaped flower, D'mico placed her nose up against the beautiful plant and inhaled.

"Mmm," she exclaimed, pleased by the scent. Down the hall, the sweetest voices came alive to her ears. Following her ears, D'mico opened the chapel doors.

No one even knew that D'mico was there. She stood invisible to the people in front of her. A man with his back to her and with his arms moving in all kinds of directions stood behind a mahogany-colored podium.

D'mico wished that she could be a part of the group. The sound of their voices made her feel so lonely and empty. D'mico closed her eyes and pictured herself on stage with them. The sound of the notes being played on the piano and the melodious harmony of their voices joining forces caused a flood of tears in her eyes. Although she was too young to understand the meaning of the song, the soft hymn to "Silent Night" made her eleven-year-old heart ache. All she ever wanted was to be loved back and experience the affection which came with closeness.

The voices along with the piano ceased. A final note was thrown off of key before D'mico opened her eyes to the shocked faces looking wildly in her direction.

Shocked beyond belief, Reverend Johnson's heart melted at the sight of the little girl standing in the center of the chapel. Immediately, dozens of questions began to enter his thoughts. *Where are her parents? Did someone bring her up here? Who is she? Where is her coat? Its twenty-five degrees outside for God's sake.*

From the look on D'mico's face, Reverend Johnson knew better than to ask her a lot of questions. The type of household D'mico came from more than likely taught her rules to remain quiet, answer no questions and assume that anyone outside of her family was a lethal threat. Reverend Johnson's assumption was right on the money.

Breaking the tension in the atmosphere, Reverend Johnson spoke in a friendly voice. "Hello, can I help you, young lady?"

Instead of answering, D'mico choked up. It was the boy with the scowl on his face that made her feel uncomfortable. Shoot, she ain't never been too proud to beg, but again the boy made her nervous. Quickly Reverend Johnson sent everyone to the back for refreshments.

"Let's say we take a break. Denise, honey, will you show everyone to the hot chocolate and donuts in the reception area, please?"

Denise must've been the beautiful Indian standing in the front row. With a motion of her hand, she complied with her husband. "Come on, everybody. I know ya'll been waitin' on a break, so let's roll out."

Pretty as a flower with a warm smile on her face, she looked towards D'mico. "How about you, baby? You want some? There's plenty."

"Yes, ma'am," D'mico answered timidly.

The congregation rushed towards the back with their hands over their mouths while whispering discreetly.

"I thought you said that we wouldn't eat until we

finished?" a voice called out over the piano.

"Well, I changed my mind. Now go on back there with your mama and the others. Go on, Tyreke," Reverend Johnson ordered.

D'mico's eyes fell on the boy whose skin was as smooth as peanut butter. Reluctantly, he took several steps before looking over his shoulder, giving D'mico a once-over. Out of nowhere, he cheesed big and wide like the Kool-Aid man. Whoever the girl was, she was nothing like the girls who sweated him at school. She didn't have on expensive clothes, just enough makeup to not get her ass beat by her parents, tight jeans, or the look of adolescence in her eyes. She looked like she'd been through it all, and Tyreke knew that he had her by a few years; he was fifteen. Despite her three-sizes-too-big shirt, old jeans and wasted away sneakers, she was beautiful. She had a distinct face that he would never forget. Believe me when I say never.

Embarrassed, to say the least, D'mico tugged at her shirt and hung her head low.

"Tyreke, hurry up and tell your mama that I said to bring that hot chocolate and them donuts right away," Reverend Johnson spoke up, taking notice of Tyreke's change in demeanor. *I swear, that boy see a girl and his whole mind go blank!* Reverend Johnson thought to himself as the boy rushed out of the room.

Amazingly, God knew all of D'mico's needs. Reverend Johnson asked few questions and made D'mico feel secure. He even offered her a ride home. And to top it off, Denise combed her hair in small triangles just like her daughter's. Denise also took her to Walmart and bought her a coat. D'mico was so happy; it was the first gift anyone had ever given her. She couldn't help but smile inside and out.

Pulling into the dilapidated apartment complex, Reverend Johnson turned around in his seat, "D'mico, I wantchu to call me if you ever need anything, and if your parents don't mind, maybe you can spend Christmas with us." He gave her his business card. "Have your mama call me. Me and Denise will pick ya'll up, okay?"

D'mico accepted the card and slid it into the pocket of her new coat. *She gon be so happy*, she thought to herself. Cheerful like never before, D'mico reached for the door handle.

"See you later," Tyreke called out coolly. D'mico's lips parted into a genuine smile.

"See you later, Tyreke," she said. Once she got out of the car, she waved good-bye and walked reluctantly to the filthy place she knew as home.

D'mico walked inside her stuffy apartment, which reeked of crack cocaine, with a big smile on her face and a full stomach. Her mother would be so proud of her, and D'mico couldn't wait to see the smile on her face once she saw that she'd brought home Christmas. D'mico set the bag of food and clothes down on the living room floor.

"Mama!" D'mico called out going from room to room. "Mama." There was no answer.

All of the sudden, the lights in the apartment went out. "Oh no!" D'mico mumbled, hoping it was something else other than the expected. Stunned, she opened the front door and there hung an orange cut-off notice around the doorknob. All too familiar with this little orange paper, D'mico removed the slip, plopped down on the stained mattress and waited for her mother in the darkness.

* * * *

BANG! BANG! BANG!

D'mico woke up to the powerful sound of someone trying to beat down the front door. Wiping the corners of her eyes, the sound repeated over and over. On alert, D'mico broke for the door.

"Mama?" she said, yanking the door open with a smile. June stood outside the door with a dumb look on his face. Next to him stood a white woman dressed in a business suit. Confused, D'mico wondered where her mother was; she was with June earlier. *Where could she be if June is right here*, she thought, inching the door closed. With his eyes, June pleaded for D'mico to not say his name in front of the social worker.

"Umm, my mama ain't here. She went to the store," she lied. She thought back to what Trish coached her to say in the event that an unfamiliar face came around asking questions. "You gotta come back," D'mico stressed, easing the door shut. With force, June stuck his foot in the crack of the door. D'mico was making this real hard. He knew goddamn well that Trish's smoked-out ass wasn't at no store. In fact, he was the last one with her. She probably would still be alive if she hadn't of given him the ultimatum to leave his wife or else. With extended arms, the white lady came closer.

"D'mico, honey, I'm a social worker. I-we need for you to come with us, honey," she said sincerely.

"Uh-uh, my mama at the store."

Swallowing, the woman looked towards June, and then her eyes dragged back to D'mico. "D'mico, your mommy is in heaven." Caught off guard, D'mico recalled what the word heaven meant.

"Noooooo...but we gon spend Christmas together. Noooo. Get away from me," D'mico wailed, trying to force the door shut. Her eleven-year-old body quivered with every push and shove of the door. Everything from that point on within D'mico's soul flew away into the cold air. D'mico collapsed.

* * * *

Tyreke spotted D'mico slouched over the top railing in deep thought. The chandelier above her head illuminated the level of distress she wore on her face. And boy did she wear it well. *Where did we go wrong?* he thought, taking in her presence.

Chauncey locked eyes with D'mico also, examining her smooth skin. "What's next?" Chauncey asked, licking his lips.

"So far, everything is good except for the south side. The fuckin' Feds is all over that area."

"What? All the money you payin' these muthafuckas and—"

"Don't worry about who I'm payin' and what I got goin'. Your job is to make sure you clear out the areas I tell you to, aight?"

Chauncey slid both of his hands in his pockets and nodded in agreement. *"Yeah, aight, nigga. I'ma clear yo ass out here shortly."* Chauncey thought to himself.

Taking everything into account, Tyreke remembered what he intended on talking to Chauncey about.

"Did you give my cell number out?"

"Nuh-uh, why?"

"Chauncey, don't make me fuck you up in front of these fancy-ass white folks. Some bitch called my phone and asked for you. Who you give my shit out to?"
Chauncey searched for an answer. No sooner did he pause, he came up with a response. "Oh, I forgot. I told LeeLee to call me on your cell the other day when my battery went dead. I didn't think you would mind, my bad."

If you ask me, Chauncey was begging to get his ass whooped. And the nigga was pushing all of the right buttons to send Tyreke over the edge.

"Of course I mind. The fuck you mean you didn't think I would mind?" Tyreke mimicked. He stopped in the middle of his lashing and pointed to Chauncey's busted lip. "Who fucked you up?"

Chauncey had to let out a laugh, a laugh that annoyed the fuck out of Tyreke. You see, because of Chauncey's tendency to indulge in abusive sexual acts with D'mico, the man acquired multiple bruises and scars. Fortunately, the busted lip was the only thing visible on his body aside from the bite marks and scratches on his backside.

Chauncey allowed his eyes to graze over D'mico's face. "I got this new chick. Let's just say that she workin' a nigga overtime."

Tyreke followed Chauncey's gaze. Immediately his brow lifted in a manner that said that he'd been disrespected. He moved in on Chauncey like an animal stalking its prey.

Feeling the threat, Chauncey stepped back and raised both hands. "Whoa...Ty, chill. The woman I'm talkin' about you don't even know," he said, trying to ease Tyreke's discomfort.

Tyreke slammed his finger into Chauncey's chest. "If I ever catch you looking at my woman, I will cut yo fuckin' nuts off and feed them to you for breakfast, lunch and dinner. Nigga, you better know and remember who you work for," Tyreke barked, grinding his teeth.

Chauncey's jaw hit the floor in shock as if he didn't have the slightest clue as to what Tyreke's problem was. With nothing else to say, Tyreke shoved his half-empty glass of champagne into Chauncey's chest, spilling a small amount of bubbly on his white button-up dress shirt.

"Tell the driver that I'm ready," Tyreke concluded, leaving Chauncey standing there.

Embarrassed like a muthafucka, Chauncey slammed the glass on a nearby table full of food and exotic fruits. With a smug look on his face, he watched Tyreke and D'mico as they walked the entire way out the door.

I can't wait to lay his ass to rest.

* * * *

D'mico swayed her hips side to side down the long,

narrow hallway. She had her peach, Victoria's Secret night gown parted slightly, revealing nothing underneath but blessed skin and a matching thong set. Tyreke converted the lower level of the house into a lounge area for guests a year ago. It had all your essentials, including a six-seat theater. The 1,760 square foot entertainment chamber was fully equipped with a loaded bar, kitchenette, two restrooms and of course a video station for the fellas.

D'mico busied herself behind the bar. She pulled out Tyreke's stash of Purple Kush and handled the sour apple cigarillo like a vet. First she made a slit, and then she removed the tobacco contents. Once she had it rolled, she poured herself a glass of Clos d'Ambonnay and took a seat on the big, plush sofa. Pressing the play button on the surround sound stereo system, Anthony Hamilton's song "I'm a Mess" shook her thoughts. D'mico had so much shit on her mind, and she hoped the "fire" in her hand and a glass of wine would heal her broken heart. *I'm a mess right now...I can't eat. I can't sleep.* It's amazing how much the opposite sex can affect your state of mind because D'mico's thinking was foggy as hell. After everything she'd been through in her past, Tyreke had the fuckin' nerve to play her close like some chickenhead. What she wanted to do was confront his two-timing ass. But Chauncey told her not to. He said to let things play themselves out. Man did she want to though. The more she looked at Tyreke, the angrier she became. How stupid could he be? He had steak at home but chose to settle for a damn bologna sandwich.

Yeah. She was sleeping around with Chauncey, so

what? What's your point? Dammit, it was Tyreke who started this mess, remember? Two wrongs don't make a right, but shit, if he could run around and fuck anything with a heartbeat, why couldn't she master his equation? Yeah, that's what I thought. Tyreke had to be out of his damn mind if he thought she was going to stay at home doing crossword puzzles. "Where they do dat at?" D'mico choked on the "dro," becoming more and more relaxed. Weed always made her problems seem like nothing. She just wished that the problems would vanish when her high came down. That was the flipside to reefer. For the moment, she let it run its course as Scottie beamed her up. Her mind shifted to Chauncey. Chauncey had that "wake you up in the morning" type of dick. Every chance she got she wanted a sip of his Folgers—strong and black. She wondered if the nigga had a special gadget attached to it by the way he slanged his new jack.

Fantasying about him fucking her, D'mico slowly ran her hand down the center of her thighs around to her private parts. She closed her eyes, took another drag off her weed and opened her legs.

"I see you found my shit. Must be the chronic 'cause you look like you enjoying yo'self over there."

D'mico jumped from the sound of Tyreke's voice, nearly dropping her half-smoked blunt. Looking over her shoulder, she rolled her eyes, turned back around and closed her legs. She went back to her smoke session and took a long pull as if Tyreke weren't there. D'mico didn't know what Carmelo Anthony looked like half naked, but face-wise, him and Tyreke could pass as twins. Tyreke stood in the cut in his boxer briefs gazing at the woman he loved. D'mico was ignoring him. He laughed to himself before pulling all of his 185 pounds off the wall.

"Can I sit with you?" he asked, nudging her leg. Instead of putting up a fight, D'mico's silky legs parted without protest. Tyreke fell between her legs with ease. The warmth of her body pleasantly heated his backside. This was their ritual on a day when they weren't mad at each other. Every night, Tyreke would rest his back against D'mico while she played therapy as she massaged his scalp. They would talk about everything. Not anymore. Nowadays, they used body language as a form of communication and words as a way to hurt each other.

Tyreke reached his hand out for the blunt. Adding extra suction, he pulled on the fire dro until his lungs were full and the bridge of his nose tightened. Then he let out the potent cloud of smoke.

D'mico noticed Tyreke's new tattoo. *When did he get that?* she thought to herself, admiring the detail work. Tyreke had several tattoos in numerous places, like his arms and chest. But this one was definitely new. In the center was a Glock surrounded by bloody C-notes with the words "All or Nothing" above the Glock. The blood dripping off the money looked so real. D'mico started to reach her hand out to trace her finger along the bills, but quickly she thought against it.

What did it mean? she wondered.

"Can you live the rest of your life with that?" Tyreke asked, knowing she was looking at his tat.

D'mico stared at the words "All or Nothing" in silence. She didn't know what to look forward to. However, she was almost certain that her future with

Tyreke would end shortly. The crazy thing about that is not even three months ago she couldn't picture a happy life without him. Amazingly, the tables turned fast. Now she was planning on setting him up for Chauncey. Hey, there's a thin line between love and hate.

Tyreke looked over his shoulder at D'mico. "You not goin' to answer my question?"

"Ty, I really don't want to talk about this right now."

"What? Yo, D'mico, what the fuck is yo problem?"

"You!" D'mico snapped. "You're the damn problem." She shoved his back. "Move, dammit. I was doing perfectly fine until you brought your ass in here."

Tyreke damn near choked. "What?" He turned around full circle.

"You know what, just move. Let me up. I wanna go to bed."

"Oh, now you want to go to bed. But you don't wanna tell me what all the attitude is for? Fuck that! You can go to bed after you tell me what the fuck is going on. What, you mad about something?"

The fact that Tyreke wouldn't get out of her way and allow her to get up pushed D'mico over the edge. She was now yelling and expressing her aggravation with a shove here and there to his firm chest.

"Move, Ty. Get the fuck outta my way. You done already violated me enough for one night. First, you put your hands on me, and then you took me around those filthy people. You know I hate cops. Did you care? Of course not. If you cared anything about me, you wouldn't be fuckin' other bitches! LET ME UP!"

D'mico was so loud that the neighbors could hear her

through their soundproof walls. Tyreke stared at D'mico with cold eyes. Who was this woman in front of him? And what the hell was she talking about?

Although D'mico had every right to be upset about him putting his hands on her, Tyreke thought the issue was resolved. Plus, he knew about her fear of cops, but shit, that shit happened to her years ago. Yeah, he took on her baggage and promised her everything life could offer—excluding the bullshit they were going through now—but damn, she was trippin' for real. As far as him fuckin' around, he killed that noise years ago. The only thing that made his dick hard other than her was money. That's what's wrong with females these days. They be worried about the wrong things. If you want to stay close to your man, stop pushing him away. D'mico was doing just that, pushing him far the fuck away.

"D'mico, I'm not cheating on—"

SLAP!

"You're a liar," she screamed, a little scared by her outburst.

Boiling with anger, Tyreke had had enough of her shit. Some females be begging to get their asses kicked. He jumped to his feet, grabbed her shoulder and pinned her into the sofa.

"Bi-Eh, if you don't want me to beat your ass, you betta keep your hands to yourself," he said with as much venom as the smack to his face carried.

"I'm not playin' with you, Ty."

"I'm not playin' wit' yo ass either," Tyreke countered.

"Does putting your hands on me make you feel like a

man? Do it? Well, you can take that shit to Coco or whatever her name is. Where you meet her at, a strip club?"

Tyreke remained on top of D'mico. What was she smoking 'cause it damn sure wasn't the same shit he'd been smoking on. D'mico was acting like one of them psycho broads, all crazy an' shit.

"Coco? Are you fuckin' drunk? Yeah, you gotta be drunk or straight cuckoo. Where you getting your information from? Whoever dishing that shit out to you gon be the cause of you getting fucked up." Tyreke used his body weight, pressing D'mico further and further into the sofa. "If I was cheatin' on your simple ass, you'd be the first to know. Do you think I would be fuckin' wit' another bitch and still keep yo bipolar ass around? Maybe I should go find some bitch to lay up with because hearing that seems to satisfy you."

Tyreke released his grip. He got up and stood over D'mico like a roach on the floor. All possibilities of coming into the theater and making love to her went out the door. He would rather take a cold-ass shower and go to bed with a stiff dick than be around her deranged ass.

"Puttin' my hands on you is on me, but all this shit you stirring up is on you. What makes me feel like a man is having my woman at home where she need to be instead of ripping and running the streets like a nigga with a dope sack. Once you start acting like the woman I fell in love with, then I'll start treating you like a woman. Till then, grow up. I'll be in the guest room," he finished, walking away.

Once the door slammed behind Tyreke, D'mico

started to cry. She didn't know words could hurt so much. Yet they did. They hurt a lot. One minute you think you know someone, and then the next you have no idea. Deep down, that's what hurt their relationship the most. Not knowing.

Chapter 2

"Sooo...Who is he, gurl?" Leslie stressed, making her words sound drawn out. "I know you giving up the pussy, so you might as well tell me who Mr. 'don't mind getting killed' is," she laughed, referring to what Tyreke would do if he knew D'mico was seeing another man. Leslie was a hood chick. She also could be nosy as hell at times. The fact that she ran and owned her own beauty salon didn't help her inquisitive side. She always wanted the scoop on everything. D'mico enjoyed Leslie's company and all; however, it was Leslie's probing questions that flat-out drove D'mico nuts. "I'm waiting," Leslie said impatiently, applying a deep conditioner to the roots of D'mico's hair.

Unable to look her in the eyes, D'mico pinched Leslie's leg. "Bitch, don't hold your breath. I'm not fuckin' nobody but Ty."

Using the long hose connected to the wash station, Leslie started on D'mico's rinse. "Whateva, denial is the first sign of guilt."

D'mico tilted her head to the side, causing soapy suds to run down her face.

"Leslie, will you shut up? I said I'm not messing around. Stop insinuating shit. That's how rumors get started."

"Okay, okay. Jeez, calm down, killa. I believe you. Let's just hope Tyreke does," Leslie said chuckling.

"Dammit Leslie."

"You know I'm playin' with you." Leslie changed the subject.

"You know he called over here for you. He was sounding all serious an' shit. He was like yo, Leslie, where ya girl at?" Leslie heightened her voice to imitate Tyreke. "Oh, she ain't there? Aight."

Both women busted out laughing.

"For real, girl. The man love you. I thought he was going to send out a missing persons report by the way he sounded," Leslie added, wrapping a dry towel around D'mico's hair.

D'mico bit down on her bottom lip. She thought about Leslie's comment. Did Tyreke really love her? She seemed to be torn between love and hate. What was love anyway? Can two people really engage in a monogamous relationship without the worry of infidelity?

The chime of D'mico's cell phone broke the silence. She was happy that her phone had rung. It took away the pressure of having to comment on Leslie's statement.

"Is that you or me," Leslie asked, looking around. D'mico dug in her tote bag and grabbed her Samsung.

"It's me." She looked at the screen. Quickly she pressed the call button. "Hello."

"Did you find out anything?" the caller asked in a strong voice.

Pretending to be done with D'mico's wash, Leslie stuck her neck out to listen.

D'mico knew that Leslie was being nosy once again, so she spoke low and kept her answers short. One thing she didn't want was people in her business, even if Leslie was her friend. Shidd, friends will stab you in the back in a heartbeat. How true that statement was.

"Um, not yet. Actually, I'm busy right now," D'mico confirmed, yanking her head away from the comb. Leslie was being rough as hell. Normally, she handled her hair with care. After all, D'mico was tender-headed. For some odd reason, Leslie was dragging the comb along her scalp like a knife.

"What's more important than this dick?"

"My hair," D'mico said matter-of-factly to the caller while squinting her eyes and shrinking her neck. She felt like the nappy-headed, little girl in the movie *The Color Purple.*

"I guess I got to pull all of it out then. He gets jealous from time to time. Reeal jealous, mama."

D'mico smiled from ear to ear. Chauncey was crazy. He added that extra spice to her love life, and his sense of humor drove her wild.

"You so crazy," she giggled. "Can you hold on a minute?" Chauncey smiled on the other end of the phone.

"You got thirty seconds."

D'mico didn't want to keep him waiting any longer than he said to, so she diverted her attention to Leslie.

"Leslie, do you mind if I take this call outside? I'll be right back."

"Yes, I mind. Tell whoever you're talkin' to to call back. I got three more heads to do," Leslie said with a whole lot of attitude.

Sensing a cat fight on the other end, Chauncey cut the conversation short. "Yo, just lock in with me after you finish touchin' up, beautiful."

D'mico poked out her perfectly full lips. "Okay...I'll talk to you later," she pouted, ending the call. Once she secured her phone back in her bag, she went off. "Bitch, don't ever try to shit on me like that again. Five minutes wouldn't have held you up."

Leslie sucked her teeth. She tried to defuse the situation. "You know what, D'mico, you're right. You're my girl. I just got a long day ahead of me, and I was hoping to get out of here early so I can pick the kids up."

The flames in D'mico's eyes died down instantly. She was a sucker for the kids. Hell, if she was in Leslie's shoes, she probably would've said the same thing.

Leslie was dark chocolate—deep brown and rich like a Hershey's candy bar. Occasionally she wore reddish-brown highlights to boost her skin tone. She kept her hair in a chic style like the artist Rihanna. However, Leslie wasn't blessed with Rihanna's noticeable features. Leslie wasn't all that in the face. In fact, the woman barely qualified as average. Everyone couldn't be blessed with good looks. But I can tell you what God blessed her with—flawless skin, perky titties and a booty that fellas could rest their drinks on. By the way, she looked damn good to be a mother of four.

In Oklahoma, men will put you in two categories—either you're a paper chaser or a back slug. A paper chaser has the mentality of a hustler. She dominates her man by holding down her household with a steady flow of cash. A back slug? Well, a back slug has no objective. They either fuck their way out of pocket (Trick) or slowly try to rise above the cause (Prostitute). Let me tell you like this, Leslie was both a paper chaser and a back slug. Busting a nut came with a hefty price, a price that many wanted to pay. Leslie's score came with three girls and one boy. With no daddy.

It was afternoon when Leslie put the final touches on D'mico's hair. Her deep spiral curls bounced freely with every twist and turn of her head, making her baby face glow like sunshine. Leslie placed a large mirror before D'mico so she could get a better look at her masterpiece.

"Now, that's a fine bitch!" Leslie commented.

D'mico smiled partly as she eyed the reflection she hated. She didn't see the beauty that everyone else saw in her. Secretly, she saw a nobody—a woman with multiple scars, someone who men would never respect. At least that's what Lonnie told her. Lonnie was the second corrupt cop D'mico encountered as a child.

* * * *

State property is what people called children like D'mico. For the past three years she'd been in and out of foster homes, no one to love and no one to love her back. Unlike a drug dealer, Sandra, her caretaker, moved battered kids in and out of her home like a whore house. She abused the system any way she saw fit. She didn't care. Shit, she collected an average of $6,900 a month off of the kids alone, and that didn't include the pussy she sold once the girls turned fifteen. I know it sounds kinda bizarre, but even today that shit is going on. Every day little girls are being taken advantage of, and its all for that shit that keeps this world spinning. Money.

D'mico hoped and prayed that a family would adopt her before old Lady Sandra got the opportunity to rob her innocence. She was fourteen, and she knew time wouldn't be on her side much longer.

D'mico sat in the den watching cartoons with the other kids. Sidetracked by a man she'd never seen before, she took notice of the tears and hung look on old Lady Sandra's bitter face. Obviously the news the man delivered brought old Lady Sandra more grey hairs than she needed and a whole lot of sorrow.

The man stood back on one leg as his husky frame used the opening to the hallway as his support. With an expression D'mico couldn't read, he dug inside his pocket and placed a wad of cash in old Lady Sandra's wrinkled hand.

Old Lady Sandra licked her fingers, counted the money, flipped it over and counted it a second time as if what she was looking for wasn't there. She mumbled a few curse words and held out her hand.

D'mico gasped when the man straightened up his frame and charged at old Lady Sandra like an angry bull. He grabbed her by the neck and shook her violently like a rag doll.

Immediately, Lonnie let up from old Lady Sandra when he heard the squeal coming from a pretty little girl's mouth. D'mico wondered if the commotion was over Christina. The only time Lonnie or one of his associates came around was when they paid for a night with one of the girls from the house. Christina was one of the innocent who went into the hands of Lonnie. As soon as Christina blossomed into a young woman, old Lady

Sandra signed her innocence away. She always came back the next morning, but this time, things were different. Christina had left and never came back.

Lonnie knew it was his fault that Christina was dead. He was the one who killed her; it was by accident though. One night, Lonnie turned his partner from the station onto Christina. Christina was sixteen years old, and Lonnie had been knocking her off every day since she turned fifteen. Believe it or not, Christina liked the rush of fuckin' an older man. She didn't mind until Lonnie brought Matthew along. That night, she kicked, scratched and even bit Lonnie on the ear when Matthew positioned himself behind her. The two men wanted to perform a threesome with the young girl, and Christina wasn't game for the trio. Then, the unthinkable happened. Lonnie got angry and strangled Christina until her body went limp. Like I said, it was an accident.

Charging him for the two days Christina was put out of commission wasn't going to happen.

D'mico couldn't take her eyes away from the angry man. He had the greyest eyes she'd ever seen on a man whose pigmentation was so black. He smiled, licked his lips and pointed towards her. D'mico froze in place. Her heart raced and she started feeling sick. She wasn't good at reading lips, but she made out old Lady Sandra's words, "You can have her." Instantly D'mico thought about running away. She took a look at the other kids in the house. Michelle ran away, which left Serenity (nine), Desire (seven) and Kiara who was six. D'mico had grown to love the three girls as if they had the same blood running through their veins.

Serenity scooted closer to D'mico, laid her head on D'mico's shoulder, and asked her what was wrong. In order to save the other kids, D'mico kissed her dreams of loosing her virginity to her husband goodbye. "Nothin'...I just love ya'll," she stated, wiping the tears away from her face.

* * * *

Over the course of two months, Lonnie used D'mico's body like a personal garbage disposable. He did everything from beating her with his billy club to punching her in the face multiple times until she passed out. Not only did he want to disfigure her self-esteem but he wanted to disfigure her face as well. He wanted her to know that he was the only one for her. No other man would want a woman with more scars than Tony Montana. To secure his sick fantasy, he kept D'mico banged up and bruised every day. He pissed on her, shot cum in her face and hair, and a variety of other things that fed his insecurities. D'mico lay on the bed in the fetal position, still in pain from the night before. She thought back to the day old Lady Sandra sold her like a book of food stamps. She was presented with the opportunity to run away; instead, she went against the grain by sparing the other three girls. She felt like she had sold her soul to the devil, and she regretted every minute of it. She thought police officers were there to help people not hurt them. Lonnie told her that all cops were like him. Every one of them was crooked in some kind of way.

"Whatchu doin' laying down? Come undress me,"

Lonnie demanded. D'mico looked into his neutral eyes for some speck of compassion.

"Can we do it some other time? I'm hurting down there, and I have blood in my panties."

Lonnie was disgusted by D'mico's bluntness. He tapped a finger against his chin, thinkin' of a solution.

"I got a idea. Go get a towel. We'll lay it under you."

D'mico started to cry. Her voice trembled inside her throat. "But I-I don't want to. That's gross."

Lonnie backhanded D'mico across the face. She fell over. "Since it's so damn gross, then you won't mind me fuckin' you in the ass. Turn around," he ordered, bending her over. He unbuckled his uniform pants, dropped them to the floor and rammed his average-sized penis into D'mico's butt with excessive force. D'mico whimpered and cried as Lonnie cuffed his arm around her waist while he tore her rectum open.

"Look how ugly you are when you do that," he fumed, pumping faster until blood leaked on his dick and pubic hairs. After five more minutes of violation, Lonnie was finally finished. He pulled out his bloody penis and shoved it in D'mico' s face.

"Next time you won't tell me no. Ugly bitch."

Within seconds, Lonnie had his dirty dick in his pants and was out the door.

D'mico took what seemed like her first breath of air. Her tiny body shook nonstop, and blood flowed down her leg. The numb feeling in her private parts caused her body to go into shock. Seconds later, D'mico's body completely shut down, and everything went black.

Two weeks in the hospital and thirty-four stitches later, D'mico stepped outside the hospital and was greeted by Lonnie and old Lady Sandra. *When will this nightmare end?* D'mico thought, taking slow strides towards the backseat. She had a feeling that it never would.

* * * *

After the flashback from her past, D'mico paid Leslie and rushed out the door.

"Call me," Leslie yelled, holding open her shop door.

D'mico turned around, raised up a hand to block the afternoon sun and screamed in Leslie's direction. "I will. See you later."

The strong sound of Gerald Levert's voice made its way through D'mico's car speakers. The lyrics made D'mico think about Chauncey. Speak of the Devil. Chauncey was calling her.

"Hey, sexy."

"What's up? You done gettin' your hair done?" he asked.

"Yeah, I just left. I'm on my way to meet you."

"Give me a minute. I'm at my boy's crib, and I think he's waitin' on his girl. Once she gets here, I'll be there."

Chauncey smirked. From the comer of his eye, he watched Tyreke count his earnings. The money smoothly transferred into the money counter, dispensing outward in thick stacks. He then finished off the stacks with a band around the bills. Chauncey was so mesmerized by the sight of the money that he almost forgot that he was on the phone.

"Hellooo."

"Yeah."

"Dang, I said which one of your friends you talking about 'cause last time you told me that, you stood me up?"

"My man, Tyreke. Hold on."

The mention of Tyreke's name had D'mico swerving out of the lane. Dodging a red pickup that she almost reared, she regained control of her car, flashed her emergency lights and parked on the side of the street.

What kind of juvenile delinquent shit is he on? Is he fuckin' crazy? Oh yeah, he's crazy.

"Chauncey, you trippin' for real. You know what, bye!"

"Hang up if you want to. Yo, Ty, where did you say D'mico was getting her hair done at?"

D'mico boiled with anger. Tyreke got up, checked the time on his watch and frowned. D'mico had left hours ago to get her hair done, and she hadn't walked through the door yet. She probably was still holding on to their argument a few nights ago. Females had a tendency to dwell on shit until they felt like they got the last say so. If D'mico was doing that silly shit, he'd have her know that he was unfazed. She could snowball her anger forever for all he cared.

"Why?" Tyreke asked, stuffing money inside a duffel bag.

"'Cause my chick tryna get broke off with a good spot. She tired of her old one, aintchu baby?"

D'mico was so done with Chauncey that she hung up

on him. She could've easily cancelled their fuck session, but her hormones led her to the Hilton Hotel where she used the alias Chauncey gave her, paid for room 216 and slipped inside the room with a big smile on her face in wait for Chauncey.

* * * *

Tyreke's next move would be to travel to his trap house where he secretly stashed his profits. Consciously, he eyed Chauncey to see if he was paying him any attention. Chauncey was doing everything but paying Tyreke any mind. He was kicked back on Tyreke's sofa flipping through television channels. Even though Chauncey's mind was preoccupied, Tyreke put his trap house plans on hold. No one knew where he stashed his money, not even D'mico, and he planned to keep it that way. Only crash dummies display their pantry of food. Although a few of his boys knew where he lived, not a fuckin' soul but the one inside of his body knew where his money was. Niggas' bellies ached for a bite of what the next nigga had, and Tyreke had no plans of feeding the next nigga's greed.

Ring! *Ring*!

Tyreke frowned when he saw "caller id blocked" plastered across his Samsung screen.

With a hint of irritation in his voice, he answered on the third ring. "Who dis and why you disrespecting my waves calling block?" Somewhat embarrassed by the smart remark on the other end of the phone, the sweet, feminine voice answered Tyreke's question.

"I'm sorry. My phone is setup like that. Is this Tyreke?"

Giving his hands access to grab the duffel bag and car keys, Tyreke gripped the phone with his chin. "Who the fuck is this? And what the fuck do you want? I got shit to do," he stated crudely.

"This is LeeLee. Is Chauncey around?"

"Hold up! This shit 'bout to stop today. If that nigga wanted to talk to you, he would've gave you his number. Further more, after today, DO NOT call my hook up again. Hold on," Tyreke fumed, working his way back towards the living room.

Meanwhile, Chauncey was in a world of his own, laid out on Tyreke's sofa like he owned the joint. He traced circles around his belly button while he chatted flirtatiously on his phone with new pussy, grinning from ear to ear like he was a kid in a candy store.

For several shocking seconds, Tyreke just watched Chauncey. It was as if the nigga knew no bounds when it came down to respecting him.

"Eh, nigga, raise da fuck up. Why is this bitch still ringin' my horn?"

Chauncey glanced over his shoulder. Not hearing a word Tyreke said, he lifted up his index finger and returned to his x-rated conversation.

Gnashing his teeth, Tyreke hauled off and smacked Chauncey across his head.

WHACK!

"What da...whatchu do dat shit for?" Chauncey jumped to his feet. Tyreke rapped his knuckles. He was ready to mop Chauncey across the floor.

"Address whoever you're on the phone with; then address dis bitch on my phone." Tyreke stood there with a killer look on his face.

Chauncey swallowed, said a few words into his phone and then hung up. "That was money."

"Nigga, I don't give a fuck if that was yo mama. If you wanna play around wit' these hoes, by all means, have at it. The least you can fuckin' do is have one of dem add you to their calling plan 'cause you sure as hell ain't on mine, playa." Tyreke flexed.

Chauncey bit his tongue. For the time being, he was going to keep his cool. Damn...what's a phone call? It ain't like he was fuckin' the bitch in his house. "Hand me the phone."

Tyreke examined Chauncey before handing over his Samsung. "When you're done, leave it on the table. When I get my bill next month, I'll send you a copy. Let yo'self out when you're done," Tyreke said, easing out the door.

Chauncey smacked his lips. "Whateva, nigga," he said to himself. He straightened out his starch jeans, shifted into a cozy position, propped his leg up and took the phone off of mute.

"What's good, sexy?" he said, not thinking about Tyreke or D'mico, who'd been waiting on him at the Hilton Hotel.

* * * *

Tyreke dipped through traffic bumpin' the cold lyrics of UGK. He made sure to obey stop signs, red lights and the speed limit. Ninety percent of recovered drugs, guns and paraphernalia were discovered through simple traffic violations. Nevertheless, Tyreke wasn't going to fall victim to the statistics. Nearing a yellow light, Tyreke applied pressure to his breaks, drawing to a stop. Bobbing his head and taking in the view of traffic, instantly Tyreke noticed the police cruiser hidden three cars away.

"It's cool...You've done this countless times," he assured himself, turning down his beats. The light turned green minutes later. Tyreke let up off his brakes and blended in with the rest of the world like any average nigga on a typical Saturday afternoon. However, Tyreke was looking only on one side of the shield.

Officer Damon spotted the white and gold Excursion at a nearby intersection. No sooner had he saw the SUV than his quota for the month entered his mind. He planned to follow the driver. He knew that he would fuck up sooner or later.

Tyreke adjusted his rearview mirror. The three cars that were behind him either turned off or jumped onto the highway, giving the fuckin' cop access to run his tag. He knew the faggot wanted to pull him over. Guess what? It wasn't happening. Instead of going to the trap house, Tyreke had no other choice but to return to his crib.

* * * *

D'mico had enough of waiting for Chauncey. The nigga had pulled yet another whammy on her. *How can I be so stupid?* she thought, putting on her clothes. Aggravated and sexually frustrated, she dialed Chauncey's cell number and ended up getting his answering machine. Every minute that passed by pissed her off. The last time she had had sex with Chauncey was a week ago. She longed for the cream that exploded from her body when he filled up her cup. Chauncey's dick sent her on overdrive. What if he was screwin' someone else? What if the other woman fucked him better than she did? Could she handle that? All of these twisted scenarios played inside her head. She knew that she was walking on dangerous grounds, but Chauncey had her fucked up.

D'mico grabbed her tote bag and keys. She headed to her house still thinking about Chauncey and who he might've been sleeping with.

* * * *

Chauncey stroked his dick to the harmonious sound of pleasure coming from the other end of the phone. His eyes rolled to the back of his head as he jerked himself off.

"You almost there, boo?"

"Damn, you feel sooo good," LeeLee moaned, sliding three fingers in and out of her treasure box.

The sound of LeeLee playing with her juices had Chauncey's callused hand stroking his pole even faster.

"When we get the money, are we going to fuck all over it, babe?"

"Mmm-hmm."

LeeLee smiled real big. She was aware that Chauncey's main focal point was that bitch, D'mico. Shoot, that type of shit didn't faze her. The girl was their meal ticket. Nothing more, nothing less. To show LeeLee that D'mico was a bottom bitch, Chauncey gave her the earrings D'mico gave him. Stupid bitch! The girl was young, dumb and overloaded with cum. The only reason why LeeLee had Chauncey beatin' his meat in the first place was so he wouldn't have the energy to sleep with D'mico. By the time Chauncey got around to fuckin' D'mico's trifling ass, she wouldn't get nothin' anyway.

Chauncey was near his nut when he heard a car door shut. He was so busy choking his chicken that he totally forgot about where he was. He put his tool back inside his pants and wiped the sticky pre-nut running down the palm of his hand on the side of the couch.

"Chauncey, what's wrong? You're not tellin' me what to do anymore," LeeLee questioned, adding more lubricant to her now dry pussy.

"Ugh...I gotta call you back."

"Call me back? Uh uh, so you gonna stop what we got goin' for—"

"Bitch bye!"

Click

Chauncey hung up on LeeLee. He didn't want to, but she would've went on for forever and a day. He zipped up his pants, grabbed the remote and flipped through the channels. After several minutes, high heels clacking against marble changed the atmosphere. Chauncey smiled in delight and rubbed his hands together. D'mico entered the living room. When she saw Chauncey sitting there with a cheesy-ass look on his face, everything in her wanted to go left. Her hazel eyes stalked the room.

"Where is Ty?" she asked with so much attitude that it shook the smile right off of Chauncey's face.

Chauncey ignored her question and took in her presence. It was hard to believe that a woman as beautiful as D'mico was the cause of the turmoil in his life.

"Damn, you look good, gurl." D'mico rolled her eyes.

"Where's Ty?"

"He ain't here. Its just you, me, space and opportunity. Comere. Sit on daddy's lap."

"No, you stood me up."

Chauncey threw up his hands. "Gone with all of that. You know all that arguing shit ain't for us. You know I was going to call you. I got held up." He reached out his hand, beckoning her to come towards him. "Will you accept my apology?" he asked with puppy dog eyes.

Giving in to the lies, D'mico grabbed his hand. Her body slowly surrendered to his large frame.

"You gotta do more than apologize. Saying sorry ain't enough. Prove to me that you won't let it happen again," she whispered, looking into his eyes.

"Whatchu want me to do?" he whispered back.

D'mico pushed off of him. She stepped back and removed her pants. She couldn't believe that she was actually about to have sex in her and Tyreke's house. For months, all she could think about was sex. She didn't care where it occurred. Who cares as long as she got her rocks off. Chauncey's eyes zeroed in on D'mico's juice box. He hadn't even touched her, and already he could see the muscles in her pussy wink. Licking his lips, he came out of his clothes.

* * * *

Tyreke thought about D'mico. He wondered what she would do if he ever got locked up. Without a doubt, he knew she would ride out his bid with him. Shit wasn't going good with their relationship right now, but Tyreke knew her heart. He knew that she would keep her pussy nice and warm for him. She was his queen.

Fifteen miles into his drive and a few miles away from his crib, the law was still trailing behind Tyreke like a dick in the butt. I don't care how much clout you think you may have or who you got on your payroll. Being followed by the cops will intimidate anyone. Staying focused, Tyreke wiped the beads of sweat that started to form away from his face. Two more miles and he would be home.

* * * *

Being inside D'mico's pussy was paradise. Her pussy was like the Garden of Eden—tempting and tantalizing with a mixture of sin.

Chauncey tipped D'mico forward, stretching her body across the sofa and gazing at her like a work of art.

First he served her to the right, knocking the breath out of her lungs. Then he hammered to the left, hitting her stomach and kidneys.

"Uurgh...Uurgh..." D'mico moaned in short breaths. All of Chauncey's stabbing had D'mico scooting and bucking.

"Where you goin'?" Chauncey asked, grabbing ahold

of her waist.

Five minutes into their session and already D'mico was running. He had her reaching for the stars, and it wasn't even night time yet. She already climaxed twice, and he was nowhere near to being done. Fuckologist? Yeah, well you can call him that. He did everything from flipping her pussy to putting a spit shine on the bitch.

Within minutes, there was so much nut and pussy juice from D'mico that the friction against Chauncey's dick felt great. He was about to bust.

"Damn..." he groaned, fighting the rush of blood inside his penis.

Every stroke was extra sensitive. Quickly, he changed his momentum. He rotated D'mico on her back, grabbed her ankles and crisscrossed her legs. He loved this position. It made her feel tighter, and her pussy was guaranteed to get wetter. Running his hands along her cinnamon legs, he pushed her knees forward towards her lips for a French kiss. Having his way, he plunged deeper into her well, boldly and without a life jacket. In and out, he substituted back strokes with easy strokes—intervals with a tidbit of harmony. No wonder men neglected condoms. Although they are useful, preventing the risk of STDs and pregnancy, pussy felt better without them.

Negligent? Maybe. He could think about that later. For now, he had pussy to tend to.

D'mico latched onto Chauncey. He took her body for a roller coaster ride. Unlike the other times when sex with him was rough and course, this time they were having sex in her home. Chauncey was taking his time, making sure that she was pleased. Before, he would just bust his nut and go. Wham, Bam, thank you ma'am. She could literally feel his breath nuzzle against her breasts. Then he moaned. Did I say moan? I sure as hell did. Shit was that good. He still was the fuckologist though. Although he had plans to linger in her honeycomb a little while longer, the sperm shooting to the surface had a better idea.

* * * *

Tyreke swooped into his driveway. Man, that was close. From his rearview mirror, he watched the patrol car roll by.

"I'M THE GINGERBREAD MAN, BITCH!" he said out loud to the passing vehicle.

He couldn't believe the bastard followed him all the way to his crib. Then again, he wasn't surprised. TPD loved to harass niggas. Fucking lames. Tyreke killed his engine. The two cars parked side by side caught his attention. D'mico's Audi and Chauncey's Impala. Why was Chauncey still at his house? Furthermore, he didn't trust the nigga being alone with his woman. The look Chauncey gave D'mico made Tyreke want to wipe his ass across the floor in front of all those white people at the party a couple of weeks ago.

Sparing no time, Tyreke dug in his secret compartment, pulled out his handy .45 and jumped out the car.

* * * *

Approximately two minutes later, Chauncey lost control. His semen took off inside of D'mico's womb at the speed of a rocket headed for outer space.

* * * *

Fuck using the front door. If Tyreke planned on catching anything, he had to go inside the house through the back door. He used his key to the padlock, unlatched the gate and closed it behind him. He expected for his two pits, Cain and Abel, to greet him, but they didn't nor was there any barking—which was a bit strange. Tyreke was nervous and hella anxious all at the same time. His mind prepared his heart for the worse, and his trigger finger prepared itself for anything else after that.

He tucked his .45 in the small of his back, cut through the pool area, passed the basketball and tennis courts, and made his way to the back door.

"Hey, man, Whatchu doin' back here?" Chauncey called out, entertaining Cain and Abel.

Tyreke felt stupid for jumping to conclusions, but Chauncey wasn't the type of person you could put your trust in. D'mico, on the other hand, was his jewel.

Tyreke brushed his hands across his thick curls. "The question is what are you doin' back here? I came back to check on my babies. Forgot to feed 'em."

Chauncey gave Tyreke a sinister smirk. He continued to toss a small ball between both dogs.

"Well, you're in luck. These fellas is in good hands like Allstate." Tyreke cut his eyes at Chauncey and whistled. Both of the dogs ran to their owner, sitting on all fours in front of him. Tyreke knelt down and adjusted their collars.

Chauncey got a good laugh out of Tyreke. Not only did the nigga show that he was insecure about his bitch, but he was insecure over two fuckin' dogs.

"D'mico in there?" Tyreke asked curiously.

Chauncey shrugged his shoulders. "I dunno. I been out here for a minute. She might be," he lied.

As they made their way inside the house, Tyreke gave Chauncey the run down about his encounter with the law.

"Dem muthafuckas always messin' wit' a nigga. I'll tell you what you should've done." Tyreke lifted his brow with interest.

"What's that?"

"You should've bent the block, got behind his ass and made a citizen's arrest for harassment."

"What?"

"Yeah, you should've pulled his ass over. Hell...gas is too damn high to be taking a round-trip across Tulsa. The courts would award you punitive damages and mental anguish for shit like that," Chauncey joked.

Both men erupted in laughter. Chauncey passed Tyreke his cell phone.

"Here you go. I'm about to bounce. Do you need me for anything, man?" Chauncey asked.

Tyreke thought about his question for a quick second, and he couldn't think of anything off top.

"Nah, I'm good playboy," he responded coolly, giving Chauncey a pound.

On his way to the front door, Tyreke stopped

Chauncey in his tracks. "Yo, Chauncey, lemme ask you a question."

Chauncey fumbled for his car keys. He felt his stomach twist into a tight knot. *What the fuck do he want now?* he thought, turning around. "Wassup?"

"Did you handle that LeeLee situation?"

Chauncey loosened the grip on his jaws. "You know I did," he lied.

"Aight...Well fuck with me later. I got a few jobs for you to take care of later on."

"How late you talkin'?" Chauncey inquired, annoyed by Tyreke's last minute request.

"I'm not sure. Keep yo phone close." Tyreke smirked.

Chauncey turned around and grinned the entire way out the door. The last laugh would be on him.

Tyreke cracked the bedroom door to find D'mico sound asleep. Not wanting to wake her up, he eased the door shut and headed out the house to settle his unfinished business. As soon as D'mico heard the front door slam, she opened her eyes. *Damn, that was close,* she thought getting out of the bed.

Chapter 3

D'mico, Leslie, Kim and Starlet all settled in a cozy booth at Cheddar's. Patiently, their server waited for their orders.

"Umm...I'll have the lasagna trio with a glass of raspberry iced tea," D'mico ordered.

"I'll have the same," Kim said.

"Give me the chicken Alfredo with a side of toasted ravioli, no sauce. I'm hungry as shit," Leslie chimed in, rubbing her stomach. D'mico exchanged an embarrassed look with the server.

"Gurl, me too...I mean, I'm hungry too. Can I have the sirloin steak, medium rare and cheddar fries, please. Oh, can you bring some ranch dressing?" Starlet requested, handing over her menu.

The server took the remaining menus and left. Within minutes, she returned with four drinks and a basket of hot cheddar biscuits.

D'mico sat across from Leslie's homegirl, Kim. The girl was funny looking like a muthafucka. Her eyebrows were too high, not to mention she drew them on. The half circle she attempted to draw on the right side didn't line up with the one on the left.

D'mico wondered if she would be able to hold down her food without laughing in the girl's face. D'mico thought the girl could pass off as Curious George's sister.

Leslie was the first one to attack the biscuits. Steam ascended into the air after she bit into the helpless appetizer as if it were her last meal.

"Lemme tell ya'll what happened to me last night," she said, talking and smacking loud enough for the table next to them to hear.

"We right here, Leslie. Dang, why you yellin'?" D'mico commented, embarrassed.

Leslie rolled her eyes and sucked on her fingers. "Anyway, do ya'll wanna know what happened or not?"

"Yeah...what happened?" Curious George asked with the same fucked-up look on her face.

D'mico shook her head and sipped on her raspberry iced tea. Leslie washed down her biscuit with a swig of Dr. Pepper before she spoke.

"Damn, bitch, any day now..." Starlet said.

"Okay, okay, check dis out. I was suckin' my nigga off last night, right. Well anyway, while I was down there handling my business, dis nigga slipped his hand around my neck and made me choke." She bent her head down like the rest of her story was G14 classified. "I want ya'll to know that I'm no pro in that area...I'll leave that up to those cum-sucking hoes. That shit was so unexpected that I accidentally threw up all over his shit."

D'mico spit out her drink. "Ugh...Bitch, you're straight up nasty," she said, wiping tea off her chin.

"Hoe, you couldn't wait until we ate to tell us dat shit. Hell, you could've kept that shit to yo'self," Starlet fumed.

The server arrived with their entrees. She placed the plates before them, asked if they needed anything else and quickly walked away.

Curious George pushed her plate to the side. "What did you do? What did he do?"

Leslie cracked a smile. "I wiped his dick off with my shirt and dug the chunks of throw up out his pubic hairs. Nigga never knew."

Everyone laughed and shared similar stories— everyone except for D'mico. She was trying hard not to be the snobbish one, but all of these females were ghetto as hell.

D'mico hadn't said a word since leaving Cheddar's. She couldn't enjoy her meal at the restaurant with all the gruesome stories, so she took her food to go.

She sat in the backseat of Leslie's Grand Cherokee with her arms crossed and her to-go box resting in her lap. KJAMZ was jamming on the radio, and all four women bobbed their heads in unison to the beat. Even though D'mico had a funky attitude, it didn't stop her head from swaying side to side.

"Turn dat shit up," Starlet requested, rolling up a blunt. D'mico closed her eyes and enjoyed the music.

Interrupting her mellow state, Starlet offered her the

blunt, letting her know that the rotation was on her. D'mico twisted the burning cigarillo between her fingers. A potent stench burned her nostrils.

"Damn, Inspector Gadget, you gonna hit it or not?" Starlet asked, offended.

D'mico put the blunt to her lips. She paused. "Why is it wet? I ain't never smoked no blunt that was wet like this. Eitha you molested dis muthafucka or something else is wrong with it."

Leslie, who was behind the wheel, nudged Kim, who was in the passenger seat. They both fell out laughing.

Starlet rolled her eyes. She envied D'mico. D'mico was one of those females who thought she was the baddest chic out of any crew she clicked with.

Starlet held out her hand impatiently. "Of course its gonna be wet. I splashed it. Ugh...Hand me my shit please."

"Fuck you mean you splashed it? FUCK YOU MEAN?" D'mico turned her entire body around to confront Starlet.

Starlet sucked her teeth. *This bitch is extra fo sho*, she thought, taking a long, lengthy pull from the cigarillo.

"Girl, chill out. You actin' like I gave you some crack. It's just a little wet daddy. Everybody's doin' it." Starlet continued the rotation, handing the dipped weed to Kim who took two small puffs and passed it to Leslie.

D'mico was so through with their raggedy asses, including Leslie. She might not have been friends with the other girls, but Leslie was supposed to be her friend. Friends don't get you caught up into addictions; they pull you out of them.

"It's all good, D'mico. For real." Leslie assured her. D'mico poked her finger in the back of Leslie's head.

"Ain't shit all good when you dip a blunt and try to pass it to me. Hurry up and drop me—" D'mico was cut off by Starlet's strange behavior.

Starlet started removing her shirt. The smell of Coney Island onions came from under her pits.

"Leslie, do you have the air on? It's hot," Starlet asked, unsnapping her bra. Leslie fiddlcd with the air conditioner. She tried to accommodate Starlet's needs.

"There! It's on high. Are you taking off you clothes again?" Flustered, cold and angry with herself for not driving her own shit, D'mico pinched her nose from the new smell that filled the air. The scent of fish and chips caused her to gag.

Starlet had her arms spread out over the backseat, her head slumped over, and her legs cocked open. Her brown panties sat on top her lap.

"Nuh-uh...Pull this bitch over," D'mico yelled.

Leslie turned around glassy eyed. "Wha-pull over? Why?"

"Bitch, if you don't pull this muthafucka over, I'm a commence ta kickin' yo ass. Pull over NOW!"

The Jeep Grand Cherokee yielded to the side of the street. D'mico opened the car door and jumped out.

* * * *

Tyreke rubbed his freshly cut goatee, contemplating his next move. His game face was on, and at the snap of a finger, it came to him.

"Eight ball, right side pocket," he called out, removing the cue stick from under his chin. His diamond cut bracelet beamed off the light above the pool table as he struck the black and white ball.

CLACK!

Chauncey, the Chief, Damu and Dirt watched in anticipation to see where the eight ball would wind up. Confident about his strike, Tyreke held out his hand.

"Break bread, know yo position when dealing with me."

"Hold on, it ain't...shit! Alright. I gotchu," Chauncey said after seeing the eight ball go in.

The Chief was quite impressed with how the gentlemen handled the bet. He thought all black people acted like animals when they lost. In the beginning of their game, he was counting down the minutes, waiting for them to start pounding on each other; however, it never happened. Wow!

While Damu and Dirt racked up the next game, Tyreke led the Chief to his custom-made bar. Chauncey retrieved his shot glass off the edge of the pool table and followed behind them.

Fishing out a shot glass and clean towel from the cupboard, Tyreke flipped the glass upside down and proceeded to wipe around the rim.

"You said you had some things you wanted to discuss?" Tyreke questioned. He threw the towel over his shoulder and poured Remy into the glass.

The Chief wasn't fucked up enough to show the uneasiness he had around Chauncey. A nigga never shows his weaknesses. He nodded his head in Chauncey's direction for him to leave.

Chauncey glared at the Chief like he was a chump nigga off the street. "What?" he said, pretending to be clueless.

Tyreke really didn't want Chauncey around. To show some respect, he went ahead and included him in whatever the Chief had to say.

"What you have for my ears...can easily be heard by his."

The Chief flexed his jaws. With a look of concern, his ocean blue eyes wandered to Chauncey. Getting down to business, he pleaded his case.

"As you wish. I received some disturbing news about you being spotted on Edison."

"Once again, I must remind you that Edison is out of my league." Tyreke's calm demeanor changed into that of a heated bull. "Nobody's makin' moves out west," Tyreke spat.

"Really?" Chief huffed. "One of the rookies on the squad said that he followed you there and to your house. When he asked about you, if you're name was in the streets, I nearly choked on my mornin' coffee. All I'm saying is that we can't afford to make simple mistakes over a few dollars." The Chief ended his warning with a fake smile, which happened to piss Tyreke off. He was the one who signed this fat bastard's checks. His hefty salary damn sure didn't come from the department. It was Tyreke's dirty money that purchased his $1.1 million cabin in Barbados. Fuckin' pricks, always forget where they came from.

"Let's get something straight. I can go anywhere I

damn well please. I'm a grown-ass man. I gave you my word that we would stay clear from the west side. My word is solid. I mean what I say, and I say what I mean," Tyreke retaliated.

The Chief straightened out the wrinkle on his milk-white face and replaced it with a smile. His chubby hand struck Tyreke's back in a friendly manner.

"I know your word is good, son."

Chauncey and Tyreke exchanged curious looks. Chauncey wondered if Tyreke's stash spot was on Edison. If so, where? Tyreke, on the other hand, was trying to figure out why Chauncey was taking in the Chief's information by thread.

Bzz...Bzz...

Tyreke acknowledged the vibration in his pocket and fished out his cell phone. D'mico's number appeared on the screen. Pressing the call button, he answered.

"Yo."

The sound of busy traffic disrupted D'mico's recognizable voice.

"Tyreke, can you come get me?" she asked, watching a passerby.

Instead of hitting D'mico with a ton of questions, Tyreke got the location, gathered his things and told everyone to bounce.

* * * *

D'mico waited impatiently for Tyreke under the sun. Immediately, her foot let up from the flat pavement when she saw his SUV near Lewis. She unfolded her arms and glanced at her matching his-and-her watch, its pair belonging to Tyreke. For twenty minutes, she tapped her foot on the ground waiting on him.

"About time," she mumbled, walking towards the car. Tyreke sensed D'mico's attitude. He knew off top when she was mad or irritated. She did this sexy thing with her lips that made him smile—a twisted curl to the left. She also would roll her neck and eyes as if she had a permanent tweak. How was that sexy? You had to be a fly on the wall to know where Tyreke was coming from. Eh, it was sexy as hell.

D'mico approached the car like she was the toughest chick in the world. Everything about her aura screamed, "Don't Fuck with Me," and he loved it.

Tyreke reached over the passenger seat and pushed the door open. He slipped Bun B into the CD player. "If you need love, I'm lovin'...If you need a thug, I'm thugin'...If you need a hustla...Whateva you need, gurl, I'm gonna hold you down..."

The lyrics flowing through the speakers had no special meaning to D'mico. Three months ago, she would've thought different.

Tyreke gave D'mico a side glance. Although she was giving him the evil eye, a radiant glow peeked through her malevolent demeanor.

In alliance with her self-esteem, D'mico's head dropped down, and her hazel eyes gazed at her feet. Tyreke never fully understood how D'mico went from happy to hateful. Her attitude, smart remarks and distance started three months ago. Luckily for her, he was a man of understanding. He knew that she went through a lot as a child, and he assumed it played a part in her sudden withdrawal.

Tyreke placed a warm hand across D'mico's thigh. Trying to figure her out, he tilted her chin up to face him.

"Baby, what's wrong? Please, talk to me," he said softly. Everything within D'mico wanted to tell him about the text message and why she was so upset, but what good would it do them now? The damage was done. She was playing for keeps. She didn't want to share Tyreke with another woman. She shouldn't have to.

If she couldn't have him to herself, she didn't want him at all. Besides, her future with Chauncey looked promising. Refusing to acknowledge the electricity transferring from Tyreke's body to hers, she removed her hand.

"Nothing is wrong. I just feel a little sick," she said truthfully.

Feeling rejected, Tyreke looked away. She had his heart bleeding like a muthafucka, and he couldn't stop it.

Tyreke let up off his brakes and merged into traffic. They drove the rest of the way in silence. No music, no words and no eye contact. Just silence.

* * * *

Reverend Johnson woke up from another bad dream. His entire chest and face was drenched in sweat. For the fourth night in a row, he had the same reoccurring dream about his son, Tyreke, being killed by a masked man. This time, the man didn't have a mask on; he also had company. The only problem was when Reverend Johnson approached the killers to get a good look at their faces, he would wake up.

Slipping on his house shoes, he made his way downstairs. He turned on the living room lamp, grabbed his Bible and took a seat. First he prayed out loud, asking God to spare his only child. Then he prayed for understanding. Instantly, his heart was set on Proverbs 7:14. "She threw her arms around the young man, kissed him, looked him straight in the eye and said, 'I made my offerings today and have the meat from the sacrifices, so I came looking for you...'" Reverend Johnson closed his Bible. Was this the warning? If so, how did it relate to Tyreke?

Chapter 4

"Pregnant!" D'mico screamed. She couldn't believe it. She looked back at the instructions to make sure she'd read them right. Sure enough, she did. D'mico sat on the toilet seat in complete shock. She was going to have a baby. Wow! The thought of her sharing a baby with Chauncey caused her heart to flutter. What would Chauncey say about all of this? She knew he would be happy too. They were in love. A baby would complete their relationship. Flushing the toilet, she threw the pregnancy test away, washed her hands and made her way to her bedroom. Wondering how Chauncey would handle her news, she picked up the phone and dialed his seven-digit number. With the phone glued to her ear, she tried to control the butterflies in her stomach. "Nervous as hell" didn't even come close to describing her emotional state. Already baby names were popping into her head. Finally she could experience having her own family.

On the second ring, Chauncey picked up.

"What's up?" he answered incoherently while enjoying the head game LeeLee was putting down. LeeLee slurped on his long dick like an ICEE from QuikTrip.

"Are you busy?"

Chauncey looked down. If only she knew. Hell yeah he was busy. As a matter of fact, he was too damn busy, especially for her, but he couldn't tell her that.

"Nah, I ain't busy."

"Good 'cause I really want to talk to you about something," D'mico said, beating around the bush. This wasn't as easy as she'd expected.

Chauncey tapped LeeLee's shoulder and motioned for her to get up, but LeeLee kept at it. She opened her mouth wide and filled her jaws with hearty meat.

"Ab-about what? Nuh-uh...Stop. Stop!" he yelled, shoving LeeLee's face away from his lap.

Chauncey felt like smacking the shit out of LeeLee. She was doing good until her teeth scraped the skin off his dick. If anything, baby girl needed to stick to the little leagues because sucking dick wasn't her forte.

LeeLee wiped slobber from the corners of her mouth. She threw Chauncey a devilish look before getting up and leaving the room.

"Chauncey, what are you doing? Stop what?" D'mico asked, trying to listen to the commotion going on in the background.

"Oh, I was watching the game. I just turned it off. Whatchu wanna talk about?"

D'mico smiled. "Well, I don't see any easy way to say this, so I'ma just say it." She took a deep breath before saying, "Chauncey, I'm pregnant."

There. It was out and she felt so much better.

Chauncey frowned up, "Congratulations. Whatchu telling me for?"

"Chauncey, I'm pregnant by you."

"D'mico, are you screamin' this shit 'cause I haven't talked to you in a while? Damn!" Chauncey cursed.

Chauncey lowered his voice. He did his best to manipulate the situation. "D'mico, I told you we're going to be together. Saying you're pregnant won't get me to stay. I'ma fuck with you regardless. That shit ain't cute."

"You can't be serious. After everything I done for you, this is how you gonna play me? What kinda woman do you think I am? Do you think I would pin a baby on you and lower myself to get close to you?" she responded with eyes full of tears.

Unfortunately, Chauncey wasn't taking the news as well as D'mico predicted. In fact, the idea of D'mico having his seed made Chauncey sick. Was she crazy? Shit, consequences and repercussions. He should have worn a condom. Damn.

"Look, I don't know what you would do, aight? But I do know that we're losing focus on what we got goin'. Do he know?"

"No." D'mico cried softly into the phone. The future of having a little Chauncey went straight down the drain. Once more, she tried to make Chauncey see things her way, but he wasn't having it. The only option he gave her was an abortion.

"Please, Chauncey. I wanna keep the baby. Don't

make me do this," she pleaded.

LeeLee stepped back into the bedroom naked. Her chocolate skin glistened with baby oil, showing off her curvaceous figure. Her hand circled her protruding belly. Although she was only a couple months pregnant, a pouch began to form, making it quite noticeable that a little one was on the way. She stood in the cut and listened in on Chauncey's conversation.

Chauncey didn't hear LeeLee enter the room.

Still disappointed, he held his face in the palm of his hand and spoke to D'mico in a self-assuring, gentle tone.

"D'mico, we can't. Plus, I don't want him to hurt you if he finds out. You claim to love me, right?"

"You know I do." D'mico sniffled.

"Then you know what you gotta do. We got all the time in the world to make another baby. How can I take care of ya'll being under him? If you love me, you'll take care of that."

Disappointment could be heard on the other end of the phone. All the crying and sniffling had Chauncey wondering whether or not he'd persuaded D'mico enough.

"D'mico?"

D'mico was having a hard time believing that Chauncey didn't want the baby. "Hmm," she answered.

"Why you being quiet, ma? You gotta know the decision I made is for the best." Chauncey went in for the kill. What had to be done, needed to be done with perfection.

"I love you," he lied.

Maybe Chauncey is right. Having a baby isn't a

smart move right now, D'mico thought. She took her hand off of her stomach and rested her ear deeper into the phone.

"You're right. This ain't the time. I'll terminate the pregnancy as soon as I can get in," she said, choking on her words. What could she say? She loved Chauncey. The impact he had on her was more than influential; it was amazing.

Satisfied with her response, Chauncey got up and turned around. He looked into the eyes of an angry woman—LeeLee. She burned a hole in his face that made him look away. Even though his back was to her, he could feel the steam rising out of her ears.

Doing his best to dodge two different arguments and attitudes, Chauncey grabbed his shirt off the bed, retrieved his car keys off the nightstand and cut his conversation with D'mico short.

"Try to handle that this week, if you can. Oh, and umm...Call me when you're no longer under the weather. Uh-huh. Yeah, aight. Okay. Yeah, we'll wrap this up. Okay. One."

Click

No sooner had Chauncey hung up than LeeLee was all up in his space.

"Did you dive in that bitch naked?" The blank look on Chauncey's face made her heart skip a beat. She threw up her hands. "I can't believe this shit. We got a baby on the way and you mean to tell me that you out there making a family with that BITCH! Oh don't tell me that yo stupid ass slipped on a banana peel and landed dick first."

Chauncey wasn't in the mood for this shit. He ignored LeeLee's obscenities and brushed his way past her. With a shocked look on her face, she followed Chauncey.

"All the shit you told me was bullshit wasn't it? Nah, LeeLee, she ain't shit. Nah, I'm not fuckin' her," she mimicked. "You're a fuckin' LIAR. She must've had some fire 'cause it took your trifling ass a whole year before you fucked me raw," LeeLee yelled, keeping up with Chauncey's pace. "I guess the apple don't fall too far from the tr—"

Smack!

LeeLee must've struck a nerve because Chauncey backhanded her like a two-dollar hoe who came up a dollar short. The sting to the side of her face caused LeeLee to fall to her knees. Her big, brown eyes widened with shock.

"Get the fuck out," she screamed, pointing to the door.

Her mother always said that any man bold enough to lift a finger against a woman wasn't worth keeping.

Unballing his fist, Chauncey dipped without hesitation. LeeLee sat on the carpet in dismay, wondering if she would ever feel comfortable with Chauncey coming back.

* * * *

Once outside, Chauncey slid his baby blue and white polo shirt over his dark chocolate frame, catching a few lustful glances from the women in LeeLee's complex.

Any minute he expected for her to start blowing up his cell phone. Numerous times she called herself kicking him out the house. Most women played that childish game. It didn't faze Chauncey though. Eventually LeeLee would come to her senses and beg him to come back like Keith Sweat. Really, the only thing on his mind was D'mico. Becoming obsessed, he thought about the last breath she would take once he put an end to her life.

Getting inside his '64 Chevy Impala, Chauncey turned the key, creating what he considered music to his ears. He loved his girl. She didn't bitch, moan or argue. His ride stuck through some of his toughest times. For that, he was more than grateful.

"Yeah, that's right. Talk to daddy." He spoke to his car, pressing down on the gas.

Vroom! *Vroom*!

After showing out, a confident smile appeared on his face when he saw the flashing light on his cell phone. It was LeeLee. Ignoring her call, he smashed out the parking lot.

"Bitches."

* * * *

Two strangers living in the same home was what Tyreke and D'mico's relationship became. For the past three weeks, they did everything from ignoring each other to sleeping in separate rooms. At night, Tyreke would gather sheets from the linen closet and carry on to one of the guest rooms on the opposite end of the house. Although D'mico pretended to be unfazed by his seclusion, deep down she was torn. She missed the good times they shared, their laughter, the beautiful smile D'mico relinquished when she entered a room and most importantly, D'mico missed the chemistry that flowed through his body to her soul.

D'mico woke up and found Tyreke gone by 7:30 a.m. Well, at least he left later than yesterday's time, which was 6:15.

Dragging her feet in an effort to catch up with the rest of her body, D'mico grabbed her needed items and headed for the bathroom.

Two days ago, she called herself going to Stanton's abortion clinic. Although she promised Chauncey to get in sooner, with the clinic's full schedule and particular procedures, three weeks was the earliest. For D'mico, the whole trip was disastrous. Catty-corner from the clinic at a nearby restaurant, she spotted Ansean, one of Tyreke's goons. It wouldn't have been so bad if the nigga hadn't made eye contact with her. There was no way D'mico would be able to pull off the abortion without Tyreke finding out. Plus, the uneasiness and uncomfortable look on Ansean's face said that he would tell it all. Left with no other choice, D'mico left.

Plan A collapsed at the clinic. Now D'mico had plan B in her hand, riding on her future with Chauncey.

D'mico closed and locked the bathroom door.

She placed the bag and its contents on the bathroom countertop and removed the items one by one: a spoon, sugar, paint thinner, a single Summer's Eve douche bottle, and a 20 oz. bottle of Pepsi. Once she had her clothes off, she mixed the paint thinner and sugar together thoroughly. After she finished, she swallowed the hard concoction in three big gulps.

D'mico took in a deep breath as she scratched away at her burning throat. Damn, it felt like someone had poured a liter of acid down her throat. All of the sudden, her hands became shaky, and her body was jittery all over. A bubbly feeling started to form in her stomach, making her feel like she had the shits. Regardless of how she felt, she had to keep going. She grabbed the douche, squeezed its contents into the toilet and wiped her forehead. Once she emptied the douche, she refilled it with Pepsi.

D'mico took a lengthy breath before propping her leg on the edge of the toilet seat. She couldn't believe that she was actually doing this. She didn't know if she would be successful in squeezing Pepsi into her cervix, but the Lifetime movie she saw years ago gave her the idea. The girl on the movie tried the same tactics, and the acid from the Pepsi was supposed to be enough to make her water break. Can somebody say, "Stupid?"

* * * *

Two hours later, D'mico woke up to a disturbing feeling in her stomach. She shifted uncomfortably in the bundle of satin sheets surrounding her aching body. The discomfort was somewhat familiar yet much worse. Fighting the intense pain shooting to her abdomen, she squeezed her eyes shut. After the second wave of intense pain, regret began to settle. Choosing to get rid of the baby growing inside of her was a big mistake.

Folding over in the fetal position, D'mico cried out in agony. Warm fluid along with a gush of blood flowed down her legs onto the bed, sending her into a state of panic. Her conscience told her to haul her ass to the hospital. However, the gullible side she often complied with persuaded her that a warm bath was all her body needed. A few steps is all D'mico was able to get in before her mind started to play tricks on her. The room floated all around her. She tried to fix her eyes on the bathroom door, but nothing seemed to be where it was supposed to be. She felt like a bobblehead toy.

The mixture of paint thinner and sugar had D'mico tripping like a muthafucka. Either her mind was playing tricks on her or she was hallucinating.

"Santy'ya," she cried out, extending her arms outward. When the small figure that wasn't really there disappeared, desperation and loneliness filled D'mico's heavy heart.

"Where's my baby?" she sobbed, taking several more steps. Everything went black before D'mico crashed to the floor.

* * * *

"How many times do I have to tell yo stupid ass that you belong to me? You still sittin' over der? Bring yo ass over here and tend to me." Lonnie got up from the bed, unbuckled the button on his uniform slacks, removed his belt and wrapped the thick material around his wrist. He was gonna beat D'mico like the cry baby she was. To think he fucked around and got her whinny ass pregnant.

He didn't care that she was seven months pregnant. Bitches can get fucked up too.

"I'm the king of this here throne," he said, making a pop noise with the belt. "You lucky I'm allowin' you to cater to my needs. You wasn't shit when I gotchu from that nasty ol' bitch, and you'll never amount to shit neither. Bring yo ungrateful ass here, I said."

D'mico shook in place as she watched Lonnie's eye color change from grey to greyish-orange. Whenever Lonnie got mad, his eyes changed colors and buckets of spit flew out of his mouth onto the floor.

The sight of him made D'mico cringe.

D'mico got up from her time-out seat and made her way to Lonnie with wobbly legs. A minute ago, he was ranting and raving about her sitting down, and he was the one who put her in the red Disney chair, instructing her not to move or speak until advised to do so. Now he was yelling like a madman and flooding the room with his saliva. Make up your mind fuckin' moron.

The saddest part about D'mico's abuse was that she learned to live with it. Moreover, she became so familiar with the inflicted pain that her brain began to process the abuse as a way of life. Love hurts. Her mother's love hurt and so did Lonnie's. The only reason why Lonnie was mad in the first place was because he found the business card Reverend Johnson gave D'mico years ago in the bedroom closet. Lonnie ripped the card up in her face and threw it away.

Lonnie didn't believe in a higher power, whereas she did.

For years, D'mico held onto the Reverend's words,

encouraging her to seek help and call if she ever ran into any trouble. Unfortunately, D'mico couldn't find the courage to dial the seven-digit number given to her. Instead, D'mico prayed. She prayed a lot. Many times she felt like her plea for God to send help her way went unheard. Despite her constant despair, she asked God for protection over her child. Although Lonnie was a child molester/rapist, she prayed that her child wouldn't inherit his mentality and abusive traits.

D'mico vowed to be all that she could be when it came down to her baby. She would love and support it to the fullest extent. Just watch. You'll see. Across her chest, D'mico felt a heavy blow to her body, causing her to trip over her feet.

"Aaagh!" she wailed, leaning forward. Then came the second strike across her forehead and right eye. Instantly her eye began to swell.

"Do you think I got all day, huh?" Lonnie yelled, kicking and hitting D'mico in her side with the belt.

It wasn't unusual for Lonnie to do this to D'mico. The poor girl took numerous beatings from him. This shit became so routine that sometimes D'mico had a belt or switch nearby so she could just get it over with. Plenty of times she just wished that he would kill her, but being the man that Lonnie was, he would never make it that easy for her. She was stuck.

With two violent strikes, Lonnie bent down and punched D'mico between the legs. Already D'mico could feel something wet and warm trickle out of her panties and down her leg. What was it? Was her baby okay?

Tears fell from her eyes as she curled up into a knot,

fighting off the pain. What was happening?

Lonnie paused in midair when he noticed how wet D'mico was. Her pants were soaking wet.

"Ah fuck, don't tell me your damn water broke?" Lonnie yelled in a fit of panic. Shit. He didn't know what to do. He tossed his belt and went for the phone. Walking around in circles with his eyes on D'mico, he waited for old Lady Sandra to answer. Damn, he needed to get his shit together before he wound up in jail.

D'mico folded over. With one hand, she clutched her aching stomach. Her contractions had accelerated within seconds, nearly drawing the breath out of her.

By the conversation Lonnie was having on the phone, she realized it was time to have her baby. Oh my God, she was about to deliver her first child. Despite the pain, a big smile crept across her face as she hoped for a boy.

* * * *

On Monday nights, Denise rotated shifts at Tulsa Regional Hospital. Four nights a week, sometimes five, she worked ICU. But one day out of her five-day work week, she pulled a double on the fourth floor—labor and delivery. Despite her aching feet from the constant standing and long hours, Denise enjoyed her job. And the cries coming from the newborn babies made her appreciate her work even more. She only had one child, but he was much older, almost grown.

As she rode the elevator, Denise's eyes traveled from right to left as she followed the orange light bouncing from floor to floor. Once the fourth circle lit up, Denise removed her eyes from the indicator and refocused on the sliding door. Clutching onto her work bag, she stepped off the elevator, walked several feet and stopped at the entrance door to labor and delivery.

She rolled her neck in a half circle.

Eight hours behind her and eight more to go. She pressed the giant, red button and waved towards the camera.

The security at Tulsa Regional was pretty good. No one could enter labor and deliver unless approved by a staff member, which normally meant a nurse. The nurses pretty much went on faces. They knew their patients as well as their family members, so getting beyond the door meant you were one of the two. Another way to tell who you were was by the bracelets you wore or the ID cards distributed upon arrival. Like I said, it wasn't easy to pull off an unauthorized entrance.

Once Betty heard the buzz, she checked the monitor. When she saw that it was her relief, she hit the appropriate button, quickly cleaned up her mess and jumped to her feet.

Denise made her way to the nurse's station with a faint smile on her face.

"Howdy," Denise said, taking her bag off her shoulder and dropping it into the chair. "I know you're ready to go, girl."

Betty smiled at her co-worker. "You know it, sister." Betty began to put items into a backpack. "Before I go, there's a new arrival in room 520." Betty lowered her voice to a whisper. "She's by herself. She's only fifteen,

Denise. Fifteen! Gosh, that's awfully young. I have a daughter who is fifteen, and I couldn't imagine her having a baby."

Denise gave Betty a look that said that it happens all the time. In the black community, young girls having babies wasn't anything that she wasn't use to. To be honest, black and white had nothing to do with it. Young girls *period* were having kids and were left to provide all by themselves.

"Anyway," Betty continued, "she had herself a handsome baby boy, I must say. Grandmother brought her in earlier, but she left once the baby came." She picked up D'mico's chart. Her blue eyes scanned the paperwork.

"Here it is. Umm...Oh, the baby arrived eight weeks early—four pounds, nine ounces. The medication the mother is on is listed. Umm...Let's see...Oh, she had an emergency C-section. Baby's heart dropped, but the doc managed to stabilize it. Well, hon, I think that's everything," Betty ended.

Denise let out a deep breath after her update. She accepted the chart and told Betty thanks.

"See you next week," Betty said on her way out the door. "Same place, same time," Denise laughed, waving bye.

No sooner had Betty left than the call light flashed. Room 520 appeared on the monitor.

* * * *

D'mico awoke in the hospital. Confusion outlined

the wrinkles in her forehead. The last thing she remembered was the beating and old Lady Sandra instructing her to breathe in and out. While she was being coached, Lonnie paced the floor, poking himself in the head and uttering incoherent words. Everything else was a blur. Her body ached everywhere. Where was everybody? Her baby? What about her baby?

D'mico placed both hands on her stomach. She immediately started to flip out. "Where's my baby?" she screamed, pressing the call button that read, "NURSE."

A minute later, a Native American woman entered the room. Pocahontas is what came to mind when D'mico laid eyes on the beautiful woman.

"Is everything alright, honey?" Denise asked.

D'mico sat up straight, adjusted her gown and squinted her eyes. *Do I know her?* she thought.

"My baby," she bellowed, rubbing her empty stomach. Denise gasped when she moved closer. It was obvious that although Denise recognized D'mico, D'mico didn't recognize her. So she dismissed the feeling of surprise and kept it professional.

"He's in the—"

"He? I had a boy?" Tears began to form in D'mico's eyes. She rested her back against the fluffy, white pillow and covered her eyes.

Confused, Denise glanced at the chart in her hand. "Yes, you had a boy. You haven't seen him yet?"

D'mico shook her head no.

Denise swallowed her own tears. She left and returned with a healthy four pound and nine-ounce baby boy with jet black hair, deep dimples, ebony skin and grey eyes.

D'mico couldn't believe that she was a mother. She wanted a boy and she got one, despite the circumstance of him being brought into the world by nonconsensual sex. It didn't matter because D'mico's love for her son would be more than her mother's love for her. She would make sure of it.

He was so fragile in her arms and tiny.

Wow. I'm a mom, she thought, admiring her son.

Denise stood back and watched D'mico for several emotional seconds, and then she left, leaving the new mother alone with her baby.

* * * *

Denise sat at the nurses station in a daze. A lot of things juggled inside her mind, like D'mico and her baby.

There were a few questions that weighed on her mind. *Where was the baby's father? When was her grandmother coming back?* As a mother, Denise knew the importance of having a family member around during and after delivery. D'mico had neither. Another thing that bothered Denise were the bruises on D'mico. By law, she was supposed to notify the police on grounds of suspicion of abuse. But due to the fact that Denise didn't have any physical evidence besides D'mico being left alone and under age, she didn't have anything to go on.

The world could be a sad place.

Flipping through several pages, Denise nosily went through D'mico's chart looking for her emergency contact information. She scrolled down the page and came across the words, "parent: deceased."

The only available next of kin was a woman by the name of Sandra Washington, no one else. Denise shook her head sympathetically and closed the file.

Lord, is there something I can do to help her? Denise thought, getting up to tend to her patients.

* * * *

Four hours into Denise's shift, her son came strolling down the hall, looking cool as ever with a large McDonald's sack in his hand.

Tyreke set the bag on the counter of the nurses station.

"What's up, my lady?" he asked Denise while planting a kiss on the side of her cheek. Denise steered her head to face Tyreke. She smiled partly and then sighed.

"Well, you know. The usual. Work, work and some more work." She grabbed the McDonald's bag and slowly removed the hefty chef salad, bleu cheese and plastic fork. Boy was she hungry, and her stomach was giving Tyreke all the praise and glory for making it on time.

"I need to get a job at that lawn service you work for; I can see that Meech is payin' you well," Denise teased, nodding her head at the brand-new watch settled across Tyreke's wrist.

The surprised look on Tyreke's face made Denise smile. "What? Girls can work on lawn mowers."

Tyreke wondered if his mom knew about his involvement in selling drugs. The lawn service was a front job. Don't get me wrong, it was a legitimate business, but it also was a backup gig for all of Mike Mike's foot soldiers. Mike Mike is who Tyreke really worked for. He took Tyreke under his wing and showed him and his friends love by blessing their pockets.

"I know girls can work there. You would never like it 'cause you don't like the heat. Plus, you too old to be pushin' a lawn mower," he joked.

"Boy, I'ma show you old," Denise responded, striking Tyreke playfully with the empty bag.

Within seconds, Denise's smile died down. The puzzled look on her face had Tyreke questioning what was bothering her.

"What's wrong? You look like you got a lot on your mind."

Denise put down her fork and looked into her son's uncertain eyes. She told Tyreke about D'mico and how she was by herself. She also told him about her bruises. At first, it took Tyreke a minute to recall who D'mico was, but when Denise mentioned her as being the girl who came into their church several Christmases back, there was no way Tyreke could hide his interest in wanting to know more about her.

"Who's her baby daddy?" asked Tyreke.

"I don't know. She's by herself."

"Mama, you can't be worrying about lost girls. You and pops can't save the world all the time."

Tyreke wasn't trying to hurt his mother's feelings, but Denise always went out on a limb to help others only to hurt herself.

Friends first, mother and son second. Denise slumped deeper into her chair. She placed a long piece of her hair behind her right ear.

"You don't think I know that, Ty? The Lord called on all of us to help the oppressed, and just so you know, we're only tryin' to save one, possibly two," Denise responded with a hint of hope in her ebony eyes.

"Whateva, everybody's problems ain't ou—"

Tyreke was cut off by the sound of a squeaking door. Glancing over his shoulder, his eyes fixed on a girl standing next to her room. Slowly, he lifted himself off the counter.

Damn, she hadn't changed a bit in the face. Body-wise, she was a little thicker in the hips, but everything else was just the way he remembered from a few years ago. Even the soothing feeling he felt returned.

D'mico looked up at Tyreke. *I know him from somewhere!* she thought, looking away.

"I'm sorry. The baby is out of formula," D'mico stated timidly.

Denise got up. She apologized to D'mico for not seeing the light flash and went to the storage room, leaving Tyreke and D'mico alone.

Tyreke caught D'mico before she went back into her room.

"Whatchu name your baby?" he blurted out, saying the first thing that came to mind.

"I haven't named him yet," D'mico said, turning around.

"Really? So you had a boy? That's what's up."

"Do you have any kids?"

"Nah, but I'ma have one, one day."

Tyreke smiled. Although he was only eighteen, the thought of having his own junior running around excited him.

"Do you mind if I see him?"

D'mico frowned. The thought of someone other than herself being around her baby sent chills up her spine.

Tyreke sensed her reluctance. "Oh, it's all good if you don't want me to. I understand."

Tyreke's warm smile and harmless features eased D'mico's overbearing attitude. "I guess it wouldn't be a problem," she said, leading the way.

The first thing Tyreke noticed about D'mico was the bruise under her eye. He could tell by its color that it was fresh. *What kind of nigga puts his hands on a woman?* he wondered. What she done to deserve it? No matter what, a face like hers didn't deserve to be damaged.

Once they were in the room, D'mico immediately gave Tyreke a once over from head to toe, checking out his clothes. I know this might sound a little dumb, but she'd never ever been around a guy who looked so thugged out but neat. He wore a black and red Jordan shirt over black long johns, loose-fitted jeans and red sneakers. A platinum chain hung around his neck where a closed locket dangled. On each of his wrists was a watch and a silver bracelet. A platinum ring, with black diamonds encrusted in the middle, occupied his pinkie finger on his left hand.

D'mico's eyes traveled to his face.

The boy at the church. Oh shoot, that's where she

knew the nurse from. Ah man, out of all the places, why did she have to run into them here? On top of that, D'mico knew she looked a funky mess. Why, Lord, why?

"He's over there," she directed.

Tyreke broke his eyes away from D'mico and looked to the baby bed. Once Tyreke turned around, D'mico did her best to fix her hair. She ran her hand down the center in an attempt to put away any flyaways.

"I think you should name lil dude Santy'ya," Tyreke suggested, looking down at the sleeping baby."

"What? What kinda name is that?"

Tyreke chuckled. He rubbed across the baby's back with the back of his hand. "It's my name. Eh, you said so yo'self that you ain't named him yet. Plus, I'm not tryna offend you or nuttin', but from the look of things, he's gon need someone to show him the ropes," he stated in a low whisper.

What the fuck am I doing? I don't even know this chick. Leave, Tyreke is what his conscience screamed out at him.

D'mico joined Tyreke's side. Was he the angel she'd prayed for? "San-what?" D'mico asked, taking the name into consideration.

"Santy'ya. Look, its spelled, S-A-N-T-Y-Y-A, San-Ty-ya. Yo, I was just throwin' some shit out there. That's all. You ain't gotta name him that. Shidd, you don't even know me," Tyreke responded a little offended.

D'mico stood back, her weight on one leg with one hand on her waist. "I thought your name was Tyreke?"

Surprised that D'mico knew who he was, Tyreke smiled bright.

"Lemme find out. Santy'ya is my middle name. Stop lookin' for a way out. You ain't the only one with a good memory, D'mico," Tyreke retaliated, letting her name flow off his tongue like a tidal wave.

D'mico's caramel complexion turned red. Two dimples peeked through her flushed cheeks. She hadn't been around a teenage boy in a long time. Most of the men she came in contact with were grown-ass men. Oops! Did I say grown-ass men? I meant to say perverts and chomos (child molesters). Anyway, D'mico thought about what it would be like to be with someone her own age. Then again, what would Lonnie do if he found out that she was holding a conversation with another guy? The words "whoop her ass" came to mind. With these thoughts, her dimples disappeared. It would never happen. Good things don't happen to good people. Terrible things happen to good people. At least D'mico was set on believing so.

Regardless of her situation, Tyreke wanted to get to know D'mico. She was pretty, and Tyreke saw a little potential in her eyes, but would that be enough to act on? We'll see.

"So, where's yo baby father?" Tyreke asked D'mico, putting a bad taste in her mouth. D'mico bit down on her tongue. *Dangit. Why he gotta be askin' me that?*

Denise came into the room with three four-packs of four-ounce bottles. She started to introduce herself to D'mico's guest, but when she realized that it was her son, she gave Tyreke a "what the hell are you doing in here" look.

Tyreke shrugged his shoulders and turned away

while D'mico took the milk from Denise.

"Thank you," D'mico said. She bent down and put the formula in the storage connected to the baby bed.

While her back was to Denise and Tyreke, Denise nudged Tyreke. "This is my job. She ain't like dem other girls, Ty," She mumbled in his ear.

Denise was pissed, and she didn't have no problem showing it. Tyreke didn't know anything about this girl. He wasn't just playing with fire; he was putting his whole damn hand into the flames.

Tyreke broke free from Denise's wrath. He put up an index finger and mouthed the words, "You said help one."

* * * *

For the past two days, Tyreke visited D'mico freely while she was in the hospital.

Although he knew that his mom would throw a fit about him seeing D'mico, it didn't stop him from going whenever he got the chance.

At first, he was skeptical about coming around, but when he saw that she was alone, he couldn't turn and walk away like everyone else had. He really liked D'mico, and she was fun to be around. She wasn't like the other bitches he fucked with that only fucked with him because he was part of Mike Mike's squad. Tyreke whistled his way down the cold hallway.

Occupying his hand was an arrangement of flowers for D'mico along with a large teddy bear tucked underneath his arm for little man.

Yeah, he was a sucker, a sucker for jewels. D'mico and her baby were jewels.

Just earlier, Tyreke re-upped with Mike Mike, so he had to be in and out of the hospital so he could hit them streets. The streets and the fiends showed him so much love. After all, the rubber band lump in his pocket proved hella loyal, giving him the gratification necessary to remain faithful. With that said, he couldn't stay at the hospital as long as he wanted. Outside the streets, D'mico was like a breath of fresh air on a muggy day. And she was worth the loss of a few bucks.

* * * *

Lonnie reclined his tall physique against the nurses station, looking hungrily into Betty's blue eyes. Two days ago, Lonnie pulled Betty over on a routine traffic stop. One thing that he noticed about the brown and white Aerostar van was that it was swerving in and out of lanes. Putting on his lights, he then pulled the vehicle over, got out his patrol car and conducted a thorough search. It was during the search when he recovered a shitload of Demerol, Methadone and a handful of tranquilizers. Plus, Betty's constricted pupils already told the story that she was higher than cloud nine. Worried about losing her job and going to jail, Betty went on to explain that the only reason why she was abusing the drugs was because of her long hours at Tulsa Regional Hospital. When she mentioned that she worked labor and delivery, Lonnie decided to dismiss the charges under two conditions. One, she had to suck his dick—clean and dry—and two, if he ever needed information about D'mico, she would let him know. Salvaging her future, Betty got in the police car and dropped her head into Lonnie's lap. She sucked his big dick as if she was the new spokesman for Mr. Clean attempting to put Pine-Sol out of business.

"What room is she in?" Lonnie asked Betty, removing hair out of her face. Betty nervously scanned the area before responding.

"520."

Lonnie brushed her cheek and pulled himself away from the station. He headed towards 520 to see his bitch and baby. He stared cautiously at the kid in front of him. He seemed to be happy carrying his teddy bear and flowers. The sound of whistling followed his stride. Yeah, he was happy. Lonnie remembered being that happy, but that shit died six years ago when he caught his wife, Adrianna, in bed with another woman. *Fuckin' bitch.*

518...519...520...

Lonnie halted when the kid in front of him slid inside room 520. Thinking that Betty gave him the wrong room, Lonnie started to tum around, but the sound of D'mico's voice pushed him closer to the door.

"I'm glad you came back 'cause ever since you started rockin' him to sleep, he doesn't respond to my rockin'. He cried all night. You spoilin' him." Tyreke set the teddy bear down along with the flowers on the hospital bed and held out his hand.

"Aaah...Blame me. Hand 'em here."

D'mico dropped Santy'ya in Tyreke's hands. A crescent smile appeared on her face when she saw the bear and flowers.

"Oh, Tyreke, thank you. I love lilies," she exclaimed, putting her nose up to the petals.

Tyreke turned around and smiled. A man could never go wrong with flowers. He supported Santy'ya's head and rested his tiny body against his chest. Walking around in circles, he cooed Santy'ya to sleep.

The baby felt good in his arms. Tyreke stared into Santy'ya's sleepy, grey eyes and wondered how a man could miss out on seeing his child being born. He didn't have the slightest clue as to D'mico's current situation. Although, a part of him knew that she was holding back. But what was it?

Tyreke glanced at D'mico then at the baby. Drifting off in his arms, Santy'ya's eyes closed.

What was he doing here, anyway? He asked himself that question over and over every time he arrived at the hospital and when he would leave. Did he really expect to come into D'mico's life and take over? Did he really expect for her to be problem free and single? Maybe he expected to knock whoever she was with out the way and show her that he could love her better. Maybe Tyreke was plain fuckin' nuts. The crazy thing about wanting something so bad is you'll do anything to get it. The real question is how far would Tyreke go? And where would it lead him?

"D'mico, I think we need to talk. You ain't talked about yo baby's father, your plans for the baby or nothin'. I mean damn, when you leave here, will it be the end of our friendship? Talk to me. I'm here to help." Tyreke spoke seriously.

D'mico felt like a ton of bricks came crashing down on her. One way or the other, she knew the topic would come up. Swallowing her pride, she released the flowers, walked over to Tyreke and grabbed his hand.

"I'll tell you," she said calmly.

Lonnie pushed his ear off the door. His heart thumped violently in his chest as he listened to D'mico as she told the punk-ass nigga she didn't even know his business. The bitch was trying to send him up state with all the shit she told. She spoke of him being a police officer and how she was sold by her foster mother. Periodically, the young cat would cut her off by saying "What?" "He did what?" "What kinda sick shit is that?" After getting an ear full of the gruesome things done to D'mico, Tyreke swapped his disgusted comments with comforting words like, "It's okay. I won't let him hurt you or Santy'ya."

Santy'ya? Where the fuck did D'mico come up with that name? Lonnie told her before she had the baby that he was going to name it. Now all of a sudden the bitch was going against his rules.

At first, Lonnie thought about following the kid out of the hospital when he left and then killing him, but then a mischievous grin spread across his face when he worked his way back to the nurses station. Betty. It was time that she paid her second favor.

Chapter 5

Dirt lived in the heart of the hood on Garrison block in the middle of a cul-de-sac. At any given time, he could see who came and who went out of the neighborhood. Dirt felt like a nigga of importance when Tyreke chose his crib to host their meetings.

Dirt was a fairly attractive cat. His butterscotch complexion and sleepy eyes attracted more women than he could keep up with. Aside from that, he inherited a set of black-ass lips that were full and scrumptious like the rapper Waka Flocka Flame. Standing at 5'4", Dirt had a height complex. The words "lil man," "lil dude" or "kid" would get you fucked up, no questions asked. Because of his height, Dirt felt it was necessary that he carry the majority of the weight. Everything from robbery to murder was on his wrap sheet. Hell, the nigga's record was longer than his short, stocky frame. He was down for whatever, whenever. You needed somebody fucked up or murked? Shidd, Dirt was your man. Not only did he hold the name "Dirt" because of his vicious hands, but the man was a filth maggot. His living arrangements were appalling and downright unbelievable. His shit stayed filthy, and the extra buildup didn't seem to bother or faze him at all. Nasty.

Tyreke scanned the living room for a place to sit before shutting his phone. A little irritated with the fact that D'mico didn't answer her cell or the house phone, he was ready to get down to business. The first thing on his agenda was to discuss his plans for the area he was forced to abandon and his plan to relocate.

Before he made it to a half-empty couch with clothes thrown on the armrest, Damu started bitching. "Damn, nigga, is you eva gon clean dis mufucka? This bitch is always junky. Damn." Damu kicked himself a clear path to walk on.

"Man, push the shit over. It ain't nothin'. I'll have Starlet clean up later," Dirt responded nonchalantly. Dirt removed a Doritos bag from up under him, threw it on the floor and sat down.

"Who? Nigga you fuckin' that stank hoe?" Damu didn't mind showing his distaste for Dirt's new girlfriend. "Nigga, yo dick gon fall off from fuckin' dat bitch. Either that or you gon roll over from hepatitis 2 from this nasty, infested-ass house of yours." Damu laughed. "Eh, Ty, maybe you can cut this nigga's pay in half and hook him and his broad up with a life supply of bleach."

Everyone erupted in laughter.

Damu and Dirt went at each other's throats like brothers fighting for their parents' approval. This shit was routine with these two, just another day in the hood. "Ha-ha, don't be jealous. It's enough of me to go around, pussy," Dirt retaliated.

Damu laughed more to himself than to anyone else. He turned around in Dirt's direction and grabbed a hand full of his nuts.

"Lil man got big jokes. Lemme see how I can fix that."

They went at each other back and forth until Tyreke had had enough.

"Fellas! Ya'll niggas s'pose to be grown men. When ya'll ready, we can get down to business." Dirt fell back in his seat and closed his mouth, and Damu joined Chauncey's side by the window and took a seat.

"Good. All love," Tyreke said, holding everyone's attention.

* * * *

Starlet inhaled the last of her dipped blunt. The effect that the wet daddy had on her felt like a mixture of power and sexual hunger. Today, she felt like a spy. She took on a lot of roles when she got high; it was a part of the excitement.

Starlet peeped her head around the kitchen wall. Unsure who Tyreke was, her eyes fell on the nigga everyone huddled around like a football coach. Everything about the nigga cried "money." The polo, purple, label vest he had on made him look like he was posing for the front cover of *GQ* Magazine. Conservative and sexy.

"Mmm..." Starlet lusted, grabbing her moist crotch. Starlet remembered the day she went to Cheddar's with

Leslie and her stuck-up-ass friend, D'mico. The bitch was trippin' real hard on her, talking 'bout she didn't get high on anything other than weed.

Bitch, please! *Who the fuck she think she was, Oprah*? *Word has it that Tyreke is her man. Hmph*! *No wonder the bitch was so bourgeois*, Starlet ranted to herself.

She picked up the phone and dialed the only number programmed in her memory. "About time. I thought you forgot," The caller said, answering on the second ring.

"Nah, I ain't forgot. Anyway, they're here. Tyreke, Dirt, Stacey, Chauncey and two otha niggas."

"Good lookin'. I'll give you a ring later."

"Okay. But hey."

"What is it, Starlet?" the caller asked, already knowing what Starlet wanted. Loosening a couple of buttons from her shirt, Starlet fiddled with the phone cord nervously.

"Do you still got me for that? You know, for tellin' you that they was here?"

"Have I ever lied to you? You actin' like a fuckin' nuisance, asking me the same questions over and over. We talked about this forty-five minutes ago." The sparks in Starlet's eyes dimmed.

Starlet didn't consider herself to be an addict. Addicts were crackheads and alcoholics. She was neither of the two. All she wanted was the ounce of holyfield promised to her if she made the phone call. And that she did.

"Well, I'm just askin'. Do you want me to swing by your crib and come pick it up?" Starlet asked, choosing another route.

"Yeah, Starlet. Damn. You need to get help 'cause you turning into a fiend. I gotta go. Come in an hour. Bye."

Click!

Starlet rested her body against the refrigerator grinning from ear to ear. With the phone still in her hand, she loosened two more buttons on her shirt, took off her booty shorts, panties and danced around the kitchen naked.

She was the "naked bandit."

* * * *

Two hours and four Madden games later, Tyreke headed out the door. Behind him was Chauncey, Stacey and Damu.

Damu cut through the grass and jumped in his car. He left with the usual "It's on. Yo, Ty, fuck wit' me later."

Walking side by side, Tyreke headed to Chauncey's '64 Chevy Impala. The whole way to his car, Chauncey bragged about the game.

"I think I'm gonna retire from selling drugs. I made four G's off of spankin' ya'll nigga's..." Chauncey paused at the door handle. "The shit came so easy that I'm thinkin' 'bout traveling around the world. I'm goin' to make it my next profession." Chauncey laughed, grabbing the handle. Still laughing, he ducked his tall frame into the car. Laughing with Chauncey, Tyreke slammed his hand on the roof of the car and got inside.

The glow to Chauncey's CD player gave some light inside the dark car.

"I'm going to let you have that one. You did win. Lemme tell you something, playboy. You didn't whoop my ass."

"Whatchu call seven to forty-nine?"

Tyreke chuckled and nestled his head back on the leather interior. "The only reason why the score was seven to forty-nine is because I don't sit around and play video games, and for two, those muthafuckin' roaches kept playin' hopscotch on my lap."

Chauncey cracked up laughing. Tyreke was right; there were roaches everywhere. If you had your mouth open longer than a minute, a roach would climb in and lay eggs. The place was that bad.

"I swear, I seen one of 'em givin' that nigga Dirt a lap dance. Nigga was feeling that shit too." Chauncey used Dirt to open up the topic relating to D'mico. Thumbing through his CD collection, he pulled out of the driveway.

"Didn't Dirt say that he was fuckin' wit' Starlet? Ain't that your girl's friend?"

Tyreke rolled his head to the side and glanced out the window. D'mico had been on his mind all day. Something real fucked up was going on in their relationship; he just didn't know what it was.

"I don't know. I try and stay out of her social life, know what I'm sayin'?" Chauncey flashed Tyreke a sinister smirk and got on the highway.

"How is D'mico doin' anyway?" Chauncey asked, fishing for information. For one, he wanted to know if

Tyreke recognized any changes in D'mico's patterns.

"She aight. Why?"

"I haven't seen her around in a while," Chauncey replied.

"Maybe 'cause she ain't made to be seen all the time," Tyreke countered with an attitude. Chauncey let Tyreke's words be, slipped in a CD and cranked up his system. "Above the law," by Black Superman, dominated the atmosphere, setting Tyreke's mind at ease.

The more he heard the lyrics, the more his mind drifted away to his woman.

Tyreke leaned his medium frame further against the door and pressed speed dial on his Blackberry Torch, hoping to hear D'mico's pleasant voice answer on the other end. Maybe he should treat her to dinner and a movie. Just the two of them. The biggest complaint from most women in relationships is that they don't receive enough quality time with their men. Tyreke figured if he set the streets aside for a few days and gave his woman the most precious gift of all—his time—then possibly he could diminish the tension built up in their relationship. But when D'mico didn't answer, his hope quickly faded away. Chauncey eyed Tyreke suspiciously from the corner of his eye. He adjusted the volume on his system to low and addressed the look of despair on Tyreke's face.

"Yo, dawg, you aight?"

Tyreke looked at Chauncey, straightened the crooked look on his own face and smiled.

"Yeah, nigga, I'm good," he lied. "Where we headed?"

"Stacey and the rest of the fellas meetin' at Flava. We can slide that way, check out a few bitches." Although Tyreke wasn't feeling Chauncey's plan, he agreed anyway.

"We can do that."

Still in a dilemma, Tyreke looked back out the window with D'mico on his mind. *Fuck, when did shit get so bad?* he thought. D'mico was his weakness, and any nigga equipped with an eagle eye could see that. If any nigga wanted to catch him slippin', the way was through D'mico. *Through me? Oh shit!*

Tyreke shot up from his seat. He slammed his fist on the dashboard. "Go to my crib," he yelled, removing his Glock from his waist.

Chauncey's eyes traveled across the busy traffic in front and behind him. "What?"

"Nigga, I said go to my house. Turn around. Get there now!"

Confused, Chauncey's eyes fell on the Glock in Tyreke's hand. Without warning, he slowed down and busted a U-turn in the middle of the highway, forcing cars to get over.

Immediately, Chauncey stepped on the gas and headed towards Tyreke's house.

* * * *

Chauncey arrived at Tyreke's house in ten minutes flat. Breaking out the car, Tyreke ran to the door with his gun in hand. Once he made it inside, he yelled D'mico's name as he climbed the stairs two steps at a time.

The urgency in Tyreke's stride made Chauncey follow suit. Tyreke passed several guest rooms before bursting into the master bathroom.

D'mico was face down lying in a puddle of her own blood. Shock covered their faces. Just as Tyreke began to think he was too late, he saw the slow rise and fall of D'mico's chest.

* * * *

Tyreke's entire waistline was covered in blood when he made it to the hospital. He paced back and forth in the emergency room awaiting the news on D'mico's condition. How did he let this happen? He made an oath that if anything ever happened to the ones he loved, the streets would never be at ease again. No words can express the anguish he felt inside his heavy heart.

He stalked around the room, trying to narrow down her shooter. A few years ago, he beefed with the Bamn crew over turfs, but that only lasted four months. That shit was squashed when the head bitch in charge who went by the name "Boss" ran into another beef with a Jamaican muthafucka out of California. Then there was Rodney who he ran up on a year and a half ago. Dude wasn't shit, so Tyreke excluded him from the list.

Regardless of who it was, Tyreke sent Chauncey to get the crew together. The news that he was spreading havoc across the city would be in full force by morning. Speaking of Chauncey, he wasted no time leaving when they got to the hospital. It didn't matter though, because Tyreke needed as many eyes and ears out there as possible.

The guilt of leaving D'mico at home alone in harms way caused Tyreke's eyes to well up. Tired of waiting, he worked his way to the emergency desk but was stopped when someone called his name.

"Tyreke Johnson?"

Tyreke followed the deep voice and cut in between a Hispanic lady—who appeared to be comforting a child who was clutching onto her arm—and a black woman standing behind an elderly woman in a wheelchair.

"Excuse me," Tyreke said, walking towards the double doors.

The black man in green scrubs called out his name once again through a protective mask. "Is there a...Mr. Tyreke Johnson?" the doctor said clearly while glancing at the chart in his hand.

Lifting his arm in the air, Tyreke moved swiftly to the other side of the crowded waiting room.

"Yes there is. Here I am."

When Tyreke came into the doctor's view, he asked the same question. "Are you Tyreke Johnson?" Tyreke shook his head to say yes. The doctor exhaled sharply, and then he removed his face mask from over his mouth and rested it against his neck area.

The sincere look on his face made Tyreke's stomach ball up into a knot. Often bad news was brought to him, and it wasn't nothing that he couldn't handle. However, this was different; this was something that he couldn't live with.

Following the same script used many times in his professional career, the doctor gave Tyreke direct eye contact before saying, "I'm sorry, Mr. Johnson."

Chapter 6

Chauncey sat anxiously in front of Hillcrest Medical Center awaiting news of D'mico's condition. When Tyreke packed D'mico's almost lifeless body into the car, nothing but panic could be heard in Tyreke's voice. "Come on, D'mico…Stay with me. Come on, babe. Push through for us."

Chauncey laughed to himself. The pain in Tyreke's voice and eyes was fresh in his mind. Chauncey knew first hand what panic and pain feels like. He sat behind the wheel of his car reflecting back on the last days he had with his mother. Suddenly feeling a rush of déjà vu, Chauncey stared at the hospital building. He remembered the many days and nights he had spent here before. His smile faded along with his thoughts.

* * * *

Not only was Chauncey's mind tired, his body was too. He hadn't had much sleep since his mom became sick several months ago. A few of his mother's family members would duck in and out of the hospital to show some sort of support. Chauncey was grateful for the hour or two they spent trying to lift his mother's spirits. He used the little time he had away from the hospital wisely. Fuck rest. All he wanted was a quick shower and enough time to snoop around and get some information on D'mico's background. He had made little progress so far.

After being gone for only an hour, Chauncey raced through the halls of Hillcrest Medical Center and made his way to the intensive care unit. He'd gotten a call from one of the nurses to return as soon as possible, and Chauncey developed an uneasy feeling the moment he hung up the phone.

After getting on the first available elevator, nervously, he waited for his floor. As soon as he got off, he saw his mother's baby sister standing outside his mother's room in tears.

She looked up and rushed him with open arms. "She's gone, Chauncey. She's gone." She began to sob. The world collapsed all around Chauncey. He couldn't move. Too defeated to console his aunt, he stood there motionless. Chauncey had prepared himself for this day, so it didn't come as a surprise. What was surprising was the short amount of time she lived compared to the timeline the doctors had given her. Less than a year is what they told him. Now three months later, his worse fear had surfaced, and he was sure that he would never be the same again. After getting the rundown on what happened, Chauncey was allowed to say his final goodbyes before the doctors pulled the plugs to the machines that were breathing for his mother.

Chauncey entered the room. Patricia's face had lost all color, and her eyes were closed shut. No longer able to hold it together, Chauncey broke down in tears. He thought about the letter he wrote her three days prior. He reached into his pocket and read the letter out loud.

"What is strength? It is the will to push forward, the urge to fight, and the ability to move on. You are strength and strength is in you. I love you, Momma." Chauncey choked as he folded the letter and placed it in her hand. Chauncey had planned on giving her the letter that evening, but now he'd never get the chance. He owed it to his mother to fight back. Fighting back is all he wanted to do from this moment forward.

* * * *

Chauncey snapped out of his thoughts. He needed to stay focused on his plans in order to bring down Tyreke and D'mico. He didn't know what the hell had happened back at Tyreke's house, but he knew one thing. He hoped D'mico didn't make it. He'd never seen Tyreke cry the way he did minutes ago. Imagine that, the toughest man in the streets crying over a rotten bitch.

A devilish grin appeared on his face when he picked up his phone to call up Dirt.

Dirt answered on the second ring. "What's up, man?" he answered as he watched the game.

"Some shit went down at Tyreke's spot. D'mico got hit."

"What?" Dirt grabbed his remote. He turned off the television and stood to his feet. "I don't think I heard you right. Whatchu say?"

"Naw you heard me right. Tyreke want the crew to meet up."

"What happened? She got hit where? Is she alright? Where is Tyreke?" Dirt quizzed all in one breath. It only took seconds for Dirt to get a shirt on and some shoes on his feet. He grabbed his car keys and paced around his house waiting for answers. Tyreke and D'mico were like family to Dirt, and if anyone harmed either of them, they would be bringing harm to themselves. Dirt would make sure of it.

"I only know what you know. But I do know Tyreke wants us to meet up," Chauncey repeated.

"What hospital is she at?"

"Hillcrest. I'm in the parking lot now"

"How is she?"

"I don't know. We pulled up, Tyreke got her out the car, and he told me to call the crew."

Dirt was a bit irritated with Chauncey's lack of concern. To him, it was as if Chauncey didn't give a fuck about D'mico's condition. Chauncey wasn't just the black sheep out of the crew. He was a waste to have around, and Dirt never fully understood what purpose he served.

"Where we meeting at? I'm ready now," Dirt informed him.

After Dirt got the location, he hung up with Chauncey and dialed up Tyreke. Tyreke's voicemail came on the first ring. Dirt gave a sigh and headed out the door.

* * * *

A sprinkle of tears fell from Tyreke's eyes like a cloudy day on the day of a funeral. His heart beat out of his chest, and his body grew numb. D'mico was dead because of him.

"Where was she shot at? Man, I should have been there." Tyreke placed his hands over his eyes. "How did I let this happen?" Tyreke was taking full responsibility for what happened.

The doctor looked down at his chart in confusion. "I'm sorry, did you say shot?" the doctor asked.

Tyreke's puffy eyes looked up. "Are you saying that she died another way? Did D'mico die another way?" he asked twice.

"D'mico Asberry was not shot, neither is she dead. As for the baby, the unborn child did not make it, Mr. Johnson."

"Baby?" Tyreke aimed the question more towards himself than the doctor.

Just then, Tyreke's mother, Denise, walked through the emergency doors. Still wearing her nurse uniform, she called Tyreke's name. Tyreke motioned her over.

Denise kissed Tyreke on the cheek and embraced him with a hug. "I came as soon as I heard. What on earth happened?" Denise asked Tyreke, and he only shook his head.

"He's telling me now. I don't know, Mama," he said with sadness. Denise recognized the doctor. In her profession, she met a lot of people who came through Tulsa Regional Hospital. A few years ago, the same doctor in front of her worked at Tulsa where she was currently employed. She only knew him through passing, but by word of mouth, she heard he had transferred to Hillcrest Medical for a larger salary.

"Hello stranger. Denise, right?" the doctor asked,

now smiling.

"Yes. How are you, Doctor Edwards?" Denise and the doctor shook hands.

"I am fine." The doctor's smile faded as he got back to business. "I was just telling your son that Ms. Asberry is fine. She should make a full recovery."

"She was pregnant, Ma. She lost the baby," Tyreke cut in. He still couldn't believe that D'mico was pregnant.

"Pregnant?" Denise asked in a state of shock. "We talk about everything. D'mico never said anything about being pregnant." Denise looked towards her son for an explanation. "Did you know that she was pregnant, Ty?"

Tyreke shook his head no.

The doctor held a blank look on his face. He felt awkward under the circumstances. Nevertheless, he had a job to do and other patients to see, so he moved on with the news. He read from the chart until he came to a stopping point.

"Ms. Asberry was fourteen weeks pregnant. Due to the substantial amount of blood lost, we will be keeping her under our observation for three to five days until she recovers. You will be able to see her shortly." The doctor turned to Denise. "It was nice seeing you again," he concluded, about to walk away.

"Dr. Edwards, wait. What happened to her?" Denise called out, needing answers along with Tyreke.

Dr. Edwards let out a breath of air. "Denise, you know because of special guidelines and patient privacy I cannot tell you that."

Tyreke was about to go off, but Denise stepped in front of him, controlling the situation. "I know you can't, but please, Dr. Edwards, you have my word that I won't say anything. I would never jeopardize your job. This would have been my first grandchild," she pleaded.

Dr. Edwards bit down on the inside of his lip. He didn't know Denise personally, but he had heard about her while he was at Tulsa Regional Hospital. What people don't realize is that doctors, nurses, and other staff members spend so much time around each other while working long hours that in a way they become family. On the flip side, it also made it easy for gossip to spread. Denise was one of the ones he had never heard about. Well, he did hear that she was married to a preacher and did a lot for her local community. Other than that, she wasn't the messy type. For that, Dr. Edwards felt compelled to give her just a little more information. He walked Denise and Tyreke over to a more private area. He had a feeling that his words were in good hands. Dr. Edwards addressed both Denise and Tyreke.

"We're running tests on Ms. Asberry, so as of now I can't tell you the cause and will not discuss that part with you. I'm pretty sure that Ms. Asberry will let you know. But what I can tell you both is…there was a lot of damage done to her cervix and uterus. Hemorrhaging and trauma. Because of that there is a ninety-nine percent chance that Ms. Asberry will not be able to conceive children anymore. I'm sorry folks." He let his words sink in. "Do you have any questions?"

The only questions Tyreke had were for D'mico. He brushed his hands across his thick curls and cleared his throat. "Nah, man, you've done enough. Thank you."

Denise looked stunned. "Thank you, Dr. Edwards."

Denise dropped her head in her hands. The thought of never having any grandchildren made her sick. Tyreke rubbed his mother's back as he took in the information himself. He too imagined life without passing on his legacy. All Tyreke could do was hold on to his mother while her dreams of spoiling his children disappeared into thin air. After Dr. Edwards gave them D'mico's room number, Denise went up to see D'mico while Tyreke stayed behind. He waited in the lobby as he tried to clear his head. Mentally, he wasn't ready to be around anyone. He needed some time alone.

The news that D'mico could possibly be barren was fuckin' him up. *This shit is crazy*, he thought to himself. There was a big possibility that D'mico miscarried because of him. They had fought a lot lately. Then there was that time he slapped her. *Damn*. Tyreke might've been one of the most feared niggas in the city, but right now he felt small and powerless. Tyreke remembered the last time he had felt this way. It was ten years ago—the day when his world took a turn for the worse. Santy'ya might not have been his biological son; however, the love he had for the little dude could not be disguised.

* * * *

The hot sun made the temperature outside a blazing 106 degrees, and the news forecast declared an ozone alert. Niggas who relied on public transportation as a means to get back and forth loved ozone days. It meant one thing; the buses were free. Tyreke didn't have that problem. Although he didn't own his own transportation, he drove his mother's Nissan Maxima whenever he needed it. Actually, Denise was thinking about giving Tyreke the car since he put more miles on it than she did.

Tyreke tilted his snow white Nike cap over his brown eyes as he leaned purposely against the driver side door, gawking at the Arab store located across the street from the building where he set up shop at least two days out of the week. Due to the fact that he wasn't a leaser at the twelve-story, high-rise apartment building, Tyreke dealt with his customers outside. The traffic was swift and tidy, making all sales accessible. The only complaint Tyreke had was the fuckin' heat. The sun was beginning to bake his fair skin into pork rinds.

Two fiends, a man and a woman pushing a stroller, approached Tyreke's car. "You doin' anything?" the man said, shoving his hand in his pocket.

Tyreke ignored his question, glanced at the woman pushing the stroller and shook his head in disapproval.

"What I tell you about bringin' her out here, Teresa?" Tyreke stated sternly.

Teresa looked into Tyreke's serious eyes for a brief moment, and then she drifted away towards the stroller.

"Ty, I had to—" She started to give an excuse, but Tyreke cut her off.

"Man, save it. It's too damn hot out here for that baby. Protective services is waitin' for your ass to slip up. You remember what happened last week. You already know how I feel about you buyin' with her anyway, but I know you're grown and you gon do whatchu wanna do regardless. Damn, you be makin' this shit hard for a nigga," Tyreke lectured. He looked towards the man whose only concern was for his next high.

"Whatchu talkin' about?" The man clearly was just happy to hear that they weren't going to be turned away.

"Whatchu need, man?" Tyreke asked. The man quickly answered in code.

"Do you have a fifty-dollar calling card?" Meaning a fifty-dollar rock of crack cocaine.

Tyreke reached inside the pocket of his denim jeans while scanning the area and gave the man a dab, receiving his money—which was bagged and divided into twenties—and releasing the three stones into the man's hand. After the transaction was complete, the man and Teresa briskly walked away.

Even though Tyreke gave the man sixty dollars of hard for fifty bucks, he could afford the ten-dollar loss. The way he cut up his work always left him on top. Besides, he made easier money when he showed his friends love. When he did that, they always came back, and they only wanted to deal with him. A few feet away from Tyreke's car, the man turned around.

"Hey! Thanks, man, I'll see you in a bit," he yelled, smiling.

Tyreke nodded and turned around. Just another day in the hood. Believe it or not, Tyreke hated dealing dope to his people. The real money came from college students at white private schools, corporate lawyers and undercover stock brokers. The corners Mike Mike stationed him at twice a week were a waist of time, but eh, he was new in the game, and he couldn't tell Mike Mike how to control his business. Mike Mike was known on the streets as a "hood rich" figure. He had a crafty team of foot soldiers, three expensive whips—a Land Rover, Jaguar and a Porsche, all sharing the phrase "King of the Streets" embedded in the dashboards—and two homes. One home being a mini mansion located in the hood (the only extraordinary house on the black side of town). Hood rich didn't mean shit to Tyreke. The likelihood of staying on top was slim. At any given moment, the title and materialistic woes would soon be nothing but a memory. Nothing Mike Mike did was of any value, and his lack of ambivalence caused Tyreke to venture elsewhere. After all, a man has to crawl before he walks, right?

Looking intently across the street, Tyreke was thinking of a plan that would enable him to suck up some AC and improve his pockets without the stress of passing out from a heat stroke. He thumbed through his pocket, shuffling the variety of stones. Estimating the feel of a dub rock from a larger stone, he palmed the stone in hand without exposing it and made his way across the street to the Arab store.

* * * *

Blessed with the gift of gab and a heart of gold, Tyreke managed to talk the Iranian store owner into letting him set up inside the store. Of course he had to give up the dub stone, but it was well worth it. Not to mention he got to cool off. What more could a man ask for?

After a few swerves here and there, Tyreke's pockets were two stacks richer. He had one stone left and that belonged to Amahd. Lifting himself off the sandwich and frozen foods cooler, he made his way to the front of the store. Once he made himself a fountain drink, he casually strolled to the cash register.

"We on for next week?" Tyreke asked, dropping the rock in Amahd's hand. Amahd's face saddened.

"No tomorrow? You make lots of money here."

Tyreke was always wary about being too greedy. Amahd's store was a cool getup; however, coming two days in a row would be too risky. No matter how much money he clocked in, he wasn't coming back until next week.

"Yeah, tomorrow. You know I'ma fuck with you. You my new buddy," he lied. Amahd smiled, showing a set of yellowish-brown teeth.

"Yes, yes. Buddies. Bring some more of these, okay?" Amahd asked, waving the small baggy around.

Tyreke agreed. Without leaving any money, he snatched a small teddy bear the size of a can of soda off the counter and walked out the door. In the dope game, a lot of hustlers used drugs in place of money. In Tyreke's case, his currency was crack cocaine. Selling drugs was Tyreke's biggest asset right now, and crackheads were more than willing to be their own liability.

As soon as Tyreke stepped outside, the sun played a game of tag, staring him straight in the face. He squinted his eyes against the devastating ray of heat. Shit, he knew one thing; if hell was anywhere near as hot as it was today, he needed to get his shit together quick, fast and in a hurry.

Mike Mike sat at the wheel of his spacious Land Rover peering out the front window. He watched Tyreke as he made his way back across the street to the spot that he specifically told him not to leave. How could he keep an eye on his money if the money was bullshittin' around?

This nigga betta have my money, Mike Mike thought, recovering a small mirror and a miniature Ziploc bag out of his glove box. No one knew that he had been getting high, and he planned to keep it that way. In secret, he performed his customary habit of pouring the powdery white substance across the mirror. With his pinkie, he put together a perfectly straight line. Before he snorted the devil up his nose, he stared at it in disgust. Within just a short time, getting high was all he could think of. He wanted a way out, but he couldn't think of anything that could help him. A lot of niggas in the hood looked up to him. All of that would disappear if they found out that he was using. Two years ago, a flock of broads begged to get down with the Slim Thug look-alike. His physique, neat braids and distinguished style sent bitches over the edge. Although he maintained his looks and kept his body in shape, his will power was frangible. Thoughts of getting high all day everyday were affecting not only his pockets but everyone else's.

Placing his worries in the back of his mind, he snorted the entire line until there was nothing left. I'm sure you're wondering when shit got so bad for Mike Mike. Out of the blue, Mike Mike had a sudden urge to try the demon also known as cocaine base. Most people use latex gloves when handling the shit. Not Mike Mike. Shidd, he figured that if the drugs hadn't passed into his system after seven years, then he was good. Wrong! Seven years is all it took before he was dipping his hand in his own cookie jar for the next two years. Mike Mike found himself stuck, falling victim to the myth that you shouldn't get high off your own supply.

Mike Mike checked his reflection in the mirror. He closed the compact mirror, took the empty baggy, threw it out the window and put everything away. He rubbed the remainder of the powder on his finger tips across his front and back gums and pressed down on his horn to let Tyreke know that he was en route.

Tyreke looked up. Mike Mike leaned his 245-pound muscular frame out the window while he simultaneously rubbed at his runny nose, all the while displaying a kosher smile.

"You still workin'?" Mike Mike asked Tyreke when he got a few feet from the car.

Arrogantly, Tyreke stuck out his chest. He rotated his hat to the side where it did a little "lean wit' it" tilt.

"If I'm talkin' to you, then you know I'm off da' clock," Tyreke boasted, referring to being sold out of crack. He approached the car and gave Mike Mike a pound. Mike Mike stuck his body in the car and motioned for Tyreke to get in.

"Take a ride with me then, young playa."

Tyreke glanced down at the teddy bear in his hand. Damn, he couldn't wait to get back to the hospital to see Santy'ya and D'mico. After the things D'mico revealed, he wanted to be by her side. He hated the fact that he had to leave her alone. Unfortunately, he wasn't in a position to tell Mike Mike no. He was new in the squad, and the rookies always had to go the extra mile to gain recognition.

"I drove," Tyreke informed him, pointing to his parked car.

Mike Mike wiped his runny nose a second time. "I'll bring you back. Come on. Get in. I got some shit I wanna show you."

Tyreke stuffed the tiny teddy bear in his pocket. "Aight. Let's roll," he heard himself say, walking around to the passenger side, but his mind was elsewhere.

The masculine scent of leather filled Tyreke's nostrils when he got in. He took in the pleasantries of Mike Mike's ride. The seats were cream leather with burnt-red leather inserts, and the feel of chinchilla carpet welcomed his Jordan sneakers. No wonder they called Mike Mike "hood rich." The way he lavished himself was definitely that of a hood rich-ass nigga fo show.

Tyreke's eyes settled on the dashboard. "King of the Streets" were the words staring him in the face. For some odd reason, the words seemed to jump out at him, pulling him into a fantasy where one day he would be the king of not only the streets but the world.

One day. One...day.

* * * *

Mike Mike laced every block out north with his domineering presence. At every corner, necks turned and mouths hung ajar at the sight of the sparkling red SUV outfitted with twenty-inch Lexani rims with matching lips.

Mike Mike enjoyed the feel of the summer breeze cooling his scalp between his ten neat braids which held forty clear beads.

Tyreke stared out the window in awe at the herd of bitches lining up outside Soul Brothers Car Wash as they cruised by. Suspense had their feet moving right along with their eyes.

Mike Mike brushed off the obvious stares like it was nothing and carried on to his destination. He made a right on Mohawk Boulevard then a quick left behind Lindsey Elementary School.

"I wantcha to meet a few of my folks. These niggas get a little raspy, so I wanna give you a heads up on that. Don't take it to heart, aight?" Mike Mike forewarned.

Instead of responding or asking any questions, Tyreke's head fell into a rapid nod. He listened with a level head. He took everything in like a baby being schooled on his first steps. Mike Mike came upon a yellowish-green house. Scattered garbage was dispersed across the front lawn making the house look even worse than it already did. A young dude, appearing to be in his late teens, sat comfortably on a beige loveseat with a fair amount of slits and holes. When he noticed that he had company, he jumped up from the couch and smiled.

He gave the same look a kid in the ghetto would give when mom walks in the door with groceries from her first check of the month. Love and happiness. Chucking his Black and Mild, he briskly made his way to Mike Mike.

"What's good, fam?" the young dude asked Mike

Mike, slamming his fist into his, knuckles to knuckles.

"Not shit. Hoping you got good news for a nigga," Mike Mike responded.

"Man, I'm dry as beat-up pussy," he joked, holding onto his baggy jeans that revealed his orange and blue, plaid boxers.

"Damu and Ansean off in der tryna cook up some shake. You know me though, cuzzin. I'm not fuckin' wit' it. So to answer your question, yeah, I got news, news you can use." He dug out a wad of cash.

It wasn't until the young dude pulled out his money that he noticed a second body in the car. Screwing up his face, he cuffed the money and stepped back onto the curb.

Mike Mike looked at Tyreke giving him the "it's cool" look. Then he turned around and ripped the young dude a new asshole.

"Nigga, who da fuck told you to step away from my shit. Get yo ass back over here. The fuck wrong with you?" Mike Mike flexed.

Stubbornly, the young dude reapproached the SUV, holding the same malice in his demeanor. Using his hands, Mike Mike introduced Tyreke to Dirt.

"Dirt, this is Tyreke. Tyreke, this is Dirt. Dirt, Tyreke will be your second boss. He's good; people and money cling to this nigga like their part of his wardrobe." Hearing Mike Mike tell Dirt that he was his second boss had Tyreke cheesing inside, but he didn't let it show.

"What up?" Tyreke spoke up nonchalantly.

Dirt pierced Tyreke with an angry stare and flexed his jaws. He wanted to wipe the sober look right off the nigga's face. Mike Mike was trippin', straight up. He'd never seen or even heard about the nigga up until now. The rumors about Mike Mike freebasing had to be true because this nigga was definitely missing a few of his thinking screws.

"You remember me tellin' you about my trip?" Mike Mike asked. Dirt nodded.

"Vegas, right?"

"Yeah. Ty will be the go-between while I'm gone. If you happen to get low, and I know you will, holla at cuz," Mike Mike instructed.

Dirt threw a look of disapproval in Tyreke's direction. *What kind of shit is this*? he thought.

"Alright!" Mike Mike began to get irritated as he saw Dirt trying to challenge his authority.

"Yeah, aight," Dirt responded, putting his upper body inside the car. For now, he would let that shit go. For now.

"Good. All work, no setbacks." Mike Mike leaned his seat back and recovered a bag of powder from under his nuts.

"I want four G's off of her and not one cent short. Ansean already gettin' in the habit of short changin' a nigga. I don't want you to be the second nigga I have to beat down over my money."

Dirt ignored Mike Mike's idle threats. After all, the nigga was high out of his mind. He lifted up his shirt and tucked the drugs away. "Its on," he said, placing the intended money in Mike Mike's hand. They gave each other a pound before Dirt exchanged a "watch out for me" look with Tyreke.

Tyreke didn't feed into Dirt's envy. If anything, he

shrugged it off earlier when he spoke to the nigga, and he didn't speak back. No love lost. If he was the dude, he might've been angry too. I mean, shit, the bond he had with Mike Mike seemed solid, but evidently it wasn't solid enough. The reason why the upper hand wasn't given to him wasn't a question Tyreke intended to ask.

After Dirt disappeared inside the house, Mike Mike drove off.

"Don't worry 'bout him," Mike Mike commented, sneaking a glance at Tyreke. "He cool when you get to know him. Ever since his pops got that life sentence, he been a tickin' time bomb." Mike Mike pulled into busy traffic and changed the subject. "I wantchu to look under your seat. That's for you."

Mike Mike took a peep at Tyreke's expression. Curious to know what it was, Tyreke eased his hand under the seat and pulled out a brown paper bag. From the feel of it, he could tell what the contents were.

"You gon need that. The world is messy, Ty, and when I'm gone, niggas ain't gon be trying to play fair. You know how to use a gun?"

Tyreke looked at Mike Mike like he was disappointed that he'd asked the question. In all actuality, Tyreke had never held or so much as been close to a gun, but he played it cool like the "G" he was.

"Of course I know how to use a gun. I'm not new to this kinda shit, you know?"

"Good. Now that we got that out the way, lemme show you where the niggas who don't play fair live."

Fifteen minutes later, they pulled into a subdivision of moderately nice homes. Manicured lawns, fenced in yards, working sprinklers and polished rides were a few of the things Tyreke saw passing through the neighborhood. He spotted a black man dressed in a postal uniform as he got inside a two-door mini van.

"Hard working black folks." Mike Mike's strong voice broke his stare.

"I need you to pay close attention to the things I show and tell you. I like you. You gonna go far in this world, my nigga. FAR. Millions is right around the corner for us," Mike Mike said, wiping away at his nostrils. His high was beginning to come down, and he was beginning to get jittery. He hated that feeling. Coming down that is. It made him feel sluggish and handicap.

For the first time since he'd been in the car, Tyreke faked a smile. There was no "us." One thing was for sure; Tyreke wasn't knocking Mike Mike's hustle or anything, but the way he conducted business was fucking backwards. The man was supposed to be the head, not the tail. He packed his own work and dealt out of his car. A nigga as big as Mike Mike had crash dummies to do jobs like that for him. Yet the nigga was slippin', risking his own freedom for some shit he had full control of. It just didn't make sense. Another thing Tyreke couldn't overlook about Mike Mike was his addiction. Periodically, the man dabbed away at his runny nose, which was beginning to leak with specks of blood. Meanwhile, his glossy eyes told the truth his mouth could never tell. Damn, that's too bad 'cause Tyreke really liked Mike Mike. He was a cool cat, but the fact of the matter remained the same. Mike Mike was a screwup waiting to happen.

Mike Mike pointed at a tall, dark-skinned man who was holding a baby's car seat. "You see him? He's the first nigga I want you to keep an eye on. I never seen that white chick before, but anyway, watch out for him."

The white chick Mike Mike referred to cautiously looked over her shoulder, making eye contact with their car. Tyreke tensed up. Damn, the woman resembled Nurse Betty from his mother's job. Then again, Tyreke knew better than to think Betty's preppy ass would be on the black side of town with a black man. Yeah right.

"Dude's name is Lonnie...Bastard works for TPD." Lonnie? Did Mike Mike say Lonnie?

Before Mike Mike hit the corner, Tyreke gave the man a once over. Then his eyes fell on the street sign. Woodrow Ave.

"Ty, did you hear me? You taking all of this in?" Mike Mike questioned.

Although Mike Mike's words played like mush in Tyreke's head, he heard him loud and clear.

"Yeah, I hear you, man. You said Lonnie, right?"

"Yeah, Lonnie. Anyway, watch out for dude. Him and his partner, Matt, is slimy as fuck. If I got enough time, I'll swing by Matt's crib, but for now, I wantchu to focus on Lonnie. He's the nigga callin' all the shots. Both of dem fools done pulled one too many capers on my watch dogs. They take drugs, money and guns but never make any arrests, which is good on our end, but who he think he is? Damn that. I had to sho those pussies who got the big dick, feel me?"

Tyreke sat quietly in his seat stunned. Although his body was there in a physical sense, his mind was past the moon somewhere.

"The gun inside that bag is Matt's." Mike Mike turned a corner and smiled real big like he done something spectacular. "Dirt ran in that nigga's shit and swiped it. So make sure to wear gloves if you do use it. There should be some in the bag too."

Unimpressed with Mike Mike's risky behavior, Tyreke looked inside the bag. Another reason why he couldn't be down with Mike Mike any longer than he had to. Tyreke tried his best to grasp the information given to him. However, it was all too coincidental. A feeling in his gut started to form. A feeling his pops told him to never ignore. The feel of trouble.

Rolling up the bag, he took in a few mental notes of his own: the street, what the man looked like and his crib.

"Like I was sayin' earlier, I'm leaving in a couple of days. I want shit to run smooth like cream while I'm gone. I'm leavin' everything in your hands 'cause I know that I can trust you to get it done. I don't know how you do it, but you make three times as much money as anybody else in the crew. Word up, my nigga. I'ma line you up with four kilos before I smash. I wantchu to cook it like I showed you, cut it up and do the math with them niggas.

You got an eagle eye for that shit, and you know what you're doin'. As soon as I get back, we'll flip that." Mike Mike stared out the window like a zombie.

"We can't afford screwups. Everything gotta be on point."

Mike Mike told Tyreke everything he needed to know about his trip to Vegas, except for the part about how he was in debt to the Cuban mafia for $175,000. A hundred thousand of those dollars were gambling debts when Mike Mike went to Vegas trying to splurge. And seventy-five thousand was drug money owed when he received a shipment of keys on good faith.

Mike Mike didn't even have half the money to give the bastards. Come to think of it, he didn't have a third of their shit. And he knew his ongoing drug habit was the result.

Tyreke was his plan a, b and c. With no problems, Mike Mike intended to go to Vegas, make a proposition for an extension with the promise to pay interest, come back to town and relieve everyone of their funds and stack his paper until the debt was paid off. Piece of cake. Last week, Tyreke clocked in an easy 20 G's by himself. Mike Mike didn't know his method, but Tyreke's thirst for money was killing niggas in the game. He outdid everyone in his squad put together. Natural, bomb-fuckin' hustler is what the nigga was.

Looking at the way things were going, all Mike Mike needed was two months of non-stop, bona fide hustling and his debt would be zeroed out. He couldn't wait.

Little did Mike Mike know, the Cuban mafia organized a group of ruthless, cold-hearted killers who didn't abide by extensions. Either you had their loot or you wound up on milk cartons. The choice was yours. Mike Mike's trip to Vegas would be his last stop before going on a permanent hiatus. A new "King of the Streets" would be born.

* * * *

Reverend Johnson stared at the blank television screen in a state of concentration, juggling two golf-sized, silver balls between his thumb and forefingers. He found himself doing this quite often when his son was in the streets. He tried to distract his mind with other things, but he constantly feared that he would one day hear a sudden knock at the door from the police or a dreadful phone call informing him and his wife that something had happened to Tyreke. In a twisted way, he grew accustomed to the long hours of mental anguish the wait caused.

A sigh of relief escaped the Reverend's weary lungs when the front door opened and closed.

With big steps, Tyreke made a dash for his room. *Oh shit, there he go sitting in that same spot again*, Tyreke thought as he observed his father.

"Yo! What's new for the news, old man? Anybody call?" Tyreke asked, making a quick attempt to acknowledge his pops.

Reverend Johnson placed the silver balls in their original case and glanced over his shoulder. Tyreke was almost out of eye sight when he called out for him to come join him in the living room.

"No one called but, Tyreke, I do need to talk to you."

Tyreke gripped the paper bag given to him by Mike Mike, feeling uneasy about the conversation he was about to have with his father. He went ahead and slid the hidden steel underneath his arm.

"Whatchu want to talk about?" Tyreke asked in defense mode.

"Well, come have a seat and see."

Reverend Johnson cleared a few pillows out the way. Tyreke wasn't a kid anymore, and he had to be careful of the things he said unless he wanted his words to fall on deaf ears. Instead of sitting where his pops directed, Tyreke took a seat on the chaise across from him. With an attitude, he glanced at his watch to show his father that he didn't appreciate the delay.

"I know you got things to do, and I won't take up too much of your time. I know how young folks got a lot to do."

Reverend Johnson smiled remembering his own youth, but seconds later, that smiled faded into an expression that denoted grave importance.

"Tyreke, I'm talking to you man to man. You don't have to tell me what you're out there doing, and I won't ask, because I don't want you to lie to me."

Here we go with this shit again, Tyreke thought. He had the utmost respect for his father and all, but being born to a preacher was becoming a nuisance.

Tyreke licked his dry lips and stared lazily at Reverend Johnson.

"Tyreke, I been where you're headed. I've seen and done unimaginable things. I wasn't always a man of God. I sold drugs, gang banged and done things I'm not proud of. If it wasn't for my mistakes and a murder case—"

Tyreke's eyes opened in shock.

"Yes, a murder case. They were tryin' to give me the death penalty. They didn't care who I ran with or who my parents were. All they seen was a black boy and a poor excuse of a man. But God seen something else, and although I was as guilty as the eyes judging me, God had another plan. By his grace and mercy, I hope you don't have to go through the same hell I did. Listen to me, son, when I say that your past will contradict your future."

Reverend Johnson's body language expressed the many emotions going on inside his body. His lean frame inched towards the edge of the sofa, and his hands spoke the necessary words right along with his mouth.

"All I'm askin' you to do is beware of the company you keep. Be better than the hardhead I once was. You're gifted, smart and young. You have a chance to be and do whatever you want. Pick your battles, Tyreke. Pick 'em 'cause if you don't, someone else will."

The sound of the house phone ringing interrupted Reverend Johnson.

"Are we done?" Tyreke asked, standing to his feet, directing his attention to the telephone. Sorrow outlined the wrinkles in Reverend Johnson's handsome face. He knew first hand that his words went in one ear and out the other.

"Yeah, we're done. Get the phone, Ty."
Silently, he got up and looked at his son. Tyreke now had the phone glued to his ear. Shaking his head, he went to his bedroom to pray. If he couldn't get through to Tyreke, then he knew that God would. Reverend Johnson just hoped it wouldn't be too late.

* * * *

Tyreke slammed the phone down on the receiver. A blaze of fire spreading inside his chest caused his eyes to well up with tears. He just got off the phone with D'mico.

She told him that Santy'ya was taken from the hospital, and nurse Betty was wanted for the abduction. *Damn, I just seen them. The baby in the car seat was Santy'ya. Fuck*! Tyreke thought, heading out the door.

On the way to Lonnie's house, Tyreke tried to rationalize D'mico's problems as if they were his own. He wanted so bad to erase her out of his mind, but he couldn't. He wanted to face her nightmares and destroy the monster who'd been haunting her on a daily. He didn't know what was about to transpire, but he did know that Lonnie crossed the line when he took Santy'ya. He didn't understand where Betty fit in all of this, but he sure as hell was about to find out. I can tell you one thing, Tyreke wasn't about to be on no peace treaty "Can I have Santy'ya back?" type of shit neither. Fuck that.

Tyreke slowed down when he neared Woodrow Avenue. If you didn't know any better, you would've thought the silver Nissan pushing fifteen miles per hour was about to do a drive-by. For the first time, Tyreke had something other than money on his mind. He took one glance at the red and brown house down the street. Without hesitation, he dug a black mask and gloves out of the bag given to him earlier, pulled the mask over his head and around his neck, and put on the gloves. With his mind racing and his heart beating violently in his chest, he jumped out the car, raced down the street and paused at Lonnie's door before knocking. The pistol in his hand gave him the assurance that he was doing the right thing. His father was right about one thing; this was a battle he couldn't refuse. Maybe that wasn't the advice given, but in Tyreke's mind, it was.

* * * *

Lonnie's attention diverted to the three loud knocks coming from the front. "About muthafuckin' time. I called his ass two hours ago," Lonnie mumbled while taking another long pull from his crack pipe. Coughing slightly, his face tightened as he released his oversized penis from out of Betty's mouth.

He enjoyed the combination of getting his dick sucked and getting high. Wiping his dick off with a dirty shirt on the floor, he instructed Betty to stay put. Doped up from the pills and a few puffs of crack cocaine, Betty threw the covers over her exposed breasts. She was high as hell, and she wanted to stay that way forever.

"Hold on, shit!" Lonnie cursed on his way to the door.

The knocks continued. Thinking it was his partner, Matt, he flung the door open. "Muthafucka, didn't I say that I was co—"

A fleck of fear spread across Lonnie's face when he opened his door to a nine millimeter. Releasing the door handle, he threw up his hands and backed inside the house.

* * * *

Betty could hear commotion going on in the living room. She couldn't decipher what was going on, but the mention of D'mico's baby caused her to panic. What did she get herself into? Were the cops there? Everything was Lonnie's fault. She didn't want to do any of this, but that black son of a bitch made her. He threatened to tell her job about her drug addition. He also told her that he would go to her kids' school and expose her secret to the other kids and staff members. She couldn't let that happen. Regardless of who was in the living room, Betty planned to tell the police that Lonnie raped and kidnapped her. He forced her to take the baby. Who would believe a crooked, black cop over a white woman? *They'll believe me*, she thought, putting on her clothes. Once she had her clothes on, she made her way towards the front.

* * * *

Despite the fucked up predicament Lonnie was in, he snickered when Tyreke removed his mask. *Young'n at the hospital*! Underestimating Tyreke's anger, Lonnie ran a callous hand across his hairy chest.

"Look, little nigga, I don't know why you're here, but you—" Tyreke struck Lonnie across his jugular with the butt of the gun, knocking the breath out of his lungs. With brute force, he shoved him further into the house. Lonnie stumbled over his large feet, holding on to his neck while gasping for air.

"Keep that up and you're dead. You know why I'm here."

Tyreke scanned the living room. For Lonnie's house to be in a nice neighborhood, the nigga's living quarters were a dump, and it reeked of crack cocaine.

"Who else is here. Where's Betty?"

"It's just me," Lonnie lied. His eyes darted toward the .45 he kept on his coffee table.

Tyreke followed his eyes. He smashed his gun in Lonnie's face. "Don't get any bright ideas." Lonnie was fucked and he knew it. "Where the fuck is Santy'ya, bitch?" Tyreke yelled, growing impatient. His trigger finger was ready for action. One squeeze and Lonnie was a goner. If Lonnie wanted to live, he'd better start talking.

"Man, I swear I don't know who you talking about. I don't even know anybody by that name," Lonnie lied, playing dumb.

Wrong answer.

Tyreke's ten-inch Jordan sneaker came crashing down on Lonnie's face. Repeatedly he kicked Lonnie until he was satisfied enough to stop.

"Okay, okay...Please." Lonnie gave in. Blood poured out of his mouth onto his ashy chest. "He's not here, but I do know where he is." Lonnie slumped over and gripped the carpet. He started breathing heavy as he hyperventilated on the floor.

Lonnie's life rested in Tyreke's hands, and Lonnie knew that once he told Tyreke what really happened to the baby, the result would be death. The shadow in the hallway made Tyreke act on impulse.

POP!

Before Betty was given the chance to explain her innocence, it was too late. The pale look on her face and the pool of tears said it all. Betty wasn't ready to die. Sluggishly, she dropped to her knees. Blood seeped from the corners of her mouth as she looked into Tyreke's eyes. Nooo...What about her children? What about her husband? The look of pain emerged in her eyes when she realized that she would never see them again.

Tyreke's eyes rose when he heard the loud thud. Betty's body hit the ground like a sack of potatoes. Tyreke turned his pistol on Lonnie, who was on the floor crying like the bitch he was. There was no way out now.

Chapter 7

Tyreke massaged his temples in frustration. He sat shotgun next to Chauncey thinking of a way to break the news to his boys that he'd made a false call. He never made false calls, and he didn't like the fact that he had everyone shook up over his accusations. When Chauncey pulled into QuikTrip, he added fuel to Tyreke's bad mood. Anybody who liked to be called somebody had their face at the local franchise store. It wasn't your usual "kick it" spot. The store became the place to go after the club let out. Most people mingled at the establishment before heading out to another store, and that's why Tyreke was pissed. He didn't want to be out in the open. He liked to be low key and reserved. Less trouble.

"You told them to meet us here?" Tyreke asked Chauncey.

"Do you mind?"

"Outta all the places you chose a fuckin' store? I swear your brain gotta be the size of an almond," Tyreke scolded. He adjusted and straightened out the wrinkle in his bloodstained shirt and slumped closer to the door.

Chauncey sucked his teeth. He pressed the time button on his five-disc Sony system, and the time read 1:41 a.m.

"The club must've let out early. I was tryna meet somewhere close to the hospital," Chauncey retaliated.

Tyreke threw up one hand to silence Chauncey. Chauncey huffed silently to himself while looking away. He had to restrain himself from saying anything further. Ever since they left the hospital, Tyreke had this fucked up attitude directed towards him and the rest of the world. The nigga was acting all sensitive over a no-good bitch. If anything, he should've been happy that D'mico almost died. Soon her day would come. Tyreke too.

Chauncey swept the parking lot for Dirt's car. He spotted the Chevy Tahoe adjacent to several air pumps and a water hose hook up. A group of people who were talking and monkeying around suddenly parted like the Red Sea as Chauncey's Chevy Impala glided through the parking lot.

"Hey, sexy, can I ride with you, baby?" A female voice rung out through the parking lot as they passed by. Chauncey ignored the ugly duckling and continued towards the side of the building.

Immediately, a female with a face like Trina's caught

Chauncey's attention. She strutted in front of his car while meeting his gaze with her purple contacts. The gap between her legs had Chauncey's dick standing at full attention when she turned around and waved at them. Wow! Already Chauncey was scheduling her for a one on one "get to know your body" appointment.

"Say, baby girl, any room in those jeans for me?" Chauncey asked her.

"Maybe." Her dark-colored lips parted into a smile. Any minute Chauncey expected for her lips to reach out and kiss him. They were that arousing.

Chauncey's string of words drew her to the car. Resting her arm on his side-view mirror, she lowered her head inside his window and snuck a peak at Tyreke. Liking what she saw on the passenger side, her soft voice answered Chauncey's question completely.

"There's plenty of room for your friend over there," she stated slyly, backing up from the car. She waited with confidence for Tyreke to accept the pussy platter she placed before him, but Tyreke looked the other way.

Although Chauncey was a bit jealous, he still tried to hype Tyreke up. "Damn, man, she feelin' you, dawg."

Tyreke looked at the chick and shook his head. His days of chasing bitches were long gone. Nothing about this chick was appealing to him. She left nothing to discover, and her secret garden was obviously open to anyone with a desire.

"Why we ain't movin'?" Tyreke asked, blowing the chick off.

Chauncey looked at the girl then at Tyreke. *Oh this nigga is trippin'. He betta tap that or I will.*

"What? You gon pass that up? Holla at her."

"Chauncey, get this car movin'. I don't got time for pussy or hoes," Tyreke said loud enough for everyone to hear. He wasn't trying to direct his malice at shorty, but shit, he'd just lost his first seed and almost his woman. Stressed? Hell yeah he was. Tyreke was stressed to the max. Up against those odds, the Trina look-alike didn't stand a fuckin' chance.

The girl stood back with her hands on her hips in shock. Never in her life had a man rejected or embarrassed her the way he had. As she was walking off, she turned up her nose and flipped Tyreke off.

"Fuck you. You niggas must be lovers. Damn faggots."

"You stank-ass bird. Pluck your feathers and check yo stank-ass breath, and maybe a nigga will give you the time. Till then, taste the pavement, Beotch!" Chauncey peeled off, catching a few laughs from the crowd.

* * * *

Dirt jumped out of his Tahoe and greeted Tyreke.

"Eh, I came as soon as I heard. What da fuck happened?" He took one look at Tyreke's bloody shirt and started going off. "What the doctors say? How is D'mico? We gon dead some niggas tonight?"

Tyreke calmed Dirt down. "Nah, nobody is dying. I need to make sure everybody is here before I go into details. But D'mico is good, man. She's alright."

Dirt took off his shirt and handed it to his foreman. "So, whatchu sayin' what's up?" Dirt questioned, still pissed.

Tyreke took a deep breath and swapped out his bloody shirt for Dirt's. Leaving Dirt's question unanswered, Tyreke turned to Damu. Damu hung up his phone and glanced at his watch.

"They said they'll be here in ten minutes."

"Well, they need to hurry the fuck up so we can get to the bottom of this," Dirt fumed, popping his knuckles.

Tyreke understood Dirt's restlessness; however, he wanted everyone together as a group. For eleven years, Dirt worked for Tyreke. In the beginning, they bumped heads, but that later died when Tyreke showed Dirt that he wasn't trying to take over what Mike Mike started; he was only trying to improve everyone's pockets. Dirt looked up to Tyreke, and he had mad respect for his drive to push everyone in his crew to the top along with him. Several months back, Dirt ran into some trouble. The judge assigned to his case posted his bail at five million dollars like he was working with terrorists against the United States. Anyway, Tyreke not only made his bail but he put up his expensive home as collateral in case Dirt jumped bail. He lined Dirt up with a lawyer, and two months later, all charges were dismissed due to lack of evidence. Most niggas turn their backs on you when the going gets tough. Not Tyreke. Nah, the nigga was the only reliable person you could count on through thick and thin. Tyreke looked out for him, and Dirt wanted to return the favor. It was almost as if they were supposed to be blood brothers because the two of them were inseparable ever since.

* * * *

The crew of twelve looked like the Black Mafia conducting a meeting outside QuikTrip parking lot. All of the men shared the same qualities in appearance—clean haircuts and pretty-boy attire. All except for Dirt, who was the only oddball out of the crew. His baggy jeans, white tees and latest Jordan sneakers reminded everyone around him that he was a gangsta at heart and that he didn't have time to oil up and primp like a bitch. He didn't knock anyone's style, and they didn't knock his. Their heads came together on a level that only they could understand.

After Tyreke explained what happened to D'mico—while leaving out a few intimate details about her condition—he dismissed his henchmen, and everyone gathered to leave. It was 2:30 a.m., and a few people straggled behind in the parking lot.

"It's getting late, and I want to head back up to the hospital before D'mico wakes up and thinks she's alone."

"If you don't mind, I want to slide up there with you," Dirt chimed in, not taking no for an answer. He could see the hurt in Tyreke's eyes despite the poker face he revealed to everyone else. Dirt knew better. Tyreke was grieving. Even though Dirt had only one kid, he could never imagine life without his son. He knew without a doubt that he wouldn't be the pass-go nigga he was today. Dirt slowed down a lot since his son came into the world, and his life took a turn for the better. D'mico was a good girl, and Dirt knew how much Tyreke loved her. Her vivacious aura and bubbly attitude kept his boy happy. Until now.

"That's cool," Tyreke said to Dirt. Tyreke turned to Damu and Chauncey. "What ya'll 'bout to get into?"

"Not shit. I'm gonna head to the house." Damu yawned. "I might as well get some gas though since I'm here."

"Chauncey, go ahead and smash. I'm going to roll to the hospital with Dirt."

Good! Chauncey thought, nodding his head in agreement. Hearing those words were like music to his ears. If Dirt wanted to be that nigga who caked up at the hospital with Tyreke like he was his second bitch, by all means, the nigga could have at it. There wasn't no telling what D'mico did to herself, and he wasn't trying to be the nigga to find out. He could care less.

Chauncey gave his condolences and left.

"Fake-ass nigga," Damu mumbled under his breath as he watched Chauncey drive off and disappear down the street.

Tyreke pretended like he didn't hear what Damu said, but he heard him and so did Dirt. Tyreke knew that Damu didn't like Chauncey; however, Damu put up with Chauncey on the grounds of loyalty. Loyalty to the crew.

"Alright, man, I'll see you later. I'll give you a call when I leave the hospital," Tyreke said to Damu.

"Alright, bet! Send D'mico my love."

"It's on," Tyreke concluded, getting inside Dirt's Tahoe.

While Damu got gas, Tyreke got the idea to grab D'mico some goodies out of the store.

"Pull around front. I'ma run in the store real quick,"

Tyreke said to Dirt.

Within minutes, they were in front of the store, and Tyreke was exiting QuikTrip with a bag in his hand. Tyreke threw up his hand, signaling Damu, and yelled across the parking lot. "Be safe, my nigga."

Damu looked up. He nodded and bobbed his head to the lyrics of UGK while pumping unleaded gas into his BMW X6 M. A black and gold Lexus with tinted windows eased into the empty parking space next to Dirt's Tahoe. Tyreke was about to get in the car when a somewhat familiar voice called out.

"That's him." Releasing the door handle, Tyreke turned around. Two dudes hopped out the car. Tyreke's street sense told him to reach for his burner, but he held off. He was up for murderin' a nigga with the way he was feeling. I mean, damn, let's look at the logic in this. Tyreke masturbated with the world as his lubricant, and lo and behold, here stood another potential nut. Whoever these cats were, they better have heat with them. Tonight wasn't the night to be on his bad side.

A mischievous grin outlined Tyreke's face when the Trina look-alike stepped out the car. Tyreke also noticed that one of the men who accompanied her was Ansean. Ansean is a third-rate busta who use to work under Tyreke's operation. He took on the nickname "Pinch" because of his need to take whatever he could get his hands on. Several years back, Ansean use to run dope for Mike Mike. When Mike Mike didn't return from his business trip to Vegas, Tyreke took on the responsibility of supplying the streets with base.

Only a month ago did Tyreke make the call to cut

Ansean's water off—in other words, his money. Tyreke had a motto when it came down to his money: Fuck me once, it's on me. Fuck me twice, fuck you and everything you stand for. Unfortunately, Ansean's sticky-ass fingers thought they were excluded from these rules. Whoever said thinking paid any bills?

* * * *

Damu watched the confrontation from the pump. Like a thief in the night, he worked his way to the trunk of his car. He kept his eyes on Tyreke as he prepared himself for a liquidation sale if the occasion called for one. He retrieved his Glock from under a spare tire wrapped in an oily towel and grabbed a hefty bag. It was Ansean standing next to the Hulk-looking nigga that made him act fast. Was Ansean trying to start beef because he got cut off, or was he tripping about something else? Damu didn't know; however, he was determined to find out. He used the hefty bag to cover the Glock and prevent a spill of shell casings across the parking lot, a technique he learned from Dirt. Speaking of Dirt, Damu wondered why he hadn't stepped out the car yet.

* * * *

Dirt sat behind double-tinted windows, quiet as a mouse. Dirt picked up his .45 automatic. He dressed his bitch in her finest attire. First came the bullets and then came the hefty bag. Damn, he loved to play dress up.

* * * *

Ansean's beady eyes met Tyreke's. "Whassup, Ty?" He spoke more in an antagonizing tone rather than a "happy to see you" tone.

Tyreke looked straight through Ansean like he was a piece of shit. Threatened by the look on Tyreke's face, Ansean took two steps back and scratched the locks on his head. When China, the Trina look-alike, pointed Tyreke out for being the dude who violated her, Ansean tried his best to alleviate the situation by telling his brother, Chris, to let it go. Besides, China was known on the streets for being hot and screaming "boy cried wolf." The girl was trouble. Chris was 6'4" in height, weighed 265 pounds and dude was solid and built like a brick. He was fresh out the joint with an inextinguishable desire to get into a little trouble. Granted with that mentality, he was all fucked up.

Chris did a nine-year bid for second-degree murder, and in his mind, he had a license to twist nigga's caps back. What Chris didn't know was that he was in the presence of niggas who'd killed and gotten away with it. The rules in the streets worked on a different level than the codes and regulations of Joseph Harp State Penitentiary. That's where Chris made his first mistake. Today, niggas were being laid to rest for the slick shit he was trying to pull.

"Hold on. Wait a minute. You mean to tell me this is the infamous Tyreke? The one everybody be talkin' about?" Chris asked out loud, eyeing Tyreke from head to toe. "The nigga don't look tough to me," he spat.

China's facial expression went from a "now what look" to a "oh shit" scowl within seconds. She'd heard stories about Tyreke but had never come into contact with him until now. He looked very much like a pretty boy compared to the monster she heard about. She had to do something.

"Come on, baby. Let's just go," China suggested, pulling on Chris's arm. Chris shook her off, causing her to swallow the dry lump in her throat.

"Naw, this nigga 'bout to get corrected." Chris flexed.

"I think you might wanna reconsider beefing with me over some bitch, dawg," Tyreke countered.

Chris flew in Tyreke's face. "Bitch? You's the bitch, nigga."

China cut Chris off. She was on the verge of tears. "Baby, pa-lease. It's okay, really. It's okay...He's not even the one. I made a mistake," China said, trying to salvage their lives. Chris lightly pushed China to the side.

"Naw, you didn't make a mistake. Check dis out, pretty boy...I got yo bitch right here," he yelled as he lifted up his shirt and exposed his pistol. The crowd that started to form pumped Chris's mouth full of words. He wasn't the "go toe to toe with you" type of cat. He allowed his mouth and trigger finger to fire the necessary lead in his opponent's ass. Hell, Chris wouldn't bust a grape.

"Ansean, ain't he the dude you was tellin' me about?"

Ansean played dumb. All he could do was shrug his shoulders and gaze at the ground. *Damn, Chris, why you gotta go there*! he thought. If anything, Ansean wanted to kick his own ass for telling Chris about Tyreke and his woman, D'mico.

"Imagine that! You can pay for another man's child to go to college, but you ain't half the man you claim to be." Chris turned around and laughed at the crowd. Then he turned back to Tyreke, who was beyond pissed. All Tyreke kept thinking was what's his point? *So what, nigga. You gonna funk or die? Fuck talking.*

"I'm a real man. A *real* man. Ain't that right, baby."

China looked away, not wanting to involve herself any further.

"I know one thing. My woman wouldn't be at no abortion clinic." Chris smirked, allowing his words to touch a place every man hated to expose. Everyone's jaws dropped. All that could be heard was the sound of Tyreke's bag hitting the cold pavement. Without warning, Tyreke charged at Chris.

Ansean almost saturated his pants when Dirt's car door flew open and out came Dirt holding on to a black trash bag. His 5'4" frame rushed through the small crowd. He knocked Tyreke out the way, struck Chris like a bolt of lightening, and commenced to whoop his ass. Ansean was scared senseless. Knowing what was in the bag, he pulled out and fired his burner in an attempt to save his brother.

POP!

Screams came from every direction. People scrambled and trampled over each other in an effort to leave. Damu maneuvered to the other side of the parking lot, leaping over cars and shoving people out of the way.

POP! POP!

The sound of gunfire accelerated his pace to full capacity. Within seconds, Damu stood in front of China's lifeless body. Her eyes stared up at the midnight sky. One arm extended outward while the other rested over her midsection.

Damu took slow steps as he lowered his gun. His heart plunged in his chest. *Fuck.*

"Nah, man...Nah...Not my nigga," he mumbled, kicking over the *QuikTrip* bag. It wasn't the sight of China's dead corpse that made him catch a few tears; It was the sight of his best friend, Dirt, who had taken a shot to the side of his head. Looking down at his body made everything seem like one big dream.

Eeeerrrk.

The sound of screeching tires had him on alert once again. He fired several shots at the black Lexus, hitting the side-view mirror, bumper and back window. Miraculously, Ansean and Chris got away.

Emptiness made its way into the pit of Tyreke's soul.

"Somebody call a fuckin' ambulance!" The words echoed in the parking lot. Dirt had the same look Betty had before she died. Fear. This time it wasn't accidental; it was intentional, and Tyreke was on the receiving end, cradling Dirt in his lap.

"Come on, Dirt. Fight," he coached, applying pressure to the hole in his head. Even though Dirt's eyes were closed, he could still hear the panic in Tyreke's voice. He wanted to tell him not to cry. If he could do it over again, he would. That's what real G's do, right?

Dirt knew he wasn't going to make it. His body was already icy cold. Well, that's what it felt like on the inside. If only he could know his own fate. At least then he could've told his knucklehead, paper chasin' baby mama that he really did appreciate her for taking care of their seed while he was too busy taking care of the streets. Damn...the streets. A small tear trickled down the corner of Dirt's left eye. Regret is for suckas who consciously step over their own toes. Dirt didn't regret the bullet he'd just taken to the side of his head. He just wished he could've taken it at a later time. But unfortunately, his time was done. Darkness flooded his mind as his life flashed before his eyes in quick spurts. There was his pops who was doing a life sentence behind the walls. Many times Dirt's father, Monte, tried to warn him that living the life of a thug only provided an unpredictable future. As a matter of fact, Monte was a perfect example. There was no future.

The rise and fall in Dirt's chest slowed to a minimum. Dirt saw his son. He remembered the first day he was born into this unjust world. The cries that escaped from his tiny lips gave him the initiative to grind harder. He burned his feet in the streets in order to provide for his baby mom and little dude. Now look. At the age of three, he would grow up with many barriers before him, struggling to keep up in the world as just another black man without a father, another statistic. Maybe he would overcome this obstacle. Then again, maybe not. Whatever the outcome, Dirt would never know. Last of all, Dirt saw Tyreke—a person who undeniably shared a place in his heart with his son and father. Dirt smiled partially before he stopped breathing altogether. He slipped into a world where only God welcomed or rejected.

* * * *

Because Tyreke had the Chief of Police on his side, he endured only a couple hours of questioning before he was cleared of all charges involving the murders of China and Dirt. He stuck to the code and kept his mouth closed about Ansean and Chris. It didn't matter that they got away because Tyreke had already decided to take their lives into his own hands. Meanwhile, the cops were still trying to figure out why they were unsuccessful at recovering the shell casings from the slugs found in China's body. Dozens of other unsolved cases fit the same profile, but without any leads, they had nothing to go on. Tyreke grabbed his property that the detectives recovered during questioning, slipped on his watch, rubbed his red eyes and stepped out the East Side precinct into the open air. D'mico had a lot of explaining to do.

* * * *

D'mico woke up to Tyreke towering over her hospital bed. His chestnut eyes burned with fury as he yanked her up.

"You knew you was pregnant, didn't you? Bitch, you tried to get an abortion? Answer me," Tyreke seethed, shaking D'mico by the shoulders, not giving her a chance to answer.

D'mico tried to cover her eyes in shame, but she couldn't because of the way Tyreke had his hands around her. Any minute now he was going to cause her to pass out as he shook her to death. Just when she thought she was about to throw up, Tyreke dropped her like filthy laundry.

"Thought you was slick, didn't you? My muthafuckin' homeboy is lyin' in a body bag over your s'pose to be slick ass," Tyreke yelled, pacing the floor.

So many people had called his phone hoping to hear that the news about Dirt wasn't true. As much as Tyreke wanted it to be a lie, the realization that Dirt was gone forever was as real as the situation before him; D'mico knowingly and secretly tried to kill his seed.

"Answer the question. Did you know you was pregnant?" D'mico shook her head and looked away.

"Yes...I did."

"What? Oh you did? Look at me." Tyreke twisted D'mico's chin, causing her neck to make a popping noise. She met his gaze. "You hated me that much? What did I do or what didn't I do?" Tyreke smashed the wall above D'mico's head, making her jump. "If shit was that bad, why didn't you just leave? Why did you wait till you was three months to try to get rid of a baby we planned for years."

"Three months?" D'mico was a little confused.

"Yeah, three months. Bitch, you good as hell at actin' dumb."

"First of all, Tyreke, this is a hospital, and you need to calm down. I wasn't three months neither, and if you wasn't busy cheatin' on me rather than lovin' me, you would've known what was goin' on. So fuck you!" D'mico cried, letting her hospital gown soak up her tears.

"Cheatin' on you? Oh, so now you're the victim? Miss me with that shit. How many times do I have to tell you that I'm not fuckin' with another bitch? Fuck it...You wanna know the truth? Well, here it is. Yeah, I fucked a few bitches here and there throughout our relationship. I was young when I met you, and I didn't know if I was missing out on other things, but I got all of that shit out of my system. Was I wrong? Hell yeah I was, but what can I say? I did it and it's done with. Been behind me for two fuckin' years. You want to know what got my time? You and my future, that's what." Tyreke slammed his hand into his chest to show how much he was hurt. "I been taking chances out there tryin' to establish a future and family with your silly ass. And for what? For you to go behind my fuckin' back? Guess I ran out of time...Wasn't quick enough for you, was I?"

D'mico didn't know how to respond. She was crushed beyond belief. Where was the hole she could crawl into, because right now, she wanted to get away.

"Now that that's out there, let's talk about why the doctor told me you was three and a half months. Explain that shit!" Tyreke fumed.

D'mico pushed herself off the fluffy pillow that supported her back.

"Ty, three and a half months ago I wasn't—" D'mico paused mid-sentence. All of the color drained from her beautiful face. What she really wanted to say was that there was no way she could've been three and a half months pregnant because three and a half months ago she wasn't fuckin' Chauncey. Oh no. All of a sudden, D'mico felt nauseous when she realized that all along she was pregnant with Tyreke's child. Although in the past few months she went from a size five in jeans to a size seven, she never thought twice about it. She figured the extra weight came from eating out all the time. Not to mention, she didn't work out like she use to. She hadn't felt like doing much of anything lately besides sleeping and fucking. On top of that, her period came regularly until a few weeks ago. Damn, Damn, Damn...

The award for "trifling bitch" definitely belonged to her. There were a lot of emotions going on inside the room, and Tyreke's silence and eyes full of tears spoke many words. Feeling like D'mico had pulled a curtain over his eyes, Tyreke slumped down in the brown chair positioned in front of a small oak table. He peered out the window overlooking the parking lot and wondered how and when shit got to be so fucked up. Death wasn't shit to him. People died every day. The same fate would come to him one day, but having two major losses like this in one day was unreal. *Why you take my bullet, Dirt? You had a fuckin' son.* Finding out about D'mico's sneaky ways disturbed him too. Whether or not she was responsible for taking the life of his seed was a question he didn't want the answer to. He loved D'mico and would die for her if he had to, but if she played a part in the death of his kid, he would do something to her. Something he would never regret.

Tyreke's Samsung vibrating against his waist broke his train of thought. Wiping away his tears, he took a deep breath, unclipped his phone and observed the number. He dragged his tired eyes towards D'mico, who had the look of pain in her hazel eyes. Instead of answering the call, he threw his cell on the table and closed his eyes.

"You could've answered. Was she one of the ones you fucked two years ago?" D'mico asked sarcastically. D'mico believed that the person who called Tyreke's phone was someone he was messing around with. Little did she know, it was the complete opposite.

"You know what, you're really startin' to piss me off," Tyreke mumbled, opening up his eyes. He turned to face D'mico, who had a murderous look on her face. "Did you hear anything I said earlier, or are you so selfish that you think everything revolves and rotates around yo silly ass? The female who called is probably throwin' a fit wonderin' why her damn baby daddy ain't gon be comin' home anymore."

D'mico's jaw hit the floor. "What are you talkin' about?"

"I'm talkin' about Dirt. He's dead, D'mico. Got killed a few hours ago by Ansean. The same nigga who seen you at the abortion clinic. How'd you think I found out?"

Dirt is dead? D'mico felt dizzy and sick all at the same time.

"Tyreke I-I didn't know." D'mico got up from her hospital bed and forced her body onto his. She needed him to know that she cared. She wasn't the selfish bitch he said she was. She cared. She liked Dirt, and she knew that Tyreke loved Dirt like a brother. Damn, Dirt was gone. Tyreke's mind raced as he thought back to what happened hours ago. More than anything, he wanted Ansean's head. His and his brother's.

D'mico looked into Tyreke's rich brown eyes. She reached up and pecked his salty lips and kissed the tears as they escaped his swollen eyes. As much as Tyreke wanted to push D'mico away, his heart needed her touch. The warmth of her body felt so good, a feeling that he'd been deprived of for months. He devoured the sweet taste of her tongue. Both of them knew that they had a lot of open wounds that needed healing. But for now, holding and kissing one another would be a good start.

Chapter 8

Two knocks with no answer was all Matt needed before he got antsy enough and tried the door handle to his partner's house. With one twist and a turn, the door eased open with no problem. Once inside, an eerie feeling swept over Matt. Something wasn't right. He passed the kitchen into the living room.

"Anybody home ?" he called out, hitting the light switch.

As soon as the lights came on, he spotted Lonnie lying face down on his stomach. A pool of blood slowly seeped from under his body onto the carpet. A few feet from the hallway was an unknown white woman who appeared to be dead. Matt stalked around the room in disbelief, checking for pulses. There weren't any. After he checked their pulses, he stumbled across his missing gun. This is bad. Real bad.

He used the tail of his shirt to pick up the state-issued weapon, careful not to put his prints on it. *How did it get here? And who killed Lonnie? Maybe it was a break-in. The door was open, well not technically. Shit! My prints are on the door. Yeah, this is real bad.*

Okay, okay, this wasn't a good time to panic. All he had to do was wipe off his prints, put the gun in his car and then dial 911. Matt rushed for the door.

"FREEZE! Drop your weapon and put your hands in the air."

Matt almost shit himself. This couldn't be happening. It just couldn't. He dropped the gun and turned around so slow that it seemed like it took him hours to face the swarm of police officers standing outside the door with their guns drawn.

This was no longer bad. This was fucked up.

"I'm a cop. Look, I'm going to reach for my badge." Matt tried to reason with them, reaching inside his jacket.

"No! Don't move or I'll shoot. Put your hands where we can see 'em," the officer in front yelled.

The saying "At the wrong place at the wrong time" echoed inside of Matt's head as he eased his hands in the air. Within minutes, Matt was tackled, cuffed and placed inside a patrol car.

* * * *

A whole year had gone by, and D'mico still couldn't get over the fact that her son was missing or worse, dead. She sat Indian style on the canopy bed watching the highlights of Matt's case on court TV. The jury just delivered the guilty verdict. Matt dragged his weary eyes towards a light-skinned woman with soft features and high cheekbones. Disbelief outlined her face as she mouthed the words "I love you" while Matt got carted off by two bailiffs. A teenage boy stood next to the woman. He simultaneously rubbed her backside while he whispered a few words of his own into her ear. D'mico broke down and cried into her hands. The trial was finally over.

The lights suddenly switched on, and D'mico looked

up. Tyreke stood in front of the television, blocking D'mico's view.

"Excuse you. I was watching that," D'mico said, hiding her tears.

"I know you was, shorty, but you been in this room for forever. The world needs your sunshine. Sooner or later, I'ma have to hose you down just to get you to bathe," Tyreke joked, trying to lighten the mood.

"I was watchin' that." D'mico was unfazed by Tyreke's sarcasm.

Tyreke took a seat next to D'mico. The smell of his cologne clung to her nostrils, making it hard for her to continue on with her grief. When he took her hand into his, she released her pain.

"Do you know that he would be one year old today? Why did they have to sentence that muthafucka on my baby's birthday? Why, Tyreke? Why is God punishing me?"

The only thing Tyreke could offer D'mico was his time and comfort. Sometimes in a situation like this, it's best to listen to another person's issues instead of responding. Tyreke didn't know if D'mico had a close relationship with God. He knew that he didn't; therefore, he didn't want to answer any religious questions. He was there to build her up not take away whatever faith she had left. That wasn't his style. He knew that Santy'ya's birthday was today; that's why he didn't want her listening to what the media had to say. He was glad when she decided not to go to Matt's sentencing. In a fucked up way, he wished he didn't remember Santy'ya. I know what you're thinking. However, I'm just being honest. To him, he lost a child. He was still haunted by that day when Santy'ya went missing. D'mico was a young, beautiful woman with a load of heartache, and he had no way of relieving her of her emotional distress. Two people died by his hands from her pain, and he didn't regret it one bit.

D'mico never found out that it was Tyreke who killed Lonnie and Betty. All she knew was what the media reported. A few months back, she went to old Lady Sandra's house, and the place was empty. She figured that social services and the police caught wind of her illegal acts and locked her up. Oh well...just another dead end.

Tyreke looked into D'mico's desolate eyes. She had a hidden look on her face that he couldn't read, a combination of passive withdrawal and sorrow.

D'mico broke eye contact and looked down at her thighs. *I'll bet he thinks I'm a pitiful chick*! she thought, putting her self down for the hundredth time since she'd been in his presence.

Tyreke dropped her hand and cupped her chin, lifting it so that she could meet his eyes. Beauty is all he saw. Beauty and a lack of self-esteem.

"Look, I'm in no position to tell you not to grieve over your child. I might not show it, but I'm hurtin' like crazy too." He guided her hand over his beating heart. "He'll always be in a place where there's love and energy." He then placed his large hand, along with D'mico's, on her chest near her heart. "Nobody can take that away. Not you. Not me. Nobody. You hear me?" D'mico released her hand and covered her eyes to cry.

"Cry. Let it out and then…You know what? Come on. Get up. You fixin' ta roll wit' me?" Tyreke urged.

D'mico uncovered her face. "What?"

"You gon release some of this. Being in this house all day gonna turn your pretty face sour. You gonna kill yourself with grief. Now what good would that do for lil man when he comes home?" Tyreke exhaled sharply. "I never thought I'd be sounding like my pops, but you gotta allow your higher power to see you through the storm. This is a minor setback. It's not permanent. Come on. Get up!" he insisted, keeping hope alive.

D'mico gathered herself together and wiped away her tears. Tyreke was such a supportive person. She wished there was a way to pay him back. Tyreke smiled. He reached out his hands and pulled D'mico in for a hug.

"Can I have a hug?"

D'mico smiled back. She didn't mind his scent on her. Actually, she wanted to wear the scent that came with a little sweating and panting. However, a hug sounded nice.

"Sure," she agreed.

Tyreke wrapped his stout arms around D'mico. He meshed his hard body against her thick frame until she was satisfied.

"You good?" he asked, pulling away. D'mico nodded yes.

"Good 'cause I still wanna take you somewhere. You down?"

Feeling self-conscious about her appearance, D'mico ran her hands through her wild hair, which felt like an old, raggedy mop. She looked towards the mirror at her imperfect reflection. She looked just like how she felt. Like shit.

"Don't even trip. You still a dollar piece plus fifty cents. You're beautiful," Tyreke insisted.

D'mico's heart fluttered. Tyreke was like her knight in shinning armor. He gave her the motivation that she needed in order to pick herself up, dust off the bad, and be strong for herself and her son.

* * * *

There were no words spoken in Tyreke's Chevy 1500, just the strong melody of Jaheim expressing the love and passion he had for the lucky woman that he would go far and beyond for.

D'mico shifted in the passenger seat uncomfortably. When a man played certain songs in the presence of a woman, it normally meant that that was the way he felt about her. D'mico wanted to believe that Tyreke would give her anything like Jaheim's lyrics. She also wanted to believe that he was feeling her, because lord knows that she was feeling him.

Tyreke snuck a quick glance at D'mico. He was hoping that she caught on to his song choice.

When Jaheim's song ended, "Read Your Mind" by Avant played through the speakers, making the temperature in his truck rise from sexual tension. D'mico bit down on her bottom lip and let out a soft giggle. Her flirtatious eyes beamed at him as she laughed at what seemed to be nothing in particular.

"What? What's so funny?" Tyreke asked, smiling

from ear to ear. D'mico gave him her best smile, showing off her sexy dimples.

"So, what am I thinkin'?"

"I dunno whatchu talkin' about," Tyreke lied.

"You know. Tell me before I forget and start thinkin' about something else," she teased, looking into his eyes.

Damn she's gorgeous. Tyreke took his eyes off of D'mico and placed them on the road. He then turned onto a dirt road. "Let me tell you what I'm thinkin'."

D'mico hung onto his words. Her eyes narrowed as she spoke lustfully. "What's that?"

"We're here." He grinned, easing his shifter into park. D'mico flushed with embarrassment as she leaned her body in an upright position. Tyreke jumped out the truck and made his way to the passenger door. Whoever said that gangstas couldn't be gentlemen?

Tyreke massaged D'mico's hand as he helped her out of the truck.

Instantly D'mico's jaw dropped. "Wow! This is beautiful, Tyreke. How did you find this?" she exclaimed in awe, taking tiny steps around the landmark.

With her hand in his, Tyreke guided her to a large rock overlooking the city. They enjoyed the view that separated them from the rest of the city in silence. It was actually relaxing to watch the different range of activities going on beneath them. The view made D'mico feel like she was on top of the world, and there wasn't a man or woman alive who could reach her.

The afternoon breeze caressed her skin, causing her to scoot closer to Tyreke.

"I knew you would like this. I know I did when I first

came up here. Great minds think alike."

D'mico blushed. She lifted up her head and saw the serious expression plastered across his face. He was so perfect yet undeniably smooth. She had to admit that she was attracted to Tyreke. He was doing his thing too. He had grown exponentially within a year, financially as well as mentally. He'd purchased a small condo which she shared with him. However, they slept in separate rooms. He bought two vehicles—a car and a truck—and he barely stayed at home during the day but came home every night to check in and make sure that her needs were straight. D'mico didn't know what he did for a living, but she wasn't no dummy. She knew that whatever he was involved in had to be illegal. Although, he was well mannered and generous. D'mico would bet her soul that this mystery man came with a few long, tearful nights and heartache. In her mind, every man did.

"You know I really like you, D'mico, right? One day when you're ready, I would like for you to be my queen."

"Your queen, huh? Why not your girl or your woman?"

Tyreke was confused. D'mico's self-esteem had been so severely crushed that she couldn't see herself ranked above anyone else.

"If I called you anything other than that, I would be speaking in low regard."

"Sounds like you believe in fairy tales." She ran her hand through her shoulder-length hair and twisted it into a ponytail. "I don't believe in fairy tales. Those dreams died years ago," she said, catching feelings.

"You know what? You're right. Fairy tales are only

forms of manipulation, taking away a woman's right to be loved by a real man with no motive to gain. No man or woman deserves the right to be treated like a human being. Love is prosperity. Who would want that?" Tyreke concluded.

Sometimes Tyreke had a way with words that made people feel small. He wasn't trying to knock D'mico's beliefs, but the girl just didn't believe in love, and he knew that her past abuse was the cause.

D'mico looked deeper into Tyreke's eyes. What she saw in them were love and honesty. "All I'm sayin' is love hurts. Why waist your time with someone you've never slept with?"

"What don't kill me will only make me stronger. I want you," Tyreke said honestly. "D'mico, I know it's hard for you not to look at every man as a nasty pig, but lemme tell you somthin', baby girl. I'm not your average nigga. Pussy don't motivate me. Girl, if only you knew." He shook his head. "Wasting my time? Don't you know that the sweetest things come to those who wait?" he asked while staring her down. Too weak to speak, D'mico leaned her body forward. She stopped a couple of inches away from his lips and stared at their thickness. She wondered if they tasted anywhere near as good as they looked.

Tyreke couldn't hide the lust in his eyes. He knew he wasn't the only one fighting temptation because D'mico's wandering eyes stared at his lips like they were Salisbury steaks. Quenching her thirst, Tyreke moved closer and joined her lips with his.

Blackberry cobbler. He tastes like blackberry

cobbler, she thought when Tyreke connected his lips to hers. It seemed as though his heart was in sync with hers. The sound of their heartbeats thumped the same tune as their private parts. Tyreke guided her hand onto his growing erection. Trying to pry herself away from their lip-locking bliss, D'mico's fear of another man hurting her broke her desire to give it up to Tyreke.

"What's wrong?" Tyreke asked, confused as to why D'mico backed away from him.

D'mico glided her hand down the center of his chest as her lustful eyes traveled to his package. "I told you that love can hurt. Come on. Let's go," she insisted, walking to the truck.

What? What the fuck happened? Tyreke thought, looking down at the stiff bulge in his pants. It was then when he realized that D'mico was talking about his dick. After all, the stiffness in his pants proved her to be right. Love hurts like a muthafucka.

"Fuck!" he mumbled on his way to the truck.

Chapter 9

Time is fuckin' money, Tyreke thought as he stared lazily at a cat who went by the name of Black. Black was chatting frivolously about a whole lot of nothing. The last thing Tyreke could remember coming out of the nigga's mouth was the day and time he would come by to re-up. Everything after that deliberately got tuned the fuck out. What Tyreke really wanted to say to the nigga was, "Thank you for making me fifty-five stacks richer. Now shut up and get yo monkey lookin' ass out of my establishment so I can go invest this shit." But because of his people skills, Tyreke remained neutral, hoping that by constantly looking at his watch Black would get a hint that he had shit to do. Dirt's funeral was twenty-four hours away, and he still had some loose ends to tie up with Shayla, Dirt's baby mama.

"Yo, my nig', this is whassup," Black commented, admiring the inside of the 4,500 square foot building filled with punching bags, closed-in lockers, a weight room and a boxing ring that was settled in the middle of the physical education center. "You got a nice place here.

When are ya'll niggas gonna have your next tournament?" Black asked, climbing the three steps to the ring. He ducked under the rope and circled the ring while running his hand along the thick rope.

Chauncey twisted his face in a knot and glanced at his watch. *Do this nigga ever shut up?* he thought, throwing his head back in bewilderment. Gaining Tyreke's attention, Chauncey pointed to his watch indicating that they were going to be late for Tyreke's three o'clock appointment up town with the funeral director.

Tyreke returned the same disgruntled look, checked his watch and motioned for Damu to grab the bag of money next to his foot.

"Umm...I'm not too sure if we're gonna open back up, man. Dirt was the mastermind behind all of this. Openin' this place was a way to give back to the community and to his son. He always said that he wished that a boxing ring would've been available when he was growin' up. He wanted to give teens a place where they could blow off some steam and feel safe. Now that he's gone, I don't know what I want to do," Tyreke said.

Tyreke ducked under the rope and joined Black. "Word? I didn't know that nigga had a heart like that." Black swung his arms effortlessly at the air like he was in a match with an opponent. "Check dis out." He swung left and jabbed to the right. "If you thinkin' 'bout sellin', fuck with me." He stopped swinging and twirled around, looking at the many contents before his eyes. "Yo, son, I know this muthafucka would clock in some change, real shit. Plus, we can keep that nigga's memory alive, na mean?"

Tyreke gave some thought to the shit Black was spitting. Of all people, he should've been the one who wanted to keep his boy's memory alive. It shouldn't have been an outside nigga who only knew of Dirt through passing. Black's suggestion to keep the gym open whether Dirt was dead or alive was enough for Tyreke to reconsider his decision.

"Nah, I ain't sellin'. Me and the fellas will figure something out," Tyreke finally decided.

Black looked disappointed. Nevertheless, he knew that niggas like Tyreke didn't have the time nor the patience to babysit a boxing ring. Sooner or later, Tyreke would come around and sell. Most of the businesses he owned were from hustlers who were tired of doing one thing and antsy to find what they believed was their next niche. It happened all the time.

Bzzz...Bzzz...

Tyreke felt his cell phone vibrate against his hip. He turned his back to Black and answered.

"Yo."

"Hey, baby. The doctor just discharged me. He said that once he gets my papers, I can leave. I called mama to come and get me, but daddy said that she went to bingo," D'mico whined on the other end, referring to his parents as her own.

"Aight. Give me about twenty minutes and I'll be that way, alright?"

"Okay. I love you, Ty."

Silence.

"Tyreke, did you hear me? I said that I love you,"

D'mico pressed, annoyed that Tyreke wasn't responding to the way she felt about him. Truthfully, she expected him to return the gesture. Tyreke scanned his surroundings before answering.

"Youza trip. The longer I spend on this phone, the longer it's gonna take me to get to you." He grabbed his jacket and motioned for Black to follow. "Did the doctor say that he was prescribing anger management?"

"Cute. Change it up if you want to." D'mico looked up at the clock on the wall. "Mr. 'I can't tell my woman that I love her back,' I'll see you in seventeen minutes."

Tyreke chuckled. "You got problems. Whatever happened to my other three minutes? Since you getting all feisty an' shit, I s'pose I can make it in seventeen minutes."

D'mico gave in to Tyreke. However, she still was a little disappointed that he couldn't tell her that he loved her.

"Alright, I'll see you in a bit," she said.

"Boss lady?"

"Hmm?"

"I love you more than life itself," Tyreke expressed. D'mico smiled from ear to ear.

"Bye," she said.

"Bye." Tyreke hung up the phone.

"Wifey?" Black asked, eavesdropping.

Tyreke looked over his shoulder and answered proudly. "Yeah, you could say that."

Black smiled. "Must be nice. Eh, she got a single sister?"

* * * *

Once Black got inside his blue Jag and drove off, something about the atmosphere didn't sit well with Tyreke. His slanted eyes narrowed as he examined the area carefully.

It being daytime, it didn't take long for him to pinpoint what his conscience had already labeled as a threat. He stretched his arm out to its full length to stop his entourage.

"Hold up!" he called out, eyeing the suspicious car. "Who's shit is that?"

By that time, Damu had rotated the Gucci bag full of money to his other hand in an effort to have better access to his eagle. "I dunno, but we 'bout to find out," he informed.

Tyreke jerked his head in the direction of the car. "Chauncey, go check it out."

The grey El Camino with tinted windows parked across the street from Tyreke's establishment piqued everyone's curiosity. As far as Tyreke was concerned, it could have been Ansean trying to catch him slippin'. It was Sunday afternoon, and normally the only activity on his turf was from his squad. Not too many people crossed the line just to pass through for that very reason. And when they did, by the end of the day, they knew not to do it again. Tyreke made sure of that.

* * * *

Gene studied the door to the red brick building from the seat of his car. The continuous line of nice cars instilled a spark of envy. He had no money, and he was ready to get down with the get-down. From what he was told, his target was one of the most prominent niggas in the city, besides the Bamn crew. Shidd, he didn't give a fuck if the nigga was Obama. His only concerns were for *dineros* and the opportunities that brought him more *dineros*. After all, he was a nineteen-year-old young head with a hard dick to make a dollar.

Gene retrieved his Verizon mobile from his console, scanned the phone's contacts until he came upon the number he was looking for, and pressed the call button. He still had his eyes on the building when the squeaky automated answering machine delivered the news that the caller was unavailable. Frustrated as hell, he waited for the beep.

"Eh, man, I been up here for over an hour now, and dude don't look like he gon be coming out no time soon. If you changed up, you need to let me know what's up. Call me back, man. Aight then...It's on."

Click. Gene hung up.

"This nigga got me fucked up," he said out loud to himself, guzzling down the remainder of his lean. The mixture of Nehi peach and codeine had him feeling agitated and sleepy. A tingling sensation traveled through his scrotum, making him jump upward. Fighting the urge to go take a leak, he glanced at the building once more for reassurance. Thinking that he would only be gone a second, Gene placed his burner in his seat and slid out the car with ease.

* * * *

After Chauncey gave the signal indicating that no one was in the El Camino, he let out an extremely lengthy breath of air. Beads of sweat started to cascade down the side of his chocolate face as he made his way back across the street in distress.

* * * *

Gene whistled while spraying piss across his beat-up K-Swiss sneakers. In a rush, he shoved his tool back inside his pants and proceeded back to his car. As soon as he hit the side of the building, he realized this job just took a turn for the worse. He felt like 2Pac, *All Eyez on Me,* when a group of hungry, lurking men met his gaze. Feeling like a damn fool, Gene schemed his next move. If he hadn't been so damn dumb by leaving his piece in his car, he would've went out like that broad Cleo in the movie *Set It Off,* but this was some real life shit, and he had to think "reality."

Feeling like his back was against the wall, Gene did what any nigga in his current position would do. He ran.

All it took was a look on Tyreke's face, and his goons were on Gene like white on rice. Tyreke grabbed Chauncey by the arm before he took off.

"Bring dat lil nigga back to me," Tyreke instructed with authority in his voice. Unable to afford any losses, Chauncey was the first to be on Gene's heels.

Being a track star in high school was an advantage that Gene had over the niggas chasing him. The thrill of the chase caused adrenaline to pump at full speed. Every time he cut a corner or dodged them, he gave their asses a taste of the pavement. He ran like his life depended on it. And in all actuality, it did.

Gene thought back to the day he won the National Championship. The pressure of being number one had his coach on edge. He remembered the speech given moments before the race.

"Son, you got the speed everybody lookin' for. Don't look back. You're already ahead. Just run."

Fighting the burning in his chest, Gene jumped over a four-foot fence, landing on both feet. He ran with excessive speed, hitting another corner. It was then when he realized that being broke could even cripple a strong, healthy man like himself. His two-year-old, red and white K-Swiss sneakers blew out as he fell to the ground. Suddenly, it felt as if hot coals scorched the undersides of his feet. Picking himself up, he figured he lost his pursuers because he no longer heard the sound of feet behind him. The nigga who hired him did a good job schooling him on what route to take if some crazy shit popped off. And boy was he glad that he was able to get away. Just for the hell of it, he looked over his shoulder. Not one soul was in sight. Smiling from ear to ear, feeling like a champion again, he slowed his pace and examined his torn sneakers.

The ominous sound of a cocked gun clicked in his ear.

Reluctantly, Gene turned around. Instantly he relaxed

every muscle in his body when he saw the familiar face.

"Damn, nigga, don't be creepin' on me like that," Gene said, returning his attention back to his busted shoes.

He laced his shoe strings, brushed himself off and stuck out his foot. "Man, why you still pointing that muthafucka at me. Put dat bitch away and look at my shoes. I'm gonna need full compensation for these." He changed the subject. "Eh, nigga, did you see dem fools? I was ghost on they asses."

Chauncey looked over his shoulders nervously, making sure no one would hear or witness what he was about to do.

As far as he was concerned, Gene fucked up. All he had to do was stay in his raggedy shit until Tyreke came out, follow him as long as need be to his stash spot, and relinquish the nigga's whereabouts. What was so hard about that? Consequently, relying on Gene to push his course could've resulted in the both of them being screwed. Sadly, the only one being fucked and rocked to sleep today would be Gene. Either way, he had to go.

Chauncey pointed the gun at Gene's chest.

"The only thing you gon need is a three-piece suit."

"What?" Gene balled up his fists. "Come on, Chauncey. I'm goin' to get shit done, man. Trust me." Chauncey moved closer.

"Nigga, I don't even trust myself." Then Chauncey let off a single shot.

POP!

Gene's eyes widened to the size of golf balls. He used his hands to shield his body before he crashed to the ground. Not that it did him any good.

Seconds later, Damu hit the corner. His mouth hung open in shock when he saw what Chauncey had done. Smoke was still coming out of his pistol when he tucked it in his denim jeans.

"What da fuck you shoot him for?" asked Damu.

"Either it was him or me."

Chauncey thought about putting a hot one in Damu, but thought against it.

"Look, we need to bounce—"

"Fool! Ty said to bring him back. How we gon find out why he was snoopin' around if you killed him?"

Not giving a fuck, Chauncey pumped another piece of lead into Gene's face, just to be on the safe side.

"The nigga said that Ansean sent him. Unless you plan on goin' to jail, we need to shake this spot."

Skeptical, Damu peered down at the dead body. He found it hard to believe that Ansean hired someone to kill Tyreke. Everybody in the hood knew that Ansean wasn't workin' with no major paper. Dude was barely making it before the Dirt incident. Broke niggas either run into or run away from messy situations. Chauncey was too determined to put an end to whoever this nigga was. Chauncey reeked of deception. His odor was so horrible that in due time it would surface, and when it did, Damu wanted to be the one to get rid of his smell.

* * * *

Tyreke pulled up at the hospital two hours later than his expected time. He knew that D'mico would be mad because he was so late, but a lot of shit was going on, and he didn't have the time or the patience for loose cannonballs. Anxiously, he watched through the glass window as a nurse wheeled D'mico down the corridor. He would have done it himself, but the hospital said that it was procedure for all discharged patients to be escorted to their respective vehicles.

Damu immediately moved from the passenger seat to the backseat out of respect. He tried to put aside Chauncey's uncanny behavior, but unfortunately, he couldn't. Something had to be said.

"How do you feel about the way Chauncey handled things back there?" Damu spoke up.

"Whatchu mean?" Tyreke inquired with his eyes on D'mico and the nurse.

"That shit he did was foul, Ty. He the only one claimin' that he didn't hear you when you looked that nigga dead in the face before you said it. I think you was wrong about that nigga. Ty, he ain't right."

Tyreke turned his head partly towards the backseat. "No matter how we look at it, Chauncey did us all a favor. Stacey sent that El Camino to the chop shop, and he said that lil nigga had a burner in the front seat. Ansean and his punk-ass brother got me fucked up. I hear whatchu sayin' 'bout the nigga, but what's done is done."

"So you think Ansean sent him?" Damu asked, wishing Tyreke would see the big picture.

"You damn right. Who else would it be?" Tyreke said defensively.

Damu leaned against the back of the passenger seat.

Wake up, Tyreke. Wake up, nigga, before you end up

getting us all killed. Damu thought.

"On your turf in broad daylight? Come on now. We're talkin' about Ansean, right? The same nigga who can't give you, me, or anybody else with a dick eye contact? We talkin' 'bout him, right?" Damu paused for a second. "All I'm sayin' is that it don't look right. It's fishy. Everything I learned from you and Dirt tells me different. We have to think ahead of our enemies. Ain't that what you said when we bumped heads with those Louisiana cats? If it wasn't for you thinking ahead, it would've been Dirt burying us, not us burying Dirt. I just think that Ansean—"

"That Ansean what? You don't think Ansean gave that dusty-ass nigga a couple hundred dollars to get rid of me? I bet you didn't think Ansean would've blown my nigga's cap right in front of our fuckin' faces neither. It's a lot of fuckin' thinkin' going on. Either you think you on my side or you not."

Damu let out a breath of frustration and threw himself back into his seat. Tyreke was trippin' for real. "Ty, you know me better than that. This ain't about sides."

"Oh yeah? Well something is on your mind. Either spit it out now or hold your peace because when D'mico gets into this muthafuckin' car, I don't wanna hear nothin' else about it," Tyreke spat.

Damu bit his tongue. He'd been in the game long enough to know that he had to step back and let Tyreke handle this one, even if he had love for the nigga. Damn, it was as though Tyreke was holding some kind of guilt related to Chauncey, giving the nigga one too many pikepasses. Whatever happened to his eye for bullshit?

Tyreke fell back in his seat and brushed the bridge of his nose. The past couple of days seemed like a nightmare to him, and he wished things to be normal again. In the world he lived in, that type of shit just didn't happen. Damu was shooting out some good advice about thinking ahead of your enemy. Shidd, he was the one who drilled that shit into his crews' head. Because of that, they were able to make more money and remain untouched. Checking out the nigga who was sent to lay him to rest wouldn't be hard. He had the best syndicate of niggas, and they had the means to find the kid's identity and anything else connected to the dude. After the funeral though.

"Yo, Moo? You my nigga, and I know you just lookin' out for the kid. I'ma check on that dude who was snooping around and see what's up, aight?"

Damu grinned. He leaned forward and connected knuckles to knuckles with Tyreke. "All love, my nigga." Quickly, Tyreke jumped out the car to help with D'mico's belongings.

Damu observed Tyreke and the way he reacted to D'mico. His demeanor and body language belonged to a man so different than the nigga he was on the streets. It was almost as though the streets vanished when she basked in his presence. D'mico was a beauty, no doubt. However, the way Tyreke sweated this woman could be deadly. Her skin was flawless like a ripe, golden apple. Even with her hair neglected and pulled back into a ponytail, she still held the qualities of a dime piece. She was the kind of fine that looked better without makeup.

Hiding her beauty behind shades of blush, eyeliner and lipstick would be a waste. The hot sun beamed sandy brown highlights on top of her hair, and specks of jade gleamed around the edges of her hazel eyes. Damn, it almost seemed impossible, but Damu managed to break his stare away from D'mico's soft face.

* * * *

Thanks to Chris keeping in touch with a chick by the name of Cresha while he was locked up, Ansean had a place to shack up. Although Chris decided to stay elsewhere, Ansean was good as safe in the small, one-bedroom apartment on 4th and Harvard St. Ansean stopped pacing the dingy carpet and took a look around. Cresha's taste in decor was far from cozy or lavish. There were sheets covering every window where there should have been curtains, two mismatched sofas seated opposite from another, and a lamp with no bulb for light. Nevertheless, this was home for Ansean.

Cresha entered the apartment carrying a Warehouse Market bag. She briskly walked past Ansean into her closet-sized kitchen. Immediately, Ansean noticed the unwanted look on Cresha's face, so he followed her into the kitchen.

"What's up, Cresha?" Ansean asked, trying to make conversation.

Cresha placed the bag on the counter along with her keys and turned around. She looked at Ansean from his head to his toes. "Not a damn thing," she responded dryly, turning back around.

Ansean scratched the top of his head. He stared at Cresha's back before walking off to the living room where he plopped down on the mismatched couch. His head slowly fell into his hands. He was filled with dread at the thought of Tyreke finding him, and at the rate he was going, it wouldn't be long before he caught up with the devil. He went from living like a prince to hiding in a roach infested apartment with a chick who was mad because he wouldn't fuck her. Chris told him that all he had to do to keep Cresha happy was to dick the bitch down real good, but every time Ansean attempted to fuck her, his dick wouldn't agree with the girl's face and body. It was crazy. She was six inches taller than Ansean's five feet nine inches, and she had a serious muffin top. To Ansean, Cresha resembled a busted condom. So it didn't surprise him that Cresha was beginning to act like she was working up the nerve to tell him to leave.

This was a time in Ansean's life when he wished that he could think with the head below his waist. In the meantime, little man wasn't budging.

Too bad for Ansean.

* * * *

D'mico strapped on her seat belt and crossed her arms over her breasts. Like an angry child who didn't get her way, she stuck out her bottom lip and peered out the window.

Tyreke wasn't a few minutes late from picking her up; he was hours late. The ultimate disrespect.

Tyreke glanced at D'mico. He could tell that she was angry. Any minute now he expected her to throw a fit. Although he arrived at the hospital late, D'mico needed to understand that stumbling blocks could emerge at any given time. If he hadn't taken his time, he might not be sitting next to her. As much as he wanted to give her an explanation as to why he was late, he couldn't. He never involved her or stressed her out about his problems. Therefore, her only option was to trust him.

After getting a good distance from the hospital, D'mico broke the silence. "Ty, I know you're a very busy man but don't eva be late picking me up again, or it's going to be yo ass, Mr. Postman," she said, cutting her eyes at Tyreke. She turned around to face Damu. "It'll be both of ya'll's asses."

Damu shrunk in his seat while holding his hand to his chest. "Who me?"

"Yeah, you. You and him." D'mico smiled, reaching over to pinch Tyreke's arm.

"Ouch...Why you pinch me? Pinch Damu. He was late too," Tyreke yelled with his hand still on the wheel. He leaned over and landed a wet kiss on D'mico's cheek. "Sorry, baby. It won't happen again," he whispered against her warm skin.

D'mico's face softened and her heart melted. Instantly her anger disappeared into thin air, and Angela Winbush's song "Angel" took over the mood. "Love is Great" were her thoughts as she cranked up the volume.

* * * *

Tyreke had fifty G's in his possession that needed to be put up. He just dropped Damu off, and he anticipated on doing the same thing with D'mico, but he suddenly had a change of heart when he looked towards the passenger seat and found her sound asleep. Doubt hung over his head like a grey cloud of smoke. Nevertheless, the need to stash away his unmarked bills led him to his stash spot.

It was no secret that chicks were hoodwinking niggas more often than usual. You had your good apples and your bad apples. Tyreke didn't know where his woman fit. So, the possibility of his woman being a rotten apple could destroy his future. Who knows. Only time would tell.

Before getting out the car, Tyreke found himself watching the rise and fall of D'mico's chest. Quietly, he grabbed his money bag out the stash box built into his floor panel, grabbed and tucked his pistol in his waistband and darted off in the direction of his stash house.

Moments later, D'mico woke up to find Tyreke gone and the car still running. She sat up straight and wiped the loose drool from the corner of her mouth.

How long was I sleep? she questioned herself, looking around. When she came to the realization that she was at Tyreke's father's church, immediately questions were doing laps inside her head. Tyreke hated churches. The man didn't even make exceptions to attend his father's services. So why were they here? There were no parked cars in the lot, just his. So what was really going on? If it weren't for the fact that D'mico knew Tyreke had a strong aversion for churches, D'mico would've thought nothing of her being left alone to sleep in the car. However, her gut told her that something was definitely up.

Minutes later, Tyreke came out the building with a dirty looking bag.

Finding Tyreke's behavior suspect, D'mico reclined in her seat, closed her eyes and played sleep.

Perfect timing, Tyreke thought as he slowly slid into the driver's seat. D'mico was still asleep. Quietly he placed his burner along with the empty bag in his stash box and drove out of the church parking lot.

With her eyes closed shut, red lights went off in D'mico's head when she discovered that Tyreke had been using his father's church to stash his illegal money and drugs. Never in a million years would she have thought his stash spot would be there of all places. Was Tyreke fuckin' crazy? His father would put down his Bible and kick the living shit out of him if he knew Tyreke was threatening the safety of the community.

Ironically, D'mico wanted to hold Tyreke's secret. It was time for her to boss up and take ownership of her "rider rank." After all, it was the least she could do after the trifling shit she'd done with their baby.

Chapter 10

Tyreke stood back from the lengthy floor mirror and examined himself. Any other day, he would've thanked Mitch, his tailor, for making him look like a fly-ass nigga fresh off the front cover of *Jet Magazine.*

Unfortunately, today wasn't the day to be throwing out props. Today was Dirt's funeral. In less than two hours, he would be saying good-bye to the realist nigga known to man. Damn, life can be fucked up at times.

* * * *

An overweight man wearing the fuck out of a white polo vest over a button-up long sleeve sung the hymn to "Gangster Lean" by D.R.S. He lured everyone to their respective seats where they cried mournfully while gripping the seven-page obituary made and designed to look like a mini book. Dirt was loved by many and hated by few, despite his lifestyle. Shayla, Dirt's baby mama, sat quietly on the family bench in utter shock with a Kleenex in her hand.

It was no secret that the two were still having sex before the day of his demise. Shayla knew that Starlet was his new roni, but she didn't care. She loved her baby daddy. There wasn't a man on Earth who could complete her the way he did. Many times she used money as a means to spend time with him. All it took was for her to say that their son was in need, and without a doubt, he came running. More than anything she wanted to be with him, but his relationship with the streets and continuous cheating habits led her astray. One day, she figured that Dirt would come around and leave his fast life behind, but that day would never come. Dirt left the streets behind like everyone else she knew, including her brother Rat. They left in a body bag. Shayla looked towards her son. She lifted the Kleenex to her nose as she cried softly.

Dirt's mini-me looked like a little man in his two-piece suit. His mahogany eyes and butterscotch skin were the spitting image of his father. He sat obediently in Tyreke's lap with eyes full of tears. Too young to understand his emotions, the tears he worked up were a response to the many tears his mother shed. He clung onto Uncle Tyreke tightly as his curious eyes stayed glued to his father. His daddy was sleep.

D'mico stared at the star etched in Dirt's son's hair. She had to concentrate on something else rather than his tears, so she focused on his haircut. Watching him reminded her of all her past failures and regrets. She wondered over the years how her son looked. Was he alive or was he dead? If he was alive, did he think about her as much as she thought about him? The unknown seemed so gut-wrenching that it started to eat away at her soul. After staring at Dirt's son for ten long minutes, she studied Tyreke. Tyreke had been wanting children for years.

Yes, she deprived him of that, but it wasn't intentional. She made a bad call. That's all. At least that's the bullshit she fed herself every day. Chauncey was a bad call too. For three months she gave her body to him freely whenever and however he wanted, and not once did he attempt to call or stop by the hospital to check on her. He played her like the fool she was, putting her in a category of unimportance. That's okay because from this point on, anything she had with Chauncey in the past was done. He was a tragic mistake that she was ready to recover from. She just had a bad feeling that things wouldn't be that easy. D'mico scanned the packed church and spotted Chauncey sitting on the opposite side three rows from the pulpit. A corny smile appeared on his lips when they fixed eyes on one another. He'd been watching D'mico from the moment she stepped foot inside the church. With her upper lip curled up in disgust, D'mico rolled her eyes, adjusted her blouse and turned around.

With a few minutes to spare before Reverend Johnson delivered his eulogy, D'mico excused herself to get a drink of water and some fresh air.

Two rows from the exit door, she spotted Leslie and her bourgeois-ass friends, along with a crying Starlet, dressed like they were attending a concert rather than a funeral. D'mico stuck her nose in the air like she didn't see them and continued out the door.

* * * *

Bang! Bang! Bang!

Ansean tensed up from the sound of pounding on the front door. He put down his bowl of Cookie Crisp, got up from the couch and made his way to the door. He glanced through the peephole. No longer hesitant, he removed the multiple bolts and chains that kept intruders out and opened the door.

"What's good, ba-bee! Here, I brought you some clothes," Chris said, handing Ansean a GQ bag.

Ansean accepted the bag. "Thanks."

"No problem. You need it. You look like you mournin' the nigga's death. You know his funeral is today, don't chu?"

Ansean ran his free hand through his kinky dreads. "Yeah, I know. I seen it in the paper," Ansean responded dryly, returning to his bowl of cereal. Chris observed the pallet laid out in front of the twenty-seven-inch television set.

"Eh, is you hittin' that bitch off like I told you?"

Ansean balled up his face in total disgust. There was no way he was fucking a bitch who favored Craig Mack.

"Hell no. Man, I'm cool on all that. I'm not sleepin' with her. Her body look like a saggin' diaper." Ansean got up with his bowl of cereal and went into the kitchen. Chris followed.

"Whatchu mean you ain't gonna fuck with her? Nigga, don'tchu know that that bitch will get tired of you being here? I didn't say fall in love with the trick; I said to serve her."

Ansean shrugged his shoulders while adding a drip of Dawn liquid soap to the bowl.

"I ain't gon be able to do it."

Chris felt like Ansean was being ungrateful. He'd lined Ansean up with one of the bitches who held him down while he was in the joint, and Ansean took his kindness and kicked it to the curb. Chris knew what it took to make Cresha happy because not too long ago, before he was able to stand on his own feet, he was faced with the dilemma to either fuck or go. In Ansean's case, he was in no position to say what he didn't want to do.

"So what do you plan on doing, Ansean? You gonna hide out in this shitty-ass apartment until you feel like the big bad wolf ain't lookin' for you no more, or are you gonna get out and come get you some of this?" Chris stood over Ansean and flashed a wad of cash in his face, making sure he got an eye full of the crisp C-notes piled on top. Ansean exhaled, rinsed the bowl and placed it on the towel used as a drying rack.

"It's not that easy. Look, man," Ansean turned around, "shit ain't how it use to be years ago, aight? I use to work for Tyreke, and I know how he get down. I'm just tryin' to survive."

Chris waved off Ansean's words. "Aah, fuck that nigga. He ain't tryna see these hands."

"Do you think this shit is a game, Chris? Nigga, you need to wake the fuck up and grow the fuck up. None of this shit would've happened if you hadn't..." Ansean shook his head. "You know what...Nothin'. You just don't get it," he said, walking to the living room.

"As a matter of fact, I do get it. You're right about one thing; you went from having heart to being a scary-ass bitch. I didn't spend years locked behind bars and get out to be running from one nigga who think he's runnin' the streets. I been making money freely on his grounds, so you tell me whose king?"

"Nigga, don't you know that he's just waitin' for the

funeral to be over? That's how he operates. He don't disrespect the dead. After today, everything you think you gettin' away with…" Ansean's bottom lip quivered from the thought of what Tyreke would do. He worked in his slaughter house, and he'd seen some gruesome things. "You can hang it up, Chris."

Chris looked at Ansean with downcast eyes. "Who are you? You're worse than these muthafuckas on the streets. There's no way in the world we share the same blood. You're a disappointment to our mother and to our dead father, nigga. You go ahead and hide in this nasty mu'fucka, and since you got this nigga down to a science, you need to try and get Cresha down with you 'cause sooner or later, she gon get tired of yo ass and put you out. And when she do, don't come runnin' to me for help." Chris brushed past Ansean and slammed the front door behind him.

Hearing those words come out of Chris's mouth felt like salt in Ansean's wound. Chris wanted to play a dangerous game with some niggas he had no knowledge of, and all Ansean wanted to do was stay alive. With a blank look on his face, Ansean stood motionless in the middle of the living room. In all sincerity, Chris was kind of right. It was only a matter of time before Cresha put him out. He had to do something, and he had to do it fast. However, he didn't know where to start.

* * * *

The three-tier church owned by Reverend Johnson served his community for over twenty years. Directly above the water fountain in the reception area were the Ten Commandments mounted on the wall. "Thou shall not kill" stood out in bold, black letters for everyone who entered or exited the church to see. It was a commandment that many took to heart once they laid eyes on the blatant phrase.

That was the reaction it gave D'mico. Something about the four words penetrated her spirit with conviction. She stared at the bronze plaque like it was a new language that she was determined to learn. *What are you trying to tell me, Lord?*

"Thou shall not kill. Hmm...touchy."

D'mico backed away from the wall and met eyes with Chauncey.

"How you doing?" he asked smiling, showing off pretty white teeth surrounded by a set of chocolate lips.

Just because Chauncey looked like he was delicately handpicked and set aside to be dipped in a personal bowl of chocolate, his reason for speaking to her still was enough to make D'mico sick. She rolled her eyes to the ceiling, bent down and took a sip of water from the fountain.

"You mad about something?" Chauncey asked in a low whisper.

Once the cold water washed down her throat, D'mico rose up and wiped the corner of her mouth. "Mad? Never that. More like sick and tired of lame-ass niggas who only come around when it's convenient for their ass."

"So now I'm lame? So you wanted me to get us both killed by comin' up there? That is what this is about, right?"

Realizing that she still was in the place of the Lord, D'mico had to check her temper before she wound up going off on Chauncey's sorry ass. Not to mention if she wasn't careful, someone could easily catch them conversing.

"Cut the bullshit, Chauncey. You never loved me. You didn't call or come by because I wasn't shit to you. But you wanna know something? If it wasn't for your sorry ass, I wouldn't have been able to get closer to Tyreke. You was a mistake. I'm sure your parents thought the same thing."

Chauncey flexed his jaws. He jerked D'mico so close to him that her neck snapped back.

* * * *

Leelee watched Chauncey and D'mico behind two five-foot-tall elephant ear plants. What she didn't understand was why Chauncey reacted so violently to D'mico's words.

Chauncey was turning what was supposed to be business into a personal vendetta. There was something strange going on, and she was about to find out exactly what it was.

* * * *

D'mico tore Chauncey's hands off of her shirt. "Keep your fuckin' hands off of me. I'm serious. We're done. I want you out of my life," she spat. Chauncey wasn't having it. D'mico had to be a plum fool if she thought that he was done with her. He might be done sexually, but physically she would feel his wrath.

"Check this out, you nothin' ass bitch, Ty don't give a rat's ass about you. No man does. If your nigga was all that, you wouldn't have destroyed your womb for me. By the way, was it a boy or a girl?"

D'mico spat in Chauncey's face. Chauncey removed the thick phlegm and smiled devilishly. Furious, he was about to charge at D'mico and grab for her neck when Damu rounded the corner.

"Yo, what's goin' on?" Damu asked, staring Chauncey down like he was out of his mind.

Chauncey put his hands down, turned around and forced a smile. "What's good, Moo? Ain't nothin' goin' on. I was just tellin' D'mico that we're all goin' to miss Dirt." Chauncey turned around to face D'mico. "Ain't that right?"

Damu looked at D'mico to confirm Chauncey's answer. Despite the look of "help" written on her face, with a short nod, she agreed.

"Umm. Yeah. He's right," she lied, swallowing her fear. Damu took it for what it was and dismissed what looked like a bad episode from *Jerry Springer*.

"Well, I don't think it's wise for ya'll to be talkin' alone. I'm not Ty, but I'm sure that if I was, two more funerals would be goin' on right now. We don't want him making assumptions now do we?" Damu stated bluntly.

"You're absolutely right. I was out of line." Chauncey turned to face D'mico, and then he turned back towards Damu. "I been doin' a lot of fuckin' up lately."

Chauncey didn't even stay for the funeral. He paid his respects and left. When Chauncey walked out the door, Damu directed his attention to D'mico.

"I'm far from stupid, D'mico. Whatever it is you got with that nigga, cut it off. At the rate he goin', he'll be a dead man real soon."

"But I'm not—"

"That's all I want to say. Tyreke sent for you. Service is about to start," he finished.

* * * *

LeeLee, also known as Leslie, stepped away from the plants. Pissed and upset, she flipped up her Verizon cell phone and dialed Chauncey's number. His unworthy ass had a whole lot of explaining to do.

* * * *

Monte stepped out the white Department of Corrections vehicle shackled from his hands to his feet. He inhaled the scent of freedom and made a short attempt to pull down his ashy-grey, state-issued pants. At the age of forty-five, he still maintained his youth by preserving it in the rec room on the yard, lifting and bench pressing weights. His worn face and puffy eyes diminished his handsome looks, which were identical to Dirt's. He was grieving hard. A few feet from the church door, a familiar face came out. Both of the men locked eyes as the guy exiting quickly looked away, glancing at his phone which he placed in his pocket. It wasn't until Monte reached the church steps that he remembered Chauncey.

Forgetting that he was in handcuffs, he spun around to catch Chauncey, but the nigga had already left. The C.O.'s grabbed ahold of his arm. "Do we have a problem?" one C.O. barked.

"Nah...There's no problem. I thought I seen someone I knew. I apologize. It won't happen again."

"Remember, Daniels, there will be no talkin' to your family or we're authorized to bring you back."

Holding on to the memory of Dirt and not wanting to miss his final goodbyes, Monte didn't object. Somehow he had to get a message to Tyreke though.

Chapter 11

Three Weeks Later

"I'm sorry. You have reached a number that is disconnected or no longer in service. If you have reached this recording in error, please hang up and try the number again."

Monte slammed the phone down in aggravation. He glanced down at the piece of paper that had Tyreke's number scribbled across the center. He shoved the paper in the pocket of his penitentiary Dickies. Even though his son was gone, Tyreke still remained loyal and kept the maximum amount of 500 dollars on his books weekly. At first, he thought about sending Tyreke a kite, but then he later found out that the address on the money orders was bogus. All he had was the phone number that Dirt gave him months ago, and just like the address, it turned out to be a dead end.

"Shit," he mumbled, frustrated by the whole situation. He got up from the stainless steel barstool that connected partially to the payphone and contemplated his next move. Halfway to his two-man cell, a hint of hope and a half smile materialized. He had a plan, and it involved Kendale, his celly.

Kendale stood erect looking out the window like the only thing that separated him from his freedom was the thickness of the four-inch glass. Ten years ago, he thought of a million and one different ways to escape the barbed wire, twenty-three-hour lockdown and the screams that echoed throughout the facility in the middle of the night. Most of the niggas on the yard were so use to dodging their responsibilities that they actually considered prison to be home. Not Kendale. He still had unfinished business out there.

One thing that he learned about being in the state of Oklahoma was that it was racist as hell. He came to the redneck state on vacation. Now he was about to leave the bitch on probation. Kendale backed away from the window when he heard movement coming from behind him.

"What's good, yo," he said with a New York accent. He picked up his latest book titled *BY MEANS NECESSARY* by Rain. "Did you get ahold of 'em?" he inquired, flipping a page.

"Nah...The number was disconnected," Monte responded dryly.

"Word? Damn. Told you to keep dat muthafucka in rotation, son." Kendale kicked off his shower shoes. "I figured ya man would've switched up jacks. All hustlers do, na mean? At least I use to," he carried on. Monte got a little irritated with Kendale. He had a problem with young heads who thought the world came in tune when they came out of the womb. Shit, little nigga still had breast milk on his breath, and here he was stunting, talking about what he use to do. He reconsidered putting Tyreke's life in the hands of another man. It wasn't just about Tyreke; it was about Kendale too. He might have been a little wet behind the ears, but dude was solid, and Monte got attached to the young thug. Within several minutes, the old man's face aged about ten years.

"Check dis out, young blood. You been my celly for, like what, seven years? You know that I'm not the one to ask for favors because asking leads to regrets." He paused and gazed at the ceiling. Asking Kendale to put his life at risk was harder than he expected. In less than a month, Kendale would be released to the world with a fresh start, and he was about to ask him to risk that.

Kendale saw the seriousness in his celly's face. He put down his book and stood to his feet. "Yo, you my fam. Whateva you wanna ask me, you can ask with a clear conscience. That's my word."

If Kendale was good for anything, the New York bred nigga was diligent like a muthafucka. If he banked his word on something, more than likely he would see to it that it got done. Monte took a seat and gave Kendale the scoop on Chauncey and Tyreke and what he wanted him to do.

* * * *

Thwack...Thwack...Thwack...

"That's it, baby. One more time. A little stronger," Damu coached. While Damu held a punching bag in an upright position, the young kid swiveled to the right then whisked to the left and delivered a quick punch to the bag, knocking Damu off his heels. Damu smiled. "Hell yeah!" he said, excited by the kid's strength. Tyreke cracked his knuckles and placed his hands behind his head in deep thought. He thought about Dirt. His crew had kicked in every door known to man that might possibly be hiding Ansean, and yet the nigga seemed to have slipped through the cracks. Another thing that bothered Tyreke was the kid who Chauncey smoked.

Tyreke found out that the little nigga couldn't possibly know Ansean. Someone had a ticket on his head. The question was who. Tyreke had a major deal coming up with the Chief and the Commissioner of State to oversea a multi-million-dollar operation importing and exporting diamonds outside the U.S., and the last thing he wanted was for his obscenities to leak and for them to think that he wasn't cut for the job. Meanwhile, his goons, along with a few stray mutts, were on the lookout for Ansean. Although he had to kill the nigga on the hush, Tyreke wasn't going to let Ansean go. Fuck that!

"Ty, there's a lady here to see you," Damu informed Tyreke as he stood in the doorway. Tyreke gave Damu a "I don't want to be bothered" look.

"What she want?"

"I dunno. She don't look old enough to have any kids, but who knows." Damu stepped inside and pointed towards the lobby. "That's her. She fine as hell. I wouldn't mind makin' a few babies wit' her sexy ass," Damu lusted.

To Tyreke's surprise, the woman was a chocolate dream. She had the face of a school teacher and the body of a stripper. He couldn't keep his eyes from roaming all over her cocoa skin. Nor could he help his attraction to the stranger. Normally he preferred yellow bones, but there was something about this chick that gave his sweet tooth a craving for some chocolate. Damn! Secretly she looked over her shoulder at Tyreke as she felt his lustful stare. Tyreke noticed the worried look she wore on her face. She looked like a withered flower destined to blossom in the spring.

"Send her in. I got a minute to spare," Tyreke said.

Damu tapped the window and waved her inside. She gradually made her way to Tyreke's office with her tote bag tucked underneath her arm.

"Hi, my name is Serenity."

Tyreke stood up to shake her hand. "What can we do for you, Serenity?" he asked, waving her over to a chair.

Serenity sat down.

"Well, I seen your commercial on TV, and your age requirements start at the age of thirteen, and my little boy is nine, about to be ten, but he really looks and acts older. Plu—"

"Oh, we can't take nine or ten-year-olds. Insurance won't allow us to," Damu cut in crudely.

Serenity frowned. "I was hoping that you could help me out. Maybe he can just practice and hang out until he's of age. He loves boxing, and every time your commercial comes on there's a twinkle in his eye. Please."

Tyreke wanted to say yes, but rules were rules, and he didn't like to bend them even if he did make them. Once you break your own rules, other muthafuckas think they can do the same, and he wasn't up for that.

Serenity removed her tote bag from around her arm and placed it on her lap. She came for a reason, and she didn't plan on leaving without a fight.

"Before you say no, Tyler is a good kid. He got suspended from school a few times because he said that the other kids ain't on his level. To be honest with you, his school wants me to homeschool him, but I can't because I work six days a week, nine, sometimes ten hours a day. If I had the money, I would send him to an advanced school, but me and him is barely making it," Serenity said, putting her business out there.

"So you askin' us to babysit for you?" Damu asked in a disgusted tone.

Serenity cut her eyes at the rude gentleman and looked towards the man with the adorable baby face.

"Look Mr...I'm not expecting for you to babysit. Tyler needs a role model to look up to. Positive energy. Ya'll look like educated black men, and Tyler could use that," she stressed.

"As much as I want to help you, miss lady, I—" Serenity didn't even give Tyreke the chance to tell her no. She immediately stood to her feet as her tears began to sting her eyes.

"My name is Serenity. Forget it. I'm sorry for wasting your time. You gentlemen have a nice day." She picked up her bag and stormed out the office.

Tyreke and Damu sat there lost for words.

Getting up from his seat, Tyreke caught up with Serenity outside the arena.

"Serenity wait!" Tyreke called out, jogging to catch up with her.

Serenity turned around. There was something in her body language that intrigued Tyreke. She was unique and held a certain confidence about herself that he admired.

"Yes," she said with a little attitude.

"Serenity, we started off on the wrong foot, and I want to apologize for what went on in there."

Serenity held her head up. "Don't sweat it." She dug in her purse and pulled out her bus pass. "I want to apologize for askin' you to break your rules." She watched several cars pass by before speaking again. "There's no hard feelings," she said truthfully.

Tyreke was so attracted to Serenity that he didn't want her to leave. He knew he was out of line for the way he was feeling, but he wanted to see her again. On a regular basis if possible.

"I know, but I want to help. I was thinkin' that we can work something out." Serenity's eyes lit up like the Fourth of July

"Really?"

"Yeah, really," Tyreke said, enjoying her smile. "You said your son's name is Tyler, right?"

Serenity paused before answering. "Yes."

"Cool. Bring him by this weekend. You'll have to fill out some paperwork, and then after that he'll need a physical, but don't worry about that. My staff will provide transportation and cover the cost."

Serenity stared at Tyreke and her eyes lingered for several seconds. He was very lucid and handsome. Nothing like the other guy inside the arena. His self-possessed demeanor as well as his attractive features caused the place between her legs to throb.

"I didn't get your name," she said, breaking the lust-filled stare.

Tyreke shook off his illicit thoughts. "Tyreke. You can call me Ty for short." Serenity eyed him from head to toe.

"Tyreke sounds nice."

Serenity flashed a million-dollar smile, and Tyreke fell in pursuit. He didn't care that his gut was experiencing guilt or the fact that he had a woman. Something very powerful was going on between him and Serenity, and it felt damn good. However, reality gave him a smack in the face, and Tyreke had to kill D'mico's suspicions of him cheating on her. Besides, a woman as beautiful as Serenity deserved a man all to herself. She deserved a man she could bear healthy children with. She didn't need America's most dangerous gangster. He would only add to her problems.

Tyreke stepped back and glanced towards the gym.

"It was nice to meet you, Serenity. Don't forget. Seven o'clock, aight?"

Serenity noticed Tyreke's eagerness to go. The flame burning inside of her died. "Nice to meet you too. Trust me, I won't forget," she said coolly.

They departed, both anticipating the weekend.

Chapter 12

Diamonds are forever. The phrase alone hit it on the nail for Tyreke. Unlike the drug trade, the taste of diamonds was far too complex for his palate. Diamonds were far from being a speedy process.

Jose sat on a pearl-white chaise lounge picking up every diamond one by one with a pair of tweezers. He examined them thoroughly under a microscope, twirling them under a fluorescent light. Jose's entourage stood off to the side covering every square inch of the living room that overlooked the beach, making sure the diamonds didn't come off as short or pass as phony.

Finally, Jose removed his gloves. With a friendly smile, he spoke to Tyreke.

"My friend, everything looks as it should be. You are a very lucrative man," Jose commented.

Tyreke sighed with relief. He got up from the comfortable sectional with nailhead trim and shook Jose's hand. Jose shook his hand in turn. "Enjoy Costa Rica, my friend."

Tyreke took Jose's friendliness with a grain of salt. He understood the gesture was a part of business and nothing more. If he failed to deliver Jose his products, the man wouldn't hesitate to put his henchmen to work on his black ass. Therefore, friend, compadre or associate had no meaning in the world of illegal trade.

As soon as Tyreke gathered his bags of cash, a private plane awaited him to return him to the States.

* * * *

The night air was crisp and cool against D'mico's skin. It crept inside her bedroom window and caressed the back of her neck. Sluggishly, she got up and worked her way to the window, shutting out the stiff breeze and the agonizing sound of chirping crickets.

D'mico picked up the phone, dialed the first three numbers to Leslie's cell and then hung up. She slammed the phone on the receiver and threw herself back on the bed where she stared at the ceiling. Quickly, she dissolved the thought of making up with Leslie. Having friends could be a pain in the ass anyway. Just when the sexy lyrics to Usher's "There Goes My Baby" kicked in, D'mico looked up at the six screens on the monitor, catching every entrance and exit door to the house. She spotted Tyreke's silhouette. Glad that she no longer had to be home alone, she scrambled for the remote to give him a grand entrance that he couldn't refuse.

* * * *

When Tyreke arrived in the States, he met with a few of his niggas, and then he linked up with the Chief to go over his trip to Costa Rica. Although the Chief was skeptical about whether he could shuffle both the drug trade and the exporting business, he had to give it to Tyreke for pulling it off. Plus, he loved the fact that Tyreke was punctual as well as precise about when and where and how he was going to get what needed to be done, done. After paying a few people and collecting his earnings, Tyreke was beat. All he wanted to do was retreat to his crib, kick off his shoes and count some z's. After he punched in his code to his home security system, he steadily made his way up the stairs and to his bedroom. His plan to catch up on some z's changed dramatically when he entered the room and saw D'mico butt naked. Her body looked beautiful stretched across the king-size bed, favoring a work of art. She lustfully worked her hands across her nipples, tracing her areola while exposing her hairless mound.

Lust was in her eyes, and the taste of dick was on her tongue. With no spoken words, Tyreke stepped out of his clothes. His tool had risen to full length, and he was ready to take a rain check on sleep and claim his prize. *That's how you welcome your man home*, he thought diving head first.

* * * *

Sounds of pleasure echoed inside the dimly lit room. "Urgh. Urgh...Hell yeah, bitch. Work that pussy, D'mico."

Leslie's eyes fluttered open in disbelief. She was actually enjoying the hammering Chauncey was giving her until he called her by another woman's name. D'mico's name at that. What kind of shit was that?

He graduated from talking about this bitch all day to calling out her name while they were making love. Leslie wanted to cry. More than anything she wanted to smack his fuckin' face, but instead, she lay motionless on her back while he continued to do his thing.

"Argh...D'mi-co...Argh," he groaned in her ear.

In Chauncey's mind, he was inside of D'mico. In actuality, Leslie's pussy was nowhere near as good as D'mico's. However, he loved Leslie a lot. He was so caught up imagining D'mico's body that he didn't see the tears and the uncomfortable look on Leslie's face. He saw D'mico—the woman who shattered his life.

Acting on his emotions, Chauncey's movements intensified. Leslie's eyes bulged out of her head as Chauncey moved coarsely inside of her now dry pussy. Suddenly, he took her on an unexpected ride, causing her to grip the sheets. With both of his hands on Leslie's neck, he tried to squeeze the life out of who he thought was D'mico.

"Chaunceee," Leslie screeched, falling limp under his massive hands.

Chauncey didn't stop. He moved faster and squeezed tighter. In his mind, she was D'mico and D'mico had to go.

* * * *

With deep breaths, D'mico massaged the back of Tyreke's head. His curly hair flowed loosely through her fingertips as he sucked, nibbled and licked on her protruding clit. If only men knew the effects they have on a woman's body.

On the brink of ebullience, D'mico closed her eyes and worked her shapely hips to the rhythm of Tyreke's tongue. Tyreke buried his face deeper into D'mico's melting pot until the taste of honey settled on his tongue. He sucked, licked, tickled and finessed her pussy, sending a stream of juices flowing off his lips and chin onto the bed. He loved it when D'mico trembled nonstop from his tongue skills. Everything she did let him know that he was hitting all her special spots. What's the use of performing oral sex when it's mismanaged? Tyreke wasn't afraid to admit it; he loooved eating pussy. No forks, spoons or napkins needed, just his long tongue and a girl ready to give up at least three orgasms. He was a grown man, and he demanded a full course meal.

After devouring D'mico's juices for twenty minutes strong and loving every minute of it, the flood was far from over. A pillar of clouds formed in D'mico's dreamy eyes as Tyreke slid his girth inside her fountain, creating a constant flow of ecstasy. D'mico rolled her head side to side and arched her back as Tyreke shook the foundation of her walls. The way he climbed in and out of her pussy was tortuous. A melodic falsetto escaped from her quivering lips.

"Ooooh, Oh, umm...Tyrreeke, oh yes," she moaned,

wrapping one arm over his 185-pound frame. She steered her pelvis against his tool, grinding nonstop to the sound of their juices.

Together their bodies fought a battle of physical gratification. Every time D'mico contracted her muscles, Tyreke shifted into high gear.

A drop of sweat trickled down his spine to the masculine curves that sculpted his well-toned body. Putting in work on his woman's body was what he took pride in. Slowing down his pace for a minute, he marveled at the masterpiece before him.

D'mico smiled. "Do you like what you see, daddy?" she cooed.

Damn right he liked what he saw. Her body was silky and smooth with no rough spots. Her firm breasts resembled two large cantaloupes sitting above her itty-bitty waist, and the areolas in the center of them were the color of brown sugar coated with a special blend of maple syrup. Whenever they made love, D'mico perspired on the sides of her face and the back of her neck, causing her hair to dampen. She didn't look greasy or sweaty; she looked like an exotic fruit splashed with a little water ready to eat. Many times Tyreke watched the sweat spill from her face while her eyes were closed. Tyreke felt like the luckiest man in the world to have a stallion as fly as D'mico. For now, he couldn't think of any other woman who measured up to her rank. Call it lost in the moment, but Tyreke was ready to make the biggest decision of his life. He couldn't say for sure that making love to D'mico didn't play a part in his wanting to marry her, because it did to some degree. However, he was ready to put a ring on her finger and call it official.

Tyreke lifted D'mico in the air and pecked her lips. He used his lower body strength to balance their bodies against the bedroom wall. His deep voice vibrated a sensual tone in her ear. "I love what I see and I love you," he whispered, turning up the juice. Their lovemaking was timeless, and he had all night to show D'mico its meaning. Tonight, she had his attention. All of it.

* * * *

"Chauncey STOP!" Leslie squealed, swinging her arms in the air, fighting for both her life and her unborn child.

Returning back to earth, Chauncey broke out of his psychosomatic trance. He looked down at Leslie with sympathetic eyes. He freed his hands from around her neck and rolled over onto his backside without explaining his deranged outburst. He was going crazy over D'mico and he knew it.

In a rush with eyes full of tears, Leslie scrambled for her clothes.

"What is wrong with you? You could've hurt the baby and me," she yelled.

Chauncey gazed at the ceiling in silence. After all, what the fuck could he say? Hell, he was in shock his damn self. He was battling over mixed feelings he had for a woman he planned on killing. Nevertheless, the taste of revenge was more powerful than her pussy.

Once Leslie was fully dressed, she looked towards Chauncey with regret. To a certain degree, she understood why Chauncey choked her; she knew he envisioned her as D'mico. However, the man was losing his damn mind. Pretty soon he would lose her as well. After spending three miserable years with Rodney, her last boyfriend/baby daddy, Leslie was almost positive that when Chauncey came along that she would never endure the kind of pain that came with her past relationship. Instead of bringing home money or gifts for the kids, Rodney brought home the gift that keeps giving. STDs.

To add to the list of drama, females played on her phone all hours of the night. If she dared to get jazzy or question Rodney's sneaky behavior, he would kick Leslie's ass, which he did every day anyway.

Leslie wanted to move forward in her life, not backwards. Chauncey was supposed to be the powerful force in her life that would wipe away her pain. As a matter of fact, their relationship was pretty sturdy until Chauncey introduced D'mico into the picture. Sad as it was, Chauncey had some twisted kind of obsession with the woman. It would be easy for Leslie to say that she didn't want to fuck with Chauncey anymore, but words are easier said than done.

Besides, Leslie fell victim to love like everyone else. Plus, she'd invested so much in Chauncey.

Leslie grabbed her keys. She stopped at the door and looked over her shoulder at the python resting lightly across his thigh. His big, black, dangerous serpent would be her biggest downfall in the future. Knowing that she couldn't get enough of it, she walked out the door. Disgust settled in her stomach when she came to grips with the truth—she would never actually leave.

Chapter 13

Normally Damu would be at the arena closing up at this hour, but Tyreke closed the arena today. He wanted to reserve the evening for Serenity and Tyler. With a few minutes to spare, Tyreke ducked under the rope to the boxing ring and put on a set of boxing gloves.

A full graffiti sketch of Dirt's face was stretched out on the wall in front of him. He began to warm up, burying his feet in the canvas of the ring as he looked into the eyes of the portrait. In a sense, he felt like he let Dirt down by not finding Ansean or his brother. Whatever it took, he was going to get them. He just hated the wait that came with his vengeance. Once Tyreke gained his ground, he quickened his speed, letting all of his frustrations spill out of his pores onto his black wifebeater.

* * * *

Serenity stood outside the arena nervous like a kid on

her first day of school. Butterflies swam in her stomach as she shot Tyler a serious look.

"Behave, okay? Can you do that for me?" she asked, looking into his resentful eyes.

Tyler fiddled with the straps on his backpack before answering. "I gotchu."

Serenity shook her heard. *Lord, what am I going to do with him,* she thought, pressing the intercom button.

Buzz...Buzz...

Tyreke was taken from his thoughts when he heard the sound of the buzzer. Peeling off his gloves, he grabbed a towel, dabbed his face and neck, and then laid the thick cloth across his shoulders.

A big smile appeared on his face when he opened the door. Instantly he was drawn to Serenity's face, which was warm and friendly.

"Hi, I'm glad you made it," Tyreke said truthfully as his eyes wandered aimlessly across her body.

He wasn't trying to be a hound in front of this woman, but the perfect name for Serenity would've been "Divine Chocolate." Her ebony skin conveyed purity, and the way she smiled spoke many words. The yellow halter top and low-rise jeans she wore embraced her coke bottle figure to the T.

Damn she got it goin' on!

Following Tyreke's eyes, Serenity blushed. "Can we come in?" she asked.

"Yeah. Of course. I'm trippin'." Tyreke led her inside. He closed and locked the door behind them. "You just look so different from the last time I saw you."

"Thanks to Walmart. I do what I can when I can,"

Serenity stated, not ashamed of her taste in clothing.

Perhaps it was Serenity's boldness that Tyreke took a liking to, or maybe it was the fact that Serenity had no problem with being in her own skin. She was comfortable with who she was, and she clearly showed that she had no intentions of changing.

"Walmart? Well from the looks of it, Walmart doin' big things."

Serenity giggled. She was beginning to fall under Tyreke's spell. She placed two hands on Tyler. Clearing her throat, she introduced him to Tyreke.

"Tyreke, this is Tyler. He likes to be called Ty for short." Ty was so quiet that Tyreke forgot the reason why Serenity came by. "Ty, this is the nice gentleman I was tellin' you about," Serenity said in a motherly tone.

Tyreke and Ty locked eyes. Man to boy, they sized each other up and stared each other down like hawks. Although Ty was a kid, he looked like someone Tyreke knew. He couldn't put a finger on it, but the kid's grey eyes held some sort of resemblance to...someone. Studying his features, Tyreke eyed him cautiously.

Ty bunched up his face and bit his bottom lip.

"Ty, what's wrong with you? Say hello," Serenity griped.

A sour expression outlined Ty's face. He cut his eyes at Tyreke and turned in the direction of the ring.

Embarrassed, Serenity tried to apologize. "Tyreke, I'm really sorry."

"Sorry for what? He cool. I use to be like that when I was younger. It's natural. Trust me. He didn't do anything wrong."

Serenity lightened up. "Yeah, you're right."

"Follow me. I got some papers for you to fill out." He turned towards Ty. "Eh, why don't chu take a look around. Make yo'self comfortable, lil daddy. Since you took over my nickname, you family now."

Ty gave Tyreke a small smile. He threw his backpack to the floor and began to check out the place. Serenity placed her hand over her chest and mouthed the words. "Thank you."

Lately, Ty grew so accustomed to being the root of every problem that his attitude, disrespect for authority and resentment dug him deeper into trouble. Serenity was the closest thing he had to family. So the way Tyreke stood up for him meant a lot.

* * * *

Ansean was the only nigga walking around with a pullover jacket and a stocking cap in the middle of summer. He was left with no other choice but to find the nearest store and get some damn food. That or he would starve to death. Cresha flipped the switch on him when she stopped bringing food home. At first, Ansean figured the chick was suffering from dick withdrawals, but then Cresha stopped coming home altogether. For the past three months, he'd been on the run, dodging Tyreke and his squad. Fed up, powerless and tired of running, Ansean felt like meeting his maker. Chris was out there somewhere living life to the fullest or worse dead. At the end of the day, Ansean's will to stay alive took over his desire to give up.

Ansean didn't hesitate to break into his styrofoam to-go box filled with potato wedges, chicken and BBQ burritos on his way back to the apartment. He wolfed down the greasy potato wedges like they were his last meal. Up ahead, on the steps to the apartment, a dice game was going on. Ignoring his rising blood pressure, Ansean tried to make his way to Cresha's apartment on the sly in the hopes that no one would recognize his face.

"Seven, eleven. Come on, baby. Roll daddy a pair of Jordans," a dude called out with his knees to the ground and his feet supporting his butt. He blew life into the palm of his hand before releasing the green and white dice onto a crisp, white T-shirt surrounded by sweaty tens, twenties and hundred-dollar bills. The guy next to him eyeballed Ansean crudely as he made an attempt to get to Cresha's apartment.

Everybody else had their attention glued to the dice game, waiting to see if Mr. Dice lucked up with a nice seven or would he go home with a pair of snake eyes. But not Mr. Dice's friend. Nah, he couldn't take his eyes off of Ansean. Quietly, he whispered something into Mr. Dice's ear. The crowd chanted when they saw four dots on one dice and three on the other.

Ansean cramped up when the dude with the dice ceased his next roll. Violently, his heart jumped out of his chest for cover.

Like a blazing grass fire, the news that Tyreke had a ticket value on Ansean and Chris spread through every hood and metropolitan area in a 500-mile radius, and muthafuckas knew that Tyreke was a man that paid and paid well. It came as no surprise to Ansean that Tyreke was on the prowl. If anything, he counted his blessings for being able to stay alive this long.

The dude with the dice screwed up his eyes to get a better look at Ansean. "Nah, that ain't him," he said, returning back to his roll.

Ansean kept his gaze straight ahead and calmly walked towards the apartment, trying to attract as little attention as possible.

Once inside, he double bolted the locks and leaned his back against the door. A stream of tears fell from his eyes as he wondered how much longer he would be able to keep this up.

* * * *

Kendale stepped outside the penitentiary gate gripping his bus ticket. He sucked in the cold morning air as a free man. The first thing on his agenda was to find Tyreke. He promised his bunkie that he would find him. After all, a nigga without his word ain't never been shit.

Chapter 14

The repeating sound of the telephone ringing woke Tyreke up in the middle of the night.

"Yeah," he answered in a groggy voice, still half sleep.

"Sorry to wake you up, man, but I got some info that you'll take a liking to. Do the name Ansean sound familiar to you?"

"What?" Tyreke glanced at D'mico. She lay comfortably next to him in a deep sleep. "Can you hold on for a minute, Moo?" he said, removing D'mico's arm from around his waist.

The green indicator light on the surveillance monitor beamed on his half-naked body. Wearing only his Calvin Klein boxer briefs, he made his way to the bathroom.

"You said that you got some information. Can I act on this information, or did you call me at three in the morning to hear my voice?"

"Well, my sources say they know where he is."

"Where you at?" Tyreke asked, preparing himself to leave.

"At the speezy."

"I'm on my way. Nobody leaves until I get there."

"I gotchu. One!" Damu pressed the end button on his Samsung. He slid a chair across the room. "Sit. Everything you told me better be on point, shorty," he said, gritting his teeth.

Cresha ran her acrylic nails through her long micro braids. Her shit was beyond on point. When she found out that Ansean and Chris were worth 50 G's a piece, she didn't hesitate to drop the bomb on their black asses. Hell...for 50 G's she'd give up her own mama. Hey, there was a recession going on, and a sista was looking to get paid.

Cresha crossed her lanky legs. "Mister, neither your time nor mine will be wasted," she said in a sexy tone.

By no means did Damu find Cresha to be attractive. From now on, he would think twice about not wearing condoms. Cresha's long neck, beetle-looking eyes and bucked teeth were the result of a good nut gone bad.

"Yeah whateva," he said, shaking his head. "Do me a favor and shut ya fuckin' mouth until he gets here. And another thing, quit tryin' to be sexy. Dis right here is business, and you startin' to tear my damn stomach up with all of that extra shit."

Cresha curled her upper lip and rolled her eyes. She was getting tired of being everyone's special kind of fool. What was up with brothers these days? She addressed Damu's lame ass with a little bit of sense, and what did he do? Talk shit to her like she was less than a food stamp. Fuck him. She knew that she had it going on. Who was about to be a hundred thousand dollars richer? She was. With that kind of money, she would be able to buy any nigga she wanted. *Fuck him,* she reminded herself again.

* * * *

Cresha toyed with the silverware in her hand. A broad grin appeared on her face as she chewed her food while staring into Ansean's sorrel-colored eyes. The sound of J-Friday and Alex B. flowed smoothly throughout the small dining room that attached to the living room. All day Cresha had been on some "let me cater to you" type of shit. Not only did she fill up the refrigerator with all of Ansean's favorites, but she fried some catfish and French fries that made him want to smack his mama.

Ansean got up from the table. "Thanks, Cresha. That was the bomb, girl. Damn, I didn't know you knew how to cook like that." He reached for their plates. "Lemme put these dishes away. It's the least I can do."

Cresha jumped up from her seat. "No-no, that's okay. I got it." She took the plates out of his hand. "Why don't you chill? You thirsty? I got some Hine Antique in the kitchen. You wanna glass?" she asked, stacking the salad bowls on top of the plates.

"Sure."

When Cresha walked away, she added an extra dip to her hips. Ansean gave Cresha a suspicious look. The sudden change in her demeanor made him a little apprehensive as he checked out his surroundings. Her attitude adjustment was a nice change and all, but to a nigga who grew immune to her isolation, Ansean knew better than to sleep on Cresha's cunning behavior.

Within minutes, Cresha returned with two half-filled glasses of wine. "Thank you," Ansean said, taking one of the glasses.

"Lemme ask you a question, Cresha. Why you actin' all nice and shit? Last week you couldn't stand a nigga, so what's the occasion?"

Caught off guard, Cresha took a sip. "Let's just say that you're the occasion. I was buggin'. And I want to apologize for that. Do you forgive me?" she said innocently.

"No hard feelings. I understand," he said, reclining back in his chair.

Cresha sat her glass down and started to massage the back of Ansean's neck. Ansean kept his eyes closed and enjoyed the feel of Cresha's hands. It had been months since he felt the warmth of a woman's body. Cresha lifted up his shirt and worked her hands across his chiseled abs. "You like that?" she enticed, adding long strokes to the movement of her hands. She unbuckled his pants and pulled out his tool.

Ansean sat in silence with his dick in Cresha's hand. She manipulated his tool to full erection. On bended knees, she trained her lips and tongue to navigate the most pleasurable places on a man's body. It was what she was good at.

What Ansean didn't know was that this blow job

would cost him his life.

Cresha took in the sight of his tasty tool. There were no discolorations on or around his dick. His enormous mushroom-shaped shaft smoothly hit the back of her throat as she moved Ansean in and out of her mouth. Too bad this would be Ansean's last blow job, because Cresha was enjoying herself.

"Uhh..." A short groan escaped Ansean's lips. Cresha handled his dick like she was the rightful owner. For a split second, he wondered if all ugly women mastered the skill of giving mean skully. He grabbed a handful of her micro braids and forced his dick further down her throat, drawing more saliva onto his thickness. Although Ansean was in the process of fuckin' Cresha's mouth, he had to make sense of the present. A man's dick can be his worse enemy, and Ansean wasn't prepared to face anything alone if things went south. Despite the abundance of pre-nut seeping out of his penis, Ansean fought his selfish propensity and got up from his seat. His dick loosely fell out of Cresha's mouth.

"What's wrong now?" she asked with irritation.

Ansean gazed at Cresha who was on her knees with a dumb look on her face. He tucked away his limp gold mine and zipped up his 505 denims.

"Ain't shit wrong, Cresha. I got a lot on my mind, and this ain't gonna solve anything." Ansean extended a helpful hand to help Cresha up. She stared at his hand in discontent. "Come on, Cresha. Don't be like that. It's not you; it's me." Cresha accepted Ansean's hand. Oddly, she was beginning to take a liking to Ansean. But this wasn't the time nor the place to grow mushy over a dead man.

Besides, the only feeling she would experience would be the feeling of a hundred thousand in her hands.

Biding her time, Cresha kept the conversation flowing.

"There was truth in what I said earlier. I was trippin' actin' that way towards you, and I wanted to show you how sorry I was with some action. That's all. A man as fine as you shouldn't be mind boggled by Tyreke."

Ansean felt his heart plummet. "Tyreke?" He never mentioned Tyreke's name to Cresha. Lately their conversations were limited to short replies and avoidance. So how did she know about him and his beef with Tyreke?

Ansean stepped back in bewilderment. His head spun around in circles along with his insides. Fuck. He should've known better than to assume that Cresha was green from the rest of the muthafuckas out there trying to find him. The bitch was crimson red with yellow caution tape wrapped around her neck.

Damn. He'd been sold out.

Cresha nervously moved closer to Ansean. Did she let her mouth overload her ass? "What?" she asked, pretending to be stuck on stupid. "What?" she repeated.

"Tyreke? Cresha, I never mentioned that name to you, so where did you get it from?"

"You didn't have to mention it to me. Chris told me. He tells me everything. Are you forgettin' that I rode it out with him for years?" Cresha lied.

"You know as well as I do that my brother wouldn't tell you no shit like that. And if he did, he fed you some bullshit. I'm not mind boggled over no one. I'm here because I ran into some financial problems."

"Okay, whateva you got goin' don't have shit to do with me," Cresha countered firmly.

Ansean stared into Cresha's lying eyes. He knew that she was full of shit; he could see it.

"I gotta use the bathroom," Ansean said, wanting to get as far away from Cresha and her apartment as possible.

Cresha stared at Ansean's backside with troubled eyes as he went into the bathroom and closed the door. She wondered if Ansean bought her story. She couldn't wait for this to be over. In less than fifteen minutes, it would be.

* * * *

Ansean secured the bathroom door and glanced around the small bathroom. He went to the sink, turned on the water and splashed his weary face. Water ran down his hand, to his wrist, and onto his eleven thousand dollar Cartier watch. Disgusted, he slipped the worldly item off his wrist and into his pocket. It was his greed and unlawful deeds that led him to this stage in his life. If it weren't for the fact that he had sticky hands, he'd still be on the same team as Tyreke instead of being on the opposite side. But no, he stole, robbed and pinched from everyone he came in contact with. He was obsessed with the finer things in life.

Ansean pulled back the plum-colored, vinyl shower curtain and stepped inside. Only so far up was a small window positioned within his reach. Ansean knew the window would lead him down a fire escape because he checked it out months ago. Unsure of the treachery Cresha schemed behind his back, Ansean would be long gone before he ever found out.

While Ansean's body dangled partly out the window, he stopped abruptly in his tracks when he heard the low rumble of his brother's voice.

"Chris?" he mumbled to himself, stepping back inside. He leaned against the door and listened.

"Bitch, you said it was an emergency. Where the fuck is my brother?" Chris demanded to know. He drilled his index finger in Cresha's forehead. "I'm not playin' with you, girl. He better be here."

Violently Cresha shoved Chris's hand out of her face. "Calm the fuck down. He in the damn bathroom," she said, pointing towards the bathroom. "Whose dick do I need to suck in order to get some respect? I'm tired of niggas yellin' at me in my shit," Cresha stressed with her hands on her hips.

Chris began to grope all over Cresha, grabbing her by the waist where she eased into his comfort.

"C'mere, you know I got love for you," he said, squeezing her ass. He placed her hand on his dick. "You want some of this?" he asked as he slobbered on her neck.

Cresha giggled. *Finally, some attention.*

Ansean staggered backwards into the bathroom. Chris was receiving head from the same bitch that had his dick in her mouth. Oh well, hoes will be hoes. Even though Ansean was upset with Chris for leaving him for dead, he was relieved to know that he was okay.

Maybe Chris did tell Cresha about Tyreke. From the looks of it, he had been keeping in touch with Cresha. However, Ansean had to keep it moving. The game of survival never been a respecter of ill-timing, no way. You know what I'm saying?

Ansean eased out the window with caution. Halfway down the fire escape, the violent sound of a gun being cocked back made him jump.

Chink! *Chink*!

"Goin' somewhere, Ansean?"

A disgruntled look outlined Ansean's face as he came face to face with death. No more rash decisions, camouflaging his identity, or worries. This was it. The end of his life.

Fuck!

* * * *

The smell of crack cocaine, roach spray and marijuana filled the vast hallway leading to the limited amount of space some considered home. The muffled sound of baby cries, music and televisions echoed behind the walls of the living quarters.

The time on Tyreke's Rolex read 9:33 p.m. He planned and anticipated on hitting his mark, and Ansean and Chris would be no more.

For safe measures, he had a group of niggas spread throughout Cresha's apartment. Every floor, window and exit was covered.

By no means would Ansean or Chris escape Tyreke's hands. Minutes ago, Cresha gave the signal that both

Ansean and Chris were in her apartment. With everybody in position, Tyreke was ready to knock Ansean and Chris off the map.

Hiding behind a black ski mask, Tyreke stood off to the right side of the door while his henchmen waited eagerly for his cue with guns in their hands and ski masks over their faces.

Tyreke lifted one finger in the air followed by a second one. Then a third.

"Let's do this," Damu called out, sending his twelve-inch boot into the door. BOOM!

* * * *

Chris was enjoying the feel of Cresha's slithering tongue on his balls when the door burst off the hinges. Pieces of dry wall landed only a few feet from where he was standing, which was over Cresha's face in a tea bagging position. The ear splitting blast had similar effects to a bomb going off inside a tiny balloon, causing Chris to hunch forward.

Immediately Cresha took off in the opposite direction to a corner in the living room. A mob of men wearing masks with AKs and semi-automatics rushed inside. In every direction they surrounded Chris.

A voice of authority spoke behind the ski mask that concealed the man standing in front of Chris's face.

"Sweep every room," he ordered.

Even though Cresha was given the rundown on what would go down, she still played her prescribed role.

"Hey, what's goin' on?" she asked in a rehearsed

tone. Black figures swept her apartment in a military fashion with no words given.

When Cresha called Chris an hour earlier and told him to hurry over, he wasted no time tending to her needs. Instead of listening to the voice inside his head that said something wasn't right, Chris came right over anyway. Thinking of Ansean, he dismissed the peel of bells going off in his head.

Chris watched the men rummage through Cresha's apartment like filthy rats. He locked eyes with Cresha, letting her know that he was about to make a move. However, Cresha cowardly broke his gaze. She stared up at the man with the beretta aimed at his back as if he was her superhero.

When the realization kicked in that this wasn't a random robbery, Chris began to wild out. Fumes came out of his ears while his rage-filled words shot daggers in Cresha's direction.

"You dirty fuckin' bitch!" he spat.

Chris looked over his shoulder slightly while speaking to the masked man with the gun on him.

"My man Tyreke." Chris laughed. "How was the funeral?" he asked with a wide grin. Acting off of impulse, Tyreke snatched off his mask and vaulted Chris into the air with a punch to the mouth.

"Let's talk about you and Ansean's funeral, funny man," Tyreke countered, striking Chris repeatedly with the butt of his gun. Tyreke continued to pistol whip Chris until he lumped up like oatmeal. Between breaths, Chris yelled out for his brother.

"An...Sean...Run!" he yelled through the pain of the

blows.

Damu, along with a few others, rushed back into the living room. Hating to be the bearer of bad news, Damu spoke behind his mask.

"Yo, dawg, the room and closets is clear and so is the bathroom. Man, I hate to tell you this, but unless somebody caught him outside, I think he got away. A window was open in the bathroom," Damu confirmed.

Chris lay on the floor breathing heavy and laughing. Ansean got away. Funny.

Tyreke drowned out Chris's laughs and Damu's news. He walked over to Cresha and jerked her up to face him. "Was both of them niggas here or one?" Tyreke drilled.

Trembling with fear, Cresha answered. "B-both," she stuttered, shaken up.

Tyreke looked around the room, wanting someone to tell him that Ansean had been found. With all the niggas he had flooding inside as well as outside Cresha's apartment, there was no way on God's green earth that Ansean got away. No fuckin' way. After dropping Cresha to the floor, Tyreke expressed his anger with a strong hand across Cresha's face.

"Ugh," she uttered, toppling forward.

Tyreke's nostrils flared with vexation. He turned away from Cresha and got on his walkie-talkie.

"Catch any fish yet?" *Beep. Beep.* Tyreke waited patiently for a response.

Chauncey was the first to answer in code. "No fish." *Beep. Beep.*

Tyreke sighed in frustration as the other calls came in

informing him that Ansean hadn't emerged. "No fish." The last call chimed in. Tyreke placed the walkie-talkie to his mouth while speaking behind clenched teeth.

"Keep lookin'. Keep your eyes open. This is the season for biting. Keep lookin'." *Beep. Beep.*

Tyreke glanced at his watch, and already they'd been in Cresha's apartment eleven minutes too long. Speaking into the walkie-talkie for the last time, Tyreke told everyone to be in the van at their scheduled time.

Seeing how angry Tyreke was made Cresha cry even harder. Her dreams of collecting one hundred G's would never come true. She knew that she wouldn't get Ansean's cut because, from the sound of it, he got away. So that left her with only 50 G's. Oh well, fifty G's is better than nothing.

"Lemme ask you again, in case you're dumber than you appear. Exactly how many niggas were here before you gave the signal? Think long and hard before you answer my question," Tyreke pressed Cresha, refusing to believe the inevitable.

Cresha bit down on her swollen lip, pondering over Tyreke's question. The last time she seen Ansean, he was in the bathroom. She assumed that after he finished he went into her room to lie down. Where he went? She didn't have the slightest clue; she did her part.

Either way, Damu was adamant that Cresha be punished if she failed to deliver both brothers. Maybe Tyreke would cut her some slack and pay her for one. Wrong!

"Both of 'em was here. I swear to God. Please don't kill me. Ansean was here. Honest. I won't say anything to anybody. I promise," she bellowed.

With no sympathy, Tyreke stuck out his gun towards Cresha and squeezed the trigger, sending her brain matter across the wall. Chris started throwing up on the carpet.

"Put both of 'em in the van and burn the apartment," Tyreke instructed coldheartedly, stepping over Cresha's lifeless body.

Once Cresha and Chris were carried off, Damu worked the jug of gasoline around the apartment. He wondered how an inferior nigga like Ansean had the ability to get away clean without anyone's help.

Shaking his head in disbelief, Damu struck the match.

* * * *

It was one of those nights in the projects when people decided to stay inside their apartment. Neighborhood dogs barked viciously in the distance. Ansean wondered how the projects could be sleep at a time like this. Discreetly, he stuck his head around the corner.

Niggas were camped and spread out everywhere. Any place they thought he would be, they were looking, even in the dumpsters and sewer drains.

Just to be on the safe side, Ansean went as far as slowing down his breathing in case the lynch mob of niggas—who at one point in time were his friends—heard the air escape his lungs.

Caught up in the havoc that surrounded his life, he poked his head around the apartment building a second time, and Chauncey was waiting for him. Running off of impulse, Chauncey rushed Ansean. He grabbed him by the collar of his shirt and whirled him into the brick wall.

"Nigga is you crazy? What the fuck you think you doin', huh? Do you wanna get yo'self killed?" Chauncey flexed, popping out question after question. "Stick yo shit out there like that again and I'ma hand deliver yo black ass myself."

"My fuckin' brother is in that apartment," Ansean yelled, shaking Chauncey off of him. As far as he was concerned, Chauncey was one of them. His whole "let me help you" demeanor was all too suspect for a nigga who was sent to lay him to rest. Chauncey gave him a look that clearly read "dumb ass."

"You care about your brother that damn much? Then follow the yellow brick road, Dorothy. Climb yo ass back up that window. I'm sure they'll be happy to see you, believe that! You heard the man; he said to head to the van at our scheduled time. That can only mean one thing."

Fearing the worst, Ansean cut him off. "What do you mean, that can only mean one thing?"

"It means your brother is dead. You need to start thinkin' about yo'self. I see why Tyreke cut you loose. You got to be a retarded muthafucka."

Ansean felt like he had been knocked into a state of confusion. He knew that his brother was probably dead by now. Everything within him wanted to go back inside the apartment just to check, but his legs felt like they were cemented to the ground. He didn't know whether to shed a few tears for the sake of Chris or to go completely the fuck off.

"What is it to you...Why are you tryin' to help me 'cause, nigga, I don't need shit from you," Ansean said in almost a whimpering tone.

Subconsciously looking over his shoulder, Chauncey grabbed his gear. The toothpick in his mouth rotated to and fro. "Let's just say that I am your guardian angel." He grinned devilishly. Chauncey was far from being heaven-sent. He was the devil himself hiding behind human flesh. One thing was for certain, with Ansean still breathing, it would not only buy him some time with D'mico, but it would keep Tyreke from making any logical decisions. Tyreke was the type of person who didn't like unfinished business, and Chauncey could use Ansean as his crutch. It seemed like lately Tyreke was trying to prove to himself that he was in fact "The Man." He would chase Ansean down until he took his last breath, if that's what he had to do. Chauncey wasn't trippin' though. Tyreke could be "The Man." The same man that would eventually run himself into the ground. Meanwhile, Chauncey would watch from his courtside seats.

Ansean wasn't going to let Chauncey's smooth talk affect him. Clearly he could see past the bullshit. As the old saying goes, real recognizes real and fake recognizes fake. Whatever Chauncey's M.O. was for letting him go was his business. Since he was the nigga getting a ghetto pass, he could care less.

Imitating a greyhound on the prowl, Ansean sniffed the open air. "Do you smell dat?" he asked.

Chauncey took in the scent himself. "Shit!" he said,

glancing at his watch. "Okay, check dis out, nigga. In about five minutes, dis whole apartment building will be in flames."

"In flames?"

Chauncey ignored Ansean by peeping his head around the building to see if anybody was lingering around. He was three minutes behind schedule, and he knew that Tyreke would never let him hear the end of it. Once he saw that the coast was clear, he retrieved a wad of money from his sock and threw it to the ground.

"You should know the drill. That right there should hold you over. It's only six grand, but it's enough for a bus ticket. If you wanna stay alive...stay outta the projects and away from gold digging-ass bitches, ya dig?" Chauncey turned around to leave. Remembering that he left out important information, he turned back around to face Ansean for a brief second. "Oh, just so that we're on the same page, the next time he finds out where you are and I'm the one who finds you, it'll be nighttime. Understand?" Ansean swallowed the lump in his throat. He wiped his hands over his face while shaking his head up and down. If Tyreke was burning the apartment, Chris was indeed a dead man.

Chapter 15

Kendale woke up in a haze to the sound of car doors shutting. He pulled himself out of his drunken state and sat up straight. Since there was a liquor store almost on every corner out North, he purchased a small bottle of vodka to pass the time. Somehow he must have fallen asleep on the bus stop bench outside the arena. A few curse words could be heard in the distance coming from a man who didn't mind expressing that he was angry with someone or something. Kendale couldn't tell who he was yelling at directly because all of the men were staying clear of his wrath. But he did know the man was pissed. No sooner did the angry man enter the arena than an unmarked van pull up. The driver to the van emerged and greeted the men from the previous car in a brotherly fashion with pounds and half-hugs. Their silhouettes moved rapidly in the darkness towards the rear of the van.

Kendale crumpled the brown paper sack in his lap and chucked it over his shoulder as he looked on at the scene going on before him. At first, he thought the niggas were engaging in a drug transaction until he saw a man being escorted into the building at gun point.

"Oh hell naw! What kinda funny business is this?" Kendale questioned, stunned.

From past experience, Kendale knew that whatever was about to happen inside the arena wouldn't be good, and Kendale didn't want any part of it. He hadn't even been free a full twenty-four hours, and already he could hear a choir singing the hymn for his homecoming. Kendale wanted to haul his yellow ass back to his roots. It was his word to his bunkie that glued him to the bench.

Looking on in silence, Kendale was beginning to rethink the whole "my word is my bond" motto. These days the cultivable phrase was nothing more than a five-letter word backed by trouble.

* * * *

Meanwhile inside the arena, Chauncey relaxed his

arms loosely over the boxing ring rope listening to Tyreke bitch and complain over Ansean getting away.

The man was going on and on as if his complaints would deliver Ansean to his doorstep. Chauncey laughed to himself.

"Out of thirteen niggas, nobody seen him?" Tyreke asked. The veins in his forehead and neck bulged out vehemently with every word. "Not one of you fools seen him? How is that possible? Somebody tell me that much. How the fuck is that possible? The most feared niggas in town and muthafuckas is skating by you like it ain't shit. I know. Maybe I need to start eliminating muthafuckas like that nigga right over there," Tyreke said, pointing his bloody pliers at Chris's dismembered body.

Damu's eyes wandered to the milk crate that contained Chris's body parts.

Everyone in their turn explained how they were at fault in the situation. Every excuse known to a black man was thrown Tyreke's way. Every excuse except for one. Tyreke instantly took notice of the look of comfort in Chauncey's posture. His arms swinging freely in the ropes indicated his lack of interest in the matter at hand. Turning away from his malicious wrath towards the squad, Tyreke directed his attention to Chauncey. On no account would he allow Chauncey to disrespect him the way that he was.

If he had to keep these niggas up until sunrise to show them that life wasn't a game, then so be it. Not one soul inside the arena would get any sleep. Although Tyreke's appearance appeared to be levelheaded, his anger was far from subdued.

Twirling the pliers in one hand, Tyreke walked over to the milk crate that contained Chris's body, picked up something, and walked over to Chauncey.

"What's your excuse? You been quiet since we got here, playboy. That ain't like you," Tyreke pointed out to Chauncey. Chauncey stood to his full height in confusion.

Fuck he talkin' 'bout? Chauncey thought.

"Nigga, you deaf or what?" Tyreke goaded.

A little embarrassed by Tyreke's sudden outburst, Chauncey dragged his eyes across the arena at the others. A few niggas stared at the ground, happy that it wasn't them who Tyreke was belittling.

A soft chuckle escaped Chauncey's lips. "Whatchu talkin' about, Ty? I'm just chillin', man."

Tyreke got in Chauncey's grill. Another step and Tyreke's lips would be making contact with Chauncey's nose for a kiss.

"I can clearly see that you're chillin', nigga. You and everybody else is chillin'. Again, what's your excuse, and it better be a good one."

Chauncey sucked his teeth. He didn't know whether to laugh, cry or spit in Tyreke's face. But I know one thing; Tyreke was serious as shit, and he wasn't up for giving Chauncey, or anyone else for that matter, any passes. Tyreke was at the end of his rope with Chauncey, and everyone knows what the end of the rope means—cut off.

Chauncey definitely thought Tyreke was on some other shit talking to him like he was a lesser man in front of the others. He didn't feel threatened or anything, but it was obvious that Tyreke was trying to downsize him.

Tyreke tapped Chauncey's shoulder with the bloody pliers, shaking him out of his thoughts. "We got all night in case you thinking of something good. Take all night if you got to. You seem to have had all night considering you was nine minutes late to the van. These sleepy fellas won't mind waiting on you." The tension in the arena increased tenfold. In many ways, the clock stopped. There also was a lot of activity going on despite the silence. Everyone's tired gaze swept over Chauncey, wanting so bad to beat his ass themselves. Some glanced at their watches, giving Chauncey the hint to hurry the fuck up, while the others bunched up their angry faces and ground their teeth.

Instantly it registered to Chauncey that Tyreke had passed blame solely onto him. Indeed, the man was right.

Chauncey cleared his throat. "When you said to meet you at the van, I took it upon myself to look around for Ansean. I was late because I wanted to backtrack. You know, to be on the safe side in case dude slipped up."

"You took it upon yo'self?"

"Yeah."

Not only was Chauncey's excuse overall brown-nosing, but the nigga had the audacity to tell Tyreke, and everyone else, that they weren't capable of the jobs given to them.

Damu jumped up from the crate. "Bitch-ass nigga, whatchu tryna say?"

Tyreke hushed Damu and the slew of curse words that followed. "Hold on...Hold on. Since you said fuck making it to the van on time and fuck my instructions, what did you find? Where is Ansean, you good ol' fuckin' Samaritan?"

"I didn't find nothing."

"What? Say that again," Tyreke retorted, placing his hand behind his right ear.

Chauncey swallowed. "I didn't find nothing."

"Oh I know you didn't." Tyreke gestured towards the crew with his hand. "We wouldn't be here if you did, negro."

Tyreke smiled thin. He looked directly in Chauncey's eyes while he wiped his bloody pliers on the red "J" on Chauncey's Jordan T-shirt.

"You didn't mind me doing that, did you?" Tyreke grinned. Acting unaffected by the treachery used to test his manhood, Chauncey held his chin up.

"Nah, it's all good," he lied.

The calm look on Chauncey's face was only a mask covering the fury burning within him. The nigga was so pissed that he could hardly contain the shaking in his hands and the tears that hid behind his eyes. From the corner of his eyes, he could see the stone-cold faces around him. Damu sat on an empty milk crate with a broad grin on his face. Chauncey knew that Damu didn't care for him. All bullshit to the side, the feeling was mutual; he didn't give a fuck about the nigga.

"Since you like taking matters into your own hands, I'm sure you won't mind getting rid of the bodies and cleaning up this mess. I want to send a message, so don't take the bodies to the slaughterhouse. First thing's first; clean this shit up."

Tyreke left no room for Chauncey to refuse. In the event that Chauncey had a problem with Tyreke's request, he would leave the arena in the same condition as Chris. In pieces.

"By the way, you'll need an extra hand when you're done," Tyreke ridiculed, dropping Chris's chopped off hand into Chauncey's palm.

After Tyreke turned around, he made it clear that Chauncey no longer had a part in his squad. There were no spoken words. They weren't necessary. The venom in Tyreke's responses spoke a thousand words. Chauncey had been nipped and tucked to the back. There goes his rope.

* * * *

The sun slowly progressed through the morning clouds, giving the world an extra push to get their asses up and start their day. Kendale woke up with a pounding headache and a cramp in his back. He didn't know what was worse, sitting on a cold bench for nine hours stalking another man or waiting for the guilty verdict. Above all, Kendale was sick and tired of waiting. He picked the boogers out of his eyes and sat up straight.

Finally, there was movement. Kendale's eyes fell on a man with broad shoulders sharing his height and build. Two milk crates stacked over the other occupied his large hands. Kendale took out the 4 x 6 photo given to him by his bunkie and put it at arms length, pairing up the picture with the man across the street.

"Yeah, that's him."

By accident, Kendale tipped over his bottle of vodka, causing it to fall to the ground with a loud splat.

Shit!

* * * *

Chauncey set the smelly crates on the roof of his car, wiped his bloodstained hands on the sides of his shirt and removed a variety of keys from his pants pocket. It took hours for him to clean up the waste produced by Tyreke. The way Tyreke embarrassed him tonight called for a good ass-kicking and then some. Once he had the appropriate key, Chauncey grabbed the crates and opened the trunk to his car. He hated the stench of dead flesh. It was something that he just couldn't get use to.

Immediately Chauncey covered the crates with a sheet and closed his trunk when the resonant echo of a broken bottle interrupted his ruminating. Following the alarming sound, Chauncey made his way across the street towards the man responsible for holding him up.

From the corner of Kendale's eyes, he saw a pair of thirteen-inch sneakers while he was bent over picking up scattered pieces of glass.

Great, way to go, Kendale. Why don't you tell the nigga that you're here because he's slimy! Kendale said silently to himself. Thinking about the picture in his hand, he balled up his fist in an attempt to hide it from Chauncey's view.

"Yo, what's good? I been getting clumsier by the day," Kendale said when he rose up, acting as normal as can be. Chauncey nodded towards the paper sack on the ground.

"You should pick that up. This is a good neighborhood. Plus, it's a little too early to be drinkin', don't you think?"

Kendale picked up the bag and threw the pieces of broken glass inside along with the picture. "No disrespect, fam'. My lady was on some bull shit last night." Kendale lifted the paper sack in the air with a forced smile on his face. "If you knew my lady, you'd be lost in the bottle too. Word up."

Chauncey eyed the stranger as if he was another bum. He gave the man a once-over, studying his hand-me-down clothes and 1964 Reeboks from back in the day.

Avoiding the "I know you" expression Chauncey wore on his face, Kendale looked away towards the ground where he spotted some more broken glass. Cautiously, he bent down and scooped them up.

"You look familiar. Do I know you?" Chauncey asked, waiting for the stranger to finish his task.

Kendale placed the pieces in the bag. "Naw, you don't know me."

"You don't sound like you from around here. Where you from? Where do you and yo woman stay at?"

Kendale couldn't believe that Chauncey asked him where he was from and where he laid his head. Neither of the two was any of his business. Questions were another reason why he hated the state of Oklahoma. Niggas were too damn friendly, and they felt like they could drill you with a shitload of questions like their business would become yours and vice versa. In New York, you lived by the code "mind your own and you'll live long," something this nigga knew nothing about. Personally, Chauncey didn't know him from a monkey's balls, yet the cat was fresh in his mix like pancake batter.

"We stay around the way," Kendale answered flatly.

"Around the way, huh? Well as you can see, you around my way," Chauncey stated, claiming Tyreke's territory as his own.

Kendale could see that Chauncey was on some power trip type of shit. All he wanted to do was inform Tyreke about the maggot and bounce. "My broad dishin' out enough problems. I don't mean no disrespect." Kendale stood to match Chauncey's stature. He could see a stone-cold killer in Chauncey's eyes. Vengeance was written all over his face. There was no way that he could match that. His skills were rusty, and only being the messenger, he didn't have a leg to stand on. Chauncey gave Kendale a distasteful look before walking away. Making his way back across the street, he thought about the pitiful look on the brother's face. The argument with his woman probably had a lot to do with the fact that the dude was an alcoholic.

* * * *

Chauncey rotated his watch while checking the time. The law would be changing shifts in thirty minutes so that gave him exactly twenty-five minutes to deliver the bodies to their final destination. I know you're probably wondering why the twenty-five span, right? Well, it's like this. All day long police officers work around the clock shaking up folks. We're talking eight to twelve hours straight per day. Not only does the job call for high expectations but the officers are underpaid as well. With that in mind, the last half hour of their shift consists of kicking back, sipping hard-ass coffee, and bullshit. And all of this information was given to Tyreke as a courtesy coming directly from the Chief.

The clock was ticking and Chauncey was wasting time. He slid his key in the ignition bringing his ride to life. He took one last look at the man getting up from the bench and it hit him. He knew the dude looked familiar. Things were starting to make sense. Someone had sent him, and he knew exactly who that somebody was. Dirt's father. Kendale had a better chance at staying in prison. At least behind bars he would have stayed alive.

Chauncey circled the block. He watched Kendale cross Denver and its busy traffic.

Every time Kendale neared a stoplight, he looked over his shoulder to see if he was being followed. Feeling like a paranoid schizophrenic, he pressed the crosswalk button.

"Come on...Come on..." he mumbled, keeping his eyes on the indicator.

Chauncey neared the yellow light. With two dead bodies already in the trunk of his Chevy, he was about to take a major leap, but what other choice did he have? He reached for his glove box and loaded his .45 with a full clip. *Two in the trunk, one more to go*, he thought, rolling down his window.

"Excuse me, sir," he called out in his best impression of a white male.

Somewhat annoyed, Kendale turned around. In broad

daylight, shots were fired into Kendale's torso, upper shoulder and right leg. The brute force sent him staggering backwards, causing his knees to buckle. Choking on his own blood, Kendale looked towards the heavens and inhaled his last breath.

Chauncey made a clean sweep leaving behind screams, a pileup and one less nigga to worry about.

Chapter 16

Route 66 Motel was nothing but a run-down slum located outside of the city.

Not even the thrift store bedspread or curtains could escape the striking scent of Asian cuisine. The room ensured your basic necessities—a full-size bed, one thirteen-inch color television with no stand, and a phone that received incoming calls only.

Feeling out of his element, Ansean plopped down on the stiff bed in distress. Although he felt lucky to be alive, the guilt of leaving Chris behind had a major effect on his soul. Over and over he replayed the events that took place. "Save yourself" were the words his conscience repeated. Each time the statement surfaced, he tried his best to overcome the deception, yet his actions proved to be the strongest, and he gave in to the six grand placed in his hand.

Every man and woman who has a part in the streets is supposed to abide by the same rules of loyalty, integrity and honor. The streets weren't the only thing

Ansean failed. He failed himself as a man and as a brother. Pulling himself out of his funk, he turned on the TV. Breaking news broadcasted on channel six. Yellow caution tape stopped the heavy crowd of onlookers from crossing into the crime scene. A cold chill traveled up his spine when the cameraman got a close-up of the navy blue house he grew up in. Please, God, let my mom be alright. His mother was the only flesh and blood he had left. Unable to listen to the two detectives describe, in their opinion, what they believed to be the most gruesome homicide in their professional careers, Ansean spotted his mother crying on the shoulder of a neighbor. She appeared to be alright but shook up.

In the background, coroner officials placed small items spread throughout the yard in black exhibit bags. The reporter identified the unknown items as the remains of 33-year-old Chris Parrel, an ex-convict recently released from the custody of the Department of Corrections. Flushed with rage, Ansean smashed the television with his fist.

The night Dirt was killed, Ansean did what any man would do in his shoes. He protected his brother. Did he mean for anyone to get hurt? No, of course not. Neither could he take the shit back. Tyreke crossed the line when he distributed Chris's body across his mother's lawn. The 5,902 dollars he had to his name weren't enough to act on at this moment, but in due season, Tyreke would feel his hands.

* * * *

Seven Months Later...

"My friend...As usual, everything looks good. Is it necessary that you must leave so quickly? Stay. There will be plenty of beautiful women arriving tonight," Jose said.

Jose's henchman, Carlos, placed a large suitcase at the foot of Tyreke's chair. Like a trained animal, he returned to his boss's side with a stern look on his face and both hands crossed behind his back.

Tyreke straightened out the wrinkle in his Armani slacks. "With all do respect," he grabbed the suitcase and stood to his feet, "business is business, and I do not mix business with pleasure."

Jose cleared the diamonds from everyone's view. Afterwards, Jose and four of his toughest bodyguards escorted Tyreke to the door. Although Jose was disappointed that Tyreke refused his offer to stay, he respected the trade of the game. Tyreke's drive to seal a deal, deliver his product and part from his company reminded him of when he started out.

"Tyreke, you are the same today, tomorrow and the next. You never change. That is why I like you." Jose stopped mid-stride. The stern look on his face was serious. "You will find what I left in your suitcase very valuable. It's a gift that I will not allow you to decline."

Tyreke's eyebrow went up. Curious to know what lay in wait, he humbled himself and shook Jose's hand in agreement.

In less than no time, Tyreke was on his private plane with a heavy suitcase in his lap.

Two punches of a button and the suitcase opened. To his surprise, a beautiful diamond the size of a nugget sat neatly on an arrangement of bills stacked in four rows of five. Not only had he neglected the drug trade for this but the beautiful asset smiling at him proved that all of his hard work had finally paid off. He eased the case shut, leaned back in his cozy seat and relaxed every muscle in his body. A crescent smile was sketched across his face when he thought about what he would do with the diamond.

* * * *

"Everybody get ready...Here we go! Ten, nine, eight, seven, six, five, four, three, two, one, HAPPY NEW YEAR!"

Pow! Pop! Pow!

Fireworks went off, horns were blown, confetti drizzled everywhere and champagne bottles overflowed with bubbly.

Staring lustfully at one another, Tyreke and D'mico shared an intimate kiss under the stars while Maxwell sung , "This Woman's Work."

Fort Lauderdale, Florida was the place to be. The weather was nice and the atmosphere welcomed everyone. Ten of Tyreke's closest friends and family members gathered on a luxurious yacht to bring in the blessing of another year.

Reverend Johnson and Denise danced nonstop. The couple moved gracefully across the floor in a world of their own. Their bond was unbelievable. Twenty-eight years as husband and wife brought hope for Tyreke and his future relationship with D'mico.

Feeling as sensual as the cool breeze, Tyreke secured D'mico's waist as they watched the waves crash into the Atlantic Ocean. D'mico's smell, the feel of her skin and the way she balled up like a kitten when he wrapped his big hands around her made Tyreke smile. Never in his adult life had he felt this way about a woman before. On occasion, his folks would preach to them about getting hitched. On the other hand, love isn't something to be rushed. Love is patient. Tyreke compared love to opportunities; they only came around once in a lifetime, and he wanted the opportunity to be right. Tyreke lavished D'mico with kisses. He nuzzled his nose in the nape of her warm neck.

"Happy New Year, sexy," he whispered.

D'mico spun around. The twinkle in her eyes matched her smile. "Aaah...You're so sweet. Happy New Year to you too, daddy. I love you," she cooed.

D'mico loved the fact that she got to witness her man's sensitive side. There was no way in hell the man in front of her could be capable of some of the things she had heard about. Unable to hold back, she pecked his lips. Tyreke held her at arms length. Suffering from butterflies, he stepped back and got on one knee. Nervously, he stroked D'mico's arm. Looking into her eyes, he pulled a small purple box out of his pocket.

"I love you too."

Tears of joy spilled from D'mico's eyes. "Is this…Are you for real?" she asked with a hand over her mouth.

"Yeah, baby, it's real," Tyreke said, opening the box and exposing a radiant cut center ring with round diamonds in platinum—worth $298,000.

Everyone began to form a large circle around them. Denise clutched her husband's hand, and tears of joy fell from her eyes.

"Every time I look at you, I see a piece of myself. You're my spine, legs...my heart, my everything. I would die for you, and I know you would do the same if the shoe was on the other foot." Tyreke paused for a second. *Love is patient* went through his mind once again. "D'mico, you're the piece to my puzzle. Not only am I asking for your companionship but I'm asking for your hand in marriage." Another pause. "D'mico, will you marry me?"

On the verge of passing out, D'mico bent down and wrapped her arms around Tyreke's neck chanting "yes" in excitement as he lifted her in the air.

After several minutes of long kisses, the women watching managed to pull D'mico away from her fiancé.

Reverend Johnson embraced Tyreke with a warm hug. "No more shackin' up, huh? Congratulations, son. We're proud of you."

"Yeah, man, congratulations. You doin' the right thing," Damu added, giving his foreman a strong pound. Tyreke wrapped his arms around his father and Damu.

"I hope this is right. If it ain't, it'll never be," he said, watching D'mico twirl around like a black princess.

* * * *

D'mico was on her way to Sunday service in her brand-new red and black 2010 Aston Martin, courtesy of Tyreke. She wasn't complaining about the car, but she was beginning to hate the smothering gifts Tyreke threw her way to make up for his shortcomings. Like I said, she wasn't complaining; it's just that he made her feel like one of those materialistic females who only saw her man as a come up. Although she was living the fairy tale she dreamed of as a child, she wasn't completely satisfied. A void that couldn't be filled continued to press on her heart. No gifts, hugs or soothing words could release the numb feeling she endured on a day to day basis. The days she lost her mother, her son and herself were the worst days of her life.

Her self-esteem did a domino effect shortly after. Now Tyreke...oh he was great, too damn great sometimes. Every year on the same day, like clockwork, Tyreke would be there to lift her spirits up. Of course, he ran the streets on his spare time, but overall his time was devoted to her happiness. All of that came to an end today. Santy'ya's birthday.

If the man wasn't away on business, he was at the boxing ring investing his time and effort into a bunch of kids from the ghetto with no future. The choice to reopen the damn place was a wasted investment if you asked her.

Shoot, it ain't like the place paid any bills. Tyreke didn't need the extra money anyway. D'mico didn't know what Oprah clocked in every year, but she bet the money that Tyreke was earning was damn close. Okay, maybe she was exaggerating a bit. Tyreke wasn't rich rich, but the nigga's pockets were fed beyond belief. The moral to the story was he *chose* to be there. What could be more important than her? Yeah, yeah. So you think D'mico is selfish and self-centered? Well, in a way, she was. She couldn't help it. Tyreke was her everything. Hell, who am I kidding? The man was her only thing. She was three weeks into her engagement, and already she felt like a piece of shit.

Wiping the few tears that rolled down her cheeks, D'mico gathered her feelings. She couldn't wait to get to church so she could feel better. God's work is like magic. No matter what you're going through or where you been, he has a way to make all of your problems disappear. Only if you seek him.

When D'mico arrived, the church was jam-packed. Every available parking spot in the first, second and third rows was occupied with vehicles, leaving her with no choice but to park in the back. She eased in a spot next to a new Camry and an older model station wagon sitting on twenty-inch rims. These days, people saw fit to put anything with a steering wheel on rims. It could be a hearse. They wouldn't care. Throw some d's on that hoe. D'mico stepped out her car looking like a tall glass of champagne. She slid on a pair of Versace shades to hide the morning sun. She looked towards the door. From where she was standing, it seemed as though the door was a mile ahead. Taking a deep breath, she made her way to the entrance.

* * * *

Starlet stared out her car window at D'mico, contemplating whether or not she should approach her. She couldn't help but wonder how a woman so beautiful and put together could fuck Tyreke over for a nigga like Chauncey. Yep, she knew all about their little fuckscapade. Chauncey was a no-good-ass nigga. Chauncey had his share of women. He was an egotistical jerk who not only manipulated D'mico but had her girl Leslie brainwashed as well. Shidd...he even took her for a loop once. She didn't know Dirt then. Now Dirt, he was her baby. He wasn't supposed to go out the way he did. It was D'mico's slutty-ass ways that got him tricked off. All of this was D'mico's fault, and everyone's lives had been ruined in the process. I guess it was too late to be crying over spilled milk. Ever since Dirt's funeral, Starlet's urge to get high grew weak. Maybe it's fair to say that Dirt's funeral brought some change in her life. Starlet believed that this was a perfect opportunity for a second chance. With her second chance, she wanted to make right with all the people she had wronged. She didn't feel like she had done D'mico any wrong on her own, but she was holding some information about two people who had. If God could show her favor, why couldn't he do the same when it came down to D'mico?

* * * *

Starlet had the toughest job in the 9-1-8. No, she wasn't a cop or a firefighter. However, serving hungry-ass thugs and scallywags after club hours was a bigger job than protecting Obama from the Ku Klux Klan. Chicken Hutt was the only kick-it spot where you could cop something to eat, catch a few numbers, grab some bootleg liquor and possibly luck up on a cool booty call. All of this took place between the hours of 10 p.m. and 5 a.m. in the morning. Working under the table was the only reason why Starlet risked her life on the weekends. Feeding niggas who either disrespected her every night or looked at her as a mere hook-up took a nice chunk out of her sanity. She was paid to handle the toast, put butter on it, slice it diagonally, place it in the appropriate box when it was ready, and then call out the four-digit number on the receipt. That was it.

"Yo, bitch, where da fuck is order 0-1-9-1? Why is my shit taking so long? Niggas before me is comin' and goin' and still my shit ain't ready."

Starlet ignored the greasy-looking dude who cursed her between clenched teeth. She sung the song playing in the background silently to herself and continued to load bread into the toaster.

"Bitch, I know you hear me talking to you. How long is it gonna take for your simple ass to make a hot link sandwich? If I give you two extra dollars, will your skank ass have it ready then?" the dude yelled, pressing his face against the tiny window that separated him from the employees. Starlet closed the serving window. What part of "she only did the toast" did these niggas not understand? Having had enough and on her last straw, she stormed towards the back.

She grabbed a frozen hot link out the deep freezer, chopped it in half, gathered the same sloppy-ass salad served to everyone else, loaded two untoasted pieces of bread into the to-go box and called out the number.

"0-1-9-1."

Big Greasy puffed up his chest as he marched to the front line like he was VIP. "'Bout muthafuckin' time. My shit betta be hot too." With a hand full of change, he chucked the pennies and nickels through the window, hitting Starlet on her pinkie. "Buy yaself something nice." He laughed and snatched his food. For several shocking seconds, Starlet just stood there.

"That's it! Fuck this shit. I quit!" she fumed, feeling humiliated. She took off her stained apron and slammed it on the counter.

"What? You can't quit. I already paid you," Joe, the store owner, called out.

Starlet unraveled her thick, brown, curly hair. "Like hell I can't. Fuck you, yo stankin' ass chicken, and your week-old grease. Fifty dollars ain't nearly enough for the mental anguish dis shithole done put me through. You want yo money back? Well, check dis out. You ain't gonna get it back. Sue me!" she yelled on her way out the back door.

Since there were no running buses at three o'clock in the morning and she didn't have any transportation, Starlet had no choice but to walk. The Chicken Hutt was only a few blocks from her friend Leslie's house. She would crash at Leslie's crib overnight until she woke up to take her kids to school in the morning. *Yeah, that's what I'll do*, she thought.

Starlet and Leslie had been friends for fourteen years. In school, people referred to the girls as "twins" because they were so inseparable. It was only when Leslie started popping out baby after baby when they were no longer as close. Leslie hooked up with her abusive, leech-ass baby daddy, Rodney. Rodney not only controlled the amount of air Leslie could take in, but he manipulated and disrespected anybody who Leslie associated with. Their whole relationship was only based on sex, if you asked Starlet. Her homegirl was so sprung over Rodney's dick that she couldn't tell whether or not if she was coming or going.

"Gurl, I'm kinda busy right now. Me and Rodney got into it earlier, so I gotta give him that make-up. Call me back tomorrow, alright?" That's what Leslie would say to her friend numerous times over the phone.

Just to put you up on game, "make-up" meant sex. Nine times out of ten Rodney did something wrong, which wasn't a surprise coming from a bum-ass nigga like himself. He would later make Leslie feel like the reason why he was out contracting STDs and cheating on her was all her fault. Slowly, he would reel her back in, knock her up to the point where she wouldn't want to move around, and then carry on with his same old philandering ways.

"That's a damn shame," Starlet said to herself, thinking about the BS her homegirl was dragging herself through. Approaching Pine Street, Starlet spotted the greasy-looking guy from the Chicken Hutt across the street. His body hanging out of his car window indicated that he was looking for someone. Starlet knew that he was looking for her. Being attentive and keeping her eyes on the dude who turned in the direction of the Chicken Hutt, Starlet crossed the street and nearly got hit by a Chevy Impala. With her heart leaping out of her chest, she threw up her hands and mouthed the word "sorry." The driver rolled down his window.

"Eh, you alright?" the driver asked with concern.

"Yeah, I'm okay."

"Damn, lil mama, I thought you seen a ghost the way you just jumped out there like that."

Off top, Starlet noticed the pretty set of teeth that gleamed from the man's mouth. She wasn't a fan of dark-skinned brothers, but Mr. Chocolate Drop made her want an autograph. His strong features drew her closer to his car.

In her mind, she was already running down the scrub test. If the dude offered her a ride, then he was a gentleman, but if he didn't, he was another pussy-sniffing scrub ready to give her countless babies and bad credit. Even though Starlet would decline his offer if he offered her a ride, she still wanted to know where his head was at.

"Where you goin'? Lemme give you a ride, shorty."

Holding the "hard to get" look on the outside, Starlet smiled on the inside. "Nah...I'm cool. Thanks though. I'm a big girl. Plus, my mama told me never to ride with strangers."

"You're right and ya mama taught you well. I just

would hate for that nigga who you was running from a minute ago to catch up with you. He look like the type of cat that'll gobble yo fine ass up alive."

On that note, Starlet hauled ass around to the passenger side door. With a stunned look on her face, she strapped on her seat belt.

"Good choice. Just so ya know, Starlet, my name is Chauncey."

Chauncey could tell by the way Starlet gasped and reached for the doorknob that she was about to split.

"Relax," he said, grabbing her arm. "Your name tag on your shirt says Starlet. That is your name, right?" Starlet looked down at her tag. Loosening her grip, she busted out laughing.

"I'm sorry. I thought..." She waved at the air. "Never mind."

"Where we going?" Chauncey asked.

"Second block on the left on Seminole."

Minutes later, Starlet pointed a single finger at a cream-colored house with a carport over a black Regal.

"That's me right there."

"Do you live here by yourself?"

"Nah...this is kinda like my second spot. This is my homegirl's house," Starlet informed him.

"Oh, that's cool." Chauncey knew that Starlet didn't live around this area. In fact, he knew more about Starlet and her friend Leslie than they knew about themselves. Although Starlet beat her friend in the looks department, "the closest always gets the mostest," and Leslie was his first pick. One reason why Chauncey wanted to use Starlet to get to her friend was simple. Chauncey needed to get close to Tyreke. Leslie was D'mico's hairstylist. After working under Tyreke for four years, he learned that D'mico looked forward to her visits with her stylist. She also didn't have any steady girlfriends, which made it harder for him to get her attention. So that meant one thing; all of D'micos' problems, ideas and secrets went to Leslie. The only thing about Leslie was that she couldn't see past her damn baby daddy.

When Chauncey saw that Starlet had quit her job at the Chicken Hutt, he stayed in the cut and watched her get a couple of blocks before making his move. I know what you're thinking. You're thinking...damn this nigga is physco, but it ain't nothing like that. Sometimes you got to step out of character in order to get things done. Did he want to watch three women? Yes and no. Yes, he liked to watch them in some of their intimate and vulnerable moments, but he hated what he had to do. Shidd, believe it or not, his mom did raise him better than that. Yeah right!

One thing about hood chicks, as long as you supply them with fire dro, they're like that Lauryn Hill song "Nothing Even Matters." Chauncey watched Starlet long enough to know that she was just another chip off the old block, and he had plans to take Starlet straight to fool's paradise.

"You smoke?" Chauncey asked, adding fire to the potent stick.

After dealing with hundreds of hungry vultures at the Chicken Hutt, Starlet didn't mind getting blowed. Actually, chiefing on some weed sounded damn good for a bitch who hadn't choked all day.

"From time to time I do," she responded, kicking back in her seat.

Chauncey grinned from ear to ear expecting those words to come out of Starlet's mouth. He shifted his gear out of park into drive.

"Let's take a ride, sexy. You down to roll?"

Going along with the flow of things, Starlet shrugged her shoulders. "Yeah, I'm down for that. Let's roll."

Chapter 17

Disturbing memories from Starlet's past made her want to vomit. She had given into pure pressure and suffered major repercussions. The first time she smoked anything other than weed was the night she met Chauncey four years ago. The small vial filled with fluid took Starlet for an unexpected ride. She wanted to believe that Chauncey was into her, so she did what most girls her age did when it came down to men.

Whatever they asked.

The lack of interest Chauncey had in Starlet was no secret. In fact, he probed more into Leslie's life and career than he showed interest in the relationship he shared with Starlet. Yeah, that's right.

For a couple of months, Chauncey and Starlet dated. If that's what you want to call it.

Starlet tried to justify it when Chauncey scandalously hooked up with her best friend. They hadn't slept together, so what was the big deal? To Starlet, they weren't serious. Besides, Leslie finally got over her baby daddy, Rodney, and she smiled more when Chauncey came around. Hey, she looked at it like this; men were like bus stops. If one rolls by, you can always catch another one at the next corner. So why trip? Leslie was happy with Chauncey, and Starlet was happy with her wet daddy woostick.

Starlet got out of her car to catch up with D'mico. Lightly she tapped her shoulder. "D'mico, can I talk to you for a minute?"

D'mico turned around like she saw a ghost. When she noticed that it was Starlet who frightened her, she reached for her pepper spray keychain. She gave Starlet a look that said "what."

"I want to apologize for the way I acted towards you. We started off on the wrong foot, and it was my fault. I tried to getchu high on somethin' you knew nothing about, and I was wrong for that."

"No love lost," D'mico said sarcastically.

Starlet searched for the right words. The bored look on D'mico's face made her feel uncomfortable and unsure whether or not she was doing the right thing.

"You know, it took a lot for me to approach you, and your standing over there with your head in your own ass."

"Starlet, you're not on my favorite list, and I know dang well I'm not on yours," D'mico said with an attitude.

Starlet stood their baffled by D'mico's childish attitude. Damn, she wasn't expecting for the woman to forgive her overnight, but all of the extras were uncalled for. Here she was trying to make amends with the woman, and D'mico was acting like she was faultless, like she never took a shit or wiped her own ass. Ugh...No wonder everyone labeled her ass as a stuck-up phony. Just like the rest of the world, she was sure D'mico had a few skeletons in her closet.

"You know what? Maybe I was wrong about you," Starlet said.

"Maybe you was," D'mico barked, rolling her hazel eyes.

Starlet took a deep breath. Why couldn't she just punch the trick? But that wouldn't solve anything. She reminded herself why she was there. Her drug counselor gave her three important things to do to stabilize her addiction. The first thing was for her to seek God then find forgiveness. The last thing on her agenda was to apologize to everyone she might've hurt during her addiction.

"Why don't you take a second out of your "woe is me," selfish-ass attitude and listen to what I gotta say, damn!" Starlet said.

D'mico bit her tongue. Standing back on her left leg, she folded her arms over her breasts and gave Starlet the stage. She hated to admit it, but Starlet was actually really pretty. Her Chinese bangs, long Yaky hair and chinky eyes complimented her chubby cheeks, making her look like that chick LisaRaye but better. Starlet's curly eyelashes fluttered as she pleaded her case.

"It was the message Reverend Johnson delivered at Dirt's funeral that made me want to take back my life. The person you knew was heavily addicted to drugs. I'm no longer that person anymore." Starlet took a breath before continuing. "Dirt loved you and Tyreke. Shoot, Dirt talked about Tyreke all the time. I know he wouldn't let nothin' happen to neither of ya. And because of that, I know what I gotta do. D'mico, you have to open your eyes. You've hurt more people than you think.

D'mico's eyes roamed all over Starlet's face. She could tell there was more that Starlet wanted to say, yet the cat that held her tongue wired her mouth shut.

There was no easy way for Starlet to tell D'mico that her best friend's man, her ex, and D'mico's secret lover had it out to kill her and Tyreke. Starlet was facing a tough dilemma which involved D'mico and Leslie. Who would she choose?

In a hushed tone, Starlet whispered, "Just be careful about the men you encounter. Everybody ain't for you. The one to trust is the one who stuck by you from the beginning. Remember that," Starlet finished. She threw her purse over her shoulder and walked away.

D'mico stood in the parking lot scatterbrained. If it wasn't Tyreke who she'd hurt, then who was it? Chauncey was the only other person she had any contact with. Besides, their relationship was quiet. No one knew about the two of them.

Starlet was buggin', she said that she was no longer doing drugs, yet D'mico thought different. It had to be all those drugs that made Starlet lose her fuckin' mind. Just say no.

The church bells sounded.

D'mico continued inside the church without giving thought to Starlet's warning.

* * * *

Tyreke wondered how well D'mico was holding up without him. He dipped early just so he wouldn't have to face her. He knew that right about now she would be dragging her feet around the house moping. Every year on Santy'ya's birthday, she did the same thing. For years

Tyreke attempted to soothe her guilt by showering her with gifts and giving her as much attention as needed. Although he empathized with her pain, he sorta was fed up with pulling D'mico out of her ongoing funk. Selfishly, he was beginning to think that she liked the attention to use Santy'ya as her personal crutch . All of that shit got as old as a lemon, and Tyreke decided to do something productive today that didn't involve shaking up the streets, counting money or babying a grown-ass woman.

Tyler, who only answered by the nickname "Ty," won first place in his third Golden Gloves title.

Ty had something to be proud of, so Tyreke rented the Rose Bowl Center to celebrate.

Giving the center a visual sweep, Tyreke closed his phone shut. He watched proudly as Ty paraded around the spacious building with his three-foot trophy. Watching little daddy was comical as hell. The thing was heavy and half his size, coming up to his chest. Although Ty struggled to hold it up, he didn't want to put it down.

Tyreke grabbed his attention. "Ty, comere, lil daddy."

Ty walked anxiously over to Tyreke, showing off his brand-new sneakers and fresh Koogi outfit that Tyreke bought him a week ago. Tyreke started to notice small things about Ty that seemed weird. For instance, his little button nose and bright smile were exactly like D'mico's. Ain't it crazy how God works? Although D'mico and Ty didn't know each other, it was as though they were one and the same.

"Don'tchu know your arm gonna fall off if you don't

put that thing down sometime today?" Tyreke joked, grazing the top of Ty's head with his hand.

"Nah...I got this," Ty boasted, lifting the trophy to his chest.

"Okay, lil daddy. I believe you. Where's Serenity?"

"Umm..." Ty scanned the building. He pointed to the lady's room. "There she go," he said, running off to go play.

Serenity instantly captured Tyreke' s attention. The first thing he noticed about her was her striking brown eyes, full lips, chocolate skin and the beauty mark placed on the far right side of her chin. She took two bold steps before removing her bangs away from her must-see eyes. Each leg crossed over the other in a steady stride, showing off her cocoa legs which simmered with baby oil. Serenity was seasoned just right. She was more than a package deal for any nigga to play with. Nah, Serenity was quality, a grand finale made especially for a man who could handle everything that she had to offer. Tyreke watched Serenity's angelic features from across the building like a scene from a movie.

Did Cupid shoot his arrow? Well, that's the question Serenity asked when she exited the restroom and locked eyes with Tyreke. Damn, he was so fine. His strong, handsome features took her breath away. His once curly hair had been replaced with sexy, deep waves cut into a taper fade. He still had the same goatee except for the sides were trimmed thinner around the edges making his perfect, luscious lips broader, fuller and exceptionally suckable. If being fine was a crime, Tyreke would leave this Earth by lethal injection.

Serenity couldn't help herself from checking out the way the man carried himself, which seemed like a dream come true to a woman who spent many nights alone with no one to officially call her own.

Sadly, the men Serenity encountered over the years were already in serious relationships or lying about not being in one. Giving every man the benefit of the doubt, Serenity was still waiting for Mr. Right. Knowing that Tyreke was in a relationship came as no surprise to Serenity. If anything, she respected him even more when he announced that he was very much involved with someone. Contently, he stood off to the side wearing a dark brown G-Star jacket rested over a cream-colored G-Star button-up. His brown LRG denim jeans looked as though he had no problem stepping into them. They weren't too tight or too baggy.

Lord help me! she thought, making her way through the central passageway that extended through glass, double Dutch doors.

"Look at you. Wow, you look great!" Tyreke complimented Serenity when she got to him.

"Thanks. This is really nice, Tyreke." She looked around in awe. "Must've cost you a grip." She frowned, not wanting to be a burden on Tyreke anymore than she had already.

"It's all good. Ty's my nigga for life, so it was nothin'."

"Where's Damu? I haven't seen him around. Is he coming?"

"Nah, he couldn't make it. Had some business to take care of. You're probably glad he ain't comin' anyway,"

Tyreke teased.

Serenity gave him the eye. "You know it ain't nothin' like that."

"Oh yeah?"

"Mmm-hmm, anybody Ty likes is cool with me. He told me that when he grows up, he wants to be just like you two."

Tyreke scratched his head. "He gonna be better than me!"

"Can I ask you a question?" Serenity asked, getting serious.

"Sure. Ask me whatever you want."

"Doesn't Damu mean blood? You know, like the gang?" It wasn't a surprise that Serenity wanted to know the same thing a lot of people asked throughout Damu's entire life.

"Do you think we're gangbangers?" Tyreke asked.

"Well, I dunno. Ty looks up to you. Are you?"

Tyreke completely lost himself in Serenity's mocha eyes. She was one of them chicks who could keep a nigga's nose wide open. She didn't pass off as being nosy at all, just cautious enough to not piss him off. Careful to not incriminate himself, Tyreke ignored her last statement. He might not be a gangbanger, but he was a thug all the way.

"Damu does mean blood. If it quacks like a duck but smell like fish, do we automatically assume it's a duck? Of course not because it's neither. Damu was named after his late father who was affiliated with a gang known as Piru. His mother wanted to pass on his father's legacy when he got killed. It's kinda wicked 'cause most of the cats Damu looked up to were Hoover Crips. To him, his name was a curse, never being accepted by either set. Over the years, he had to learn that it's impossible to please everybody. That's why he's straight and to the point. Do that answer your question?" Tyreke answered in a nutshell.

Serenity felt bad for judging Damu's passive-aggressive behavior. Instead of searching for the goodness in his heart, she judged a book by its cover.

"So, what was it?" Serenity asked Tyreke.

"What was what?"

"Well, if it wasn't a duck and it wasn't a fish, then what was it?"

"Nobody knows. That's why it's best if we don't assume."

Serenity was quite impressed with Tyreke. She liked him, and I mean she liked him a lot. He might've not been a gang member, but he sure as hell was a thug.

"Cool" by Anthony Hamilton reverberated throughout the center, hyping everyone up to dance. Even with his trophy glued to his hands, Ty danced along with the other children.

"Tyreke, I love this song," Serenity shouted over the music in excitement.

Tyreke took in the visual pleasantries of watching Serenity do her thing by closing her eyes and gyrating her hips to the rhythm of the song. Serenity did this thing with her hands as she mouthed the words "If you're cool, then I'm cool," pointing towards Tyreke and then herself. The effect Serenity had on Tyreke was crazy. He wanted to take her into his arms and hold on to her forever. He wanted to be the body interlocked with hers, the combination to her safe. Hell yeah, he went there.

Serenity's entertaining groove came to an end when the song was over and the next song by UNK, "Walk It Out," took over. Serenity opened her eyes and a universal smile appeared on her face. Tyreke looked down at his engagement band only to feel guilty about his new feelings for another woman.

"I haven't heard that song in months. I'ma share a secret with you. Music is my mask. No matter what type of mood I'm in, good or bad, if the lyrics is on point and the beat is nice, that's where I'll be until that five minutes is up." Serenity bobbed her head like the song was being replayed inside her mind.

Clearly Serenity felt comfortable around Tyreke to run her perspective on music to him. She had a free spirit, and Tyreke was really enjoying her company. For the life of him though, he didn't understand how a woman so beautiful could be single.

"What do you hide behind?" Serenity asked, wanting to know more about Tyreke than he'd already revealed.

Tyreke fished for lost words. He hid behind a number of things. Serenity's question made him look deep into his life. To name a few, he hid behind his power, his lifestyle, the preacher he had for a father and even D'mico. Anything that wouldn't remind him of his past, the life before the corruption. The life D'mico didn't know.

"I hide behind life and everything in it. Everybody does. It's the way of the world."

Serenity was positive that Tyreke was hiding behind

something deep. Deep and hurtful. Who was she to think that he would share his darkest secrets with her. She wasn't his woman. He probably shared that intimacy with her. There in Tyreke's eyes hid a needy look. Going against her morals, Serenity started to lay her feelings on the table.

"Tyreke, there's something that I want to tell you. I know that you have a woman, but the way you make me feel...is…"

Tyreke inched closer. The smell of his Cartier cologne brushed Serenity's nostrils causing an explosion to go off inside her panties. Tyreke sealed her lips with his finger.

"Shh...I already know. I feel that way too," he said in a whisper so low that the base in his voice tickled Serenity's soul.

Tyreke felt like he opened a big present on Christmas day when his lips met Serenity's. Back and forth their tongues twirled, glided and trailed over the other as they enjoyed the savor of their special kiss. Tyreke dismissed the negative thoughts concerning D'mico.

All kinds of things went through Serenity's mind as Tyreke grazed her chin with his thumb. *Damn, this feels good*! she thought. No matter how wrong this was, she couldn't stop it.

Unfortunately, as Tyreke's cell phone rang, they both realized that this moment was a gift that neither of them could keep. Talk about bad timing.

"Shit!" Tyreke barked, watching Serenity bolt to the bathroom. "Ain't this a bitch. What?" he yelled into his phone.

"Ty, I tried to cop some sandwiches from the deli, but Moo said the shop was closed for business," Chauncey complained on the other end.

Chauncey used the term sandwiches in code for keys of cocaine. The deli meant the person who Tyreke used to distribute the product—that person being Damu—and the deli being closed was pretty much self-explanatory. Damu was told by Tyreke to cut Chauncey off, and that's exactly what he did.

"And, nigga? What's your point?" Tyreke asked in a stiff tone.

Chauncey shuffled to get his mind in order. He knew what time it was. "I just wanna know what's goin' on."

"As you can see, nothin' is goin' on." Tyreke diverted his attention to Serenity who was coming out of the bathroom. With an embarrassed scowl on her face, she looked away when her eyes fell on Ty.

"This conversation is finished. If you want to discuss anything further, you know where I'll be," Tyreke finished, hanging up before Chauncey could respond. He shoved his phone in his pocket and stared at Serenity.

She ain't for you. Don't ruin this one.

Just as quick as Tyreke felt warm and bubbly over Serenity, Tyreke washed those feelings away. No time to play around with his emotions. The hardness within him emerged. Tyreke walked around, shook a few hands, said a couple goodbyes and grabbed his henchmen's attention. Within minutes, he was gone, leaving Serenity wondering if he left because of her.

Serenity closely watched Tyreke get into his whip and smash off as two well-dressed brothers fell in pursuit, following behind him in two separate cars like they were escorting the president.

Watching Tyreke leave was the hardest thing, but she turned around, put on a fake smile and became the life of the party.

* * * *

After all the shit Chauncey went through to get close to Tyreke and his bitch and this is how it was going to play out? Desperate wasn't the word. Chauncey was in a state of despair. He paced the floor in his luxurious bedroom, tripping over the conversation he just had with Tyreke.

"Do he know who the fuck he fuckin' with?" Chauncey vented, stalking around the room in circles. "I'ma show that pussy that he's not kin to the Untouchables." He shot a somewhat painful look at Leslie. "Don't even trip. I'ma do something." Leslie nodded and remained quiet.

Everything she worked so hard to build with Chauncey came tumbling down like humpty dumpty. She was addicted to the life of living good. Now that that was in jeopardy, she didn't know what to do. She took in the sight of their master bedroom which she took pride in decorating herself. The enveloping richness of red damask tempered with unbleached muslin were chosen as curtains for the windows. Their king-size canopy bed with sheer lace hanging from the ceiling to the floor offered shelter for the many nights when Leslie felt like getting freaky with Chauncey. All would soon be a memory. Leslie wanted to scream, kick and throw a fit.

Chauncey promised her and her children security. Now they were about to be kicked out of their beautiful home onto their asses because Chauncey's money flow had now ceased. What was even more embarrassing for Leslie was that she would have to return to the ghetto with nothing to show for herself except for another baby. What a shame.

Chapter 18

Owen Park embodied such beauty. It's scenic view of tall trees, blossoming flowers and freshly cut grass gave peace to anyone who went there to clear their head.

Tyreke traveled around the pond where the Chief sat peacefully on a park bench feeding a flock of ducks from a bag of bread crumbs. He threw several pieces in their direction. He looked at them in deep thought as their beaks dabbled away at the water.

The Chief looked up and saw that Tyreke was approaching. He spread out the remainder of the crumbs, stood to his feet and wiped his meaty palms on his slacks.

"Let's take a walk. This meeting won't be long," he advised Tyreke, leading him down a bike trail.

Tyreke glanced towards the elementary school located only yards away. Kids laughed, ran and enjoyed the playground equipment under the afternoon sun.

"What's up? Talk to me," Tyreke said, kicking pebbles along the path.

"Jose speaks really highly of you. He's more comfortable with you than anyone else. Which isn't a surprise—"

"Keep talkin'," Tyreke cut in. He ignored the speckle of doubt in the Chief's eyes. The Chief exhaled sharply while rubbing the corners of his mouth, which happened to be dry as sawdust.

"Jose owns several homes around the country, and the next drop will be Venezuela. The government is sleazy and they hate Americans. We won't be able to fly over their aircraft in a private plane because they might take us as terrorists. So we'll use the regular airlines. The security can be slick, and we can't afford screw-ups. Election is right around the corner and—"

"Andrew, cut the shit. What's the ticket?" Tyreke asked, no longer walking.

The Chief picked up a loose stick on the ground. "Ty, there is a lot of money involved this time. We're talking millions of dollars. That's a lot of money to trust one man with."

"One?"

"Yes, Jose only wants to deal with you or the deal is a no-go."

Tyreke held back his anger. The shit boiled down to this. Instead of the Chief coming out and saying that his political buddies didn't trust a black man with their money, he was taking him around the world with some diplomatic bullshit.

"Whatchu tellin' me is that your crooked-ass friends don't trust me?" Tyreke shot back. The Chief broke the stick in half and continued to walk.

"Ty, it's nothing like that. If you make one mistake...Tyreke they'll kill you. I don't want to put you under that kind of pressure. We've been in business together for what, five years now? If anyone knows you, it's me," he said throwing the twigs. He exhaled sharply. "Okay, listen closely. This is what we're going to do."

Despite his expressionless face, Tyreke was smiling real big inside. It was the Chief that insisted that Tyreke leave the drug cartel. He told Tyreke that if he wanted to taste "real money" he needed to cross the other side of the fence. It took months before Jose agreed to meet Tyreke. Secretly, the Chief needed Tyreke to keep the heat off himself. The peanuts given to Tyreke not only insured his job but deflected any suspicions of his involvement with illegal dealings. But Tyreke doing a job this big alone worried the Chief. The fear of Jose cutting him off was heavy on his mind. If Tyreke had gained this much trust from Jose in such a small amount of time, it would only be a minute before he took over completely, leaving the Chief and his partners to find another source of money. Real money that is. Hey, whoever said a black man can't rise to the top?

* * * *

Tyreke used his foot to kick the oriental rug over the obvious space that held his prime possessions. Also inside the small hole were the diamonds given to him by the Chief. For years Tyreke stashed his drugs, deeds and money at the bottom of the staircase inside his father's church.

I know what you're thinking. Honestly, I don't give a fuck. Neither did Tyreke. Choosing the church was a good look, despite what people say. Look at it this way. Who in their right mind would heist a church? Exactly, NOBODY! Well, no one who is even remotely sane. All that shit about niggas fearing Tyreke was true to a certain degree. You know as I do that money and jealously will drive any man to the edge for a quick come up. But one thing is for sure, EVERYBODY fears God. Even the ones who don't believe in him. Mention "Father God," "Lord and Savior" or "Jesus" and everybody will get to running. Now you tell me. Was it a good look? You bet your pretty ass it was.

Tyreke opened the chapel doors. He sat in the pews seated across from the pulpit. For a few seconds, he took in his surroundings. Damn, life can be so crazy. In a few months, D'mico would be walking down the same aisle to accept his hand in marriage. And he was more nervous than a muthafucka. Not to say that he was getting cold feet, but he wanted shit to be right. Even a young nigga in his late twenties whose feet is in the streets wants things to be on point. Another thing that tugged at him was Serenity. She made him have second thoughts. The kind of doubt that made him want to wake up and reevaluate his life. Damn, this girl was starting to weigh heavy on his mind. Then again, maybe he was trippin'. D'mico didn't deserve a delay because he was mixing what he thought was love with lust.

The chapel door made a squeaky noise.

"And the son said unto him, Father, I have sinned against heaven and in thy sight and am no more worthy to be called thy son. But the father said to his servants, bring forth the best robe and put it on him, and put a ring on his hand and shoes on his feet."

"For this is my son...Was lost and is found. What's good, pops? Didn't hear you come in," Tyreke said over his shoulder.

Reverend Johnson smiled and took a seat next to Tyreke. "I see you still remember that story. The Prodigal Son. It was your favorite," he said, waiting on a response from Tyreke. When there wasn't one, he kept the conversation going. "Service was good on Sunday. So many people showed up. Me and your mother were so happy to see all the young folks of all ages congregate under one roof to give praise to the only person worth more than you or myself. D'mico showed up too. She's missed a few Sundays, but she's been getting back on track. Maybe you could come with her next Sunday. You know...like old times."

Give 'em an inch and what do they do? They take a whole damn mile. Tyreke's eyes fell on the maroon carpet. All he could do was shake his head in disagreement to his father's wishes. For a few minutes, there was perfect silence. No crossed questions nor crooked answers. Reverend Johnson looked diagonally from the podium. In the corner was a beautiful grand piano. Midnight black, flashy and untouched. Just looking at it made his lips part into a smile.

"Do you remember the Christmas party we had a

while ago? The very first one?" Tyreke lift his head. He leaned back in his seat and reminisced with his father.

"Yeah...That was the day you had us working our butts off. How could I forget."

"Practice makes perfect, remember? After we came back from dropping D'mico off, you got on that thing and showed out." Reverend Johnson laughed, referring to the piano. "We thought the Holy Ghost hit you or something." Tyreke laughed too. In a way, the Holy Ghost did hit him. He met an angel that day. His soon-to-be wife.

"Was it that obvious?" Tyreke asked, getting more relaxed. He leaned his arms over the seats in front of him.

"Sure was. Do you think you'll ever play the piano again? When you played, everybody listened. God gave you a gift, a gift to bless the people around you with. It still amazes me how, unlike other people who take classes, all you had to do was sit down and release the seed God planted inside of you. You nourished spirits. I miss those days."

Tyreke exhaled a deep breath of air. He shook his head nonstop to the words pouring out of his father's mouth. He knew the old man meant well, but damn, why did he have to go there? Shidd...he was beginning to think his father was a walking Jehovah's Witness. Everything was "God this" or "God that." His parents could walk around like everything was copasetic if they wanted to, but he knew better than to believe the hype. God had let everyone down. Him, his parents and Amyah. So before you start thinking that Tyreke is a jerk, why don't you ask God where he was when Tyreke was fifteen. Where was he?

Reverend Johnson invited the whole community to attend an annual Easter egg hunt slash barbeque. The mention of free food had folks piling in like roaches. They even invited a few people of their own. So many people came that Reverend Johnson had to go to the grocery store to keep up with the demand for bologna, hot dogs, baked beans, coleslaw and his famous ribs. Mothers, daughters, fathers, sons, crack addicts, boosters...everybody participated. Not only was Reverend Johnson known for stuffing jelly beans and mini candy bars inside the plastic eggs, everyone knew that 200 dollars in cash was scattered around the church. Once Denise released the flag, people ran in every direction screaming and yelling in excitement.

Standing next to his sister, Tyreke watched everyone take off. It was the older people pushing the younger kids out of their way that made Tyreke laugh in amusement.

"Bubba...I wan' egg," Amyah whined, tugging at Tyreke's pant leg.

Tyreke looked into the eyes of his baby sister. They were big, brown and full of innocence. How could he say no? Amyah batted her long eyelashes while tugging at Tyreke's pant leg a second time.

"Please."

Tyreke looked around for Denise, and he didn't spot her. She specifically told him not to participate due to the fact that the event was for the community. Going against the grain, he took his baby sister by the hand and held up one finger.

"One egg and that's it."

Amyah's face lit up like the weather—sunny and bright. She followed behind Tyreke with her pink Easter basket. Something long and hard rubbed against Amyah's white jelly sandals. Curious to know what it was, she dropped Tyreke's hand and observed the funny looking object. Falling behind, she sat down her basket and picked up her new mystery toy.

Clear as day, Tyreke spotted a purple and green Easter egg for his sister underneath a shade tree.

"Look, Amyah, there's one," Tyreke shouted. He turned and noticed that his sister was no longer around. He turned to the left and right and she wasn't there. *Where is she?* Worry settled in the pit of his stomach. How could he be so careless?

Tyreke spotted Amyah's pink dress in the distance. What he saw caused his heart to sink. It was like his brain was noncompliant. Amyah was lying face down on the ground. By the time Tyreke's brain kicked in and told him to move fast, it was too late. She was already dead and unresponsive. Unfortunately, Amyah's mystery toy turned out to be a dirty needle thrown in the grass by one of the addicts attending the event.

While playing with the sharp object, Amyah accidentally stuck herself in her main carotid artery. Beautiful Amyah died at the age of three. Tyreke blamed his careless behavior for the death of his baby sister. More than anything he blamed the man upstairs. How could he not protect his own people? Everything his pops preached about God being their safety was a bunch of bull, and for that, Tyreke vowed to never step foot in another church. Two years later, he bumped into Mike Mike.

Mike Mike turned him onto a lot of things. Bitches, money and the world of crack cocaine. From then on, his life was sweet.

* * * *

Tyreke faced his father. For a brief moment, he entered into the old man's feelings. He knew his pops knew what he did for a living, so why was he wasting his breath? Although Tyreke stared into the eyes of the Reverend, the Reverend was looking into the eyes of his past. Such a sad case.

Reverend Johnson could preach until he was blue in the face, but would Tyreke listen? Of course he wouldn't. Force could never impact the desire to change. Tyreke had to want to change, not his father. However, Reverend Johnson wasn't going to give up on his son.

"Tyreke, you need to forgive yourself for the past. The longer you hang on to this spirit and beat yourself up, it's—" Tyreke's face wrinkled above his brow.

"Forgive myself? Wait a minute." He jumped to his feet while slamming a violent finger in his chest. "I'm not beatin' myself up over a damn thing. I'm sick and tired of you tryin' to hold my hand. I'm a grown-ass man. Every time you come around, I gotta hear your shit. Honestly, I'm beginning to think that you're using me for your own guilt."

Reverend Johnson's eyes bulged out of their sockets while gravity pulled his mouth ajar in shock. *No this boy didn't just disrespect me.* Peering into Tyreke's angry eyes, Reverend Johnson spoke. "Boy, you might be tough on the streets, but that don't mean nothin' to me. I'm the one who helped bring you into this world. Don'tchu ever forget that. I don't care if you never listen to another word I say, but I do know one thing. You better not ever speak to me like that again like I'm some—" Reverend Johnson was on the verge of going off. He gave Tyreke a once over from head to toe. "You better be thanking God that I'm a changed man. I might not have pounds of useless gold around my neck, diamonds in my ears that cost more than my car, a Jag or ten bedrooms in my house that I'll never sleep in, but I am rich." Reverend smiled so big that it spooked Tyreke. "Yes, sir. I am rich indeed. I have a beautiful wife, two vehicles that aren't up with the Joneses but they take me to and from where I need to go, and I have just enough money to pay my bills. And sleep? Oh I can sleep peacefully in my home without the worry of thugs kicking in my door. In God I trust. More than anything, I am rich in the Lord. What about you? What do you have that's worth smiling about besides drug money? You failed to reach your calling, and nothing will ever be enough for you because you're too selfish to see. Do you even care how your days end in this world? Do you care whether you live or die, Tyreke?"

Every bit of hope Reverend Johnson had for Tyreke to do right turned into hot coal. The Reverend was so quiet that you would've heard a mustard seed drop to the floor.

Tyreke's entire face went numb. His heart was beating slower than a muthafucka, and tears tumbled down the side of his caramel cheeks, dripping one by one as his heart was carried away by a rush of guilt. Never in his life had his pops crossed the line like that. Over the years, they had a pretty good relationship. Mainly, the demon that haunted Tyreke every day of his life went unnoticed. His parents swept Amyah's death under the rug, and so did he to a certain extent. Reverend Johnson spoke of forgiveness. How can a man who couldn't even forgive God forgive himself? Did he care whether he lived or died?

Come on now. Was that a rhetorical question or what? The life he lived came with day to day trials. I mean damn, he cared somewhat. Wasn't that good enough? Every day Tyreke stuck his neck out there making some of the toughest decisions in order to survive, and right now there were two words that weren't on his plate: losing and death. If Mr. Joe Black happened to knock on his door while he was in pursuit of this white man's world, then what other choice would he have but to throw his towel in?

What did bother Tyreke was his father's statement about his destiny. The realization that he was just another nigga ready to be zipped up in a body bag with a bunch of other muthafuckas chasing the same dream hit him like a lifetime of bricks. What were riches exactly? Were they what his pops described, or were they the material possessions we see plastered across the TV screens and magazines? Were riches pursued only by niggas who thought plenty was never enough? Something to think about, huh? All I know is, for the moment, Tyreke was being served silver platters stacked with green.

Without saying a word, Tyreke regained his composure. He gathered the remainder of his dignity and walked away from his father before he wound up saying something he would later regret.

"It's never to late, Tyreke," Reverend Johnson called out in his last effort.

Tyreke stood in place for a brief second and then continued towards the exit, ignoring his father's final plea to lead him in the right direction.

In God we trust.

Chapter 19

The telephone ringing at three o'clock in the morning interrupted Tyreke's deep sleep. He turned over on his side and looked at D'mico, hoping she heard the constant ringing, but just like the state he was in, she was out cold. After the fourth ring, the ringing stopped and then started all over again.

"Whoa?" he answered in a groggy voice.

"Tyreke, I'm sorry to call you so late, but I didn't know who else to turn to. Ty is gone. I went in his room to check on him, and he wasn't there. He's gone."

Tyreke's mind couldn't quite register what was going on. However, the sniffles on the other end of the phone caused alarm bells to go off inside his head.

"Sin? What did you say?"

"He's gone. I-I don't know where he is." Serenity's voice cracked as she sobbed uncontrollably into the phone.

Déjà vu was the only word to describe how Tyreke felt. The last time he got a call like this was the day he laid Lonnie's bitch ass to rest, so he didn't know what to make of Serenity's news.

"Tyreke, what's going on?" D'mico asked in a concerned tone.

"Nothing. Everything is fine. Go back to sleep," Tyreke said, kissing D'mico's forehead. He diverted his attention back to the phone.

"Sin, everything is goin' to be okay. Do you trust me?"

Serenity sniffled. "You know I do. Tyreke, I wouldn't know what to do if—"

"Eh, don'tchu even say that. There's power in our words. I asked you if you trusted me, and you said you did."

"I do," Serenity confirmed, sitting on Ty's bed in distress.

"Okay, when did you last see him?"

"It was like...I don't know nine thirty maybe."

"Nine thirty? Okay, listen. I need for you to stay home in case he come back, and stay by the phone. I might know where he's at."

The assurance in Tyreke's voice was like a heavy dosage of Valium for Serenity. "Please find him, Tyreke," Serenity said before she hung up.

Already out of bed and on his feet, Tyreke punched in a few numbers and waited for the caller to answer. "Yo, Moo."

D'mico was so busy watching Tyreke pace with the phone to his ear that she only got the tail end of his conversation. The conversation before he called Damu. His voice was so low and reassuring that she knew without a shadow of doubt that he was on the phone with another woman. *What the hell did he mean by, "Do you trust me?"* Those words were meant for only her.

Tyreke had the phone glued to his ear, balanced by his shoulder. D'mico eyed Tyreke suspiciously as he zipped up his pants. She listened as he instructed Damu to get a few of the fellas together for what sounded like some kind of search. Once he ended the conversation with Damu, Tyreke punched in the six-digit code disarming the alarm system; pressed a button on his keychain, which was used to start his car from inside the house; and out the door he went.

Just like that, Tyreke left without a single word as to where he was going or what was going on. D'mico stared at his shadow on the surveillance monitor. In frustration, she threw the covers over her face and sulked until she drifted off into a deep sleep.

* * * *

Ty sat on the curb outside the arena. The bright lights beaming in his direction blinded his vision, causing him to look away. Tyreke was relieved to see Ty. He cut his engine and jumped out his SUV.

"Lil nigga, is you crazy? Do you know Serenity is worried sick about you?"

Loaded with sadness, Ty stared into the darkness. His premature deep voice echoed in the night. "She ain't worried 'bout me," he replied, resting his head in his lap.

Tyreke was unsure of the reason why Ty decided to run away; however, the shit he pulled was totally unacceptable. It was none of Tyreke's business as to who Ty's father was, but in spite of that, he wished that whoever the nigga was would man-up and accept his responsibilities as a father. If only these knuckleheads understood the importance of a male role model. Tyreke wasn't Ty's father, but just like the bond he shared with Dirt's little one, Tyreke acquired the same affections for Ty. There is something impeccable about the way men influence the minds of our children that a woman can't replicate. I'm not saying that women don't take care of business, because love and nourishment is what a child craves. It's irreplaceable, but we're talking about the authority of a man. Guidance. An issue that has been overlooked for many generations.

"Whatchu talkin' about? Serenity do love you. She's your mama and she would die for you."

"She's not, but whatever." Ty lifted his eyes towards Tyreke. "If she loves me, then why do she cry every night? I know she cry because I messed up her life. I did her a favor when I left." A small tear fell from Ty's eye.

Tyreke wondered how a person so small could think so big. Ty wasn't supposed to have any worries; he was a child. Yet he proved that just like adults, kids not only have problems but they deal with everyday obstacles too.

"You got every right to be angry, but you running away won't solve yo problems. What if somebody snatched you up? It's a lot of sick people out here roaming these streets. Sometimes, as men, we think selfishly. We don't think about the feelings of the women in our lives. Ty, I never lied to you, and I don't plan on it. Serenity loves you."

Ty cut Tyreke a razor-sharp look, the same look every kid gives you when they want you to shut up. Tyreke couldn't help but laugh. Ty had a hard head and a soft ass, something Tyreke knew a lot about when he was his age.

"Boy, you know what I'll do to you if you ever look at me like that again?" Tyreke hopped around Ty in circles, throwing punches over his head. "When you give a man a look like that, you gotta be ready to get down," he teased. Ty snickered in his sleeve. Watching Tyreke parade around him, swinging at the open air, was funny.

Out of breath, Tyreke popped a squat next to Ty. Even in a pair of jeans and a white T-shirt, he looked out of place sitting on the sidewalk. He looked into Ty's smoky-grey eyes. In them he saw the past. Where did Ty fit though?

"Man...I don't know 'bout you, but all of this looking for you and fighting gotta nigga hungrier than I don't know what! You hungry?"

Seconds flew by before Ty answered. "A little bit."

"What?" Tyreke chuckled. "Eitha you is or you ain't. From the looks of yo little peanut head, I'm guessing you is." Ty jumped to his feet with a sudden burst of energy.

"I don't have no peanut head. Serenity said the ladies love me."

"Oh yeah? Whatchu know about girls?"

"I know more than you. I got three girlfriends at my school, and they all love me."

Tyreke fell out laughing. "Trust me, lil man, you in way over your head. Enjoy it while you young 'cause in a few years, them girls gon go upside the same peanut head you swear they love." Still laughing, Tyreke asked, "McDonalds is open, or do you wanna go to IHOP?" Ty was still trying to figure out what Tyreke meant about the girls. For now, he stored Tyreke's words in the back of his head.

"Uh...let's go to IHOP. I never been there." Tyreke got up and dusted off the back of his jeans.

"There's a first time for everything. You made a good choice...here." He handed Ty his cell phone. "Since you walked out the door like a grown man, you got a couple of phone calls to make. First, you gonna call home and let Serenity know you're okay and that you're sorry. Then, you gonna call Damu and apologize to him for having to look all over Tulsa for you. Oh yeah, the money I gave you yesterday, do you still got it?"

Ty lifted up his backpack which he stuffed with clothes. "Yeah, it's in here."

"Good 'cause you buyin' our food," he said, getting inside the car.

Ty sucked his teeth. "Aah man..." he mumbled, trailing a few steps behind.

* * * *

Just as Tyreke arrived at Serenity's two-bedroom house, the sun yawned sending the morning clouds on their way.

Serenity's mocha eyes followed Tyreke's SUV until he came to a complete stop in her driveway. With worry written all over her face, she got up from the porch steps and made her way to the car.

Tyreke's leaf-green Navigator was so sparkling, shiny and immaculate that Serenity's reflection winked back at her as she approached the passenger side door. She didn't doubt that by the way his ride glimmered and gleamed that he had it serviced and detailed at least twice a week, if not every day. It was that clean.

As soon as Serenity got the door open, Tyreke greeted her with a finger to his lips. "He's sleep," he whispered in a hushed tone.

For several lingering seconds, Serenity's eyes zoomed in on Tyreke's perfectly shaped mouth. His lips were full and luscious. She broke her gaze and looked in the backseat where Ty was sound asleep, snoring louder than ever. Watching him was definitely a Kodak moment. Serenity smiled as she watched the slow rise and fall of his chest.

Tyreke motioned for Serenity to get in. With his voice low, he gave Serenity a plastic bag with IHOP's logo written on the outside.

"I think it's still hot. There's some silverware in there too if you wanna eat before lil daddy wake up."

Serenity accepted the bag. The different smells coming from the plastic pinched her stomach. However, she had so much shit on her mind there was no way she would eat.

"That's okay...I can eat later. You didn't have to do this," Serenity said, lifting the bag slightly above her waist.

"Oh, it wasn't me who bought it. It was Ty." Serenity smiled. Shaking her head, she glanced at the food in her lap.

"I'm not even goin' to ask." Fighting off her nervousness, she redeemed herself by paying Tyreke homage. "Thank you. I owe you big time. You're always around when I need you, and you don't know how much that means to me."

"Don't sweat it. As long as I got breath in my body, I'ma look out for your son."

Serenity felt like she was suffocating. Tyreke looked out for her like he was her man. He went to all lengths to make sure Ty didn't want for a damn thing. School clothes, shoes...the whole nine. Serenity, on the other hand, hadn't been completely honest with him. Unable to look him in the eyes, she turned away from his baby face. She allowed the voice within her inner woman to speak.

"Tyreke. Ty, isn't my son."

Tyreke felt like a man on *Maury* when the woman reveals to her baby daddy that the baby they share isn't his. He was dumbfounded. I mean damn, why the fuckin' lies?

"It's really a long story. I was gonna tell you sooner but—"

"It's six o'clock in the fuckin' morning; we ain't got shit but time. Whatchu mean he ain't yo son? What, he yo little brother or something? Is his name Tyler, or did you con that shit up too?"

Tyreke was pissed. One thing he hated more than anything was a fuckin' liar. Especially one who gave you direct eye contact like Serenity's ass was doing right now. Damn, this chick deserved an Oscar. Shit, she was good.

Serenity looked over her shoulder. Ty still had his head resting against the door, sleeping peacefully. "Do you kiss you mother with that filthy mouth?" she shot back in a low snarl.

Every bit of Tyreke wanted to dismiss Serenity's lying ass. Serenity placed a warm hand on Tyreke's thigh and pressed the issue. "Can we talk about this before you make the choice to X us out of your life?"

Tyreke looked deeper into Serenity's eyes. The hard look of wear and tear hidden behind her pupils began to relinquish all of the skeletons in her closet. Looking into Serenity's eyes was like the power of sex; Tyreke would never know if she was faking it until it was over.

With an ill look, Tyreke flexed his jaws and shifted into reverse. "I got a place where we can go. If you know what's good for you, you won't ever lie to me about something like that again. And no, I'm not threatening you. Shorty, that's my word," he said, sliding out the driveway.

Serenity knew that Tyreke was talking out of anger. She was just happy that he was willing to let her explain herself. Instead of adding fuel to his fire, she strapped on her seat belt, leaned back and went along for the ride.

* * * *

The last time Tyreke had been to his thinking quarters was the day after Ansean slipped away and went into hiding. He had a lot on his mind that day, and it seemed like the stress he endured over the months was starting to get worse.

Tyreke killed his engine and got out. Following suit, Serenity unfastened her seat belt. She got out the car wondering where Tyreke brought her. Feeling like she was on top of a mountain, Serenity took in the glorious view of the landscape beneath them. The houses of varying colors, passing cars and billboards resembled a scattered bag of Skittles.

Serenity joined Tyreke's side where he sat on a large rock staring off into space like he had a lot on his mind.

"Start talkin'," he said, breaking the silence.

Serenity swallowed the lump of air in her throat and started from the very beginning.

* * * *

D'mico swung the covers off her tired body in a fit. Tears ran down her angry face as she tore the room upside down, knocking makeup off her vanity onto the carpet and dropping pictures of her and Tyreke to the floor. At first she didn't want to believe Chauncey when he told her that Tyreke was with another woman, but when he said he had proof, D'mico wasted no time destroying their bedroom and then sliding into a pair of simple sweats.

Thirty minutes later, D'mico was in the front seat of Chauncey's Chevy.

"Where's your proof?" she demanded to know.

"Damn. No 'how you doing?' or 'I miss you?'"

"Proof. Where is it?"

Chauncey ran his tongue across his teeth. He grinned with malevolence and smashed on the gas pedal, sending D'mico's head jerking backwards.

Chapter 20

Tyreke embraced Serenity's weeping body with all of his strength and comfort. He watched the well of tears cascade down her eyes onto her ebony cheeks. Lost in her revelation, Tyreke gave some thought to what she confirmed to be true. Serenity's experience growing up in an unhealthy foster home and being viewed as an outcast to society were a couple of things she mentioned. The only thing she ever knew about her parents was that her mother gave her up for adoption after finding out that the truck driver she secretly had been sleeping with for over a year was married with children. Ain't that a bitch? Anyway, Serenity's foster mom, a lady who was known as old Lady Sandra, passed away six years ago, leaving behind her only grandson. The only thing Serenity ever heard about Tyler (who's real name was Santy'ya) was that his mother unfortunately died after giving birth. Everything, including the woman's name, Sandra took to her grave.

Consequently, the passing of Sandra left Serenity to take care of Santy'ya by herself. All she wanted to do was protect him and give him a better life.

Tyreke believed everything about Serenity's story except for the part about Santy'ya's mom being dead. Ironically, Tyreke knew exactly who and where Santy'ya's mom was. For now, he would withhold that piece of information until the time was right for Santy'ya, Serenity and D'mico.

This was just too much.

"Tyreke, I really wanted to tell you sooner. I just didn't know how," Serenity said, crying into her hands.

Tyreke squeezed her tighter. How could he hold her accountable for being overprotective? Truth be told, he exonerated her from her guilt the moment he got lost into her soft brown eyes.

Tyreke pulled Serenity together, holding her at arms length. Serenity removed several tears. She looked up at Tyreke. "Look, none of this is your fault, shorty. You did what you had to do." He removed a few of her tears as well. "Come on now. Go slow on the tears. What type of nigga would I be to lose a friend like you? I'm not mad. We'll get through this, aight?" Tyreke ended with words of honey, wrapping his arms back around Serenity while cradling her head against his chest. Serenity felt ten times better knowing that she had someone like Tyreke around. From now on, she was going to cherish their friendship.

* * * *

From a distance, jealousy tore through D'mico's scornful eyes as she witnessed Tyreke holding another woman in the spot he held her in years ago. It was the day she accepted his heart. Her hazel eyes burned with betrayal. The look she sent in their direction could rip the both of them to shreds. Tyreke was supposed to be her lifeline. The air in her lungs, not the flatline to her monitor. Their love was supposed to be bigger than the universe, and now Tyreke was sharing that moment with someone else.

Chauncey quickly sped up, breaking D'mico's glare. He cupped her chin while maintaining full control of the steering wheel.

"So, what's up? You gonna help me now?"

Although Tyreke had already disappeared in the cloud of dust, D'mico turned around and looked down the narrow road as her heart plunged to the floor.

Bright as day, she had her proof.

Even though D'mico loved Tyreke more than herself, he left her with no other choice but to swallow her feelings and even the score. Chauncey might've not been her first choice in the love department; however, he was somebody, and somebody sounded better than nobody.

D'mico faced Chauncey who was eagerly waiting on her response. "I know where the stash spot is, but first I want to square away a couple of things before I tell you."

D'mico's words were like music to Chauncey's sensitive ears.

"Okay, that seems fair." With his eyes on the road, Chauncey's lips parted into a broad smile.

Finally, justice would be served.

Chapter 21

"All rise. Honorable Judge Bradford presiding," the bailiff announced in a husky tone.

Judge Bradford climbed two squeaky steps, fastened the last button on his black robe and gave the courtroom a visual sweep. Once he straightened his robe, he took in a deep breath and sat down. In a rehearsed tone, he instructed everyone to take their seats. The rustling sound of bodies moving, library whispers, and a few strong coughs could be heard throughout the crowded courtroom.

CNN and *Court TV* set up their cameras in the back corner of the courtroom to shoot the high-profile case.

Forty-five minutes ago, a recess was called for lunch.

Now that everyone was full, it was time for the defense to cross-examine the D.A.'s witness.

Attorney Kevin Harris was a handsome black man with a reputation for winning ninety-five percent of his cases, fitting the profile of a Harvard graduate. He stood up in his expensive Armani suit and clutched his expensive blazer as if it would suddenly fly open. With his game face on, he stalked towards the witness.

"Hello, Mr. Davis. How was your lunch?"

Mr. Davis shook his head up and down. "It was okay," he replied.

"Good. Well, I won't keep you very long. Mr. Davis,

earlier today you testified that the weapon you tested was in fact my clients. Is that correct?" Harris asked.

Having done this a million times plus two, Mr. Davis leaned forward to speak into the microphone. He gave the men and women of the jury direct eye contact before answering.

"That is correct."

"Did you do a ballistic test, Mr. Davis."

"Yes, sir. We conduct that on all of our cases," Davis replied.

Harris went to the defense table and shuffled through several pieces of paper before turning around.

"Mr. Davis, can you tell the jury whose fingerprints you discovered on the murder weapon in question?"

Davis looked towards the D.A. for a way out. "Uhh..." Stalling for time, Davis shifted uncomfortably in his seat.

"I'm sorry, Mr. Davis. Maybe lunch was a bit much? Let me repeat the question. Whose fingerprints did you find on the murder weapon issued to my client?"

"Objection, your honor!" the D.A. screamed out loud.

"Overruled! Answer the question, Mr. Davis," Judge Bradford ordered.

Backed into a corner, Davis answered. "Deontae Crenshaw."

This is where things got tricky for the D.A. The only reason why Deontae Crenshaw's (A.K.A Dirt) prints were on the gun was because he broke into Matt's crib a while back. The whole purpose of breaking into Matt's home was to send a message, a message that later was relayed to Lonnie and Matt. Just because their asses wore a badge didn't mean that they could go around doing whatever they wanted, whenever they wanted. Dirt gave the gun to Mike Mike. Mike Mike held onto it and then gave the same stolen gun to Tyreke. However, Mike Mike and Tyreke were smart enough not to put their prints on the gun. Dirt, on the other hand, wasn't too smart. Didn't matter anyway, Dirt had an alibi. But Matt didn't.

Matt sat behind the defense table stressed. He had a feeling that his missing gun would surface. But he never imagined that it would come back to haunt him like this. He thought he was in the clear when he reported his gun missing. Apparently not. A few times he and Lonnie had hemmed up Mike Mike's crew. It was Lonnie's idea to strip all of the drug dealers who worked for Mike Mike of their dope sacks and money. Dirt was one of the many who were a part of Mike Mike's crew. Lonnie was so far on drugs that he involved Matt in a lot of shit, but fuck, Lonnie was Matt's partner. There was no way he would turn him in to the department. Instead, Matt accepted his portion of the cash and kept his mouth shut. Greed can be a bitch.

"Nineteen-year-old Deontae Crenshaw. Imagine that! A man known by the TPD as Dirt. Also known for his hot temper and stream of violence around the city. Is that correct?" Harris asked, nailing the question over Davis's head.

"Objection, you honor," the D.A. yelled over the mumbles coming from the jury box. "Mr. Harris is making accusations that don't pertain to this case."

"Sustained. Mr. Harris, stick to the relevance of this case," Judge Bradford said behind clenched teeth.

Thinking of another approach, Harris licked his dry lips while he flipped through several more sheets of paper.

"Mr. Davis, on September 6, 1999 at approximately four o'clock in the evening, my client reported his state-issued weapon stolen. As a matter of fact, it was you who handled the paperwork at the time. Am I right or wrong?" The D.A. jumped out of his seat.

"Objection, your honor. This is beyond ridiculous. Mr. Harris is trying to lead the jury into believing that a mystery man, who by the way got arrested for traffic violations the time of the murders, kidnapped and committed a heinous crime against the victims. The defendant was caught red-handed with his own gun in his hand. Not Deontae Crenshaw."

"Sustained."

The D.A. was on Harris like a bad weave. Not only did Harris open up a can of worms but the judge told the jury to disregard his statement. Everything he had to work with was backfiring. With nothing else to say, he went back to the defense table.

"I have no further questions, your honor," he said before leaning over to whisper in his client's ear.

After days of back to back testimonies, it was time for the jury to deliberate.

Matt felt defeated. He knew the outcome wouldn't be good. Not even the expensive lawyer his wife hired by selling their home could get him a freedom card. He was looking at life without the possibility of parole for three felony murders and one count of kidnapping. The kidnapping and one murder count were against D'mico's little boy. Which was straight bullshit!

Meanwhile, the niggas he sent upstate for crimes they really didn't commit would be waiting on his arrival.

"Fresh meat" is what they would scream while he carried his Ziploc bag of hygienic products and wool blankets down the corridor. Dozens of payouts would go out to the first nigga who could turn the crooked cop into sushi. Matt wasn't afraid to go to prison. Nah, he was afraid of the fate that awaited him inside the desolate place.

Despair and despondency were written all over Matt's face when he looked towards his son, Chauncey, who had been consoling his wife, Patricia.

Poor Patricia. She cried nonstop during the entire trial. She felt like her whole life had been slipped from under her feet. Hearing Matt's coworkers destroy his credibility broke her heart into a million tiny pieces, especially the little girl's testimony. Her hazel eyes never broke from Matt. Not even once. Every time the D.A. hit her with a question, she directed the response to Matt.

"Please just give me my baby," she pleaded over and over. D'mico showed up every morning at 8:15. Sitting in the front row, she locked eyes with the man wearing the bright orange jumpsuit. Every day she did the same thing. Every day except for the day of deliberation.

Where is she? Patricia wondered, looking around for the young girl. Was her husband the monster everyone portrayed him to be, or was he the family man she knew? Of course Matt was a family man. He wouldn't hurt anybody, right?

Bound by grief, Patricia rested her head on her son's shoulder to cry.

For months, Chauncey kept an eye on D'mico. The nerve of the little whore to take his family through all of this shit. Where was the nothin' ass bitch anyway? Look at the pain she was taking his mom through. Continuously she cried on his shoulder mumbling things like "What are we gonna do without your father?" Chauncey didn't know how his pops got caught up in D'mico's lies, but he did know his father, and he knew he wouldn't have done half the shit D'mico told the world. Plus, Chauncey knew some vital information about Miss Innocent D'mico. Mmm-hmm...That's right. Get this. Her boyfriend, Tyreke, was friends with the cat whose fingerprints were found on his father's gun.

Dirt was his name. Dirt was Tyreke's second in command.

Chauncey didn't have the slightest clue as to the connection they had with his father, but a nigga was gonna find out.

One thing was for sure. If his father's verdict came back guilty, he was taking court straight to the streets. In cold blood. Somebody was gonna pay. The only way Chauncey would accept payment was if they were paying with their lives. Crossing his fingers, Chauncey waited with everyone else for the verdict.

Chapter 22

Tyreke waited for the garage door to shut behind him before he got out of his vehicle. With his pistol tucked away in the front of his pants, he punched in his home security code and made his way through the quiet halls feeling better than a muthafucka. He felt like not only could he redeem his relationship with D'mico and restore her years of heartache but he also wanted a relationship with God again. Finding Santy'ya was almost heaven sent. Crazy as it sounds, Tyreke wanted to put the streets behind him. He didn't believe in the myth that carried a lot of niggas to their graves. "Death or jail is the only way out the game." Fuck that mythological bullshit. He created the game; the game didn't create him. And even if it did, he was the hand to his mouth, the foot to his work. There was no stopping him. He had made up his mind. Upstairs in their bedroom, D'mico sat in front of a large vanity brushing her hair with long strokes.

Tyreke kicked off his shoes. Marveling over

D'mico's reflection, he complimented her on her beauty that always put sparks in his eyes.

"Good morning, beautiful." He kissed the top of her head. "You're sexy as hell. You know that?"

D'mico ignored Tyreke's gesture. She spoke to the mirror. "Good morning, Ty." She glanced at the clock on the nightstand. "Or should I say good afternoon? Glad you remembered where home is."

Tyreke's smile faded a bit but still held the same "I'm happy to see you" look. For the most part, he was in a good mood. He looked towards the clock, and sure enough, it was a quarter to twelve. Shit, he didn't realize he'd been gone that long.

"Yeah well, I got tied up in some important business," he said, removing his clothes, hoping to heighten D'mico's mood. Instantaneously, D'mico stopped brushing her hair, but she managed to keep her cool.

"Business? Hmm...interesting."

Although the room temperature was cool as the wind, everything God gave Tyreke simmered with warmth.

With every breath, his nice set of abs did a little dance underneath his caramel skin. He knew D'mico was being sarcastic, but he wasn't trying to go there with her. He could've easily told her where he'd been, but he wanted to line things up first.

"Yo, hop in the shower with me."

"No thanks. You go ahead," D'mico responded nonchalantly, refusing to acknowledge his hint that he wanted to have sex.

Having a woman as unstable and hostile as D'mico

could be frustrating as hell. One minute the girl was cool and neutral and then the next she was all muggy and hot.

Niggas hate that shit. The least D'mico could do was speak whatever the fuck was on her mind so the remainder of the day could press on. Otherwise, the only one who would be walking around with a stuck out lip would be her damn self.

"There you go with the extras. I didn't ask you to take a shower with me...I told you to. Finish whatchu got goin', and then meet me in the bathroom," Tyreke said, not taking no for an answer.

D'mico cut her eyes at the mirror as she peered at his reflection. She sat there for a minute stunned. The only time she put a pep in her step was when Tyreke talked to her crazy, and sadly, it was the only time she would listen and do whatever he asked her to do. What a shame.

* * * *

After their shower was complete, Tyreke stepped out the bathtub, grabbed a towel and reached for D'mico's hand. As bad as shit seemed at the moment, D'mico's 5'5" curvaceous frame fell into the towel freely, though the steam from the hot shower had yet to melt the cold look off of her face. She watched Tyreke put all of his effort into making sure her body was fully dry. First, he started with her chest. He brushed the towel against her left nipple and nuzzled against her right breast.

Working his way downhill, the towel circled across her smooth stomach. Moving further down, Tyreke's journey rested on her narrow honey dip. She could feel his warm lips sink into her hip bone. Everybody has a spot that drives them over the edge, and D'mico's hip bone was like her g-spot. Once you get near it, it's all she wrote.

Standing in the middle of the bathroom naked, half wet and with a hard dick, Tyreke stroked D'mico's swollen clit like an instrument needing a tune-up. In slow increments, he finger-fucked her pussy until she neared an explosion, causing her clit to jolt against his fingertips. While his hand was busy looking for a different kind of wetness, Tyreke savored the taste of her plump lips.

"Is this what you want?" he asked, speaking into her mouth and adding an extra jolt inside her pussy. Just like that, D'mico was slippin' away like quicksand. Lost in a world of nonexistence. How can a man who makes her feel like the only woman in the universe cause her so much pain? The love he had for her, was it only based on sexual pleasure? Fuss, fuck and fight...Fuss, fuck and fight...

Maybe she could overlook Tyreke messing around if he just admitted to it. D'mico broke free from Tyreke's hold.

"Where were you last night?" she blurted out.

Cut off, Tyreke inhaled and exhaled a deep breath of irritation. He picked the towel up from the floor and wrapped it around his decreasing erection.

"What? I told you I had to take care of some business." Knowing that wasn't enough, he tickled her ears. "Why did you carry this issue all the way up until now? You know you can talk to me about anything. I'm 'bout to make you my wife." He looked into her hazel eyes. "Last night, one of the kids from the gym took off. The call I got was his sister asking for my help. I drove around for a minute and wound up finding lil daddy at the gym. We talked for a while, I took 'em to IHOP, dropped him off and that's it."

Tyreke was a real live character. His mouth might have aligned with his words, but D'mico knew her eyes did not lie. She knew what she saw, and it was as real as you and me.

"So you're tryna tell me you was with a kid all night?" she asked, fishing for another answer.

"Ain't that what I just said? How 'bout this, next week when I finish this deal, I'll introduce you to him. Is that cool?"

Shaking her head in disbelief, D'mico stormed out the bathroom, leaving Tyreke in a state of confusion. *What the fuck just happened?* he thought, looking around the empty bathroom.

* * * *

Five Days Later

Damu leaned against his 2010 black on black Rolls-Royce Ghost with a cold hand in his pocket. Every time he exhaled, his breath ascended into the bitter cold. He wished he had the mindset of one of those cats who didn't mind the smell of cigar smoke inside their ride. However, his OCD wouldn't allow it to go down. The only smell he wanted to greet him in his spacious, luxurious ride was the smell of black ice air freshener. Damu was choking on his vanilla Black and Mild when Tyreke stepped outside the rinky-dink coffee shop located twenty minutes away from the city. Snapping out of his haze, he flicked his cigar.

"Everything good, my nig? You ready to roll?"

"Everything is everything...let's roll," Tyreke insisted, getting in the passenger seat.

Everything was official. The weather might've been cold and dreary outside, but the sun kindled with excitement inside of Tyreke. He had everything he needed for his trip, including his passport and fake IDs. In less than twenty-four hours, he would be saying good-bye to his old life. Over the course of eleven years, Tyreke took the crumbs given to him and turned them into loaves and loaves of bread until he accumulated a whole bakery. He hustled the streets, conned bitches, shed some blood and caused many tears. He knew the game didn't discriminate. Shidd, it would carry on with or without him. Let me tell you what the problem is. The problem is a lot of cats lock in the game thinking they can change shit up, like all the bullets and haters in the world is on their side.

Yeah, fuckin' right! Wishful thinking is what I call that. Wishing on falling stars will only guarantee the same result; a falling star.

Hell, Tyreke was fortunate enough to have made it this long without the bullet wounds or scratches his crew inherited under his supervision.

Tyreke glanced proudly at Damu, who was bobbing his head to the music. If it wasn't for foot soldiers like him and Dirt—may he rest in peace—Tyreke would've gotten knocked off years ago. The word "appreciation" could never define Tyreke's gratitude. The nigga was loyal, straight up!

Tyreke tipped his head to the side. Quietly, he stared out the window thinking about his queen. A sense of calm swept over him from the thought of going legit.

Chapter 23

Tyreke had two hours to grab the diamonds and haul ass to the airport. He tried once more to reach D'mico. He came to a dead end when the answering machine delivered the news that no one was home. With two empty garbage bags in hand, he entered his father's church.

In less than no time, Tyreke had the plywood placed back over its original spot and three duffel bags of diamonds loaded into the empty garbage bags. Checking his watch, he was still on schedule. After all, time is money. On his way out the door, he noticed movement in the entrance hallway. Who could it be besides his father?

"Yo, pops...Is that you?" Tyreke called out, placing the bags behind a large plant.

There was no answer.

"Pops, is that you?" he called out a second time, his hand inching towards his waist.

When Tyreke got to the entrance door, he checked the knob. As expected, it was locked. *I know I seen something*, he thought. As soon as Tyreke turned around, he collided with a figure lurking in the shadows.

D'mico threw up her hands as a hard blow was delivered to her chin.

"Who da...fu-D'mico? What the fuck you doing here? How in da fuck did you get in?" Tyreke fumed, pushing her out the way.

Looking dumbfounded as ever and still rubbing her chin, D'mico followed Tyreke's stride like a baby duckling.

"I'm sorry I scared you. I was just tryna—"

"You didn't scare me, aight? Gurl, I could've killed yo ass for sneakin' up on me like that. What if I thought you was some nigga tryna catch me slippin', then what?"

"Well you didn't. I had a lot on my mind, and I thought daddy would be here so I could talk to him since you're never around anymore for me to talk to you," D'mico countered.

"You thought he would be here on a Saturday? On a Saturday, D'mico?"

D'mico opened her mouth to speak, but no words came out. Tyreke loved D'mico and all, but she was really starting to piss him off with the lugs she threw his way almost every day.

Dismissing her answer, he glanced at his watch. One hour and thirty minutes is all he had left to get going. Being the punctual dude that he was, he knew that being on time was important. He had millions in his possession, and he didn't want Jose screaming incoherent, twisted shit at him that he couldn't comprehend.

"Look, after today, I promise you that we can do whatever you want. I'm not neglecting you on purpose, D'mico. I'm tryin' to take care of things for our family. The only way I can do that is if I get out there and get it. Like I said a minute ago, after today, I'm all yours. You won't ever have to worry about nothin'. For now, I got shit to do. For us, for our family," he emphasized.

Tyreke left his words to sink inside D'mico's head. Carrying on like she wasn't there, he recovered the bags of diamonds he hid behind the plants. It didn't matter that D'mico was around nor did it matter that his spot had been revealed because after today, everything he'd ever done in the dark would be a closed casket. With his back to D'mico, Tyreke said a few more words on his way out the door, but his words went unheard.

D'mico's scorching eyes followed the bags in Tyreke's hand. *Is it filled with money?* she wondered.

All she could think about was Chauncey's soul-stirring words. "After we get the money, it's you and me," he reminded her. The craziest thing about all of this was the fact that D'mico didn't even love Chauncey. The only thing that bound her to him was sex. It was the sex alone that altered her mind into thinking that Chauncey gave a rat's ass about her. Which was sad. A pang of venom paralyzed the true affection she had in her heart for Tyreke.

D'mico's heart was beating so fast in her chest that she felt like it was expanding, making her even more nervous. Shaking like a leaf, her caramel complexion flushed as she reached for the small of her back. This was it. There would be no turning back. She cocked and aimed the small revolver given to her by Chauncey at the back of his head.

"Drop the bags and turn around." The cold steel pressed against the back of his dome caused Tyreke's eyelids to flutter. *What the fuck?* His eyes narrowed in confusion as his head jerked slightly to the side.

"What?"

"Tyreke, don't make me do this. Turn around," D'mico demanded. The bags hit the floor with a strong thud.

Slowly, Tyreke turned around to face the woman who he thought was the love of his life. All he kept thinking was that this had to be a joke. But in reality, there were no flashing lights or cameras, and he damn sure knew that he wasn't being punk'd. I guess at the end of the day, all you got is a bitch who don't even love herself. FUCK! How could he not see fault in D'mico? Of course he placed her on a cloud of perfection. She was his woman. But shit, you don't fuck a nigga blind like this. Never in a trillion years times two did he expect this. He'd seen this type of shit plastered across the TV screen all the time. Fox 23, channel 6 and channel 8 aired robberies and murders more than McDonald's and their dollar menu. That's how thug town was getting down these days. Just to keep it green with you, Tyreke was responsible for persuading more than half of those cases. And that's just the clean side of it. Why was he surprised that D'mico turned? Hmph, good question. Tyreke wasn't about to go down like this. Already he was weighing out his options. He could snatch the gun out of her hand and beat her ass with it. Then again, she might panic and wind up pulling the trigger. The million-dollar question did little dances inside of his head. Who did she sell him out for?

The look Tyreke cut into D'mico eradicated any respect he had for her. His hands was itching to knock the dog snot out of her ass.

"Bitch, you better make sure that you leave no

witnesses," Tyreke threatened with so much intensity that D'mico staggered backwards a few inches. Like a child, she started to squirm as if she was being forced.

Stupid...Stupid...Stupid...

That's what you're thinking, right? Well, it's not even like that. You'll never fully understand the pain and self-hatred going on inside of D'mico until you've walked a mile in her shoes. Yeah, yeah, you got your feet kicked up saying, "I don't want to be in her shoes." You're right. You don't. Let me be the first to tell you that it is a long road, and her Jordan sneakers are looking like flip flops. Her and Chauncey weren't planning to kill Tyreke or anything; Chauncey gave his word. All they planned to do was strip him of a little cash. Nothing he couldn't recover from.

"I'm sorry" is all she managed to say before Chauncey came strolling down the entrance hallway with a grin wider than I-40.

Tyreke licked his firm lips as he took the strong blow to his heart. So it was Chauncey who had D'mico brainwashed. Imagine that! A nothing-ass coward for a coward-ass bitch. He should've known better than to trust a weak-ass bitch around Chauncey's spoon-fed ass.

"Remember me? You don't look too happy, playboy," Chauncey mocked. "What's wrong?" He took D'mico's gun and pushed her forward.

"Raise up his shirt and get his burner, then grab the bags."

Immediately D'mico went for Tyreke's shirt. After she had his gun, she wasted no time dragging the bags away from his feet where they rested against the wall.

Tyreke's scornful eyes never left the pitiful-looking D'mico. He practically eye fucked her without a rubber. He couldn't believe how low she went. She looked more pathetic now than ever. Nine times out of ten Chauncey would knock her to sleep right along with him. Yep, I said it. D'mico would die too. There was no way in the world that Chauncey would let them live. D'mico was just too stupid to believe it. But Tyreke was no dummy when it came to the "leave no witnesses" rule.

Besides, surviving Chauncey's hands was the least of Tyreke's worries. Once Jose got word that he didn't step off the plane with his diamonds, all hell would break loose. Either way, in the next forty-eight hours, Tyreke would be cold fish. A dead man.

"Open the bags."

D'mico followed Chauncey's command. She tucked Tyreke's pistol, got down on one knee and poked a small hole next to the tight knot Tyreke had made. Inside the garbage bag was another bag. Only this bag was smaller, dookie-brown with a touch of yellow stitched along the edges. Most drug dealers used less noticeable, inconspicuous luggage bags to transport drugs and money, and D'mico had seen that same ugly bag numerous times before.

"What's in it?" asked Chauncey.

"It's another bag," D'mico informed.

"Whatchu waitin' for? OPEN IT!" Chauncey pressed.

D'mico cut her eyes at Chauncey. She didn't like the tone in his voice, and she damn sure didn't appreciate him pushing on her minutes ago. Freeing the hair from her face, she unzipped the bag. Lustrous crystals dazzled her eyes, causing her to gasp in surprise.

"Looks like big chunks of ice," she informed Chauncey, standing to her feet.

Chauncey kept his gun on Tyreke while he leaned in for a better look. Already dollar signs gleamed in his eyes, and his smile lit up like the Fourth of July. Diamonds? Not only was Tyreke infecting the streets with poison but he was supplying diamonds too? Damn, I guess greed is a muthafucka. Maybe the man didn't think he had enough. Oh well, maybe he could help Chauncey out with that. Hopefully the other bag had money in it.

"Look in the other bag," Chauncey instructed. D'mico promptly moved to the second bag.

"Same thing. Those ice chunk lookin' things," she called out.

Chauncey was getting antsy and growing impatient. Although he could do a lot with the diamonds, it would take him months to find a connect to get rid of them. The downside to that was that he didn't have months. He only had a couple of weeks to get his father's lawyer paid before he backed out of his appeal.

"Where's the money?" Chauncey asked Tyreke, sticking him in the temple with the gun. Tyreke bit down on his bottom lip and grit his teeth.

"You and that bitch can suck my dick."

Chauncey's face screwed up. With two powerful blows, he struck Tyreke across his face with the gun, splitting the skin above his brow. Tyreke sucked in the air as he came up from the second blow.

Real niggas bounce back, were his thoughts when the

pain kicked in.

D'mico's shaky hands flew over her eyes. She shook her head side to side. She couldn't watch Tyreke inflict so much pain on himself. *Just give him the money, Ty!* she thought.

"Where is the money?" Chauncey reiterated.

"I said, suck my dick, nigga."

Chauncey laughed. He clearly could see that Tyreke was trying to be the hard-ass nigga that everyone thought he was. Yeah, the nigga might've had heart, but even a heart will stop beating. Chauncey stepped back a notch and pulled the trigger.

POP!

D'mico's screams bounced off the walls. "Chaaunceee...you said we wasn't goin' to hurt him. You promised...You promised." She started to cry hysterically.

Tyreke tried to push himself off the floor, but the gunshot to his arm pulled his weight back to the ground.

D'mico looked at Tyreke. Her eyes welled up with tears. Truly she was hurt. She never meant for any of this to happen, and she wished that she could take it all back. I know she said those words before, but this time she was serious.

In a fit, she rushed Chauncey. "You gave me your word, Chauncey. Let's just take whatever's in that bag and go."

Chauncey shook his head. "Nah, I know there's money here, and I ain't leaving until I get it." He grabbed a handful of her hair and chucked her into the wall behind Tyreke with brute force. Like a rag doll, D'mico slid down the wall in a daze. A short moan escaped from her lips as she tried to make sense out of what just happened. She should have known better than to trust a penny-licking man like Chauncey.

In the midst of all the chaos, the chapel door crept open, and out came Leslie dressed like a nightwalker. Her short bob cut bounced with every step. She had on a pair of black leather pants with a matching jacket, gloves and knee-high boots. Licking his lips, Chauncey smacked her ass as she passed by.

The clamorous sound of Leslie's boots breaking into the floor panel stirred D'mico out of her shock. Leslie bent over, smoothed D'mico's loose hairs away from her face and smiled.

"Damn, girl...you look a mess," she ridiculed. "You didn't think you was going to live happily ever after wit' my man, did you? My child's father?" Leslie's upper lip curled in disgust. "Oh you did, huh? Oops, your bad. Girl, you wasn't shit from the get go. Getting pregnant sure as hell wasn't gonna keep him. That's fo damn sho." Leslie continued to burn words into D'mico, words that had been bottled up for a long time.

"Tyreke shoulda kicked your tired ass to the curb when you did that trifling shit to yo'self. Now look at you. You'll never know what it would be like to have a child. You should've accepted the fact that you lost only one baby..."

D'mico's thoughts drowned out Leslie's words. All of a sudden, she felt numb, wrapped in outrage. She'd known Leslie for years. She had confided in her and Leslie confided in her too. When Leslie's baby daddy,

Rodney, was kicking that ass, it was D'mico who she called in the wee hours of the night. It was Tyreke who made him pack up and leave for good. Yeah, I know. What goes around comes around, but Leslie and Chauncey? They had a child together? Unfuckin' believable. It was because of Chauncey that she would never be able to have kids.

D'mico thought about the gun tucked inside her pants, poking the small of her back. Chauncey was so busy being greedy that he must have forgotten all about it. Otherwise he would have taken it by now. All she needed was the right opportunity. Then she was going straight for Chauncey's dick and Leslie's fat-ass mouth. Secretly, she waited in perfect silence for her chance. Tyreke's head shot up in disbelief at Leslie's spill of words. The more she flapped her gums, the more he realized that she was the same female who had called his phone numerous times looking for Chauncey. Hmph.

The odds of that. Immediately cement formed a wall around Tyreke's heart. He no longer had any compassion for D'mico. She was gullible, naive and foul, just like her friend. There were two things D'mico done that he would never overlook: killing his seed and setting him up. Leslie snapped her fingers to get D'mico's attention.

"Get yo silly ass up," she instructed, jerking D'mico up by her long, silky mane. With a handful of hair, she spoke to Chauncey. "I know where the money is. I saw him in it." Leslie pointed a skinny finger down the hall. "It's by the stairs. Underneath a rug."

A half smile spread across Chauncey's lips. He took his gun and slid it under Tyreke's chin. Jabbing upward, he forced him to get up.

Reluctantly, Tyreke moved to his feet, clutching his wounded arm close to his chest. Reverend Johnson's words spun out of control inside his head. "Nothing is ever enough with you because you're selfish. I am rich. Rich indeed. What about you?"

While Leslie led them to the money, D'mico attempted to get Tyreke's attention, but Tyreke ignored her. She wanted to die in her own shoes for giving up a good thing for a pipe dream. She knew he would never forgive her for killing the baby. Hell, she couldn't even forgive herself.

"All it took was one text to snatch up your bitch," Chauncey bragged. "D'mico, you so dumb, you fell for the shit." He laughed. "Didn't your parents ever tell you not to trust your friends?"

D'mico stopped walking. She turned and looked over her shoulder in confusion. She looked at Chauncey for an explanation, but Leslie punched her in the back and told her to keep walking.

What text? Text...text...text...What text? What was Chauncey talking about?

Tyreke gave Chauncey a "I don't give a fuck" look. He could care less about the chump's motives. Either he was gonna funk or die. I'll tell you one thing; Tyreke was prepared to go out with a bang. He was going to funk all the way. The greed in Chauncey's eyes and the fact that he'd cut the man off said enough.

Already he could sense that Chauncey would be on some power trip type of shit. As a result, Chauncey would try to defile him as a way of payback for all the times he controlled him. In addition to that, it would be Tyreke who Chauncey would want to pass over the money. Tyreke bet his life on it. Fortunately enough for him, he moved his money days ago. The only thing left in the stash box was a .380 automatic loaded with purpose. Actually, the gun was left as a precaution. And a good thing it was.

"I wantchu to give it to me. Remove the rug," he demanded, pointing his .380 special at Tyreke's temple. Tyreke acted like he wasn't with it even though he was more eager than a muthafucka.

"What? Nigga you can give orders, but you can't take 'em? Open the bitch, now!" Tyreke threw up his hands in surrender.

"Aight, nigga. Aight," Tyreke said, lowering himself to the ground. After he pushed the rug over, Chauncey yelled.

"Wait!"

Tyreke's hand released the plywood. *What now?* Chauncey's big eyes wandered to D'mico.

"After I kill him, I'm gonna kill you too. I've waited years for this day, and it ain't even about the money. Nah, it's bigger than that. You killed my mother, and you and this fool tried to put away my pops forever. This shit right here is court in the streets. The money? Oh, well that's for punitive damages."

No one said a word.

Chauncey talked over everyone's head. The shit he was saying was Greek, and the only one who understood where he was coming from was his damn self. Even Leslie had this look on her face that read, "This nigga done went nuts."

D'mico hid behind her bewilderment. She was stunned. What the fuck was Chauncey talking about? Her hazel eyes dragged across the room. For the first time since she turned on Tyreke, he was matching her gaze. Although she had his attention, the disturbing look on his face revealed unforgiveness. He also had an eager look in his eyes that she couldn't fully read. No matter what was going on inside his heart, she'd learned how to read his eyes. What she saw was enough to make the hairs on the back of her neck stand up. Breaking eye contact, she looked at Leslie who appeared to be annoyed. Bitches like her only care about one thing. Yep, money. It was the slap to D'mico's face that tore her eyes away from Leslie and to the ground.

Tyreke jumped up at first, but then he fell back, realizing that D'mico was no longer a part of his worries.

"Did you hear me, bitch?" Chauncey screamed, shifting his gun. Then he took off his belt.

The thick leather came down on her face. *Whack!* "This is whatchu respond to, ain't it?"

D'mico balled up. She reached out for Tyreke, but he wasn't there to help her. This time he stood back and watched. Repeatedly Chauncey hit and kicked her between her legs with his fist and belt buckle.

"You told the jury he done this to you, didn't you?" he fumed.

"Chauncey, that's enough." Leslie spoke up.

Chauncey snapped out of his crazed state, breathing heavy. D'mico might've been on Tyreke's bottom scale of dislikes right now, but he did still love her. Shit, love don't change over hours. There was no way in hell he was going to allow Chauncey to dehumanize her in the way he just done and get away with it. Yeah, D'mico proved that she wasn't loyal, but she still was a woman, and Chauncey was beating her ass like she was a man. With his eyes on everyone, he inched towards the stash box.

D'mico was in and out of consciousness. She was on the verge of blacking out. It felt like her ribs had been crushed, and between her legs was so sore that she couldn't even feel her private parts.

Like a deranged maniac, Chauncey started wiggin out again. Instead of going after the money, he wanted Tyreke and D'mico to feel his pain. From the middle, he told his story. Once he got that off his chest, then it would be time to cancel their asses.

Chapter 24

Tubes ran in every direction from the breathing machine and small monitors into Patricia's frail arms and mouth. The spacious hospital room was decorated with roses, lilies and dandelions to make her feel more comfortable with her extended stay. Despite her condition, the flowers and cards made her smile every time she opened her eyes. The soft cries from family members were what made her smiles fade away. It was as if she was already dead and gone. To make matters worse, it was her son, Chauncey, who she worried about the most. He would slip in and out of the hospital at weird hours of the night. When he would return, his words never changed. "Yeah I'ma get them muthafuckas" he would say while clutching onto her loose hand like a baby blanket.

Get who, baby? Oh, Lord, help my child.

With the long tube in her mouth, it was impossible

for her to speak. Even if she wanted to question her son or try to soothe his anger, she couldn't. Talking seemed to take away all of her energy. For now, she would just enjoy the last days they had left together.

After all, he was all she had left.

Chauncey stared into his mother's soft brown eyes, which were turning a shade of blue in the center. He wiped saliva off the corners of her mouth with a rag. Damn, it was killing him to see her like this. Her once beautiful face was sunk in from months of chemotherapy. She looked like the life had been dragged out of her. To tell you the truth, it had. She was robbed of her happiness. As much as he wanted to hug her and tell her to fight, he couldn't. Fuck. He couldn't even hold her hand without her releasing an agonizing wail, as if he was breaking her bones. Damn right he was pissed about it. He loved his T-Jones. She was a good mother and wife to his pops.

Only a year after he was sentenced to life without the possibility of parole did she find out that she had cancer. The nasty illness got a hold of her at a vulnerable time in her life. All because of D'mico. Why you say? Well, let's take a look at it. In the past, Patricia had fought off the same disease.

The difference between now and then? Oh, that's easy. Back then her support system was larger, and she had tons of motivation. Now, all she had was the title of being "the bad cop's wife." She also had a shitload of bills, an overdue mortgage payment, and a husband who would never again wake up as a free man. At the end of the day, the finger pointed straight to D'mico. She and Tyreke had been spending a lot of time together lately, like they didn't have a fuckin' care in the world. What happened to her tears, huh? How about those fake-ass tears that moved the jury to give his pops a guilty verdict? Fuckin' bitch! She was counterfeit all the way. A fraud. It was all good though 'cause one of these good days, he would see her tears. And when he did, they would be real. Oh, they would be real alright.

Chauncey took Patricia's cold hands and placed them over one another so that they rested on her stomach. Her eyes were already closed and she was sound asleep. With a short peck, he kissed her forehead.

"Good-night, Mama," he said. Then he got up and left. That was the last day he saw his mother before she passed away.

* * * *

Granite State Penitentiary became Chauncey's second home. He never missed a week of visiting his father, and he never would. As far as Chauncey was concerned, he was serving a life sentence himself. Only difference was, he got to go home every day.

Halfway through the metal detector, the alarm sounded, alerting the female guard in front of Chauncey. Taking two steps backwards, he dug into his pockets.

"Fuck. Eh, my bad. I forgot to put my keys in the tray," he confirmed.

The guard gave him an unsure look before motioning him to go on through. Chauncey smiled. Shit, he was a regular face up in here, so he knew she wasn't about to trip. He emptied his pockets completely putting everything in the tray, including his pack of Winterfresh gum which he knew wouldn't go off in the metal detector. What the hell, might as well show these muthafuckas that he didn't have shit to hide. Casually, he made his way back through. Nothing. The guard turned around. She bent down. Her navy blue uniform showed off her assets. She rotated her hypnotizing ass in his view. Her round dumpling was fatter than the meat on a pig. The chick definitely had a "donk."

Seconds later, she pulled out a handheld metal detector shaped like a wand. "You can't be serious," Chauncey said, embarrassed.

The guard gave him a look that said that she was serious like a heart attack. "Please step over here, sir," she instructed.

Chauncey stepped to the right. *Damn, this broad is trippin'. I just went through the metal detector, and it didn't go off. What the fuck is her problem? Underpaid-ass trick.*

During the search, she teased her D cup breasts up against his chest. Slowly, she worked her way below his midsection with the wand, nuzzling her face against his package while taking in his scent.

Chauncey jumped when her face settled on his dick.

"Damn, mama, did you find what you were lookin' for?" he exclaimed, looking at her like she was crazy.

If this trick was getting down like that with visitors, it ain't no telling how much dick chastising the bitch was doing with the inmates. Guess they gotta get their rocks off too.

"Sorry about that." She grinned.

After getting some dry head from the guard, Chauncey was escorted past the visiting area by another guard, which was a bit odd because he always remained in the big room filled with tables, chairs, vending machines, sad and happy faces, and kids refusing to fall into the arms of the men who they were no longer familiar with.

"Excuse me." Chauncey tried to get the guards attention. "Why we going this way?"

Leading the way was a hulk-looking white guy with a receding hairline and bulky arms. He did more walking than talking.

"Dunno, just following orders. You got a special visit," the guard answered dryly. A special visit? What kind of special visit would his pops need? After going down the long main passageway, they turned into a breezeway where the guard radioed in the call to open the sliding door. Once it opened, they walked down another hallway with fluorescent lights. From the looks of it, not to mention the drop in temperature, they were now in the infirmary. The sign on the wall confirmed that he was in medical.

Chauncey's weary eyes traveled to the glass rooms lined against the wall. Separating the inmates from one another was a six-foot, lime-green curtain. People in scrubs walked up and down the hallway, going from one room to the next. A bad feeling started to form inside Chauncey's stomach. Call it intuition, but his gut told him that this was no field trip. Was his pops sick? Nah, of course not. He was fine. Absolutely fine.

The guard stopped walking and got on his walkie-talkie. After speaking in two or three security codes, he turned around and pointed a meaty finger two doors down.

"Your visit will be in there. He has his own room." He looked at his clock. "Your visit starts now. Got thirty minutes."

Chauncey skipped the questions. Immediately he went into the room where his pops was facedown on his stomach. Heating pads covered his entire backside.

"What the fuck! What the fuck happened?"

Matt looked over his shoulder. Hot tears fell onto the small cot they called a hospital bed. "I was jumped. You know these niggas been tryin' to get me since I got here," he choked.

Chauncey burned with fury. His father's black eye told the story. However, the heating pads spread across his back and anus said a different tale.

"What happened?" Chauncey asked, wanting the truth.

"Chauncey, that's not important. I told you I was jumped." Matt refused to worry Chauncey with his problems. The boy already been through enough for God's sake. Plus, how could a man tell his son that he'd been gang raped, and two of the men who raped him had AIDS. How? How do you say that to a teenager who'd been through more shit than a grown man?

* * * *

It was common for inmates to do work around the facility. It was another way for the system to fuck you in order to save a dollar. While the system ran game on the inmates by giving them two cents an hour, the inmates were dominating the system in full force. They had some of the officers on lock.

Anything you can think of that a man locked up would want, they had. In prison, niggas never ratted on each other. They might compete when it came to race or representing different gangs, but when it came down to busting the system wide open for drugs, cell phones and minor shit here and there, they came together as one. The women officers were their pride and joy. Not only were they something to look at but they were the ones bringing the shit in. Having an officer on your team said one thing—you had pull. Not only was Old School's son one of the most promising niggas on the street, the young dude had major pull inside and outside the penitentiary. Dirt made sure Old School—also known as Monte—had the latest of everything, including pussy.

Old School was in the infirmary working the dust mop when he overheard the mention of his son's name. Pushing a few pieces of lint and hair towards the sound of the voices, he lingered around to see if his ears could catch anything of interest.

Old School's bunkie worked the medical ward as well. He was doing his routine trash check when he came out of the room with a bag of garbage. Right away, Old School hit him with the question.

"What up, young blood? Who off in there?"

Kendale rotated the bag of garbage to his other hand like it was heavy, but it was just a tactic he used to speak with his hands.

"Ol' boy who got raped last night. The pig. Dude an' his son in der choppin' it up about an appeal or some shit."

Old School nodded and Kendale carried on to the other rooms.

Old School made his way to the pill line window with the dust mop. It was Keasha's attention he was after. Keasha was sexier than a muthafucka. She had small lips, sky-blue eyes and long auburn hair that fell down her back. For a white chick, she was sugar to the eyes. Her titties sat perfectly above her small waist for the inmates to look at. Even though they were hidden behind the blue fabric, they still poked out for the eyes to see. Everyone on the yard knew that Keasha was Old School's bitch. Well, one of them. Anyway, she backed him one hundred percent and made sure that he was satisfied to the best of her ability. It took several long minutes for Keasha to notice Old School before she turned her back to the line which she was patrolling. Knowing that the inmates in the line were probably cheeking their medication by now, she immediately gave Old School one look that told him to meet her in their usual spot—the utility closet. Then she turned back around.

Old School waited in the utility closet for fifteen minutes before Keasha came rushing inside. "I'm sorry, baby," she whispered, grabbing his crotch. Old School grabbed her wandering hands.

"We ain't on that right now. Whatchu know about the dude who got the special visit?" Disappointed, Keasha stepped back.

"Well, his dad use to be a cop. Guess that's why he

was raped. Anywho, the warden pulled a few strings for him to go through his appeal with his son. His son said something about him being set up or something. I dunno. Why?"

Old School had all he needed for now.

"No reason. Make sure you keep your ears open."

"Okay, you know I got your back, baby."

"You ready for some of dis black dick?"

Keasha ran her tongue across her lips, pulled down her pants and purred like a kitten. "Ooww...Yeeess." She bent over doggy style for her daily dosage. Damn, she loved her job.

* * * *

Chauncey checked the time on his watch before he walked into King's Catfish. For the first time he would be meeting up with Tyreke, and he didn't want to be late. After being greeted by a server, he was lead to his table where he waited for what seemed like an hour. Periodically, he checked the time on his watch. Dude was late. What was he doing here anyway? He didn't know shit about slangin' no rocks. Just when he was on the verge of leaving, a group of niggas shuffled inside the cozy establishment. Following their stride was the strong scent of marijuana. Chauncey played himself cool and sipped from his glass of coke.

Tyreke took in his surroundings. Shrugging off the jacket from his medium frame, he scanned the restaurant for the nigga who Stacey lined up. Stacey was one of the few from his crew. Reading Tyreke's mind, Stacey pointed in Chauncey's direction.

"That's him." Tyreke looked away.

"Keep 'em waiting," Tyreke said to Stacey.

Stacey kinda frowned. What was up with the delay? Within minutes the gentlemen were greeted by a waiter and seated by a spacious window with the view of the streets. After ordering some of the bombest catfish in the city, Tyreke's eyes fell on Chauncey's backside. Patience is everything. Patience can also tell who a person really is. One thing a muthafucka hates the most is to be kept waiting. Five entrees and seven beers later—enjoyed by him and his crew—Chauncey was still seated in the same spot, sipping from the same watered-down beverage. Leaning further back into his seat, Tyreke addressed Stacey.

"Where you say you met him at?" Stacey's eyes wandered towards Chauncey.

"You know my sister Charlene who work at the pen? Well she fuckin' with dude. She really like the nigga, asked me to hook him up."

"Charlene with the fat ass?" Dirt cut in.

Stacey cut his eyes at Dirt for a brief moment. Then he turned his attention back to Tyreke.

"Like I was saying. She asked me to hook the nigga up. I talked to the nigga a few times. He aight. Still wet behind the ears, but overall, he can be broken in if you know what I mean," Stacey finished.

Tyreke eyed everyone at the table. Even though he called the shots on when, where, how and whatever, he still liked to include his crew on some of his decision making. Because of that, he was given a lot of respect in return.

"Who all game for the nigga?" Tyreke asked everyone at the table.

All he needed was a single no, and Charlene's little buddy would be SOL, "shit outta luck." Dirt, Stacey and Ansean all tipped their hats in agreement. Damu, on the other hand, burned a hole in Chauncey's backside like he had personal beef with the nigga while sucking suspiciously on his cinnamon toothpick. Something wasn't right about the dude, and it didn't sit well with him. For thirty long minutes, the man sat there with a stiff neck like a damn mannequin. He had to know that they were peeping his weird ass out, yet he chose to sit there like a lump of shit.

"So what's up, Moo? What's your answer?" Tyreke asked, wanting a quick response.

* * * *

Chauncey had his back to Tyreke and his team of sergeants. The waiting process was beginning to be ridiculous and pretty fuckin' annoying. How long was the nigga expecting him to wait? Even the tramp who waited on his table was ready for him to bounce. Twenty minutes ago she placed his check on the table and left without a word. Rude bitch! Ten minutes later, Chauncey felt a light tap on his shoulder. He looked up and Stacey was standing over him with the look of good news spread across his face.

"Come on, nigga. Ty ready for you." Stacey said, dropping two twenty-dollar bills on the table.

"I only had a soda."

Stacey laughed. "Nigga, that ain't shit. Time is money, and you wasted a lot of lil mama's time. Come on. And whatchu mean SODA? Nigga, it's called POP. Let me find out that you all proper an' shit. Don't worry my nig. That won't last long." Stacey chuckled, leading the way to their table.

Tyreke examined Chauncey from across the table. So he was looking for work, huh? Yeah well, the nigga better be prepared to work around the clock. If he expected sleep, he would never get it. Shidd, fiends didn't sleep, so neither would he. Tyreke planned to keep him so busy that he wouldn't even have a chance to wipe his own ass. Yeah, he would work him alright.

Tyreke stared awkwardly at Chauncey before speaking. "I hear you lookin' for work. We ain't knocking on doors selling Boy Scout cookies, you know?"

Chauncey ignored Tyreke's sarcasm. "I know. That's why I'm tryin' to be down with ya'll."

"Tell me, nigga. What makes you official?" Tyreke asked.

Official? Huh? What the fuck did he mean by that? Everyone stared at Chauncey as if he was a fuckin' idiot. The only thing that came to Chauncey's mind as being official was him wanting the man dead.

Tyreke smiled, showing off perfectly white teeth. "Relax. I'm just fuckin' with you. Stacey tells us that you're dating Charlene," Tyreke probed. Chauncey cleared his throat and answered.

"Yeah, we been talking for a month or so now."

"Hmph...for a month or so?" Tyreke asked as he looked over to Stacey. A month wasn't shit to judge a nigga on. Dude could be anybody working for God knows who. Just when Tyreke was about to tear into Chauncey's ass, his phone rang.

"Say love," he answered. "Hold on, mama, will ya?"

Tyreke didn't even excuse himself. He just got up and walked outside, leaving the five of them at the table. Chauncey couldn't deny his jealousy. The things he would give up to see his mom again. Life seemed like such a blur with her gone. What would she say if she was alive and saw him with the same man who ruined their life? Knowing his mother, she would probably tell him to forgive Tyreke. Fuck all that. He wanted revenge. Tyreke returned minutes later. Instead of taking a seat, he stood in place.

"Wrap dis shit up. Stacey, plug Chauncey and show him how we do thangs. Get ready, playboy, 'cause you just signed yo soul over to the devil," Tyreke said with a smirk.

Everyone got up from their seats. Stacey placed his large hand on Chauncey's shoulder. "All work. No play," Stacey added, walking Chauncey out the door.

* * * *

Two years later, Chauncey moved from being a corner boy to Tyreke's henchman. Tyreke kept him on the streets long enough to see what side of the toast he buttered. Break him down a bit. Chauncey done everything from running the work to delivering the product. He even had to kill a few people in the process. But not once did he show weakness in the midst of the storm. He was on a mission.

Ring...Ring...Ring...

Chauncey scrabbled to get his phone, knocking over the lamp on the nightstand. With a banging-ass headache, he answered on the fourth ring.

"Hello."

"Now I know you ain't sleep."

Chauncey ran a hand across his chest. Shit. His head was pounding like Kenwood speakers. Last night was crazy, and the bitch laying next to him reminded him of how crazy it was. Racheal was her name, a stripper from club Cloud Nine. Man, she fucked his brains out like whoa.

"Nah, man, I'm not sleep. I was actually just getting up," Chauncey said, looking at the beautiful woman sleeping next to him.

"Good 'cause the early bird gets the worm. I got a job for you," the caller said.

Chauncey exhaled. Those were Tyreke's favorite words. Always running a nigga ragged with some "do this and do that" bullshit. Did the man ever do anything himself? Probably not.

"What's up?" Chauncey asked, biting his tongue.

After getting Tyreke's instructions, Chauncey was up, groomed and on his way to his destination.

* * * *

"Leslie's Hair and Nail Salon" is what the pink neon

sign out front read. Beautiful wasn't the word. The female who stepped out the salon was gorgeous. D'mico? Damn, Chauncey didn't even notice her from three years ago. She definitely didn't look like the broke-down bitch who testified against his father. Uh-uh, she looked like she bathed in hundred-dollar bills. Judging by her outfit, hair and nails, Tyreke spoiled her with the best and nothing under that. This was the first time he'd seen her since court. Tyreke did a good job of excluding her from his business, making sure she stayed away from the niggas in his crew. One slip up was all Chauncey needed for Tyreke to get comfortable and he would be in there, and guess what? He was in. Immediately he rolled down the window. It ain't no way in the world he was going to get out and open the door for this bitch, so he did what disrespectful niggas do—stay in the car and honk the horn.

D'mico was way better looking up close than from a distance. She was a jewel to any man's eye. Gay or straight. For several minutes, Chauncey deliberately stared at D'mico through the mirror, but she never noticed. Quietly, she sat in the backseat of his car, occupying her own thoughts. Periodically, she would go through her text messages. Not once did she look up to make eye contact with Chauncey.

To Chauncey, it was strange being around D'mico without laying a violent finger on her or causing her bodily harm. After all, she was the cause of his family's grief. Regardless of how Chauncey felt, he couldn't let his feelings ride on his father's future.

Finally, D'mico's captivating eyes looked up and

met Chauncey's gaze.

Damn she fine, Chauncey thought, looking deeper into her cat eyes. Transfixed by her beauty, his long tongue traveled across the top and down the bottom of his thick lips. Instantly his dick rose inside his pants. The physical attraction was so apparent that Chauncey let the strong desire slip from his mouth.

"You're so beautiful."

Bunching up her face, D'mico shoved her Blackberry in her tote bag. She placed one hand behind her right ear and stuck out her neck.

"Excuse me?" she asked. "What did you say?"

Not wanting to ruin any opportunity to get close to her, Chauncey tore his eyes away from the mirror and fixed them on the road. Shit. What was his problem? He was trippin' for real.

"Umm...Oh, I was just commenting on the weather. It's beautiful out today. Don'tchu think?" he lied, hoping she wouldn't say shit to Tyreke.

D'mico had heard exactly what the man had said, and it didn't relate to the weather. Naturally, Tyreke's friends fell into the custom of not speaking to her at all. Either they were afraid of Tyreke or had a high level of respect for her man.

Nevertheless, to them she didn't exist. Not to say that she was looking for their attention, because she wasn't. Tyreke had that on lock. This might sound a little hoeish, but getting a compliment from a fine-ass man like her driver made her blush. Ain't nothing wrong with compliments. *Who is he anyway?* she thought. Hmph, only time would tell.

* * * *

Coming in as a newcomer wasn't easy. Chauncey endured the thick of it all. Now, he was one of Tyreke's close henchmen. The job didn't call for a pat on the back or no shit like that. So hold your applause. When Tyreke said that he'd sold his soul to the devil, boy was he right.

The shit he saw would make a blind man praise God for not having the ability to see. Tyreke had the world fooled. The nigga was a straight up natural-born killer. Instead of having a warm hand and a cold heart, Tyreke had a cold hand, a cold heart and icy eyes. The baby face everyone saw was his makeup. The shit Chauncey witnessed Tyreke do was too explicit for words, but the up part of it was that Chauncey got close to Tyreke, which is what he wanted. He'd even gone as far as to get close to D'mico. D...Mi...co. Hell yeah! He was thirsty like a muthfucka for the yellow-bone. And I ain't talking 'bout thirsty for a non-alcoholic beverage neither. Nah, he wanted to get tipsy off of her apple pie. He could tell by the look in her eyes that she had some intoxicating pussy.

Among other things, he was on the money. A while back, Tyreke sent D'mico over to his crib for a pickup, which was his second mistake. What was his first mistake you ask? Are you following the story? The first mistake was made when he sent him to pick D'mico up from Leslie's salon. I know its impossible for someone to walk a straight line, but fuck, a bitch as fine as D'mico who was use to being a homebody should never be left in the hands of her man's workers. Tyreke must've thought that

D'mico was exempt from all the other bitches in the world. Funny. Sure, women be screaming that, "I'm a down bitch," loyalty bullshit, but just like niggas, women got feelings. I'm talking about the feeling to want something new and fresh. Lock them up, take away all the things they're use to and let 'em out. Man, they'll go crazy. A woman might've had it in her mind to be faithful. She probably couldn't even imagine life without her man. She probably even promised to love till death do you part, but fuck up once and all the feelings she ever had will go in the shade. D'mico didn't react to Chauncey's compliments in the beginning because she was still in her happy zone with Tyreke. Over time, all of that changed. The first episode was while Chauncey was in the back getting the bags ready for D'mico, he spotted Tyreke's cell phone on his nightstand. He'd meant to return it to him, but then it dawned on him. Instead of dragging out this thing with Tyreke and D'mico, why not get the ball rolling. He would pose as Tyreke, send D'mico a text using Tyreke's phone, and play on her feelings. Ten minutes later, his plan worked. Not only did he have her mind in the palm of his hands but he had her panties to the floor. Every chance Chauncey got he made sure to fuck her nice.

Funny thing about that is he even went as far as telling her that he was into all of that kinky shit them white folks be into just so that he could slap her around while he was tearing her good pussy up. Dumb broad.

I must admit though, there were times when Chauncey lost focus. Reluctantly, he was able to get himself out of it. The love he had for his parents would never redeem her as being anything other than a rotten bitch he intended on destroying completely. Besides, good pussy came a dime a dozen, and there wasn't shit beneficial about her pussy that someone else couldn't master.

It wasn't until three months ago that shit started getting hectic. In the beginning, things were looking real good with Matt's lawyer and the appeal. Then all of sudden, the lawyer stressed that he needed more money, claiming that he needed it for necessary paperwork. Damn, you would've thought seventy-five grand was enough. What kind of paperwork required seventy-five stacks? Paperwork my ass. Every dime Chauncey made off the streets went into the man's greedy hand. Sure, there was extra change he made from Tyreke. So what. By choice, Chauncey settled Leslie and her kids in an uppity neighborhood across town. Also, he splurged on a few strippers here and there, popped a few bottles and even decked out his ride just the way he wanted. But shit, he didn't anticipate to stay in the game this long. He wanted to finalize his father's appeal and then kill Tyreke and D'mico.

Last month, Chauncey went to visit his dad, who by the way moved to another maximum facility two hours away. Matt looked like death as if he was sick or something. No matter how much Matt tried to assure Chauncey that everything was fine, Chauncey refused to believe him. He didn't look like his normal self. Matt had open sores on his face and on the back of his neck. Gory looking sores. All Chauncey kept thinking was how he couldn't let his father die behind bars. Every time he left his father behind, he felt defeated. He hated the new facility where his father was. It looked more like a hospital ward rather than a prison. The sons of bitches even had a cemetery adjacent to the prison. A constant reminder to anyone doing a life sentence that prison was their final destination.

Muthafuckas! If he had to go broke without a pot to piss in to spare his father's life, so be it. At least he would be free.

Like I said before, things got out of control. It went from bad to worse. Due to the fact that he was several minutes late getting to the van, Tyreke cut him off like he was a piece of broken thread. There wasn't a nigga in town who would even consider doing business with him. He was desperate, willing to do anything. It was then when Chauncey realized that he could no longer play cat and mouse. He was ready to tidy things up and get the ball rolling.

* * * *

Killing time behind the wheel of his car, Chauncey eyeballed Tyreke. He found himself following Tyreke from day in till day out. Wherever and whenever. Shidd, he didn't have a life. Tyreke took that away. If Tyreke went to the store, Chauncey was there too. If the nigga went over his parents' house. Guess what? Chauncey was there. Everywhere. It was in the middle of the night one time, and he found himself trailing behind Tyreke to the arena.

A short distance away, Tyreke jumped out of his

SUV and ran directly to the little boy that was sitting in front of the building with his head held low. From the looks of it, little daddy had run away from home, considering the hour and the fact that he'd already been there when they pulled up.

Whatever Tyreke was saying to the kid must have nurtured his spirit because he was no longer looking down. He had his head up and a big smile on his face.

Chauncey remembered seeing the kid a few times before when he passed through the gym. He also remembered the woman who brought him up there. Shorty was fine, a chocolate dream. To think Tyreke said that she was nothing more than a friend. Nigga had to be crazy. Friend my ass. Ain't no way he could look at her sexy ass every day without all of that chocolate melting in his mouth.

Anyway, Tyreke was spending so much time with this little nigga that you would've thought the nigga was little man's substitute father. Tyreke a father? Yeah right. The man was the biggest hypocrite in America. Then again, look at D'mico. She was far from having any type of motherly skills. That's why Chauncey chose Leslie's baby over hers.

Wait, hold up. Chauncey took one more glance at the little boy. *Think...think...think. Oh shit. Get the fuck out of here. Couldn't be. Or could it?* This was big. Reeeal Big. The kid was—

Chapter 25

Leslie must have sensed that Tyreke could reach the stash box because she abandoned D'mico and made her way towards Tyreke. I take it that she got tired of listening to Chauncey like everyone else had. Whatever the cause, Tyreke was already quick on his feet and swift with his hands. On the hush, he swept up his .380 and snatched Leslie by the arm. A low shriek came out of her mouth which was too quiet to be heard over Chauncey's blabbering mouth. Surrendering to the cold steel, Leslie's back fell into his pistol as he whispered a lethal threat into her ear.

"Shhh…Scream and you're gone, bitch."

Leslie's head moved up and down in four quick nods. She was scared shitless. She knew Tyreke wasn't the type to be fucked with. She looked at Chauncey for a way out, but he was too busy blaming D'mico for his sad life.

Although D'mico was battered and beaten, she still managed to listen to what Chauncey had to say. Even though Tyreke felt a hint of compassion for D'mico, the fact still remained the same. She had put herself in a situation that she couldn't get either of them out of.

D'mico cut Chauncey off right before he was able to tell her about Santy'ya. Too bad she did because she would have gotten the answer she had been wishing for. "You fuckin' son of a bitch!" she cursed, reaching for something behind her back.

Tyreke was trying to make out what D'mico had up her sleeve. He could tell that she was making an attempt to reach for something. But what? Then it dawned on him that she had his gun. As a matter of fact, Chauncey had given it to her. Guess he forgot.

Tyreke saw Chauncey lift up his hand to shoot. Knowing that D'mico was unskilled and too slow, Tyreke was already on his feet making sure that she wouldn't catch a bullet. Even after her betrayal, his loyalty to her was still too strong.

Tyreke threw himself in front of D'mico as her personal body shield. His adrenaline was so fierce that he didn't feel the slug penetrate his flesh. Halfway in front of D'mico, Tyreke felt his chest open up. He felt like someone had taken gasoline and poured it into his exposed lungs and lit a match. The combustion in his chest was so intense that he wrapped his hands around D'mico's waist to remain standing.

After that, everything happened so fast. It wasn't until Chauncey fired the next shot towards Tyreke that he realized that he'd been hit. First time in the ribs, and the next shot missed.

BOOM!

The third shot rung inside of his ears. *Fuck*. He got hit again. Only this time the bullet came from D'mico's gun. While attempting to defend herself, D'mico pulled the trigger, and the bullet went straight towards Tyreke's face. Tyreke's body jerked and crashed. On his way down, Tyreke fired a shot at Chauncey, not knowing whether he hit him or not.

D'mico fell to her knees. Her apologetic cries echoed throughout the church. "I didn't mean to. I didn't mean to. Please, Tyreke don't die. I didn't mean to. Oh God!" she wailed.

What was she apologizing for? Shit, it was a little too late for apologies. Hell, it was too late for a lot of things.

With the bags in his hands, Chauncey dodged Tyreke's bullet. If it hadn't of been for him reaching down, he would've been a dead man. He rushed to Leslie, shook her out of her comatose state and gave her one of the bags. It didn't take Leslie long to snap out of it. She secured Chauncey's side, looking for an emergency exit. Even though they didn't get any cash, she was content with the diamonds and the breath she had in her body. After all, she did have kids. The spray of bullets going on around her reminded her of how she wanted nothing more than to make it out the church alive.

Stopping in her tracks, she gave D'mico a pitiful look. The girl might've been a prize to the eyes, but deep down she was dumber than a box of rocks. Leslie still couldn't believe how she made it easy for Chauncey by shooting Tyreke in the face. Good for you, girl.

Chauncey wanted to put an end to the final chapter in this nightmare. He turned around with his gun to

D'mico's back. He was about to pull the trigger when Leslie stopped him.

"No, Chauncey."

"Whatchu mean? I been waiting a good while for this," he said, staring at her backside.

"You kill her and you'll be letting her off easy," she reasoned. "Do to her what they did to your father."

For years, Chauncey wanted to be the one to send D'mico to her grave. He wanted justice for his family more than anything. What better way to get it than through karma? He pictured the cops running in the church with their guns. D'mico would be right where she was now, on the floor next to Tyreke's dead body with the weapon in question laying next to her. She would sit in prison for the rest of her life screaming that she didn't do it, like his father. Karma is what it all boiled down to. And everybody knows that karma is a bitch.

D'mico was so torn by her mistake that she didn't hear what Leslie and Chauncey conspired behind her back. Neither did she notice the gun put on the ground a few inches away from her feet.

Tyreke's heart started racing like crazy, and his face was numb. He was dying on the floor of his father's church.

Thump! Thump! Thump!

Thinking about dying on the same ground as his baby sister caused his eyelids to close. Tears and blood ran down his cheeks. He said a silent prayer to himself. At this point, what did he have to lose? I guess he still had faith after all. Look at him now. He was drowning in his own blood, fighting the devil just to get a few words in to the man upstairs. God tried to warn him in the past, but Tyreke had gotten too hardheaded to listen. Would God listen now? Tyreke remembered his father telling him how great God's love is. Did he have enough love to spare for Tyreke, a man who put God aside for the streets?

The sound of sirens hovered above his head.

Thump! Thump!

Tyreke's heart grew weak in his chest. D'mico placed her trembling hands on his ice-cold face. Crazy thing is, he no longer had hatred in his heart for her. He should have known better. He should've been more careful with the lives around him. Tyreke took on her baggage without finding out how heavy her load really was. It wasn't sex that bound him to her. It was love. He loved her from the first time he saw her.

Tyreke worked up enough breath to tell D'mico to go, but she didn't budge. Sadly, she sat in place crying her eyes out to God right along with him. Tyreke's eyes fluttered open and he saw his baby sister dressed in her cute little Easter dress. She mouthed some words to him. Her big eyes glowed as she extended two arms outward in his direction, motioning for him to pick her up.

"Amyah," he said in a hoarse tone. Heavy as his eyes were, he tried to keep them open. "I love you." Amyah mouthed the soothing words to Tyreke. Then she was gone.

Like a baby, Tyreke cried as the blood in his mouth came to the surface.

A while back, Reverend Johnson asked Tyreke if he cared whether he lived or died. At the time, Tyreke couldn't give a clear answer. No one in his position could answer a question like that. All they see is where they want to go, not where they're headed. Mike Mike never made it back home from his trip to Vegas and just like him, neither would Tyreke. Just when you think the riches of the world come with no price, the world surprises you and spins at a different speed. Back to his pops question. Tyreke had an answer.

Thump!

In God We Trust.

To find out more about Tyreke's fate and the people around him, be on the lookout for the upcoming story.

THE POWER OF
REVENGE

Part II

No escaping

Coming Soon

By Rain

www.ingramcontent.com/pod-product-compliance
Lightning Source LLC
Chambersburg PA
CBHW071207250626
47159CB00001B/229